Jordan unveiled the sculpture, watching her reaction closely.

The man's body was brilliantly carved to show each muscle and rib, and except for a cloak, the figure was naked from head to foot. There was no way she could ignore *that*. If, as he thought, she was Emily Fairchild, her reaction would be dramatic.

Dramatic indeed. Her mouth dropped open and her eyes widened, and she blushed, filling Jordan with satisfaction. She was Emily—she had to be.

After a moment of stunned silence, she said in a hushed whisper, "My word, he's magnificent."

Magnificent? He nearly choked. "You're not shocked?"

She shrugged. "Why should I be? I'm from Scotland, where the men wear nothing under their kilts." When she peered closer at the carving, he actually found himself jealous. "The man is quite well rendered."

Well rendered? Did she mean well hung? Deuce take her!

Other **AVON ROMANCES**

THE BELOVED ONE *by Danelle Harmon*
THE DARKEST KNIGHT *by Gayle Callen*
KISSING A STRANGER *by Margaret Evans Porter*
THE MACKENZIES: PETER *by Ana Leigh*
THE MEN OF PRIDE COUNTY: THE REBEL
by Rosalyn West
ONCE A MISTRESS *by Debra Mullins*
UNTAMED HEART *by Maureen McKade*

Coming Soon

MY LORD STRANGER *by Eve Byron*
A SCOUNDREL'S KISS *by Margaret Moore*

And Don't Miss These
ROMANTIC TREASURES
from Avon Books

BECAUSE OF YOU *by Cathy Maxwell*
ON BENDED KNEE *by Tanya Anne Crosby*
UPON A WICKED TIME *by Karen Ranney*

SABRINA JEFFRIES

The Forbidden Lord

AVON BOOKS ◆ NEW YORK

This is a work of fiction. Names, characters, places, and incidents either are the product of the author's imagination or are used fictitiously. Any resemblance to actual events, locales, organizations, or persons, living or dead, is entirely coincidental and beyond the intent of either the author or the publisher.

AVON BOOKS, INC.
1350 Avenue of the Americas
New York, New York 10019

Copyright © 1999 by Deborah Martin Gonzales
Inside cover author photo by René William Gonzales
Published by arrangement with the author
Visit our website at http://www.AvonBooks.com
Library of Congress Catalog Card Number: 98-93535
ISBN: 0-380-79748-8

First Avon Books Printing: February 1999

AVON TRADEMARK REG. U.S. PAT. OFF. AND IN OTHER COUNTRIES, MARCA REGISTRADA, HECHO EN U.S.A.

Printed in the U.S.A.

WCD 10 9 8 7 6 5 4 3 2 1

To all my wonderful fellow writers in the Heart of Carolina Romance Writers, and especially Judy, Judith, and Theresa, who helped critique the book: Thanks so much to all of you for welcoming me into your chapter.

Chapter 1

Derbyshire, England
March 1819

> Children, I grant, should be innocent; but when
> the epithet is applied to men, or women, it is but
> a civil term for weakness.
>
> Mary Wollstonecraft,
> A Vindication of the Rights of Women

I might as well be playing hide-and-seek in a circus, Emily Fairchild thought as she surveyed the ballroom at the Marquess of Dryden's country estate. There were hundreds of masqueraders, four hundred at least, all wearing exotic, expensive costumes far beyond Emily's means.

And none of them was her good friend Lady Sophie. Where was she, for goodness sake? Emily couldn't leave the ball without finding her; Sophie would be so disappointed if she couldn't get the elixir Emily had made up especially for her.

"Do you see her, Lawrence?" Emily asked her cousin in a voice pitched to be heard over the delightful orchestra. "You're tall enough to spot her."

Lawrence frowned as he craned his head forward. "She's over there, engaged in that absurd

1

and pointless activity society considers entertainment."

In other words, she was dancing. Emily bit back a smile. Poor Lawrence. He'd come from London to visit her and her father at Willow Crossing for the first time in years, and in return, had been forced to stand in for her father by escorting her to a masquerade ball—an event Lawrence considered "stupid, wasteful idiocy."

Well, at least he needn't be further tortured by having to dance with her. Propriety forbade her from dancing, since she was in the final weeks of mourning for her mother. Indeed, she was the lone guest wearing black bombazine, with a silk mask her only concession to the masquerade theme.

"Who's Sophie dancing with?" Emily asked.

"I believe her partner is currently Lord Blackmore."

"*The* Lord Blackmore? She's dancing with *him*?" A man of some consequence, the Earl of Blackmore was the brother of the Drydens' new daughter-in-law.

Envy quickly assailed Emily, and just as quickly she banished it. How silly to envy Sophie what was hers by birthright. It wasn't as if Emily would ever have the chance to dance with the earl herself. She was merely a rector's daughter with no lofty family connections.

She was lucky to be here at all. Lady Dryden had only invited her in payment for a small service Emily had rendered her. The marchioness had no reason to introduce Emily to any of the wealthy, sophisticated lords and ladies who'd traveled from London for the occasion.

Still, what would dancing with an earl as famous as Lord Blackmore be like? Nerve-wracking, she imagined, especially if he were handsome. Was he?

She stood on tiptoe and squinted through the slits in her eye mask, but couldn't see a thing beyond the sea of wigs and odd headdresses that swirled and churned about her.

"Do tell me what's going on, Lawrence. Are they dancing a waltz? Does Lord Blackmore seem to be enjoying it?"

"How could he? First of all, he's dancing. Secondly, he has Sophie for a partner. He deserves better."

"What on earth do you mean?"

"Lord Blackmore is a man of some substance, you know. Despite being one of the youngest members of the House of Lords, he has instituted more reforms for the poor than any other member."

"And why does that mean Sophie isn't good enough for him?"

Lawrence shrugged. "It pains me to tell you this, but your friend is a twit, wholly unsuitable for a man of intelligence and experience."

"She is *not*! What do you know of her? You only met her yesterday!"

"Yes, and she spent the entire visit snubbing me. I suppose she considered a London barrister far beneath her notice."

His attempt to sound nonchalant failed so miserably that Emily had to stifle a laugh. "Oh, Lawrence, you misunderstood her entirely. She wasn't snubbing you. She was terrified of you."

"Terrified?" There was skepticism in his tone. "Why on earth should a marquess's daughter be terrified of me?"

She cast a sideways glance at her cousin. Like many of the young men who hadn't bothered with costumes, he wore standard evening attire with his mask. But although the mask covered his straight nose and part of his smooth brow, it didn't disguise his silky auburn hair or good looks. Not to mention that Lawrence was a trifle opinionated, which in itself would cow the timid Sophie.

"Well?" he asked impatiently. "Why is she afraid of me?"

"Because, my dear cousin, you are a man. A handsome, bold, and consequently terrifying man." When he snorted in disbelief, she added, "Trust me, Sophie was only too painfully aware of your presence yesterday. That's why I couldn't coax her into mumbling more than a few words until you excused yourself from the room."

"That's absurd. A woman of her situation— pretty, rich, and well connected—has nothing to fear from anyone. At her coming out, she'll have numerous suitors clamoring after her inheritance. She'll make a spectacular marriage and go live in a grand estate with some duke or marquess."

"That may be true, but it doesn't prevent her from fearing your sex."

A sudden commotion on the dance floor roused the crowd's attention. Lawrence peered over their heads, his eyes narrowing. "Well, that put an end to that, didn't it? Doesn't surprise me, either."

"Put an end to what?" A bald man in a toga wearing a lopsided crown of laurels swayed in front of Emily and blocked her view. Goodness gracious, what she wouldn't give for a stepping stool right now! "What's happening?"

"Sophie's father just wrenched her out of Blackmore's arms. What a fool Lord Nesfield is." He leaned forward to survey the scene she couldn't see. "Now he's shouting at Blackmore."

"Poor Sophie! She must be mortified!"

" 'Poor Sophie'? What about Blackmore?" He adjusted his mask with tapered fingers. "Wait a minute. Why, jolly good, Blackmore! That's the way to handle a fool."

She rose up on tiptoe again, but could only see a giant Merlin's hat. "What is it? What's he doing?"

"He's walking away, cool as a cucumber. Nesfield is following him, ranting, but Blackmore's ignoring him, which makes Nesfield look ridiculous."

"I don't understand. Why won't Lord Nesfield let Sophie dance with Lord Blackmore?"

Around her, people were murmuring, and they seemed to share Lawrence's opinion of the Marquess of Nesfield.

"Nesfield is Blackmore's chief opponent in Parliament." An acid tone entered his voice. "The marquess believes in leaving people downtrodden, because helping them might encourage them to rise up and overthrow the aristocracy. To him, Blackmore is the worst of rabble-rousers and thus much too sullied for the pure Sophie."

"The marquess has always been suspicious of men where Sophie's concerned," she said indignantly. "Ever since she was a girl, he's been worried that some blackguard will carry her off. That's why she's so afraid of men—because he hasn't allowed her to be around boys her age, and she knows only what he tells her about them."

Lawrence cast her a skeptical glance. "I thought she had a brother. Surely he taught her better."

"Her brother ran off when she was eight. He was very young—seventeen, I think—and he and his father had a great row. He lives on the Continent, I believe. So without her brother around and with her mother dead, Sophie has only her father to guide her, and *he* has her believing that every man is suspect."

"I think you're making excuses for her, though Lord Nesfield *is* an idiot." Suddenly his face grew more somber. "Wait, she's coming toward us. While her father was haranguing Lord Blackmore, she slipped off. Now you can give her that elixir so we can go. But if you don't mind, I'll absent myself, before she sees me and grows 'terrified.' " With a sniff every bit as haughty as any he could attribute to Sophie, he stalked into the crowd of dancers.

As soon as he left, Emily saw Sophie burst through the crowd, her face mottled with shame. The poor dear. And her looking so pretty tonight, too. This ball was something of a practice for Sophie's coming out, which was probably why she wore no costume. But her lavender silk gown was fine and rich, accentuating her petite figure and raven hair. No wonder Lord Blackmore had wanted to dance with her.

Sophie caught sight of Emily, then hurried to her side in a rush of skirts. "Oh, Emily, did you see?"

"No, but Lawrence told me about it."

Her face reddened. "Your cousin saw it? Oh, I'll never live down the shame! It was horrible, simply horrible! Everyone must think awful things about me now!"

Emily embraced her poor friend. "It's all right, dear. No one will think anything about *you*. They'll only blame your father, as well they should."

Sophie's small body trembled, and Emily could tell she was on the verge of tears. That wouldn't do.

Emily set Sophie firmly away. "Chin up, dear, it's over now. You must behave as if it didn't rattle you, or everyone will talk of it in the morning."

Choking back a sob, Sophie rubbed at her eyes with one delicate fist. "Yes, you're right." She glanced around. "They're all watching me, aren't they?"

"Never mind them." Seeking to distract her, Emily added, "I brought the calming elixir you wanted."

Sophie's face brightened. "You did? Truly?"

"I could hardly resist your begging, could I?" Emily smiled as she drew the glass vial from her reticule. "You wouldn't have sneaked out to visit me yesterday if you hadn't been desperate."

Sophie took the vial from Emily and examined it, her eyes still shimmering with unshed tears. "I can never thank you enough for this, my dear, dear friend. You don't know how you've saved my life!"

"Nothing so spectacular, I'm sure, but I hope it helps." Sophie's enthusiasm gave her a moment's unease. Only once had Emily's nostrums caused harm . . .

No, she wouldn't think of that. Nothing could happen this time. The elixir was mild as chicken soup, a mere diffusion of chamomile, lavender flowers, and balm leaves.

"I know it will be a *great* help," Sophie said. "Everyone swears by your nostrums."

Not everyone. Certainly not Lord Nesfield, who would kill her if he knew she'd given this to Sophie. "If your father should find out—"

"He shan't," Sophie assured her as she slid the vial into her reticule. Her blue eyes clouded over. "Anyway, it's worth risking his anger, especially after tonight. I'm near to being a candidate for Bedlam already. Look." She held out her gloved hands, which twitched and trembled.

Emily murmured her sympathy.

"Tonight has been such a nightmare," Sophie added, her mouth forming a delicate pout that would soon be breaking hearts in London. "First,

Lady Dryden introduced me to her elegant friends, which was vexing enough. I'm sure I behaved like a complete rattlebrain. And then the disaster with Lord Blackmore!"

"Surely it wasn't a disaster until your father came along."

"Not true! I was in a perfect terror the entire time we danced! The earl is well-known for treating respectable women with coldness and contempt."

"Don't be absurd." She couldn't reconcile Lord Blackmore's reform efforts with this rumor. "Did your father tell you that?"

"Not just him. Lady Manning said that Lord Blackmore rarely attends social events, and then refuses to dance with any of the eligible women. Instead, he consorts with fancy women and scandalous widows! They say he has a heart of stone when it comes to decent women of marriageable age."

Emily rolled her eyes. Sophie was still so very young. She couldn't distinguish legitimate fact from politically motivated gossip and rumor. "You shouldn't listen to such nonsense. I'm sure Lord Blackmore is perfectly polite to every woman, or Lady Dryden wouldn't have introduced him to you, nor would he have danced with you."

Sophie worried her lower lip with her perfect teeth. "Perhaps you're right. He was quite the gentleman while we danced, though he was a bit stiff."

"Besides, if he was indeed so cruel to young women before, he's clearly reformed. If any sweet innocent could melt a heart of stone, it would be you, dear friend."

Emily thought she heard something like a muffled snort nearby, but when she glanced around, no one was there. It must have been the wind coming through the open balcony door at her back.

"It doesn't matter, in any case," Sophie said. "Papa will never let me dance with Lord Blackmore again. Not that I would want to, after Papa's horrible scene. Oh, Emily, I'll never last a day in London! I'd rather run away with one of our footmen than have my coming out. At least I *know* our footmen."

Emily groaned. "You can't mean that. Imagine your father's reaction!" As if Sophie, who thought hardship was having to peel her own oranges, could ever be a servant's wife!

"No, I . . . I don't suppose I do. But I so dread this trip to London." Sophie's chin quivered dangerously.

Emily changed the subject at once. "So you danced with the famous Earl of Blackmore. What was he like? Handsome? Charming? Or too pleased with himself to endure?"

"He was very charming and quite handsome, from what I could tell. He wore a mask, you know, like your cousin." She colored a bit, then went on reflectively, "Come to think of it, he actually *looked* a great deal like Mr. Phe—" Sophie broke off, her eyes widening in terror. "Oh, no, Papa is just over there. I'm sure he's searching for me."

Emily turned around to see Lord Nesfield's golden lorgnette aimed in their direction. Though he was squinting and obviously having trouble seeing at that distance, she groaned.

Sophie ducked down. "He mustn't see me talking to you. You know how he is."

She certainly did. Though she and Sophie had been close friends from childhood, the Marquess of Nesfield had recently discouraged their friendship. Sadly enough, Emily knew why.

"We'd best separate," Emily said, squeezing Sophie's hand. "Go on now."

"You're the dearest friend a girl could have," she whispered, then fled.

Oh, dear, what if he'd spotted her giving the elixir to Sophie? She'd best make herself scarce, before he decided to waylay her. Ducking through the balcony door, she peered back into the ballroom to make sure he hadn't seen her.

"Hello," said a voice behind her, and she whirled around in surprise, then relaxed when she saw it was Lawrence. She wouldn't have recognized him in the darkness if not for the bit of candlelight from inside that glinted off his red hair.

"So you were listening in, were you?" she said dryly. "I should have known. Well, you'll be happy to know you can finally take me home."

He stayed oddly silent.

"You *are* ready to escape this tedium, aren't you?" she said.

When he answered, his voice was low and huskier than usual. "Oh, yes. I've been ready for hours. But aren't you planning to bid our host and hostess good-bye?"

"Oh, I should, shouldn't I?" she said, ashamed that she'd forgotten such an important courtesy. "Still, I don't want Lord Nesfield to see me. Do you mind doing it without me?"

He shrugged. "Not at all." With a bow that was strangely gentlemanly for Lawrence, he headed past her into the ballroom.

While she waited for him, she strode the balcony nervously. He seemed to be taking an awfully long time. Going to the doorway, she glanced in, but he was halfway across the room, speaking to the Worthings and gesturing to her. Quickly, she darted back onto the balcony and paced some more.

Once he returned, they hurried along the shadowy gallery until they reached the last room before the foyer. Then they walked briskly through it to where the footmen awaited the guests' leisure.

Lawrence spoke in an undertone to the servants, who then scurried about, gathering her pelisse and his greatcoat as if the two of them were very important guests. How strange. The servants had often seen her here before and never treated her with such extravagant courtesy. What *had* Lawrence told them?

As a servant helped her into her velvet pelisse, she thought he regarded her oddly. Then he darted away, making her wonder if she'd imagined it. The carriage was brought to the door with amazing speed, undoubtedly because it was one of Lady Dryden's. Emily and Lawrence had been unable to take the Fairchild carriage because it was being repaired, so Lady Dryden had generously offered to send one for them.

Lawrence opened the ornate door and handed her in. She relaxed only after he'd ordered the coachman to drive on. "It was fun for a while, but I was quite glad to leave, weren't you?"

He leaned back against the seat, the moonlight touching on his smiling mouth. There was something odd about his smile. It seemed different. "Yes, indeed. So good of you to suggest it."

"Suggest it? Don't be silly, Lawrence. You've been wanting to leave that ball almost since we got there."

The man across from her went very still. "Lawrence? Who the deuce is Lawrence?"

If his surprise hadn't told her that she'd made a drastic error, his language would have. Lawrence would never use such words in front of a rector's daughter. That's why his smile looked different and why the servants had behaved oddly when she'd left with him!

"You're n-not Lawrence," she whispered inanely, her heart leaping into her throat as he frowned and quickly removed his mask.

Dear heavens. The man had Lawrence's red hair and Lawrence's build and Lawrence's attire.

And a very different face.

"Of course I'm not Lawrence," he snapped. "What kind of game are you playing?" He tilted his head, and she glimpsed his hard male jaw and clean-shaven throat before the moon ducked behind the clouds, extinguishing what little light had filtered into the carriage. "You know very well who I am. That's why you said all that nonsense to Lady Sophie in my defense."

Removing his silk top hat, he laid it on the well-padded cushion of the brocade seat, and the very intimacy the action implied sent her into a panic. What nonsense had she said in his defense? What did he mean? Obviously he meant her conversation with Sophie, which he'd clearly overheard. But they'd only talked of the girl's coming out and her fears and . . .

Goodness gracious. And Lord Blackmore. They'd discussed Lord Blackmore at length. What had Sophie started to tell her? That Lord Blackmore looked an awful lot like someone? Lawrence. That's who his lordship resembled.

It couldn't be. "Are you saying you're . . . you're—"

"Blackmore, of course. But you know that quite well."

His irritated tone drew her up short. There was no cause for alarm. This was just a silly mistake, one they could quickly correct. The entire misunderstanding was her fault anyway. She couldn't very well blame him for taking her at her word and assuming that she needed an escort home.

"No, I didn't know. I'm afraid you look a great deal like my cousin, Lawrence, who's my escort this evening. In the darkness on the balcony, I mistook you for him. It's a simple error, no harm done."

Jordan Willis, the Earl of Blackmore, gaped at the trim, attractive woman across from him. What kind of joke was this? "Your cousin?" Deuce take it. Could this situation merely be a devilish strange mistake? He'd been wearing a mask, after all, but red hair like his was rare.

He'd assumed she was merely a lusty widow wanting a private encounter with him. Yet she did seem agitated. And if she really were telling the truth, then . . . "Are you claiming that you actually *meant* all that nonsense about my reputation being undeserved?"

"Of course I meant it." She seemed bewildered by his reaction. "Why would you think otherwise?"

He stretched an arm out along the seat back. Surely the woman couldn't be so naive, given what she'd heard of him. "Because when a beautiful widow defends me in my hearing, she generally means to impress me."

"A widow? You think I'm a widow?" Flipping out her fan, she worked it in agitated motions. "Oh, dear, so that's why you came along with me so easily. Because you thought . . . I mean, you assumed—"

"That you were a widow eager for a little company. Yes." A sense of impending doom descended on him. "Tell me I wasn't mistaken."

"But you were! This is all a terrible error! I'm not a widow. I'm in mourning for my mother, who died last year."

The sense of doom roared in his head. She wasn't

a widow. She was probably some squire's virginal daughter. And he'd carried her off in his carriage without regard for who might see them.

No, he couldn't be that stupid. "You're joking. This is some sort of game."

"Not at all! I'm telling the truth!"

"Am I to understand that you're unmarried?" His stomach began to churn.

Her head bobbed furiously.

"And pure as the driven snow, I suppose." Anger exploded in his brain. How could he have acted so heedlessly? "You're right, madam. This is indeed a terrible error."

"You *must* take me back at once, now that you see I'm not the sort of woman you thought. The longer you keep me out here, the more my reputation suffers. Besides, my cousin will be looking for me."

That brought him up short. Her cousin would be looking for her. And who else; her eager father? Her scheming aunt? What if she'd lied about mistaking him for her cousin? Overzealous mamas had laid traps for him before. It was one reason he'd always given a wide berth to unmarried young women.

And what about the way she'd defended him so adamantly? What young woman would have done so if not to make an impression upon him? She must have known he was eavesdropping. She hadn't acted at all surprised to find him standing there.

Cold anger settled in his gut like a bad meal. "I suspect your cousin knows exactly where you are right now."

She dropped her fan into her lap. "What do you mean?"

He interpreted her wary expression as more indication of her guilt. "You know exactly what I mean. This was all a little plot, wasn't it? If I return to the ball, I'll find a host of people awaiting us, ready to force me into 'fixing' my indiscretion. Well, let me tell you something. If you think I shall let some clever virgin trap me into marriage—"

"Trap you into marriage! You don't think that I...that this..." She sputtered to a halt, then drew a shaky breath. "You think I purposely did this? Made you take me out in a carriage unchaperoned at the risk to my reputation?"

"What else am I to think? You defended me when you surely realized I was standing there listening. All that nonsense about mistaking me for your cousin—"

"Why, you insolent, presuming blackguard! I see that I misjudged Sophie's information entirely! Obviously, you know only one sort of woman, which explains why you don't recognize a decent woman when you meet one!"

"Oh, I recognize decent women quite well," he snapped, his ancient fear rearing its ugly head. "They play games like this to catch themselves prominent, rich husbands. They want money, position, and the chance to run a man's life into the ground, and they'll use anything to get it."

When she gave a choked gasp, he added with deliberate coarseness, "Indecent women, on the other hand, are honest in what they expect for the pleasures they provide. They're easy to manage, take little time away from important pursuits, and don't ask for more than a man can give. Oh, yes, I recognize the difference. And I prefer indecent women to so-called decent women any day."

She straightened to fix him with a frosty gaze. "You may find this hard to believe, Lord Blackmore, but there are women other than the ones you've described, women who don't need to advance their position or fortune by tricking some hapless man into marriage. I'm one of them. I'm quite happy with my own life, thank you very much, and don't need to 'run' yours to find satisfaction. And I most certainly did *not* set out to trap you. I merely made a mistake, one that appears more grievous for every moment I spend in your disgusting presence!"

The vehemence in her voice took him by surprise. She did look the very picture of affronted womanhood. But then, she'd have to be a bit of an actress to pull this off, wouldn't she?

"So you claim not to have known I was listening to your conversation?"

"I do *not* have such appalling bad manners as to allow my friend to gossip about a man within his hearing!"

"All right," he said in clipped tones. "Let's say you're telling the truth. If you were oblivious to my presence on the balcony, why on earth did you defend me to Lady Sophie when you had no idea who I was or whether the gossip was true?"

She met his gaze coldly. "I knew of your work in Parliament. That *seemed* to show you to be honest and good."

He winced inwardly at her emphasis on "seemed." Had he been too hasty in his judgment of her?

The coach lurched, throwing her to the side long enough to expose one trim and decidedly pretty ankle before she righted herself. "Besides, it's not right for people to malign a man when he's not there to defend himself. If one doesn't know the truth, one should keep silent. My father, the rector of Willow Crossing, raised me not to listen to such idle gossip."

"Your father is a rector?" His uneasiness deepened. A rector's daughter? Setting a trap for him? That seemed too unlikely. He groaned. He'd made a nasty mistake in letting his anger get the better of him. Despite her mask, he could see her eyes snap.

"Yes," she said, barely pausing to acknowledge his question. "You could learn a lot from him. He doesn't judge people without knowing anything about them. He's always quoting Matthew 7:1, 'Judge not, that ye be not judged.'"

For God's sake, the woman was reciting the Bible, chapter and verse.

"I live by those words," she went on, now fully provoked. "No one but God has the right to judge a person's behavior, not even you. And furthermore—"

"Enough, madam."

She went on as if she hadn't heard him. "There's the scripture that says—"

"Madam, leave off! I believe you."

Her expression was priceless, almost disappointed, like that of a preacher denied a pulpit. "You what?"

"I believe you." Even he, with his cynical view of the world, couldn't believe that a woman could quote scripture and plot against him at the same time. Glancing away, he grumbled, "Clearly, you're not . . . the sort of woman I took you for."

"I should think not," she said loftily.

Gritting his teeth, he added, "I'm sorry to have offended you."

There was a long, chilly silence from the other end of the carriage. Good God, he'd made a horrible mistake. He would have recognized it earlier, but he'd been so furious at being caught in this devilish position that he hadn't been thinking. Obviously, if she'd been trying to trap him, she wouldn't have told him so soon of her error. She would have tried enticing him to compromise her.

But she'd done none of that. What's more, he'd just insulted her beyond countenance. He shot her a glance, wondering what she was thinking.

She watched him with all the wariness of a cornered deer. "So you admit that I was not trying to trick you?"

"Yes."

"You acknowledge that you were completely in the wrong?"

"Yes, yes, deuce take it!"

She sniffed and drew herself up. "You needn't curse at me."

"Now you're correcting my language, for God's sake." He sighed. "You're as pernicious as my stepsister. She bedevils me until I admit I'm wrong. And she, too, corrects my language and quotes scripture in an attempt to make me mend my ways."

"Then she must spend a great deal of time correcting your language and memorizing scripture."

He stared at her, then broke into laughter. "Indeed she does." The girl had a spine, he'd give her that. No woman but Sara ever dared to criticize him to his face, although many undoubtedly did behind his back.

This rector's daughter was an intriguing little thing. Not a simpering, foolish bone in her body, unlike most of the young women foisted upon him these days. Was she pretty as well, behind that mask? The rest of her certainly looked promising.

Good God, what was he thinking? She was a virgin. "A rector's daughter quoting scripture," he said, trying to fix the thought in his head. "I've truly caught myself an innocent, haven't I?"

"Yes." She smoothed her skirts primly. "Now you must throw me back."

"Indeed I must." But he made no move to order his coachman to turn the carriage around. First they must consider the potential problems arising from his fatal error. "Tell me something, Miss . . . Miss . . ."

"Fairchild," she supplied.

He groaned. "Even your name cries out purity and innocence." As the carriage rumbled on, he crossed his arms over his chest. "How shall I get you back to the ball without ruining your reputation? If your cousin is looking for you, he's liable to be standing on the doorstep when we return."

A troubled frown marred her pretty brow. "Oh, dear, you're right. Even if he doesn't know I've left the ballroom, there are the servants. They saw us leave together."

"You needn't worry about that; I paid them well to keep our departure secret." When she cast him a look of outrage, he shrugged. "I don't like having my private affairs bandied about the country. They won't speak of this to anyone, I assure you. Nonetheless, someone else may have seen us leave together. And if we return together . . ."

She slumped against the seat. "That's true. You aren't exactly inconspicuous."

No one had ever put it quite like that before. He smiled. "I'm afraid not. Believe me, at the moment, I wish I were."

Several people were sure to have noted that she'd walked out of the ballroom with the Earl of Blackmore. And when she didn't return for some time, then entered with him . . . He grimaced. She hadn't needed to set a trap. The result would be the same. All it required was one person standing in the entrance. Then everyone would know she'd been off in a carriage with an earl notorious for his encounters with unsavory women, and she'd be ruined for certain.

He didn't want to ruin her. He had this profound urge not to hurt her in any way, and he didn't know why. Because she was so completely innocent? Or because she'd defended him with no reason but the principle of the matter?

There was a sudden thumping from the coachman above. Then a voice, muffled by the roof of the carriage, echoed back to them. "We're approachin' the main road, milord. Where to?"

"Halt here for a moment, coachman." Jordan cast her a searching glance. "Well, Miss Fairchild, what do we do? I could take you home, then come back and pretend I'd been out alone. But you'd have to brazen it out later, tell some lie for how you got home and why you left without your escort."

"I do not tell lies, Lord Blackmore," she said stiffly. "It isn't in my nature."

He bit back a smile. "I see. Then perhaps you have some plan for reentering the ballroom without being noticed?"

She toyed with the velvet cord on her reticule, then brightened. "What if you bring me to the edge of the gardens? I can slip in there and emerge into the ballroom as if I'd been walking outside all the time. Then I needn't lie. If you stay out a while longer, then come in with your tale about going for a ride alone, we might pull it off."

"In other words, you won't lie, but you don't mind forcing *me* to."

"I'm sorry," she said in obvious chagrin. "You're right, it's very bad of me to—"

"It's all right." He tamped down on the laugh bubbling up in his throat. Devil take it, he'd never met a woman so principled. Nor could he remember ever having so much fun with one. "Believe me, I wouldn't hesitate to tell a fib to save your reputation."

A wan smile touched her lips. "Thank you."

He knocked on the ceiling, then ordered the coachman to drive back to the gardens. While the servant maneuvered the coach about, Jordan returned his attention to Miss Fairchild.

She was staring out the window. Her bombazine gown was so black it swallowed up whatever faint light the moon shone on it, leaving her hands and her face to reflect the moon's glow.

And what a face, all soft curves and secrets. If only he could see more of it, could rip the mask off and get a good look at her. What he could see was exquisite. Her brow, so high and moonlight pale . . . fine rounded cheeks . . . generous lips. Her hair looked like spun silk even inside the dark carriage and—

What had come over him? He was waxing poetic, something he never did, and certainly shouldn't with the prim little Miss Fairchild. He mustn't even *think* of her in those terms. She wasn't his sort at all.

Suddenly, she met his gaze. "Lord Blackmore, I must apologize for getting you into this mess."

"No, no," he said, waving his hand dismissively, "it was an honest mistake on both our parts. With any luck, no one will ever know it happened."

"And if they do?"

She was asking if she could trust him to make it right. Suddenly, he wanted very badly to reassure her of his character. "I would do what must be done, Miss Fairchild. Don't concern yourself about that."

"I wouldn't expect you to marry me," she hastened to say, "but if you could make up some story or . . . or . . ."

"I'll do what needs to be done; don't you worry," he said, more firmly. Some story, indeed. As if any story could safely extricate them from this. "But we won't be found out. I've successfully wriggled out of far more compromising situations."

"I'm sure you have."

He smiled at her arch tone. He wished she weren't wearing that damned mask. Though the moon graced her figure with silvery light, he could only discern a little of her expression. It bothered him that she could see his face, but he couldn't see hers.

"Still," she added, "if there's any way I can make up for my error—"

"There is one way," he said, the dangerous words out of his mouth before he could stop them. "You could let me see you without the mask."

Chapter 2

I met a lady in the meads
Full beautiful, a faery's child
Her hair was long, her foot was light
And her eyes were wild.

John Keats, "La belle dame sans merci"

Emily stared at Lord Blackmore blankly. "I beg your pardon?"

"You have me at a disadvantage—you're masked, and I'm not." His voice was husky and deep within the close confines of the carriage. "I'd like to see you without your mask. Do you mind?"

She hesitated only briefly before lifting her hands to the ties. "No, of course not." It was a small enough thing to give him, and he *had* been a perfect gentleman once they'd sorted everything out.

Besides, simple logic told her he'd had every reason to misunderstand the situation. No doubt he was often pursued by silly girls eager to snag a rich earl. How could she blame a man as wealthy and powerful as he for being cautious? The least she could do was show him her face.

If she could release the ties. Goodness gracious, they were knotted. She couldn't even pull the blessed thing over her head. It would dislodge her coiffure, and if she entered the ball with her hair in complete disarray, people would suspect something had happened. "I'm sorry, but it won't come loose."

"Allow me." Despite his long legs, he moved easily from his seat opposite her to the one at her side. "Lean forward."

She hesitated. The thought of his fingers against her hair sent little frissons of alarm dancing up and down her spine. Some feminine instinct warned her that letting this man close was dangerous.

Then again, he clearly wasn't interested in her as a woman. He'd practically recoiled from her once he'd learned she was a virgin. So why not let him do this?

"All right," she said, trying to keep her voice even.

He rested his large fingers on her scalp, then gingerly began to work loose the knot. She went completely still, as if by making herself into a perfect statue she could keep from noticing the male body a few inches away.

What a joke. Never had she been this close to a man, and his every movement awakened her senses: his forearms resting against her back, the muscles flexing as he worked on the knot . . . his breath, warm and measured, tickling the fine hairs on the back of her bare neck . . . his firm thigh plastered against her backside.

Her foolish blood rampaged through her body. The long years of her mother's illness and then her year of mourning had prevented her from having suitors. Not many eligible men lived in Willow Crossing anyway, but she might have found someone if she hadn't been so concerned with keeping her mother alive.

Now Mama was dead, she was twenty-two, and

she had only Papa for company. These days, with him so distant and her activities so restricted, even Papa couldn't keep the loneliness at bay. Still, she'd taken her mind off it by keeping busy at home.

Until tonight. The man beside her would make even a nun crave male companionship. Nervously, she glanced out the window of the carriage, but that only heightened her awareness of their intimate surroundings. Out here it was so deserted that crickets whined undisturbed and owls hooted their night cries without fear of repercussion. And it was dark. Very, very dark. A dangerous environment indeed.

Suddenly the mask came free. "There you are," he murmured as he let the scrap of starched silk float down into her lap.

"Thank you." She quickly slid to the other end of the seat. He was too close, too . . . too male. Her presence might not affect him, but his presence certainly affected her. Here in this cavelike retreat, he loomed larger than life. She must escape this mess before she began to behave exactly like those girls he despised. Trying to squeeze herself into the smallest space of the seat possible, she shifted to look at him.

Dear heavens. That was a mistake. The capricious moon now flooded him with light, allowing her to get a good long look at him for the first time all evening.

Handsome? Had Sophie really used that innocuous term to describe the Earl of Blackmore?

Arresting . . . intimidating . . . overwhelming. He was all that and more. And handsome was only a very small part.

Amazing how much a mask and a little darkness could disguise. He and Lawrence had the same hair color and build, but there the resemblance ended. Lawrence's eyes were wide-set and an indeterminate brown. Lord Blackmore's were deepset and so dark they were almost black, particularly in this light. Lawrence's cheeks tended to be pale, except when he blushed, brightening them to pink. Lord Blackmore would never blush. She was sure of that.

But the way he was running his gaze over her face, as if trying to make out her features, did bring a blush to her own cheeks. Instantly she regretted removing her mask. It left her so . . . so exposed.

"It's hard to see well in this light, but you don't look like a rector's daughter." When she frowned, sure that he was doubting her word again, he hastened to add, "You *act* like a rector's daughter, mind you. You just don't look like one."

She relaxed against the seat. "And what does a rector's daughter look like?"

"I don't know. Tight-lipped. Pinch-faced. Holier-than-thou."

"You haven't had much experience with people of my situation, have you, my lord?" she said tartly. "I assure you, rector's daughters have all sorts of faces. And attitudes."

He smiled. "Thank God for that."

His tone expressed full approval of her appearance. A delicious shiver whispered down her spine. Goodness gracious. No wonder women climbed over themselves trying to trap him into marriage. What woman wouldn't desire a man who could make her weak in the knees with just a few words?

A pity he was forbidden to her.

As he continued to stare, she grew hot. Quickly she lifted the mask to her face and retied it. "I . . . I must have it on when we reach the gardens, you know."

"I suppose you must."

Did she imagine the edge of disappointment in his voice? Of course she did. He'd merely been curious about her, that's all. It was perfectly natural.

She twisted away to look out the window again, but that only made her more aware of him. She could feel him watching her, interested, controlled. She only wished she could be so controlled.

"Oh, look," she said brightly as the carriage made a sudden turn. "We've reached the gardens."

"Have we?"

Why must the man have such a . . . a rakish voice? He probably didn't even know he sounded like that. It made her very eyelashes tingle.

"Yes, we have," she said inanely. The carriage shuddered to a halt as she continued to peer out the window.

But once everything was silent, she heard it. Voices. In the garden and quite near. "Oh, no, I think there's someone out there."

He edged toward her, peering over her shoulder out the window. "I see them. They're passing the apple tree now."

The couple was a man and a woman of indeterminate age, talking and laughing as they strolled arm in arm. Suddenly, one of them looked up and spotted the carriage.

Emily jumped back from the window so quickly, she found herself practically in the earl's lap. When she turned toward him, his face was mere inches from hers. "What do we do?" she whispered.

He rapped his fist on the ceiling. "Another turn around the drive, coachman."

"Yes, milord," the coachman answered, and prodded the horses into a trot.

For a moment she sat frozen, plastered to him for fear that the moonlight would reveal her face as they drove past the couple. But when they cleared the garden, the earl said in choked tones, "You can remove your hand from my leg now, Miss Fairchild."

Only then did she realize her fingers had a vise-like grip on his thigh. Mortified beyond belief, she snatched her hand back, but not before an impression of the hard muscle beneath his superfine breeches burned itself into her palm.

He was too close, too . . . too . . . *there*. She tried to slide down the seat from him, but there was no more space. Nor did he move away. When she glanced up in alarm, it was to find him staring at her, his eyes fathomless and mysterious in the moonlight.

"Fate seems to be conspiring to throw us together," he said in a rumbling voice.

"Oh, don't say that! Our plan may still work!"

"And if it doesn't?" He was so close she could feel the ragged cadence of his warm breath on her lips.

"Then I'll deal with the consequences. Though I would prefer not to have been caught riding in a carriage unchaperoned with a man, it is mostly my fault it happened. You mustn't concern yourself with it, my lord."

"But I must. To be honest, the thought of a continued association with you isn't as . . . unappealing as it was at first." His gaze drifted down to her lips, intimate and interested.

Her pulse raced wildly. "You needn't say that to spare my feelings."

"Believe me, sparing your feelings has nothing to do with it." He lowered his head until his mouth hovered inches from hers. "The truth is, I'm having a devil of a time resisting the urge to kiss you."

"Oh, but you *must*!" she protested feebly as her head swam.

"Yes. I must."

Yet he didn't. Before she could protest or even move away, he covered her mouth with his.

It was a shock, the most sublime shock she'd ever had in her life. Who would have guessed a man's lips could be so soft ... or so fiendishly tempting? His breath mingled with hers, spiked with brandy, though he didn't seem the least bit drunk. His mouth caressed hers in such a leisurely fashion that it seduced her into stillness.

She exhaled on a sigh, then caught her breath when he clasped her shoulders to draw her closer. In a futile attempt to dispel the fog forming in her brain, she turned her lips away, but he only shifted his mouth to drop short, delectable kisses along the curve of her cheek to her earlobe, following the line of the mask.

"Sweet Emily," he whispered, his breath tickling her ear. "Sweet, innocent Emily."

Her name sounded foreign to her ears when he rasped it like that. How did he know it anyway? Oh, yes, he'd overheard her conversation with Sophie. "You mustn't c-call me that," she stammered. He nibbled on her earlobe, and she gasped. "You ... you must call me Miss Fairchild."

"All right. Kiss me, Miss Fairchild. Or I shall surely kiss you again."

"I ... I would prefer that you not ... kiss me, Lord Blackmore. It's not proper."

"As if I care about propriety." He planted a kiss on the pulse in her neck. "Remember my scandalous reputation? And my name is Jordan. Say it."

"I-I can't. It's too intimate."

"Exactly." Sliding one arm about her waist, he tugged her close, then tipped her chin up with his free hand until she was staring into his glittering eyes, her heart beating a wild, staccato rhythm.

"Say my name," he whispered hoarsely. "I want to hear you say it."

"Jordan," she breathed. If they continued this much longer, he wouldn't have to ruin her. She'd gladly rush to ruin herself. "Jordan, we mustn't do this. You . . . you mustn't kiss me."

"I want a taste of the woman who's to be my downfall." As she stiffened, preparing to protest, he caught her mouth with his once more.

There was less softness in his kiss this time. He kissed like a man with a purpose, single-minded and thorough. His mouth drew on hers hungrily, his tongue outlining the seam of her lips as his hand swept from her chin to her throat, lingering there to stroke the bare skin of her arched neck with his clever, knowing fingers. When she gasped at the sheer intimacy of his caress, he slid his tongue inside her mouth.

Some Puritan part of her insisted that she protest this latest indignity. But protest was impossible. The Earl of Blackmore was kissing her, deliciously and provocatively. She'd never even expected to meet him and now to have him kissing her like this . . .

Her mind went blank as he swept the inside of her mouth with his tongue, finding and conquering every sensitive part. His kiss deepened, grew more daring, and she became his willing accomplice. Dear heavens, the man certainly knew what he was doing. Like a ninny, she found herself welcoming each heady stroke, each masterful thrust of his tongue.

Then she was curling her fingers into the crisp superfine lapels of his cutaway, clinging to him like a wretched wanton. And she no longer cared. Like drinking champagne for the first time, the varied pleasures of his kiss roused new and unfamiliar cravings in her. She strained against him, needing those cravings answered, and he gave her more than she even knew to ask for, bending her back until she was half-reclining on the brocade seat.

Then the carriage lurched, throwing him off-balance and forcing him to break off the kiss. He stared down into her eyes a long moment, the desire leaching out of his face like color from bleached linen. A thin shaft of moonlight played over his stark features, highlighting the carved planes of his cheekbones and nose.

Her hands still gripped his lapels, but now that he was looking at her as if in a state of shock, she became painfully aware of their scandalous position. Embarrassed, she released his cutaway and turned her head.

He spoke in a tortured voice. "My God. I had no idea how sweet one kiss could be."

Sweet? It was magical! So why was he staring at her as if she were a Jezebel?

Uttering a low curse, he dragged himself off her and threw himself into the opposite seat. "What the devil was I doing? I must have lost my infernal mind."

Ashamed by his words, she sat up and tried to straighten her clothing. Never had she felt so small. It had been so delightful, she hadn't stopped to think how mundane such kisses were to him. Even with her poverty of experience, she recognized the wealth of his. No doubt he found her kisses painfully pathetic.

"I'm sorry I became so carried away," he said in a stiff voice. "I had no right to take advantage of the situation."

"Please, it doesn't matter." Tears pooled in her eyes. Now he was trying to be kind, curse him.

"But it *does* matter. You're not the sort of woman . . . I mean—"

"I'm not your usual preference," she whispered in utter mortification. "Yes, I know."

"That's not what I mean. Let's just say that your sort of woman is forbidden to me, all right?"

That wasn't true, she thought. He could involve himself with anyone if he truly wished. But he wouldn't. An earl with a nobody like her? It was unthinkable. She wasn't forbidden to him. But he was most certainly forbidden to her.

Jordan watched her, trying futilely to gather his scattered wits. Judging from her hurt expression, he was saying this all wrong. No doubt she'd expected him to swear his undying love. That was precisely why he avoided virginal, respectable women.

Experience had always been paramount in his encounters with women. A lusty woman whom he could forget as quickly as she forgot him—that was all he'd aimed for in a lover. He knew better than anyone that seducing virgins was a dangerous sport.

But with Emily . . . Good God, he could still taste her on his lips, apples and cream and a hint of champagne. And when she'd parted her lips for him . . . He sprang to life just thinking of it. Lust raged through him, tearing down the barriers of sense and reason. Even now, he wanted to toss her down on the seat and bury himself inside her. And he couldn't.

He felt like a child who couldn't get his fill of sweets, even though he knew they would make him ill. Her lavender scent filled the carriage, enticing him even further. He wanted to taste her, all of her, to strip the clothes from her and press his mouth against every inch of her pale, delicate body. The damned hunger— He clenched his jaw. It was so intense, it hurt.

"Look here, Emily—" he began, wondering how to explain his lapse in judgment.

"Please don't say any more. It's all right. I . . . I suppose the full moon affected . . . both of us."

"Yes—the full moon."

It was as good an explanation for complete insanity as any other. Only complete insanity could make him lose control. And for a prim little rector's daughter!

A prim little rector's daughter who might end up his wife if he weren't careful. He tightened his jaw as he glanced out the window. Pray heaven no one was in the garden now. Marriage to Emily Fairchild would be sheer disaster. She barely knew him and couldn't hope to be happy with him. She would chafe at a forced marriage. Being a starry-eyed innocent, she would want more from him than he could give. Before long, they'd be locked in the same kind of disastrous battle that had ruined his parents' marriage and destroyed his mother's life.

A memory flashed before him, of his mother screaming in his face that he was the reason she couldn't have fun, the reason she was in hell, the reason for her misery. And though he'd long ago realized that it was the drink that made her say that, he also knew it was partly true. If not for him . . .

Forcefully, he drove back the pain. Perhaps Emily would react differently to such a marriage. But perhaps not. Pray God he never had to find out.

Besides, for all her softness and easy capitulation to his kisses, she was still a sweet-faced gentlewoman with firm ideas about proper behavior. If he married her, he'd be making love with the candles snuffed and asking permission to attend his club. And the more he wanted her, the worse it would be. He'd rather shoot off his deuced cock than face a lifetime of that.

Still, she'd defended him without even knowing him. No woman except his stepsister Sara had ever defended him. Raged at him, yes. Gossiped about him and lusted after his money and title, most definitely. But not taken his side.

"Lord Blackmore, may I ask you one question?" she said timidly.

Her voice jarred him. Ah, so they were back to formalities, were they? Hard to believe that scant minutes ago, she'd whispered his name with something like affection. But this entire evening had been like a dream, and it was time for it to end. "Ask whatever you wish."

Her gaze dropped to her hands, clasped demurely in her lap. "You . . . said you prefer indecent women to decent women. Yet you danced with Lady Sophie."

She was too polite to call him insincere, but he knew what she thought. "Lady Dryden asked me to dance with your friend, so I did. I'm not so rude as to ignore my hostess's wishes. But that's all it was, I assure you, no matter what Lord Nesfield made of it." A smile touched his lips. "Why? Are you jealous?"

That got her dander up. "Of course not. I'm not that foolish. I know I am . . . I know this was . . . merely a fleeting flirtation for you. We move in entirely different circles. If I do manage to reach the house without being noticed, I doubt I'll ever see you again."

Her bald description of what he'd already been thinking irritated him. "I'll be here for a week more. We could—"

"Have more scandalous tête-à-têtes in your carriage? I think not." She glanced away, the fluid light catching the porcelain stillness of her face, a stillness betrayed by eyes that showed every emotion. "I don't think I could survive any more such meetings."

Nor could he. Good God, if he had another chance at it, he'd probably make a complete fool of himself. He refused to lose his head over any woman, especially an upstanding young gentlewoman like Emily Fairchild.

But the carriage was rapidly approaching the gardens again, and as the horses clopped nearer, his heart dropped into his stomach. He wished he could know her better. What a shame that was impossible.

All too soon, the carriage was slowing, and she was staring out the window. "Thank God, they're gone," she said, her relief evident.

Did she find the idea of being forced to marry him so distasteful? Of course she did. She thought he was the kind of scoundrel who could have a "flirtation" with a young woman, kiss her senseless, then send her off without a thought.

Very well. Let her think it. It was better that way.

He knocked on the carriage ceiling and ordered the coachman to halt. Then he sat back in his seat. "I'll go in first. If anyone asks me about you, I'll declare I have no idea what they're talking about. You wait a while, then stroll in from the gardens as if you'd been out there all along. With any luck, you won't have to tell any lies."

"Thank you," she said primly, then turned the handle, opened the door, and descended from the carriage.

"Emily—" he began as he followed her out, wanting to stop her, yet knowing it was pointless.

She faced him with a look of expectation. He didn't know what to say. What could he offer her? What did she want from him? Did she want him to throw caution to the winds, ask her if he could call or announce his intentions to her father? If she did, she wouldn't get it. As she'd said, this was an interlude. And he wouldn't change the outcome.

When he remained silent, she flashed him a wan smile. "Thank you for a very enlightening evening, Lord Blackmore. I shall never forget it."

Nor shall I, he thought as she hurried into the gardens, a quiet grace in her movements even as she raced to be away from him, disappearing into the night like Cinderella after the ball.

Except for one awful difference. She'd left him without even a glass slipper to remember her by. And there would be no future between them. None at all.

Chapter 3

Willow Crossing
May 1819

> *Fetters of gold are still fetters, and the softest lining can never make them so easy as liberty.*
>
> Mary Astell, English poet and feminist,
> *An Essay in Defence of the Female Sex*

Since it was the servants' day off, the rectory was still and the kitchen deserted in the wee hours after dawn. Emily stood at the stove heating watered-down brandy, glad for the solitude on this spring morning as she prepared her father's breath-sweetening tincture.

She touched her finger lightly to the glassy surface of the liquid. Good. It was finally warm enough. Turning to the table, she poured the hot brandy water over the cloves, wild sage, and marsh rosemary she'd crumbled in the bottom of a china bowl. As a crisp, festive herbal scent wafted through the kitchen, it roused memories of mulled wine and wassail . . . and feasts served at elaborate masquerade balls given by wealthy nobility.

Sticking her tongue out at the bowl, she dropped into a chair and crossed her arms over her chest.

Oh, why couldn't she banish that wretched night from her mind? Two months had passed since the ball, for pity's sake. Her period of mourning was over, and she'd been invited to countless dinners and parties since. A young man or two had even paid her some attention. By now she should have forgotten the entire incident.

Lord Blackmore had surely put it out of his mind the very next morning. Although she'd foolishly hoped he might pay her a visit in the days that followed, he hadn't taken any more notice of her.

Of course he hadn't: he'd made it quite clear that it had meant little to him. He'd even thrust her away from him as if she were some nasty troll. Obviously her lack of experience had disgusted him. She was the only one foolish enough to dwell on their kisses and savor the memory of his mouth locked to hers, his hands pressing her down on the seat of the carriage . . .

Oh, wretched, wretched imagination! Why was she so tormented with embarrassing memories?

Because it had been her first kiss. She blushed. No, not just her first. Her first and second and third. How many more might there have been if he hadn't stopped? She'd been ready to let him ruin her right there in that carriage! The man certainly knew how to make a woman's first kisses memorable.

Curse him for that. Until then, her life had been mostly content, an ordered procession of small cares, light duties, and casual friendships. She attended church and paid morning visits and tended house for Papa. What did it matter if she sometimes felt a breath of dissatisfaction in her preordained life? If she occasionally found the tedium overwhelming? Her life was better than many people's, and she'd been taught to thank God for that.

Then Lord Blackmore—Jordan—had entered her placid world, disturbing its unruffled surface and forcing her to see what she'd missed. She hadn't known a man could startle a woman's heart into joyous beating or inflict upon it a pain so intense, it was almost akin to pleasure.

Now she understood the poet Thomas Gray's words, "Where ignorance is bliss, 'tis folly to be wise." She'd been happy in her ignorance. Gaining wisdom, or experience, about men had indeed been folly. The worst kind of folly.

"There you are," came a voice from the doorway. Her father strode into the kitchen. "I should've known I'd find you here."

Edmund Fairchild was a tall, thin man who'd never looked like a clergyman. Until her mother died. After that he'd taken refuge in his work, always citing the most restrictive scriptures, the most solemn verses. The mouth that once had always worn a smile now seemed tugged perpetually downward with the weight of his grief. The hands that had often hugged her now fell limp and stiff at his sides.

Guilt settled sickly in her belly as she surveyed his rumpled clothes and blue eyes fogged by sleep. "I'm so sorry, Papa, did I wake you? I tried to be quiet. I just couldn't sleep."

Lowering his lanky frame into a chair, he threaded his fingers through his disheveled graying hair, and for once a smile softened his hard features. "You didn't wake me. Didn't you hear the carriage drive up outside? Before they could ring the bell and wake you, I came down to see who was calling at this unreasonable hour."

"So who was the rude creature?" When her father frowned, she added, "I do hope it wasn't the mayor's wife, asking for birch-leaf tea again. I've told her repeatedly to visit the apothecary, but she insists I'm the only one in Willow Crossing who can help her with her rheumatism. If it was her servant, please tell him my answer is still no."

"It wasn't the mayor's wife." Her father concentrated on rubbing his bony, arthritic legs. "You know, Emily, lately your answer to anyone asking for physic seems to be 'no.' You used to enjoy helping people with your medicines. Now you seem almost fearful of it, unless it's something inconsequential like the elixir you made for his lordship's daughter."

Rising suddenly from her chair, she turned her attention to the duck that needed plucking for dinner. Papa must never know the real reason she was afraid to dabble in medicines anymore. "I'm making breath sweetener for you, and that's a help, isn't it?"

"Yes, but it's not the same thing as making physic." When she said nothing, he added, "If this concerns your mother—"

"Of course not! I-I've merely lost my interest in doctoring." That he would even mention Mama surprised her. They'd grieved apart, neither one encroaching on the other's remembrances, as if speaking of Mama might make the world explode. Their unspoken agreement had grown more strained of late, however.

Quickly, she changed the subject. "If it wasn't the mayor's servant at the door, who was it?"

Papa slapped his head with his palm. "My word, I forgot! Lord Nesfield's footman is waiting outside with his lordship's carriage."

"Lord Nesfield? I thought he was still in London for Sophie's coming out."

"I thought so, too. But it seems he's returned."

She began to pluck the duck's feathers with

sharp, angry strokes. "And of course, the first thing he did was demand your presence at a ridiculous hour. You'd think you were his blessed servant. You'd think—"

"No, dear. He didn't send the carriage for me. He sent it for you."

The duck dropped onto the counter with a thud. "For me? Why?"

"Lord Nesfield wants you at Ormond. His footman said it concerns Lady Sophie. And you *are* her particular friend."

Wiping her damp hands on her dimity apron, Emily stared at her father. Sophie? Had something happened to Sophie? But why would that prompt the marquess to send for her when he thought so little of her friendship with his daughter?

The last time she'd seen Sophie had been at the ball, when she'd given the girl the nostrum . . . A horrid chill slinked down her spine. Goodness gracious, what if something had gone wrong with it?

No, nothing could have gone wrong. The thing had been perfectly mild. And surely Lord Nesfield wouldn't have traveled all the way from London to lecture her about a harmless collection of herbs.

But what else could have brought him here and prompted him to call for her?

Her father apparently misinterpreted her uneasy silence. "I know you don't like the man, but it would be wise for you to go, my child. He is my patron, after all."

"Yes, of course. I'll go at once." Untying her apron, she set it on the table. She had no choice but to leap when Lord Nesfield snapped his fingers.

While Papa spoke with the footman, she took a few minutes to change into her sky-blue sprigged muslin, the only one of her day gowns suitable for an audience with the haughty marquess.

When she descended the stairs, Papa was pacing the hall, the lines in his face etched more deeply than usual. "Don't let Lord Nesfield's ill humor rouse you to harsh words, Emily." He bent as she lifted her head to kiss his cheek. "We owe him a great deal. He may be troublesome, but he's still one of God's creatures. Try to remember that."

"I will, Papa. Don't worry. I'm sure this is nothing at all."

Later, however, as the Nesfield carriage rumbled up in front of the ancient mansion set amidst acres of tenant farms and forest, she found it increasingly hard to be nonchalant. The imposing facade of stone and brick with its myriad windows emanated an awesome power. The Marquess of Nesfield held complete sway in Willow Crossing. If he wanted to ruin her and Papa, he could do so with a snap of his cruel fingers. And unfortunately, she'd given him the wherewithal to do it.

A shudder passed through her. When she descended from the carriage and entered the gilt-edged foyer to find Lord Nesfield himself waiting for her, the shudder grew to a raging alarm. Something was amiss, to be sure. But what? How could it possibly concern her?

It must be terribly important. His lordship's attire, usually extravagant and self-important, was casual, mussed, and grimy. He looked as if he'd just now arrived from London. He was treading a circle around the foyer like some great vulture surveying a dead carcass, and his ivory cane beat a choppy rhythm on the marble floor.

As soon as he caught sight of her, his frown added more wrinkles to his aging brow. "At last! You took your sweet time, didn't you, Miss Fairchild? Come with me. We have much to discuss."

She bit back a hot retort. She would never get

used to Lord Nesfield's utter lack of courtesy toward anyone beneath him. He barely allowed the butler time to take her pelisse before he clasped her by the arm, dragging her to the drawing room as if she were a recalcitrant child. Dear heavens, what was going on? She'd never seen Lord Nesfield so agitated, and he made a profession out of peevishness and agitation.

As soon as they entered the lavishly appointed room, he released her. She surveyed her surroundings, discovering to her surprise that someone awaited them there. A woman of substantial proportions filled up a large wing-backed chair like a great stuffed peacock.

And with such brilliant feathers! Emily couldn't help but stare. The woman's expensive-looking satin gown was so vividly purple it made her pink-cheeked face look like a peony floating in a sea of violets. Emily judged her to be about fifty, though it was hard to tell since she wore a turban of golden satin over her hair, and the plumpness of her skin smoothed out any wrinkle that would dare to crease its surface.

One thing was for certain. Only a woman with utter confidence in herself could effectively wear such an outrageous ensemble.

Lord Nesfield broke the silence. "Ophelia, I present to you Miss Fairchild, my rector's daughter. Miss Fairchild, this is Ophelia Campbell, the Countess of Dundee. Lady Dundee is my sister."

Emily gave a deep curtsy, her curiosity thoroughly roused. So this was the formidable Lady Dundee. According to local gossip, the woman had turned down offers of marriage from an English duke and a marquess to marry her Scottish earl. Some said she'd married for love, and others said she'd married to spite her indifferent parents.

Whatever the case, rumor had it that her wit, intelligence, and forthright speech had garnered her respect and power among Scottish society despite her English upbringing.

She straightened to find Lady Dundee examining her like a jeweler perusing uncut gems.

"You're probably wondering why I've brought you here, Miss Fairchild," Lord Nesfield continued. "As you know—"

"Randolph, must you be so rude?" Lady Dundee scowled at her brother. "Let the poor girl sit down first. And call for some refreshment, for heaven's sake. We've been on the road for days, and I'm dry as a bone." With a regal nod cast loosely in Emily's direction, she added, "You must forgive my brother's ill manners, Miss Fairchild. He's very tired. We traveled all last night to make up the time we'd lost to poor weather."

Gesturing impatiently to the settee across from his sister, Lord Nesfield barked, "Sit down, Miss Fairchild," then strode to the doorway, and bellowed for a servant.

Emily did as he bade at once, not daring to do otherwise. While they waited for the tea, Lady Dundee peppered Emily with questions—about her parents, her upbringing, the sort of books she read. By the time the tea arrived, Emily was on the verge of rudely informing Lady Dundee that none of it was her concern. Goodness gracious, was this some sort of test? Or did all women of exalted society interrogate their guests?

"Now then, Miss Fairchild," Lord Nesfield began, "as you may have guessed, I've brought you here because I need your help."

Her help? How very strange. "Your footman said this concerned Sophie." Emily sipped at her tea, all too aware of Lady Dundee's intrusive gaze on her. "She's not ill, is she? May I see her?"

"I'm afraid that's impossible," Lady Dundee answered for her brother. "My niece is at my estate in Scotland with her uncle."

"Scotland!" Emily set her cup down so abruptly that tea sloshed over onto the delicate china saucer. "But I thought she was in London having her coming out!"

"She was." Lord Nesfield shoved his hands in his coat pockets, his expression grim. "Until she tried to run off with some bounder."

Emily forgot about her tea completely. "Sophie? Timid little Sophie? Off with some man?"

"Yes. Timid little Sophie, off with some man," he echoed sourly. "That's when I whisked her away to Ophelia's in Scotland. And that's where she'll remain until I find out who the scoundrel is."

"What do you mean? Don't you know who he is?"

"Unfortunately, no. One night a few weeks ago, I heard a sound and went downstairs to find Sophie sneaking out of the London house. I ran through the open door after her. A carriage awaited her in the street, but when the driver saw me, he set off at a frantic pace. I called for my horse and gave chase, but it was too late, of course. The man had disappeared. And I never got to see who he was. I still do not know." A dangerous look entered his eyes. "But I will find out. You can be sure of that."

Emily might have thought this some strange joke if not for two things. One, Lord Nesfield never joked. Two, Lady Dundee was loudly seconding her brother's vow to find the scoundrel.

But who would have believed that shy, skittish Sophie would ever attempt elopement? Then again,

Sophie *had* made that odd comment about the footman.

Something in her face must have alerted Lord Nesfield and his sister to her thoughts, for they both burst out together, "You know who he is!"

"No! Truly, I don't! It's just that . . . well, she was so nervous about her coming out that she jested about . . . running off with a footman."

Lord Nesfield's face fell. "It was not a footman, I assure you. The scoundrel is of higher consequence than that, for I have had Bow Street Runners by the score trying to discover the driver of the hired hack to no success. It is as if the bloody carriage disappeared into thin air." Lord Nesfield lifted his lorgnette to peer at her. "Didn't she tell you anything else? Write you about any man she had met?"

"If you'll recall, Lord Nesfield," Emily said stiffly, "you forbade her to write to me. And Sophie is always careful to honor your wishes."

Lady Dundee's muffled laugh provoked Lord Nesfield's anger. "Well, she wasn't so bloody careful when she ran off with that bounder!"

Emily glared at him. This wasn't her fault, after all. "But surely she was willing to tell you who it was once the elopement failed."

"No, damn it all!" His grizzled cheeks puffed out in indignation as he punctuated each word with a tap of his cane. "She won't say anything!"

"Calm down, Randolph. Your dramatics won't help the situation." Lady Dundee smiled thinly at Emily. "It seems my niece has suddenly grown a spine. She refuses to reveal her true love's name. No one can break her silence, not even me. All she'll say is that they're in love, and she'll marry him no matter what we do or say."

"I would have brought the insolent girl here to

see if you might get the truth out of her," Lord Nesfield grumbled to Emily, "but I feared that the blackguard would come here as well. At least he will not think to look for her in Scotland."

"What about Sophie's maid? Couldn't she tell you anything?"

"She, too, ran off on the night of the attempted elopement." Lord Nesfield sat down on the other end of the settee. "If I find her, I will string her up by her sassy tongue, I will. Never did like that maid. She was a bad influence on my Sophie."

Emily bit back a smile. She'd yet to see a single person whom Lord Nesfield regarded as a *good* influence. Sophie'd had six different maids in the last five years, and this one had stayed on longer than most, given Lord Nesfield's mercurial temper.

Lady Dundee reached forward to pour herself more tea. "About all we can determine is that Sophie met the man in London. How else could she have been put in the company of such a blackguard?"

"How else indeed," Lord Nesfield growled. "And we know he is a fortune hunter, to be sure. If he were respectable, he would have asked me for her hand."

With difficulty, Emily stifled a retort. Lord Nesfield's reputation might have cowed even a respectable man. Then again, elopements seldom occurred between people of equal wealth and station. Perhaps Lord Nesfield's concern was justified.

"He's probably a titled man without a fortune, or some second son eager to snatch an heiress," Lady Dundee said. "Such men would have enough family influence to keep their attempt secret from Bow Street Runners."

Clearly, neither of them thought it was simply a man in love, someone who knew he'd never have a chance with Sophie otherwise. Given Sophie's lack of experience, they could be right.

Lady Dundee leaned back in her chair, settling her violet satin skirts about her like an unfurling sail. "Now you see why we're in a bind, Miss Fairchild. My niece is eager to return to her secret suitor. If we don't discover him soon, I fear he'll make a second attempt. And he just might succeed. We can't keep the girl hidden in Scotland forever. People will talk. Her other suitors—and Randolph says there have been several—will want to know where she is. We must tell them something. But first we must unmask the scoundrel who started this."

"Then I can deal with him—offer him money to be rid of him or threaten to discredit him," Lord Nesfield put in. "But I cannot put an end to the scheme until I know who is behind it."

Emily sighed. "I see what you mean. I only wish I could help you more. But as I said before, Sophie never spoke of being in love with any young man."

"Ah, but you *can* help us," Lady Dundee said. "We're relying entirely on you." Two pairs of eyes suddenly fixed on her, and the weight of their combined power hit Emily with the same force as brilliant sunlight after the curtains are opened.

Oh, no. There was more to this than she'd realized.

Lady Dundee rose from her seat and moved to sit beside Emily on the settee. That in itself was alarming, but when the woman took her hand, Emily's fears were confirmed. Something was afoot, something she wouldn't like.

"You see, my dear, Randolph told me of your friendship with Sophie. When we set off for Willow Crossing, it was in hopes that you would know something. But in case you didn't, we made a plan for discovering the identity of Sophie's lover."

"And it involves me?"

"Yes. If you're willing to help us. For the sake of your friend."

Emily shifted uneasily on the hard settee. She cast a speculative glance at Lady Dundee, but avoided looking at Lord Nesfield. Lady Dundee might at least pretend that Emily had a choice. But Lord Nesfield wouldn't give her one. He would command that she help them, knowing that Emily daren't refuse.

"What do you want me to do?" she asked warily.

Lady Dundee's anxious expression softened. "We need a spy, dear, someone to circulate among Sophie's friends and keep company with her suitors . . . someone whom this scoundrel of Sophie's can approach to find out information about her."

"I don't understand."

"Randolph has seen men watching the house in London, and Sophie seems convinced that her young man will pursue her until he succeeds. So we need a woman about Sophie's age who can appear sympathetic to this man's plight. If he confides in her, begs her for help in reaching Sophie, we'll have the bounder."

"That is why we need you," Lord Nesfield said bluntly as he neared the settee. "We want you to be our spy."

Emily looked wildly from Lady Dundee to Lord Nesfield, who was closing in on her. "Why, that's absurd! Who of your set would confide in a rector's daughter? Who could possibly believe that *I* could help him get to Sophie?"

"You're quite right, of course," Lady Dundee said smoothly. "If we introduce you as Sophie's friend—a rector's daughter from Willow Crossing—

it will look suspicious. Even if we continue with our current story that Sophie is too ill to attend the balls, people will find it odd that you're attending balls instead of staying by your friend's sickbed."

Lord Nesfield leaned toward her with a fervent gleam in his eye. "So we don't want you to be a rector's daughter. We want you to masquerade as Ophelia's daughter."

When Emily stared at him in slack-jawed amazement, he went on eagerly, "We'll say you're in London for your coming out. You look youthful enough to pass for eighteen. Both of Ophelia's real daughters are too young yet to come out, and by the time they reach the proper age, most people will have forgotten all about you. All you need do is speak soulfully of your dear cousin Sophie and how distraught you are over her illness. A few balls, some breakfasts, and I'm sure our man will approach you."

Forgetting that she was just a nobody and they were two very important members of the nobility, she said, "You're both mad! It cannot work! Be a spy? Try to entice some man to approach me on Sophie's behalf? It's insanity!"

When they merely stared at her as if waiting for her to finish a tantrum, she fumbled frantically for some argument to convince them. "No fortune hunter would come near me, and certainly not if I pretended to be one of the family! He'd be a fool to approach a supposed family member when he knows you're all looking for him!"

"But unless you pretend to be a member of the family, he won't believe you have the power to help him," Lady Dundee said in a placating tone. "So this is what we propose. Once we reach London, we'll make it known that you and your Uncle Randolph dislike each other. We'll portray you as a willful girl who ignores her elders. That will make you seem sympathetic to the lovers, and possibly gain you the man's trust."

"If by some chance your supposed position as an heiress would attract the fortune hunter to yourself instead," Lord Nesfield added, "that would work very well, too. That would demonstrate his fickle nature to my daughter and make her abandon her hopes."

Goodness gracious, they'd thought this out carefully, hadn't they? They'd planned an entire deception around her before even asking her to help them. And now they thought she would go along with it!

"I can't participate in such a deceit," she protested. "It's not right!"

Lady Dundee patted her hand kindly. "Don't think of it as a deceit, my dear. It's an adventure, one that will help your friend. You do want to help keep Sophie out of the hands of this fortune hunter, don't you?"

"Of course, but—"

"It'll be fun," Lady Dundee went on as she tightened her grip on Emily's hands. "You'll see. Think of all you can experience. A girl like you would never get the chance for a London coming out. This will allow you to enjoy the town, to wear expensive gowns and go to the most prestigious balls." Leaning closer, she winked at Emily. "Who knows? You might even catch a wealthy husband of your own. Isn't that a temptation?"

Jerking her hands free, Emily leapt to her feet, every inch of her body bristling. "No, Lady Dundee, it is not! I don't know what sort of frivolous girl you think I am, but I don't desire expensive gowns and a wealthy husband gained through deceit and trickery!" At Lady Dundee's surprised expression, she took a deep breath, forcing herself to remain calm. "I'm sorry about Sophie's predicament, but I don't think she'd wish me to do something as abominable as this to help her. I cannot do it. I will not!"

Lady Dundee cocked her head and ran her gaze over Emily, as if seeing her for the first time. "How very interesting. A young woman with principles. It's so rare these days, I hardly recognized it." She folded her hands in her lap with a shrug. "Very well, then. I see you won't serve our purpose."

"Nonsense!" Lord Nesfield had been silent throughout Emily's emotional outburst, but now he spoke out loudly. "Leave us, Ophelia. I must speak to Miss Fairchild alone."

"If she doesn't want to help—" Lady Dundee began.

"Leave us, Ophelia!" he bellowed, making even his formidable sister jump.

With a swish of ample skirts, Lady Dundee stood. "Very well. But don't browbeat the girl, Randolph, or I shall hear of it." She cast Emily a penetrating glance. "I may not agree with her motives, but I respect them. Besides, it does us no good if she gives her help unwillingly."

"She will not give it unwillingly, I assure you," Lord Nesfield said in a low voice as his sister swept from the room. "Will you, Miss Fairchild?"

Emily's heart sank as the drawing room door shut behind the countess. She knew what was coming. "Please, my lord, you must understand my position—"

"Silence!" The marquess reached into his embroidered waistcoat, then drew out an object he kept curled in his bony hand. "I was afraid you might balk at this. Never mind that I gave your father his living, that your family has been indebted to me since the day you were born. You think to ignore that obligation. Well, I will not allow it."

He held out his hand. In it was a small blue bottle containing a few drops of fluid. She knew only too well what it was. Laudanum. The remains of the laudanum she'd made up for Mama, to help soothe her pain from her wasting disease.

The same laudanum that had killed her.

When he was sure she'd recognized it, he tucked it back in his waistcoat pocket with a grim smile. "I see you understand. Until now, I have thought it best to let everyone believe that your mother died of her illness. After all, it would have reflected badly upon me to have it known that my rector's wife had killed herself. It would have caused a great scandal."

"I don't know for certain that she killed herself," Emily protested. But of course she did.

On the horrible morning when she'd found Mama dead and the empty laudanum bottle lying on the floor beside the bed, Emily had been all alone. Unfortunately, just as Emily had found her mother, Lord Nesfield had arrived to speak to her father. He'd seen everything and had guessed the truth at once.

Distraught, she'd asked his advice. She'd wanted to confess all to Papa, but Lord Nesfield had insisted that she keep silent. He'd pointed out that hearing how her mother had really died would hurt her father deeply—not to mention what would happen if others learned the truth. A rector's wife committing the ultimate sin against God would be a scandal so far-reaching, it would ruin her father forever. So she'd agreed to tell everyone that her mother had simply died of her disease. No one, not even Papa, was to know about the laudanum.

The sour pain of guilt gripped her as it had so many times before. It was her fault Mama had died—hers alone. If only she'd been more circumspect about where she kept the laudanum! In the throes of great pain, Mama couldn't resist temptation. And secretly, Emily didn't blame her. Perhaps it was wicked of her, but she thought it abominable the way the Church passed judgment on such matters.

"Come now, Miss Fairchild," Lord Nesfield said coldly, "we both know your mother purposely took that laudanum to end her suffering. If I choose to let that be known, your father would be ruined."

Could he do that? Would he be so awful? Yes, he would do it.

On the other hand, Papa would not want her to engage in such a deception even at the risk to his future. "I-I don't know . . ."

"If you're still balking, let me point out one other matter. I have no proof that she took the laudanum herself. You might have given her the laudanum to end her suffering. This might not be a suicide after all, but a murder."

Emily stared at him aghast. He had never even intimated . . . Surely he couldn't believe . . .

Without remorse, he lifted his lorgnette to focus his gaze on her. The refractive glass made his eyes appear large and chilling. "I do not know what really happened, do I? All I have is a nearly empty bottle of laudanum. And everyone knows you dabble in physic."

"But I would never—"

"Wouldn't you? To save your mother from further suffering? Granted, some might think it a noble gesture." He patted his waistcoat pocket. "But the law does not. If I decided to unburden myself about the events of that day to ... say ... my friend, the magistrate, and made it clear that you could have done it yourself, he would be very interested. What do you think, Miss Fairchild? If it came to a trial, whom do you think they would believe?"

The room seemed to sway around her. The answer to that question was painfully obvious. She'd have no chance against Lord Nesfield's power and lofty station; there was no proof of her innocence. Besides, even if she could win such a trial—which was doubtful, given his connections—she and Papa would still be outcasts everywhere. "You wouldn't— You couldn't be so cruel—"

"Your poor father. To see his daughter brought to trial for murder. It would kill him." He gave an unearthly cackle. "It would kill *you*. And what a pity to see such a pretty girl's life cut off in its prime."

She shuddered. "You would lie about me that way? You would bring me to trial for a murder I didn't commit? How could you?" She grasped at straws. "It would mean scandal for you, to have your rector's daughter accused of murder."

"Do you think I care about scandal with my daughter's well-being at stake? You wish to protect your father." He pounded his cane on the floor. "Well, I shall protect my daughter's reputation and future at all costs."

She stared into the fire, wishing it would spill out and consume Lord Nesfield with all his nasty threats. "Why me? Surely there's some other poor girl you can blackmail into doing as you wish."

"Because you are the best person for our scheme." His impersonal eyes ran over her with the thoroughness of a man choosing a prize racehorse. "You're genteel enough to pass for nobility, and you're clever enough to learn what you don't know. No one of consequence in society knows you, so you won't be recognized by some friend. The only ball you've attended where any of the *ton* might have met you was a masquerade ball, and you wore widow's weeds and a mask. You didn't even dance, for God's sake."

Folding his arms over his chest, he said, "So you see, it must be you. No one will know you, nor care when you disappear and return to your safe little life here."

No one would know her. That wasn't true! Lord Blackmore had seen her without her mask. Of course, she could hardly tell Lord Nesfield that she'd been alone in a carriage with his enemy, a man notorious for his associations with women. For one thing, Lord Nesfield wouldn't believe it. And if he did, it would merely give him one more thing to hold over her.

Besides, she wasn't even sure Lord Blackmore would recognize her. The earl had only seen her briefly by moonlight. He'd probably already forgotten her face.

Still, others might know her, no matter what Lord Nesfield believed. "What about Lawrence, my cousin? If he sees me in London—"

"Do not be absurd. A London barrister does not attend society balls. And if you happen upon him in the street, you can tell him you came to London with Sophie."

She cast about in her mind for others. "What about the Gormans? And the Taylors?" she said, naming the two most prominent families in Willow Crossing. "They go to London for the Season, and they know me. What of the Drydens?"

"The Drydens' grandchild has just been born.

They won't leave their estate with the newborn there. The Gormans aren't going to the city this year, because they don't want to leave Mr. Gorman's ill mother. As for the Taylors, their daughter's coming out last year cost them so much they've decided not to go to town this year."

"But surely there will be someone—"

"If there is, I'll take care of it."

"What about Papa? How can I explain why I'm leaving him?"

Lord Nesfield lifted his scrawny shoulders in a careless shrug. "We'll tell him that Sophie needs you in London. It will be better if he did not know the rest, for he might object. Or would you rather tell him the truth?"

Tears sprang to her eyes. Ruthlessly, she held them back. Wretched man! This was so unfair! If she ever saw Sophie again, she'd strangle the girl for doing this to her!

No, she mustn't blame Sophie. It was her own fault—if she had been more careful with the laudanum, none of this would have happened, and Lord Nesfield wouldn't have this hold on her. This was her punishment.

Still, to actively take part in his deception would be an offense against every moral precept! Yet she had no choice. She doubted God would want her to sacrifice her life for such precepts, especially when it would mean heartache for Papa.

"Very well. I'll do as you wish." The words were wrenched from her.

"One more thing."

Her eyes burned with unshed tears. "What more could you want from me?"

"You must keep your reasons for helping me a secret, even from my sister, or I swear I will make good on my threats."

"Lady Dundee wouldn't approve of your black-mailing, I take it?"

He scowled. "I don't know. But I don't want her interference. If you tell her the truth, I swear—"

"You've made yourself quite clear." She straightened her spine. "But if I do this, you must swear to bury Mama's secret forever."

He eyed her through his lorgnette. "Certainly. Once I find my daughter's secret suitor and put an end to his pretensions, you and I will be done with each other."

"Do you swear it?"

"I swear it."

I'll hold you to that vow, my lord, she told herself fervently as he stalked back into the hall and called for Lady Dundee. *Don't think that I won't.*

Chapter 4

London
May 1819

> *Minute attention to propriety stops the growth of virtue.*
>
> Mary Wollstonecraft,
> *A Vindication of the Rights of Women*

Emily shivered and gathered her fur-edged pelisse more tightly about her flimsily clad body. Beyond the frosted window of the Nesfield carriage, London's streets glimmered beneath the spring fog. As a child, she'd visited the city only once with her parents, leaving her with vague memories of pinnacled towers and jam tarts.

This week, however, London had left a more distinct impression. Hesitant young ladies and their preening mamas in a long succession of millinery and seamstress's shops. Endless trips in the carriage through muddy, people-choked streets. And everywhere, the task of pretending she was Lady Dundee's daughter newly come from Scotland.

Why had she ever thought Willow Crossing dull and uninspiring? How she missed the pale yellow wash of morning sun on their little garden, the patchwork of open fields, the neat lanes and walks. What she wouldn't give for a glimpse of home.

Idly she rubbed a circle in the frost on the window so she could peer at the grand houses lining the streets. This was what she was—an onlooker, an outsider. No matter how Lady Dundee presented her, she'd never be part of this world.

Tonight the kind and forgiving moon was absent. There was only the feeble glow of oil lamps that transformed everyday objects into hulking shadows, serving to further lower her spirits. A long sigh crept out of her.

"You're not nervous, are you?" Lady Dundee said at her side.

"A little."

"You've nothing to worry about, child. After last night, the worst is over. You weathered the presentation at court with the proper amount of modesty. I couldn't have been more pleased if you'd truly been my daughter."

The praise warmed Emily. At first, she'd wanted to hate Lady Dundee, but that had soon proved impossible. Though the countess did say outrageous things, she was also friendly and engaging— the ideal companion. She was as different from her brother as sweet cherries from lemons.

Thankfully, Lord Nesfield rarely joined them. He and his sister had decided it would be better if he kept out of sight most of the time, especially since he and "Lady Emma" were supposedly at odds.

"Last night's presentation at court was easy," Emily said. "You told me when to walk, when to hand my card to the lord-in-waiting, when to curtsy, and when to withdraw. Even a mere rector's daughter can manage such things. But tonight won't be so orderly. There will be more chance for error."

Lady Dundee drew up her long gloves. "Pish-posh. I've been watching you, my dear. You have the natural grace and confidence that comes from good breeding, unlike some of these chits pretending to gentility because their merchant fathers have the wherewithal to keep two carriages. You were raised with the moral precepts that underlie all civilized behavior."

"Oh, yes, the moral precepts," she said bitterly. "Like deceiving good people into thinking I'm someone I'm not."

"Why did you agree to help us if you find it so distasteful?"

Emily cursed her quick tongue as she averted her gaze. "I'm doing it for Sophie, of course. What else?"

"What else indeed?"

She quickly changed the subject. "Don't mind me. I'm merely anxious about this evening. There are conventions of behavior peculiar to your station that I fear I'll omit in my ignorance."

There'd been so much to learn—a thousand little nonsensical rules. *Don't say "my lady" and "my lord" too much, or you'll sound like a servant. Never put your knife in your mouth.* Apparently, although country manners allowed it, people of high society thought it gauche. *Never overimbibe, for liquor's effects lead to a woman's ruin.*

She and Lady Dundee had repeated the order of precedence in rank so many times that she had nightmares about some great bishop recoiling from her in disgust because she gave a mere viscount precedence over him. And who could have ever guessed that learning the newly touted waltz would be so difficult?

"Don't concern yourself overmuch with the rules," Lady Dundee told her. "I can always gloss over some error by explaining that you're nervous. It's only true vulgarity that I can't hide, and I needn't worry about that with you." She patted Emily's leg. "Indeed, I may have to prod you to be *less* refined. Remember your role: you're my rebellious child. Otherwise, no man will believe you'd go against your mother and uncle to aid your cousin."

Emily fidgeted restlessly in her seat, trying to find a comfortable position in the incredibly tight corset she'd been forced to wear, the one that pushed her breasts up so shamefully. She'd never worn a corset at home, nor gowns of such rich elegance. Right now, she'd trade them all for her sprigged muslin.

And discomfort made her cranky. "I'm still uncertain what you want me to do. Should I be forward? Flirtatious? Such things are not in my nature."

"You can't know what's in your nature until it's been tried, can you? If I understand Randolph correctly, you haven't been much in society. You may find you enjoy flirting with men. I certainly enjoyed it in my day."

"But you're more flamboyant than I. And Papa always says—"

"Forget your father and his strictures. Do what you want, Emily: enjoy yourself."

"I won't."

"You might be surprised." When Emily shot her a skeptical glance, she grinned. "It's more common than you think for people to enjoy pretending to be what they aren't. You attended Dryden's masquerade ball in Derbyshire. Didn't you notice how people become different creatures when they don costumes? How they feel free to be wild?"

She thought of her wanton response to Lord Blackmore. "I did."

Lady Dundee covered Emily's hand with her plump one. "It's a common response, and this is no different. Half the members of good society live a pretense every day. One more young woman acting a part won't bother a soul, and it might save Sophie from a disastrous future." She smiled. "Lady Emma is your masquerade, merely an amusement. It doesn't change Emily Fairchild. And it hurts no one."

"I-I shall try. Although if someone engages me in a battle of wits, I'm not sure I'll be very convincing."

"Speak the first thing that comes into your head, and you'll be fine. That's what I do. Everyone's so busy trying to impress one another that honesty generally takes them by surprise."

"Be honest in my dishonesty?"

"Something like that." Lady Dundee squeezed her hand, then released it.

Emily straightened her long gloves. Well, at least she needn't worry about seeing Lord Blackmore tonight. Lady Dundee had made it quite clear that this was a marriage mart, and if ever a man was set on avoiding marriage, it was him.

Ever since they'd arrived in London, she'd dreaded the day she would cross his path. It was foolish, of course, he probably wouldn't even recognize her. Still, she worried.

But he wouldn't be around tonight, thank heavens.

The carriage slowed, and Emily glanced out the window. Goodness gracious, there was an ocean of coaches out there. This must be what was called "a crush."

Wonderful. Nothing like having a huge audience to witness one's humiliation.

Now they were approaching the front of the mansion, where liveried footmen awaited each guest's arrival. Crippling fear overtook her.

Reaching up to fluff the corkscrew curls surrounding Emily's face, Lady Dundee said reassuringly, "You'll do fine. Don't worry, I'll be at your side as much as I can, so don't hesitate to ask questions if you're confused about anything." Lady Dundee lowered her voice as the carriage halted. "Remember, you're in masquerade. You're Lady Emma Campbell, daughter of a respectable Scottish laird from a venerable old family. You've nothing to be ashamed of."

Lady Emma Campbell. It still sounded strange to her ears. They'd considered letting Emily use her own Christian name, but hadn't wanted anyone closely acquainted with Lord Nesfield to wonder at the coincidence that his niece and the daughter of his rector had the same one. Emma was at least similar enough to Emily's real name to prevent her from growing confused.

So now she was Lady Emma, miraculously transformed overnight from a common nobody to a lady of the realm. But it was all fruitless, she thought, as she and Lady Dundee descended from the carriage. She would fool no one. They could dress her in the rarest satin and put pearls in her hair. They could teach her the waltz and the language of the fan. But they couldn't make her into an earl's daughter, no matter how hard they tried. One day she'd be found out—she had no doubt of that.

Pray heaven that she finished her task before it happened.

*   *   *

With casual unconcern for the sleeves of his cashmere cutaway, Jordan leaned out the window of his carriage and called up to his coachman, Watkins, "What the devil is taking so long?"

"Sorry, milord, but there's a cart o'erturned in the lane. It'll take ten minutes at least for them to clear it."

Jordan jerked out his pocket watch and glanced at it.

"I suppose we're very late," his friend George Pollock remarked from across the carriage.

"Yes. Thanks to you and your vanity." He tucked his watch back in his waistcoat pocket. "I should have left you to hire a hack instead of waiting while you dithered over which waistcoat to wear. And how many cravats did you ruin before you could tie one to your satisfaction? Ten? Fifteen?"

"Probably twenty," Pollock said blithely. Wetting one finger, he used it to smooth a wayward lock of his blond hair into place. "What good is having money if you can't spend it on cravats?"

"You should have spent it getting your deuced carriage repaired, so I didn't have to wait for you."

"Relax, old chap. Since when do you care if we're late to a marriage mart? You're not looking for a wife."

"No, but Ian is. God knows why he has this urge to marry, but I promised to help him. I was supposed to reach Merrington's before Lord Nesfield and his daughter Sophie leave, and since it's nearly eleven already, that's unlikely, isn't it?"

Ian Lennard, the Viscount St. Clair, was Jordan's closest friend, and rarely asked favors of anyone. It galled Jordan to fail him now because of Pollock's ridiculous vanity.

"St. Clair won't mind if you're late," Pollock

said. "He's not that desperate. If you don't arrive in time, he'll merely try his scheme on her at the next ball."

"It doesn't matter. I said I'd be there, and I will. I keep my promises."

The carriage shuddered forward, and the sound of the horse's hooves clopping over cobblestones filled the air. Jordan relaxed a fraction.

"That's not what's irritating you, and you know it," Pollock retorted as he flicked a minute speck of dust off his gloves. "You don't like having your schedule upset, that's all. Everything must go precisely according to your plan, or you lose patience."

"Anyone would lose patience with a dandy like you," Jordan snapped.

His friend frowned. "I'm not a dandy, but I do believe that being well dressed is the mark of a good gentleman. Besides, I *like* dressing well. That's the trouble with you, Blackmore. You don't know how to relax and enjoy life."

"Yes, I'm a dull fellow, aren't I?"

"If the shoe fits . . ." When Jordan scowled at him, Pollock tugged on his impossibly high cravat, then went on in a mulish tone. "You must admit you can be a blasted machine sometimes. Your life is consumed with running your estates efficiently and running things in Parliament. Everything's orderly; everything's part of some plan."

"That's not true." But it was. He did like an orderly life. God knows he'd put up with enough disorder as a child without having to endure it as an adult. So yes, he hated it when things went wrong simply because some fool didn't behave in a logical or timely manner.

But that wasn't what had Pollock miffed. The man was merely peeved at being called a dandy.

"Then there's the way you treat your women," Pollock went on bitterly. "I've never seen a man who can take a mistress, then cut her off without a thought because she erred by falling in love with him. And they all fall in love with you, blast you. They don't realize your charm is merely a means to an end. They think you care. You always make them pant for you, then toss them out into the cold when they want more than sex from the arrangement."

Now Pollock was hitting a little too close for comfort. "You're still angry at me about Julia, aren't you?"

"She's my friend."

"Your mistress, you mean. If I hadn't 'cut her off without a thought,' you wouldn't have the benefit of her company now."

Pollock glanced away. "Actually, she and I have parted ways."

That caught Jordan by surprise. "Already?"

"I grew tired of competing with you for her affections."

Jordan winced. His parting from Julia had been particularly messy. "That isn't my fault. She and I had a very clear arrangement: mutual satisfaction of each other's physical needs and no more. I can't help it if she changed her expectations. I never did."

For a moment, the air was thick with Pollock's irritatingly sullen silence, punctuated only by the rattling of the carriage wheels on stone. Ever since Julia, their friendship had been a bit strained, though Jordan didn't know what he could do about it. *He* wasn't the one suffering from romantic whims.

Pollock sighed. "I don't understand you. Love isn't something you turn off and on like a damned spigot. You can't control it as you control your financial affairs. Haven't you ever wanted to lose yourself to love?"

"Now that's a dreadful thought. Relinquish everything for a fickle emotion? Not a chance. What kind of fool abandons reason, good sense, and, yes, control, for the dubious pleasure of being in love?"

Only once in his life had he come even close to losing control because of a woman. Strange how he still remembered that night in the carriage with a certain Miss Emily Fairchild. What kind of madness had possessed him? It must have been the full moon, as she'd said. That was the only possible explanation for why he'd nearly seduced the wrong sort of woman.

He'd paid for it later, too. His stepsister Sara had plagued him relentlessly with questions until he'd deliberately picked a fight with her devil of a husband to take her mind off matchmaking. A pity it hadn't taken his mind off Emily's lavender-scented hair and lithe, enticing body. Or her fascinating way of making statements that took him completely by surprise. Women rarely took him by surprise.

At least their encounter had been brief, and the illusion that he'd found the only female in England who could totally bewitch him had finally passed. No doubt if he met Miss Emily Fairchild again during the light of day—and he wouldn't—he'd find her ordinary and distinctly unbewitching.

"I'll never understand your cynical view of marriage, Blackmore," Pollock said, "but obviously St. Clair chose you well for his scheme. Any other man might be tempted to steal a winsome little thing like Lady Sophie after dancing with her. But not you—the lord with the granite heart."

"Mock me if you will, but I'm well pleased with my granite heart. It doesn't bleed, it doesn't fester, and it can't be wounded."

"Yes, but it can break if someone hits it with a hammer. One day a woman will come along who shatters it into a million pieces. And I, for one, can't wait to see it."

"You'll be waiting a long time then," Jordan said, growing bored with this subject. "And it won't happen tonight. I'm dancing with Sophie merely to oblige Ian. He thinks it'll prompt Lord Nesfield to accept his suit and thus get Sophie out of my foul clutches. Ian assured me I'd be done quickly. Good God, I hope so. These affairs are tedious."

"I don't mind them. But then I can appreciate a good party. You can't."

Pollock's insistence on making him sound like a cold bastard began to irritate Jordan. "And I'm not looking for a wife to enhance my standing in society. You are."

Pollock glared at him. "Is that an allusion to my lack of a title or connections? To the fact that my father was in trade? My word, you're pompous. You can have any woman you want, so you lord it over the rest of us."

The vehemence in Pollock's voice startled him. "That's not true. Any number of merchant's daughters would happily lead you to the altar."

"I don't want a merchant's daughter. As you so crudely put it, I want someone who can increase my standing in society."

"Why? You already move in exalted circles."

"Yes, but I want a woman who can be the jewel in my crown, a woman so stunning that my position is secured forever. And preferably someone who can love me despite my faults."

Jordan couldn't restrain his laughter. "You think to find it at Merrington's? With a lot of simpering virgins and scheming mamas?"

"Perhaps." Pollock fingered the cravat he'd spent so much time torturing into a Mathematique. "Before St. Clair set his sights on Lady Sophie, I'd planned to try for her myself." He scowled. "Then St. Clair came along and captured her fancy. He isn't even in love with her. He just wants a docile wife, God knows why."

Yes, that was curious. Jordan himself had wondered why Ian seemed so bent on marrying these days. "I wouldn't envy him his conquest of Sophie, if I were you. She's tolerably pretty and good-natured, but her father's a bastard. I fear Ian will rue the day he marries into that man's family."

The carriage drew up in front of Merrington's, and Jordan checked his watch. They'd made good time; the girl might still be here. If so, he'd give it an hour. That should be sufficient time to enrage Lord Nesfield and promote Ian's suit. Then he could go to his club and be done with this nonsense.

The two of them left the carriage and entered Merrington's handsome town house in silence. The place was all got up in spring flowers and ribbons, enough of them to make a man ill. When they reached the ballroom, Jordan paused to survey the scene. As usual, Merrington's ball resembled a ship's hold full of doves and crows, cooing and cawing and taking wing whenever they liked. White-gowned women swirled down the lines of dancers accompanied by their black-tailed companions, whose cinched waists, tight knee-breeches, and brilliant-colored waistcoats enhanced their birdlike appearance.

Hovering on the sidelines, he scanned the crowd

for Ian or even Lady Sophie. But despite the glow of a thousand candles and Argand lamps, he saw nothing but flashes of fans and trains and white slippers.

Then he and Pollock were surrounded by Pollock's friends, all of them bachelors attending the ball in search of mates. A few moments of pleasantries ensued, but they soon gave way to earnest comparisons of the young women's attributes. Jordan wanted to laugh at the lot of them. What romantic drivel these young pups spouted! If they had to have wives, at least they should choose them sensibly.

That's what he would do when the need for an heir became overwhelming. He would find some experienced woman—a widowed marchioness or some such—with taste and good judgment, who could preside over his household without a lot of fuss. A businesslike marriage. Sensible. No emotional entanglements.

The one thing he would *not* do is marry some chit out of the schoolroom who would expect him to dote on her every word and indulge her whims. Like the tittering young women the men around him were discussing.

Impatient with their talk, Jordan turned to Pollock. "Have you spotted Ian yet?"

"Just now. He's at the top of the set." Pollock nodded toward the dance floor.

"Ian is dancing? You must be joking. He hates to dance. Though I suppose he'll do what he must to secure Lady Sophie."

"Lady Sophie?" one of the others remarked. "Haven't you heard? Lady Sophie's very ill, and no one knows when she'll be able to leave the sickroom."

"You must be mistaken," Jordan said. "I heard

she'd left town briefly last week, but St. Clair told me yesterday she was back. He planned to call on the family today.''

"She may be back, but she's not out and about. St. Clair is dancing with her cousin. For the second time, I should add.''

"Deuce take it.'' So Lady Sophie wasn't even here, and he needn't have come after all. Well, he'd stay just long enough to torment Ian for missing his shot at Nesfield's girl, then leave for his club.

It took only half a minute to pick his friend out of the throng of dancers, for Ian was hard to miss. Unlike the blond, fair, and short Pollock, Ian had the coffee-colored skin of a gypsy and stood easily a head above most other men. Among the fair geldings of English society, he was certainly a dark horse.

As for his dance partner . . . Well, well. Ian always managed to snag the pretty ones, didn't he? Jordan couldn't make out her face from where he stood, but her hair was the rich, dark gold of late sunset, and the figure a randy young man's dream, even draped in pure white satin. Of course, he wasn't young or randy, not for these sweet darlings. He preferred women in scarlet . . . or black bombazine.

Good God, where had that come from? That was the second time he'd thought of Emily tonight. Matchmaking was polluting the spring air, that's all. It was bound to affect him a little.

The dance ended, and Jordan threaded his way through the crowd toward Ian, casting a warning look at the one bold matron who approached him with a simpering daughter in tow. She stopped in her tracks, thank God. Smart woman.

He should never have come. All these harpies would get the wrong idea about his attendance at a marriage mart and descend on him en masse. After talking to Ian, he'd have to beat a hasty retreat.

The closer he got to the couple, the more interested he became in the woman on Ian's arm. For a girl at her coming out, she was much too graceful. No awkwardness in the way she walked, no hint of uncertainty in her manner. Her back was to him, and a very shapely back it was, too—not to mention the exceedingly attractive derriere. And there was all that glorious hair, swept up into a chignon and studded with pearls above her long, elegant neck.

He could swear he'd seen that neck before, and all that hair, too. But that was absurd, of course. He'd never even heard of Lady Sophie's cousin, much less seen her attractions before tonight.

Then the couple stopped at the edge of the dance floor, and the woman turned toward her companion, putting her face in profile.

Devil take it. He *had* seen her before! The profile was achingly familiar. Last time it had been muted by moonlight and covered by a mask, but he could swear it was the same face . . . the same delicate nose and modest smile.

No, it couldn't be. How could she be in London at a ball like this, dressed in expensive white satin and pearls? He was imagining things. This woman merely shared some of Emily's features. And he couldn't be sure about the face, after all. He'd seen it for only a few moments in the darkness.

Still, this woman had the same height and the same figure, the same way of ducking her head when she smiled and that same swanlike bend in her neck. She even had the same color hair, though it was dressed more extravagantly. His heart thudded loudly, and he quickened his steps. It couldn't be her. But it was—he couldn't be mistaken.

What on earth was she doing here? "Emily?" he said hoarsely as he reached them. "Emily, is it really you?"

The woman faced him, a startled expression on her face. A flash of recognition seemed to touch those emerald eyes before it disappeared completely, replaced by a cold look of censure. "I beg your pardon, sir. Do I know you?"

Jordan couldn't have been more stunned if she'd hit him in the face with her reticule.

"My God, Jordan," Ian cut in. "At least wait until I introduce you before you call the lady by her Christian name." He looked from Jordan to the woman, both of whom were staring at each other. "You two don't know each other, do you?"

"We do," Jordan asserted at the same time she said hotly, "Certainly not."

Jordan gaped at her. How could she pretend not to recognize him?

Ian said with distinct amusement in his voice, "Since there seems to be some confusion on the matter, I'd better perform the introductions. Lady Emma, may I present Jordan Willis, the Earl of Blackmore. Jordan, this is Lady Emma Campbell, the Earl of Dundee's daughter and Lord Nesfield's niece." In an aside to the woman, he added, "Don't let his rudeness give you the wrong impression. When he puts his mind to it, he can charm the moon out of the sky."

Ian's humor was lost on Jordan, especially when the mention of his full name and title didn't produce a reaction from her. Lady Emma? Who the devil was Lady Emma? It had to be a mistake. This wasn't the Earl of Dundee's daughter; this was Emily Fairchild, the rector's daughter. He was sure of it.

But it had been dark that night in the carriage,

and he *had* seen her face only briefly in the moonlight. Could he be wrong?

Either way, he couldn't just stand here gawking at her. He gave a sketchy bow, then said, "I'm sorry, Lady Emma, for accosting you so boldly." He forced a contrition he didn't feel into his voice. "My only excuse is that I mistook you for someone else. Please forgive my error."

The woman arched her eyebrows in wary disapproval. "Someone else? Pray tell me who this Emily woman is." Her tone grew coy. "Don't disappoint me, Lord Blackmore, or I swear I'll never forgive you. Please tell me she's an exotic princess from the South Seas. Or even an opera singer. I'll be insulted if it's anyone less interesting."

It was Emily's voice, Emily's lips . . . Emily's blond hair. But not Emily's manner. And yet . . . "Then I'm doomed to remain unforgiven. She's a rector's daughter." He added, very deliberately, "Her name is Emily Fairchild."

He watched for any reaction and fancied he saw a faint tinge of a blush spread over her cheeks.

If so, it was quickly gone, for she smiled archly and said in a haughty voice, "A rector's daughter? Indeed, you *are* doomed. I could never countenance being mistaken for a common rector's daughter. No, no, I can't forgive you at all."

Ian was watching Jordan with narrowed eyes, but Jordan paid no attention whatsoever to his friend. "Then I must make amends. May I have this dance, Lady Emma? I can think of no other way to atone for my horrible error."

Her smile slipped. Good, he'd flustered her.

But she recovered her composure with amazing speed. Tucking her hand in the crook of Ian's elbow, she said, "I'm afraid that's impossible, Lord Blackmore. I promised the next waltz to Lord St.

Clair, and they're playing the waltz now."

For the love of God, she was refusing to dance with him. The brazen chit! What had happened to her? He flashed Ian a quelling glance. "You don't mind crying off, do you, old friend?"

With a chuckle, Ian quickly disentangled himself from the woman. "I absolve you of your commitment, Lady Emma. Even another dance in your delightful company can't compare to watching my friend dance the waltz at a marriage mart for probably the first time in his life."

A look of outrage spread over her face as Jordan held out his hand. She glowered at Ian, then Jordan. "But we have barely been introduced! You can't do this! It's not at all proper!"

Emily had protested his lack of propriety that night in the carriage, too. Jordan smiled, feeling more sure of himself now. He ignored her protest and cupped his hand about the slender waist that felt so painfully familiar. Surely he'd held this waist before and seen those same tender lips quiver as they were doing now.

Taking her small hand, he placed it on his shoulder and repeated the same words he'd said that night, in a voice meant only for her ears, "As if I care about propriety."

If she remembered, she showed no sign of it. "Oh, but *I* care," she spat back, "especially when a rude man attempts to forgo it."

He tightened his hold on her when she tried to wriggle out of his embrace. "Sorry, my dear, but this rude man shall have his waltz, and you *will* follow along. Everyone's watching, and if you refuse me, your name will be on every gossip's tongue tomorrow."

Her name would be on every gossip's tongue regardless. Already he could feel the hush that had fallen on the crowd the moment he'd taken her in his arms. Ian wasn't the only person keenly interested in observing the Earl of Blackmore break his own rules about dancing with innocents. It had been this very effect Ian had been hoping for with Sophie. And with any luck it would prod Emily into telling him the truth.

He could tell when she became aware of the eyes on them. Her hand in his trembled, though her shoulders remained stubbornly set.

"I see we understand each other," he said smoothly.

He just had time to see her pretty eyes narrow in mutinous resentment before the music began, and he whirled her off into the waltz. Casting her a grim, triumphant smile, he tugged her almost indecently close.

When her response was to step forcefully on his foot in the next turn, he had to laugh. If she thought she could brazen this out with him, she was mad. One way or another, he would find out what was going on. And no amount of petty attacks and dissembling on her part would prevent it.

Chapter 5

Foolish eyes, thy streams give over,
Wine, not water, binds the lover:
At the table then be shining,
Gay coquette, and all designing.

Martha Sansom, "Song"

Of all the wretched luck, Emily thought as Jordan waltzed her deftly through the throng of fashionably dressed lords and ladies. He wasn't supposed to be here. Or recognize her. Or waltz with her. No, definitely not.

She should have protested more strongly when he'd asked—no, commanded her to waltz with him. Lord St. Clair's sudden defection had confused her. Was it acceptable for one man to hand a woman off to another? She rather thought it wasn't. Still, who knew what rules applied to men like the Earl of Blackmore and Viscount St. Clair?

Worse yet, Jordan was a fabulous dancer. In her practice sessions with the awkward Lord Nesfield, she'd fallen all over her feet. The marquess had blamed her and she'd woefully accepted the blame, but now she wished she hadn't. With Jordan, she was as graceful as a swan. Somehow he lightened her feet until the steps of the waltz seemed as nat-

78

ural and easy as walking. She forgot to count the measure, didn't even *need* to count the measure.

Curse him for that, and for holding her so intimately. If he held her any closer, she'd make a complete cake of herself. As it was, she was near enough to see his clean-shaven jaw and the Blackmore crest on his gold cravat pin, to feel his thighs brush hers in the turns.

As usual, he looked handsome and very male. None of those silly satin breeches for the Earl of Blackmore—oh, no. His coat and breeches of expensive cashmere and his figured gray waistcoat and snowy cravat were more commanding in their simplicity than any of the extravagantly embroidered waistcoats worn by the other men in the room.

Did he know how dancing with him affected her? Of course he did. His broad hand rode her waist with shameful familiarity, and his other hand clasped hers possessively, reminding her of their night in the carriage. No wonder Papa thought the waltz too scandalous for decent people. No woman with an ounce of self-preservation would willingly put herself this near to an attractive, virile earl.

Especially after having shared intimate kisses with him. Memories plagued her—of his hands in her hair . . . his breath warming her skin . . . his mouth anointing her cheeks and neck with secret, thrilling kisses.

Goodness gracious, now she was turning red! *Please, God*, she prayed, *don't let him notice.*

She might as well have been howling at the moon. When she risked a peek at Jordan, she found him quite obviously aware of the heightened color in her cheeks. His dark eyes seemed to miss nothing, more was the pity.

"I like making you blush, Emily," he whispered wickedly.

"Emily? Why do you persist in thinking I'm this Emily person?"

"You can lie to those others, but not to me," Jordan said in that low, husky tone she remembered all too well. "Why are you here? Why are you pretending to be some deuced Scottish lady?"

She hated deceiving him, truly hated it. Still, she had no choice. "Lord Blackmore, your little joke has grown tedious. I don't know why you persist in confusing me with this Emily Fairfax creature."

"Fairchild! Her name . . . *your* name is Fairchild, not Fairfax, as you well know, goddammit!"

"You needn't curse at me," she chided automatically.

The flickering light from the candles overhead played over his gloating expression. "Seems I've heard you say that before—one night in my carriage."

Dear heavens, she'd slipped up already. "Your carriage? I have no idea what you mean."

The music crescendoed, preventing him from answering at once, but his smug expression stayed firmly in place.

This was futile. How could she possibly succeed? All her life she'd been taught how not to lie, and now she was expected to lie like an expert. Perhaps she should just reveal everything . . .

Yes, and then Lord Nesfield would have her hanged. She couldn't trust Jordan to keep her secret, since Lord St. Clair seemed to be a close friend. Lord St. Clair had spent half the ball asking her about Sophie, and he was her most likely suspect. For all she knew, Jordan could have helped the man plan an elopement with Sophie.

"Come now, Emily, tell me what this is all

about," he demanded as soon as the music allowed
him to speak again.

Suddenly, Lady Dundee's words came to her:
Lady Emma is your masquerade, merely an amusement.
It doesn't change Emily Fairchild.

This was a masquerade, not a deception. And
why should it matter if she had to lie to him? That
night in the carriage, he'd made it quite clear she
was nothing but a fleeting diversion. He too had
played a role with her—flattering her, saying sweet
things, when he knew all the time he never intended to see her again.

She cast him a frosty look. "I grow weary of this
game, Lord Blackmore. Please find another."

He glowered at her as if to frighten her into telling the truth, but when she said nothing more, he
set his lips into a determined line. "Very well. You
force me to take more drastic action."

She laughed coyly. "What shall you do to me?
Torture me? Throw me in a dungeon until I say
what you wish?"

For the first time that evening, he smiled, though
most devilishly. Angels must cry every time he
loosed that smile on unsuspecting women. "I can
think of more pleasant ways to get the truth from
you."

Too late, she realized they were dancing along
the edge of the room, where doors of cut crystal
opened onto wide, marble balconies. Somehow he
had maneuvered her there without her even noticing.

He danced her onto the balcony, then stopped.
Furtively, Emily looked back into the ballroom,
praying that Lady Dundee had seen her, but too
many people were dancing for anyone to notice
one couple's absence, especially once everyone lost

their initial surprise at seeing her dance with Lord Blackmore.

She tried to wriggle away, but he merely snaked his arm more tightly about her waist and dragged her toward the steps that led down into the garden.

"I thought you wanted to dance," she said acidly, though her heart was pounding loudly enough to be heard in China. "You behaved in a most rude manner to gain a waltz with me."

"I require more than a waltz from you, as you well know. And for what I intend, we need privacy."

Privacy. The last time they'd had privacy, he'd kissed her senseless. If he kissed her again, she was likely to fall apart and confess everything.

But Lady Emma wouldn't balk at going into the garden with him. She was much too sure of herself to do such a ninny thing. Indeed, the woman would probably delight in a private assignation with an unmarried earl of Jordan's consequence.

Centering her mind on that thought, she let him draw her down the stairs, her legs moving mechanically beside him. When they halted behind an oak that hid them from anyone who might be watching from the balcony, however, she felt a moment's panic.

"Now then, Emily." He released her arm and faced her with the expression of an older brother chastising a child. "What do you have to tell me?"

The condescension in his voice provided her with a jolt of courage. How dared he treat her like some simpleton?

"I'm sure I wouldn't know what to tell you. This is your little fantasy, Lord Blackmore." Flipping open the ivory fan attached to her wrist by a slender cord, she worked it with languid motions. "A rector's daughter? Is that who I'm supposed to be?

I don't guess you'd settle for a gypsy girl, would you? A rector's daughter is such a tiresome role."

Her reward was the stunned look on his face. "Deuce take it, woman," he growled, grasping her shoulders roughly. "Stop this pretense! I know who you are!"

"Oh, I don't think you do." Casting him a flirtatious smile despite the somersaults in her stomach, she walked her fingers up his silky coat lapel. "If you really knew anything about me, you'd lose interest in this Emily person at once."

He blinked, then scanned her again, as if to ascertain where he'd made his mistake. Then his eyes narrowed dangerously. "You won't mind if I determine the truth in the only way I can think of."

"Oh? And how is that?"

His hands closed about her waist, drawing her hard against him. "By kissing you as I kissed her."

She had no time to prepare herself before his mouth caught hers. Though she'd already half expected it, the touch of his lips came as a shock. It was exactly like that night in his carriage . . . the same dizzy pleasure stampeding over her restraints, the same hot, hard thrill linking her to the man forbidden to her. She melted and sizzled against him like butter in a hot pan.

But when his mouth left hers and he murmured "my sweet Emily" in a tone that left no doubt of his certainty, her heart sank. She was doing this all wrong. Emily Fairchild melted. Emma Campbell burned.

"It's Emma," she whispered, correcting him. Then she boldly slid her arms about his neck and drew his head forcefully back for another kiss.

He went rigid at once, though he didn't pull away. Remembering how he'd kissed her in the carriage, she opened her mouth and ever so lightly touched her tongue to his, then smoothed it along his unyielding lips in a repetition of his actions that night.

For a moment, she feared she'd gone too far. His body was frozen, as unyielding as an iceberg as she stood there on tiptoe, her mouth joined to his with embarrassing intimacy.

Then a growl erupted from his throat as he opened his mouth over hers, hungering, needy. Grasping hands anchored her against his taut, lean body, and his mouth began an assault so wild and furious it stunned her.

She rose to his kiss, a fever gripping her blood. It was easy to become Lady Emma, the bold half-Scottish lass. Forgotten was Emily Fairchild's shy uncertainty and virgin manner, blown into the distance like a bit of goose down. He'd primed her for more, and it took only a tiny shove to thrust her over the edge into passion.

So when he drove his tongue deeply, she tangled her own with it, then went further, slipping her tongue between his open lips to explore the warm, silken dangers of his mouth. His kiss grew almost brutal, as if he couldn't get enough of her. Over and over he devoured her mouth, and when that no longer seemed to satisfy him, he stamped hard, possessive kisses along her cheek and down her neck. His rough skin rasped against her, and his musky scent mingled with the flowery perfumes dancing in the garden air.

His hands roamed where they wished, gliding down her ribs and over the contours of her hips. No longer bound by any restraint, he left off kissing her neck to scatter kisses along her collarbone, then lower, along the neckline of her bodice until he reached the dip between her breasts.

She nearly pushed him away, surprised by his

forwardness. Then she caught herself. Forcing herself to arch back, she allowed him to explore the inner curves of her breasts with his firm, knowing lips.

Pleasure pooled low in her belly like warm honey. *Goodness gracious, why must wickedness be so delicious?* The more his hot mouth caressed her, the more she wanted it against parts of her body that only some future husband should be allowed to touch. She couldn't breathe, couldn't think. She was rapidly losing control of this battle.

Then he tugged at the ribbon-trimmed neck of her gown, edging it down the slope of one breast and shocking her to the core. Shoving hard against him, she backed out of his embrace and crossed her arms protectively over her bodice.

A thousand reproaches sprang to her lips as his gaze shot to hers, hard, male, and ravenous. Then she caught herself. Lady Emma wouldn't reproach a man for being a man.

It took all her will to paste a coy smile on her lips and lower her hands from her chest. "I doubt your Emily could ever kiss like that, Lord Blackmore."

She fervently prayed that the dim light dappling the garden walks hid the full effects of their encounter. If he could hear her pulse beating triple time or see her desperate attempts to draw air into her lungs, he'd know at once she wasn't truly a flirt.

Thankfully, he didn't seem to notice. As he stepped toward her, his expression slid from hot desire to pure astonishment.

Quickly, she caught up her fan. Brandishing it playfully in front of her, she danced away. "That's enough of that, my lord. I think I've proven sufficiently that I'm not this rector's daughter of yours."

When he merely continued to gape at her, she added, warming to her role, "If you'll excuse me, I'd best return to the ball before my mother finds me being naughty again."

"Again?" he choked out.

"Surely you don't think you're the first man I've kissed? I may be half-English, but I'm half-Scottish, too. And in Scotland, ladies are much more free to . . . um . . . enjoy themselves."

The look on his face was priceless. Lady Dundee was right. Flirting with a man—especially one who'd nearly tossed her out of a carriage in his eagerness to get rid of her—was enormously satisfying.

Turning her back to him, she cast him one last teasing look over her shoulders. "But don't worry. You rank with the best of the men I've kissed, I assure you." Then she strolled away, smiling to herself in triumph even as she prayed he wouldn't follow her.

But Jordan was completely incapable of following her. *What the devil? Who the deuce* is *that woman?*

That seductress masquerading in Emily's body had acted like one of the Fashionable Impures auditioning a new lover, not like the virginal innocent who'd kept him tossing restlessly in his bed for months now. He rubbed his lips. He could still taste her sweet, spiced breath and smell the lavender in her hair.

Lavender—Emily had smelled of lavender!

But many young women used lavender water. More to the point, could his sweet rector's daughter have put on such a performance? She'd balked at telling one small lie. And she'd certainly never kissed like that.

Good God, he was hard as oak from that kiss. Taking out his handkerchief, he wiped away the beads of sweat on his brow. If she were Emily, where had she learned how to flirt and kiss and drive a man to utter distraction? He'd nearly deflowered her right here in Merrington's garden.

Deflowered her! He snorted. As if that woman could possibly be a virgin. Emily Fairchild had most certainly been a virgin, but he had his doubts about Lady Emma.

Or had she merely been trying to confuse him? If it hadn't been for that kiss, he would've sworn the woman was Emily. She tasted and looked and smelled like Emily. And she had a connection to Lord Nesfield.

His blood ran cold. Yes, there was that.

Muttering foul oaths under his breath, he adjusted his clothing to cover his still-obvious arousal and walked slowly toward the house. He glimpsed a human shape in the shadows of a nearby tree, but assumed it was another couple dallying in the dark garden, and walked on, deep in thought.

If it had been Emily, she'd been awfully stubborn in her lies. Could even Nesfield have coaxed the prim rector's daughter into pretending to be his niece? And why? The man would need a strong reason for giving a nobody like Emily both a new identity and a lavish coming out.

A nasty thought cut viciously through his mind, stunning him with its ugliness. What if Emily were Nesfield's mistress? Nesfield would never marry a rector's daughter, but he might try to arrange an advantageous marriage for her once he was done with her . . . as payment for services rendered.

He shook his head. That was absurd. Nesfield could hardly have taken Emily as a mistress, then discarded her in two months' time. Nor could Jordan believe that the Earl of Dundee and his wife would cooperate in such a scheme.

Nonetheless, Emily couldn't have done this without Dundee's cooperation. And Nesfield's.

The thought of Nesfield and Emily plotting together was enough to make him doubt his suspicions. How could Emily, the girl who'd quoted scripture at him and refused to lie, be capable of such a deception?

But how could two women be so much alike? And how could he be attracted to them both?

Devil take her, whoever she is, he thought sourly as he climbed the steps to the balcony, then crossed to the ballroom. She'd knocked him back on his heels with her little display out there, then left him craving her voraciously.

He entered the clamor of the ballroom and paused, searching the roiling knots of dancers for the little chit. She'd infected him with some disease to make him want her like this—that was the only explanation for such insanity. If he had any sense at all, he'd leave at once and put her out of his mind.

Instead he stood there, scouring the room for a glimpse of her pearl-twined hair and shimmering white gown, the gown he'd pawed only minutes ago in his eagerness to taste her bare flesh.

"You look as if you've been hit on the head with a mallet," came a familiar voice at his side.

He glowered at Ian's grinning expression. "It wasn't a mallet. And the spot was a bit lower, unfortunately."

Returning his attention to the ballroom, Jordan finally spotted Lady Emma. She was waltzing with young Radcliffe as cool as you please, without a hint in her sweet expression of the scene she'd played with him in the garden. The puppy was holding her close enough to imprint his lecherous body on her skirts. Where was the chit's chaperone, for God's sake? Somebody ought to put a stop to her outrageous behavior!

Ian followed the direction of his gaze. "It's not like you to be interested in an innocent."

"She's no innocent, I assure you," he snapped.

"So you don't still think she's the rector's daughter you mistook her for?"

"I don't know what to think." White anger seared Jordan when Radcliffe lowered his head to whisper something in her ear and she laughed.

"Come, man, I met her mother, a formidable matron if ever I saw one. Why would a woman of Lady Dundee's social status put an impostor forward as her daughter, risking her husband's reputation and the future of her other daughters?"

Why indeed? "I don't know; perhaps the countess grew bored in Scotland and this is her entertainment." His eyes narrowed. "And what about Lady Emma's speech? If she's from Scotland, where's her brogue?"

"She wouldn't have one, not with an English mother like Lady Dundee. The countess probably worked with her for years to prevent her from developing an accent."

"You can't eliminate an accent that easily. She ought to have some trace of it."

Ian sighed. "Even if Lady Dundee were foolish enough to pass off a nobody as her daughter, Nesfield says the woman is his niece, too."

"So why do Nesfield's niece and the daughter of his rector resemble each other so much?" Except in their experience with men. "Strange coincidence, don't you think?"

"Perhaps. How did you come to meet a rector's daughter, anyway?"

"She was at Dryden's masquerade ball in Derbyshire two months ago."

"Was she in costume that night, wearing a mask, that sort of thing?"

Jordan sensed a trap. "Yes." He added hastily, "But I saw her without her mask."

"For how long?"

With a black scowl, Jordan returned his attention to the dancers. He could only imagine what Ian would think if he admitted he'd seen the girl's face in dim moonlight for a mere matter of minutes.

"I take it from your silence that it was a brief glimpse."

"It was enough."

Now the deuced woman was dancing with Pollock. With a jealousy bordering on idiocy, he remembered Pollock's vow to find a woman to love. *Well, it won't be her, Pollock,* Jordan thought. Pollock wasn't for her. None of them were for her. If anyone had her, it would be him, and he wasn't about to become entangled with a deceitful, coy flirt.

Unfortunately, his body had other ideas. All it wanted right now was to drag her back outside and lay claim to her like some half-witted stallion.

"My God," Ian said dryly, "this rector's daughter must have made quite an impression on you for you to remember her after so short an encounter."

Jordan met his friend's speculation with stony silence. How could he explain the way Emily had affected him that night? He didn't understand it himself. "It was enough to make me almost certain that this woman is *not* Lady Emma, but Emily Fairchild, engaged in some scheme of Nesfield's making."

"That man is the most humorless, self-important creature in all England—why would he indulge in something so risky to his reputation?"

"I don't know. But I do know the woman I met, and I'd swear that's her."

"Well, I hope you're wrong."

"Why?" A horrible thought suddenly seized him. Ian was now watching Lady Emma, and at the sight of his intent scrutiny, another ridiculous spasm of jealous anger wracked Jordan. "You're not thinking of courting her instead of Lady Sophie, are you?"

Ian shot him a sideways glance. "Perhaps. I'm ready to put an end to this search for a wife."

With a fervency that astonished him, Jordan wanted to tear his best friend into little pieces.

"Judging from your murderous expression, however," Ian went on with decided amusement in his tone, "I'd best not try it. I'm not the sort to fight over a woman."

Devil take the man. Ian had merely been gauging his reaction. "I don't care if you court the chit," Jordan grumbled, trying futilely to regain lost ground. "But don't expect me to pick up the pieces when I prove to be right."

Ian laughed. "Now that I think about it, I don't believe Lady Emma will suit me after all. Two dances with her told me that. Lady Sophie meets my requirements better. I want an easy wife, not some flirtatious, unruly Scot. I have no tolerance for breaking in wild fillies."

Jordan wouldn't mind having a go at breaking in this particular filly. Judging from that kiss in the garden, Lady Emma could make the most devout monk forswear his vows of celibacy. And Jordan was no monk.

But even if she were Emily, he needn't refrain from seducing her—for it would mean she was a designing, lying wench and not the innocent he'd thought. For some reason, that possibility infuriated him. He'd liked Emily Fairchild exactly as she was.

"Look at her," Jordan bit out. She'd taken a new partner, that idiot Wilkins. "She's an incomparable actress. Well, I will expose her little game, whatever it is."

"Why? What does it have to do with you?"

Ian wouldn't understand. It was like discovering that the unicorn you revered for its magical powers was really a horse with a horn attached. It made you want to tear off the horn and kick the horse. "If she's an impostor, people ought to know," he grumbled.

"What rot! You're not doing this for the good of society. You want that girl, and you want her badly. You're besotted with the very sort of woman you've always avoided." Ian's smug smile broadened. "What a sweet revenge for all those women who've tumbled head over heels for you and received nothing for it but a cool glance."

"Don't be absurd. I'm not besotted. I'm never besotted."

"Then it should be a singular experience for you. Beware, my friend; they say it isn't easy to dismiss love." He added, only half-facetiously, "Protect your heart if you can."

"No need," Jordan retorted. "As Pollock is so fond of saying, my heart is made of granite. No one, and certainly not some pretty chit up to no good, shall change that."

Chapter 6

In men this blunder still you find—
All think their little set mankind.

Hannah More, *Florio*

An hour later, Emily still couldn't decide what bothered her most. That she'd fooled Jordan by giving him precisely what he wanted—a reckless interlude with an experienced woman—or that she'd played the wanton with such ease. What sort of wicked person could do that, could lie to a man and tease him so . . . so scandalously?

"You're awfully quiet, Lady Emma," said a voice at her side. "Are you bored?"

She glanced at Mr. Pollock and, as she'd been doing all evening, said what she thought Lady Emma might say. "Of course I'm bored. You city folk are so sedate. In Scotland, we'd have been dancing jigs until dawn, but already this ball seems to be ending. I'm quite put out over it."

The two coxcombs who flanked Mr. Pollock laughed. He smirked at her, his eyes brightened by too much punch. "Yes, and those Scottish lads are wild, aren't they? Walking about with nothing under their kilts. I imagine their jigs are . . . enlightening for a young lady, shall we say?"

93

It was a shocking thing to say to a girl at her coming out, and he probably knew it. Tamping down on her urge to chastise him, Emily instead tapped him playfully with her closed fan. "I see you take my meaning exactly. You English should try wearing kilts sometime. It would certain liven up these affairs."

The three men laughed raucously, and Mr. Pollock the loudest. Then he leaned toward her, his voice lowering. "Name the time and place, Lady Emma, and I shall be happy to wear a kilt for you."

She ignored the decidedly naughty implication behind the comment. "I wouldn't dream of dressing you in a kilt when you already have such splendid attire."

That seemed to please him enormously, which didn't surprise her. Mr. Pollock, for all his blond good looks and devil-may-care manner, was what Lady Dundee would surely term a dandy. His head was perched above the largest number of folds she'd ever seen in a cravat, and from the unnatural way he moved, she guessed that the starched material chafed his neck. She could suggest a soothing ointment for it, but doubted he would appreciate it. Besides, Lady Emma wouldn't know about such matters, would she?

"I wonder what your mother would think of your interest in kilts," Mr. Pollock murmured.

"Mama doesn't understand me at all," she said in a conspiratorial voice. "These days she lets herself be guided by my Uncle Randolph, and he's a sour old fart."

Papa would have a nervous collapse to hear her use such language, but she secretly enjoyed shocking these pompous nobles—especially since she'd never have to suffer the long-term consequences of her outrageous behavior.

Oh, she was truly becoming wicked.

Mr. Pollock seemed to like it, however. He arched one finely plucked eyebrow. "Having had my share of set-tos with your uncle, I'd have to agree."

Her heartbeat accelerated. Could he be the one? "Really? Has he insulted you, too?"

"Warned me away from your cousin, he did."

"What did you do about it?" she asked, holding her breath for his answer.

Just then his two friends, peeved at being ignored, made their presence known. "Pollock, Blackmore's scowling at us again," one of them whined. "This time I think he's really angry."

Curse the fools, she thought as Pollock faced them, her question forgotten.

"Ignore him," Pollock said harshly.

"Ignore him! I can't ignore him. I invested in his latest concern, and I need that money. I think he—" The man hesitated, casting Emily an apologetic look. "I think he has his eye on Lady Emma, and I for one shan't stand in his way." He grabbed his friend's elbow. "Come on, Farley, I'm parched. Let's have some punch."

As the two fops left, Emily seethed. How dare Jordan scare off the other men? How would she find out who'd been courting Sophie if he frightened them all away?

Her gaze shot across the room to where Jordan stood beside a Ming vase, downing champagne and scowling at the men who'd just left her side. How she'd dearly love to crack that vase over his head! The scoundrel hadn't danced with anyone else this evening, further rousing people's speculations about his interest in her. He'd probably done it purposely, curse him.

Suddenly he caught her looking at him, and his

scowl disappeared. With deliberate slowness, he allowed his gaze to drift down her gown as if he could see every inch of what lay beneath. He might as well have stroked her naked skin with his hand, for every place his gaze touched, her body grew all hot and tingly. When his eyes finally came back to hers, they were smoldering. Then he smiled insolently, knowingly, and to add insult to injury, lifted his glass in a mocking salute.

She snapped her gaze back to Pollock in utter mortification. The miserable wretch! When Emily Fairchild had wanted his attention, he'd thrust her away, but let a wanton like Lady Emma kiss him, and he broke out his best seduction techniques! No wonder Lord Nesfield suspected him of treachery. He was a cad! He deserved to be deceived, and oh, how she would enjoy doing it!

"Why aren't you running off, too?" she challenged Mr. Pollock. "Aren't you afraid of Lord Blackmore?"

"Not at all. We're friends of a sort." He leaned nearer, two spots of color rising in his pallid cheeks. "If you have an ounce of sense, Lady Emma, you'll steer clear of him. He has no interest in a woman beyond the obvious. Don't think you'll snag him as a husband, because you won't. He boasted to me only this evening of his granite heart. Even as lovely as you are, I doubt he'll soften it for you. Beware of setting your cap for him."

"Don't worry; I find him rude, arrogant, and annoying. He doesn't interest me at all." A pity he kissed like the very devil and made her toes curl whenever he looked her over.

"I'm glad to hear it. I thought you might . . . be flattered by his attentions."

"Not at all. And if you don't mind, I'd rather not

discuss Lord Blackmore. The subject gives me terrible indigestion."

Mr. Pollock laughed. Then he began to describe his latest visit to his tailor, wringing a smile from her. Dear heavens, the man certainly placed great store by choosing the right clothes. She'd never met a man for whom examination of the cut of a waistcoat required at least an hour. How frivolous could one be? Emily Fairchild would have told him right out that he was wasting his life. Unfortunately, Lady Emma must pretend to find the tale enormously diverting.

A few minutes later, as Mr. Pollock was deep into his recitation of how he'd enlightened his tailor on the subject of waistcoats, she saw Lord St. Clair approaching beyond him. She mustn't lose this opportunity to speak with the viscount in private and determine if he could have been Sophie's love.

Waiting until Mr. Pollock paused, she said in a sugary voice, "I hate to trouble you, but would you be a darling and fetch me some punch? I'm simply parched."

"I'd be delighted." He gave her a gallant bow, then hurried off across the room. And none too soon, for she turned to find Lord St. Clair at her elbow.

He wasn't classically handsome—his black brows were rather thick, his complexion a bit too dark, and his features too coarse for that. But he stood out among his pampered, perfectly coifed peers, and not only because of his great height. It was his eyes, black as sin and far too knowledgeable for a young woman's comfort. It was hard to imagine timid little Sophie running off with him. But then, it was hard to imagine her running off with any man, so Emily supposed it could be Lord St. Clair as easily as anybody else.

The smile he gave her was genuine, if a little formal. "You seem to have acquired several admirers, Lady Emma. Every time I turn around, you're surrounded by men."

She wasn't sure she'd call them men. They were more like children, with their fawning and their petty arguments about whose horse could run a faster mile down Rotten Row. It was refreshing to speak to a man with a brain.

"I'm sure I'll fall out of fashion by the next ball," she quipped. "From what I've heard, the fashionable become unfashionable with every change of the wind."

"It does seem that way sometimes." A servant passed with a tray of champagne glasses. He took one and handed it to her. "I heard you say you were thirsty."

"Yes."

She fumbled for some way to bring the subject back to Sophie, but he surprised her by addressing a completely different topic. "I've come to apologize for my friend's behavior earlier. He can be . . . odd sometimes when it comes to women."

His mention of Jordan made her steal a glance toward the earl, who was glowering at them both. She deliberately turned her back to him. "Odd? From what I've heard, he has no use for women at all except for what they can provide him in bed."

The scandalous statement seemed to surprise him. "I see you've been listening to Pollock. Don't put too much stock in what he says. He envies Blackmore."

"So Lord Blackmore did *not* boast about his heart of granite?"

"I have no idea. It does sound like something

he'd say. But no matter what he claims, he has the same vulnerable heart as most men. He's merely erected a large shield around it."

How very sad, she thought. "It sounds as if you know him well."

"We've been friends since childhood, and we attended Eton together. There's little we don't know about each other."

Emily fought back the urge to ask him about Jordan. Instead, she should be questioning him about Sophie. Dismissively, she remarked, "Well, I think he's insolent and boorish."

Amusement flickered in his eyes. "Why? Because he mistook you for a rector's daughter? You needn't worry about that. I set him straight. He won't trouble you with such nonsense anymore."

"You don't mean to say that he still thinks I'm this . . . Emily creature!"

Did she imagine his slight hesitation? "No, of course not. Your waltz seems to have disabused him of the notion."

Thank heavens, the kiss had worked. This masquerade would be difficult enough, especially if Jordan were Lord St. Clair's good friend.

"Actually," the viscount went on, "I believe he's as interested in you as he was the rector's daughter."

Emily's pulse began a wild thumping. *Steady, now,* she cautioned her foolish heart. *It's not me that Jordan finds interesting, but that wanton creature, Lady Emma. And he's forbidden to both of us—now more than ever.*

"Well, I don't return the interest, I assure you." She tucked her hand in the crook of St. Clair's elbow. "I much prefer you to him. You don't spend the evening scowling at me."

"I'm flattered, Lady Emma, but . . ." He paused.

"But what?"

"My interest lies with your cousin."

Aha! Her flirting had finally turned up something useful. Odd that he'd announced his infatuation in such a cool manner, but Lord St. Clair didn't seem the sort to wear his heart on his sleeve.

"Does she return your interest?" She held her breath. This masquerade might end tonight if he cooperated. It couldn't end too soon for her.

"You mean she hasn't mentioned me to you at all?" he said.

Oh, dear. She scrambled to rethink her tactics. "You must understand, we've had little chance to talk since my arrival. With this illness, she sleeps all the time and only rouses to take her medicine."

The concern in his face seemed appropriate, though not excessive. "That sounds serious."

"Not really," she hastened to assure him. "I mean, it may *sound* serious, but I'm sure she'll be fine after a few days' rest."

For a woman who'd been taught that lying was an awful sin, she'd certainly learned the art of it quickly. Obviously wickedness was as easy as it was wrong.

She was saved from more lies when Lady Dundee emerged from the crowd and bore down on them like a mother elephant thundering to the rescue of her calf. "Where have you been, you naughty girl? I told you not to stray too far!"

It took Emily a second to remember her role as willful "daughter," but her response was quick. "I refuse to follow you about like a ninny, Mama. I intend to enjoy myself, no matter what you and Uncle Randolph intend."

Lady Dundee whipped out her fan and worked it furiously. "The very idea! That a young girl should think of enjoyment before her elders' wishes—what is the world coming to?" She leaned toward Lord St. Clair, her tone conspiratorial. "I do hope you'll keep an eye on my daughter. You've been so very solicitous of Sophie that I know I can trust you to be a good influence on this willful creature here."

"I'll do my best to curb her youthful impulses," Lord St. Clair answered, flashing Emily a sympathetic glance over the countess's head.

Emily bit back a smile. Obviously, the countess also believed Lord St. Clair to be a likely suspect for Sophie's love.

Mr. Pollock suddenly emerged from the crowd to join them, a glass of punch in his hand. He glanced sullenly at Lord St. Clair and the untouched champagne in her hand, then gave her the punch. "It's the last of it, Lady Emma. I think you were right about the ball ending."

Lady Dundee fixed her penetrating gaze on Mr. Pollock. "Of course it's ending. I'm told Merrington's affairs never go late. Our young ladies need their rest."

She glanced quizzically at Emily, who gave her the barest nod to indicate that Mr. Pollock was one of her suspects. Then the countess bestowed a regal smile on both men. "So I fear we must be on our way as well. We're attending a breakfast tomorrow."

"Which one?" Lord St. Clair asked.

Lady Dundee snapped her fan closed. "Lady Astramont's. Perhaps we'll see you there?"

"If I may caution you," Mr. Pollock offered, "Lady Astramont is terribly unfashionable. Only the most tedious people attend her affairs. I fear you'll be bored to tears."

"Probably," Lady Dundee said with an impatient wave of her bejeweled fingers. "But she's an old friend of mine. We came out at the same time. I can't slight her by not attending her breakfast on the one occasion when I am in town."

"That's very generous of you," Lord St. Clair said smoothly. "And may I express my hope that Lady Sophie will be well enough to attend also."

"I'm afraid that's unlikely. But she'll be fine at home while Randolph and I take Emily to the breakfast." She tugged on Emily's arm. "Come, girl, you need your rest. We don't want you falling ill, too."

Flashing Lord St. Clair and Mr. Pollock a helpless look, Emily handed each of them a glass, then went off with her "mother." As soon as they left the men's hearing, she whispered, "Do you think Lord St. Clair is the one?"

"Quite possibly, but we'll find out soon enough. Now that he knows Sophie is at home alone tomorrow, he may attempt to visit her in private. That would be a certain sign of his guilt."

"How will you keep him from discovering she's not there?"

"Don't you worry about that, my dear. The servants know what to say. Besides, Randolph will contrive to be home. He'll thwart Lord St. Clair if he attempts anything drastic." She glanced back to where the two men were still standing. "What about Mr. Pollock? Do you suspect him as well?"

"I'm not sure. He did say something odd, however, about Uncle Ran—I-I mean, Lord Nesfield's warning him away from Sophie."

Lady Dundee grinned at her. "I see you're falling into your role very well."

Emily blushed. "I suppose. But sometimes I hate her."

"Her?"

"Lady Emma." They entered the foyer, and Em-

ily glanced around to see who might be listening,
but the place was empty. "I hate her for being rich
and a flirt and making all the men like her." She
thought of Jordan's change in behavior toward her
tonight, and added fervently, "They wouldn't act
that way around Emily Fairchild. They wouldn't
give her a second thought."

"Don't be silly—they *are* acting that way around
Emily Fairchild. This is a masquerade, not a spirit
possession. Both women are you. Why, you
couldn't be Lady Emma so convincingly if her per-
sonality weren't latent in you." She brushed back
one of Emily's wayward curls in another of those
motherly gestures Emily had come to like. "Now
tell me honestly, did you hate your masquerade so
very much?"

She ducked her head, almost too ashamed to answer. "No. But that's what's so awful. I *should* have
hated it."

" 'Should have.' 'Ought to have.' Those are
words for people without minds of their own.
Thankfully, you're not one of those." The countess
smiled and added, "There's no shame in enjoying
oneself, you know. Life is meant to be fun."

Life is meant to be fun, Emily thought as Lady
Dundee went off to request their wraps and order
their carriage. No one had ever said *that* to her before. Her parents had spoken of fulfilling one's duties without complaint or of giving something
useful to the world. They'd even spoken of the importance of finding love. But no one had ever mentioned fun.

What a novel concept.

"Leaving already, Lady Emma?" said a smooth
voice behind her.

Emily froze. Why must Jordan continue to
plague her? Or was this God's way of punishing

her for daring to enjoy her masquerade?

Pasting a cool smile on her lips, she faced him. "Yes. The evening has grown tedious, I'm afraid."

"I was hoping we could have another dance." He lowered his voice. "Or perhaps another walk in the garden."

His gaze caught hers, fathomless, intense . . . tempting. Her heart did a quick somersault. Curse him! He shouldn't affect her like this! "Surely you have better things to do than dance with me—ladybirds to seduce, young girls to ignore, matrons to shock."

He raised one eyebrow. "I see someone's spreading nasty rumors about me. I wonder who it might be. Pollock? Or those pups gamboling about you all night, making fools of themselves?"

"If I didn't know better," she said sweetly, "I'd think you were jealous."

A thunderous scowl darkened his face. "Not jealous—curious. Are you hiding behind those popinjays because you can't handle more challenging company?"

"Like yours, you mean?" She fought down the butterflies that his all-seeing glances scared up. "I'm perfectly capable of handling the likes of you. I think I made that clear earlier in the garden."

She regretted the words the instant she said them, for his body went hard, his lips curved upward in a smile, and the look on his face would have tempted a nun.

His gaze was a whisper of seduction, so clear she could swear everyone in the room could hear it. When he stepped close enough for her to smell the male scent of him, she had to stiffen every muscle to keep from backing away.

He spoke softly, huskily. "The only thing you made clear in the garden is that you and I should dance your particular variation on the waltz more often.''

Her mouth went dry. Her particular variation on the waltz would no doubt lead to *his* particular variation if she ever allowed him to get her alone again. And she suspected that his variation would be a great deal more naughty than hers.

Thankfully, Lady Dundee returned just then. ''I don't know what's wrong with servants these days. I swear they can't—Oh, hello.'' She halted beside Emily, her gaze narrowing on Jordan. ''I don't believe we've been introduced, sir.''

Emily performed the introductions quickly, eager to be away from him.

''I see Lady Emma gets her looks from you.'' He took Lady Dundee's plump hand and pressed a gallant kiss to it.

Goodness gracious. Was he hinting that Emily was an impostor? Or merely paying Lady Dundee the usual facile compliments?

Whatever the case, he'd met his match in Lady Dundee. ''Of course she does,'' she said smoothly, as if she weren't speaking the most blatant lie in Christendom. ''The shape of her brows, the elegant nose . . . it all came from my line, though she resembles her father, too. The Campbell mouth, you know.''

Emily barely smothered a laugh when Jordan actually searched her features as if to confirm Lady Dundee's words.

''I must say, Blackmore,'' Lady Dundee continued, ''that you've given the lie to what I heard about you. I was told you never flattered young women and their mamas. I was even told that you preferred a more . . . experienced sort of woman.''

He shook his head in mock disappointment. ''All these unfounded rumors. As someone once told me, it's not right for people to malign a man when he's not there to defend himself." He cast her a taunting smile. "Don't you agree, Lady Emma?"

Dear heavens, she'd said those very words to him when they were in the carriage together!

"Besides," he went on smugly, "I wouldn't think of treating you and your lovely daughter so abominably, Lady Dundee. Lady Emma is the most *original* woman I've met in a long time."

So original she's invented, his gloating smile said. Emily pretended not to catch his meaning.

Lady Dundee evidently missed it entirely. "Yes, my daughter is quite original. All the men think so. Even before her coming out, I had to send several unsuitable young men in Scotland packing."

Her unwitting reference to the very suitors Emily had mentioned earlier wiped the smile off Jordan's mouth. "Did you really? I'm not surprised. Lady Emma has a talent for attracting unsuitable men."

Lady Dundee tapped her foot with impatience. "My brother would say that *you're* unsuitable, Lord Blackmore. I believe he disapproves of your politics."

"Your brother disapproves of everything about me. But your brother is a fool."

The blatant insult astonished Emily. She glanced at Lady Dundee, who surprised her by laughing. "Indeed he is. Always has been. How good of you to notice."

Just then, the footman announced that their carriage had come.

Lady Dundee drew her cloak more closely about her. "A pity I can't stay and hear more of your intriguing opinions, but we really must leave. Come, Emma."

She headed off for the entrance, but before Emily could follow, Jordan caught her arm. Bending his head, he whispered, "We'll continue our discussion when your protector is not around."

Protector, not mother. She glared at him, then regretted it. Looking at him was always a mistake. A man that handsome should be locked away from virgins.

Fixing his gaze on her, he lifted her gloved hand to his lips. When he pressed a kiss to the back of it, a shock of awareness sizzled up her arm and exploded over her like Chinese fireworks.

"You and I aren't finished," he whispered meaningfully.

"Dear me, I'm all aquiver with anticipation," she snapped as she jerked her hand free, then whirled away to follow Lady Dundee.

Jordan watched her go, every muscle straining to keep from rushing after her and shaking her senseless. She had to be Emily Fairchild. No matter what any of them said, she could *not* be this Lady Emma creature.

This alluring, infuriating, Lady Emma creature.

As Emily Fairchild, she'd tempted him with sweetness. As Lady Emma, however . . . What would taking her to bed be like? He imagined tracing each line and curve of her shapely limbs with his mouth, taking down her hair with its cloud of lavender scent and rubbing the gossamer strands between his fingers, filling his palms with her lovely ripe breasts—

Sweet God in heaven, he was hard again. No woman had ever made him lose control like this, and he'd made love to the best courtesans—the most famous, the most beautiful. Those women had satisfied his needs, but he'd never burned for them this intensely, not before, not after. He was sweating buckets merely thinking about having Emily's body beneath his, her legs spread in welcome, her skin hot to the touch as she cried his name at the height of her release.

With a curse, he strode up to the footman and ordered that his carriage be brought. Devil take her lovely face and quick mind and this strange masquerade. Was she Emily or not?

She *had* to be Emily—no other woman had ever affected him like this. She was Emily and she was lying, and he would prove it somehow.

His carriage arrived and he leapt in, his mind already awhirl with strategies as Watkins began the short drive home. As soon as he arrived at his town house, he commanded a footman to fetch Hargraves to his study at once. When the butler entered a few minutes later, Jordan was crouched on the floor, searching through the papers piled under his desk.

"My lord?" Hargraves exclaimed, peering around the desk with alarm in his expression. "Is something amiss?"

"Didn't I receive an invitation to the Astramont breakfast a few weeks ago?" Jordan tossed aside a gilded envelope and picked up another.

"Of course. It's in the pile with the rest of the discards. Lady Astramont always invites you. And you always refuse. This year was no exception."

"I've changed my mind." At Hargraves's silence, Jordan glanced up to find his butler gawking at him. "Well? Surely the flighty creature won't mind if I accept at the last minute."

"Mind? After she receives your acceptance, her ladyship will probably spend the intervening hours in joyful contemplation of the good chance that led you to decide to grace her home for the first time in a decade."

Jordan laughed. Hargraves always managed to cheer him.

Hargraves cleared his throat. "Um, milord. May I ask *why* your lordship has decided to attend the viscountess's affair?"

The Astramont invitation suddenly surfaced, its chicken-scratch script reminding him of how very much Lady Astramont irritated him. She was an effusive, bird-witted twit with the dullest guests imaginable.

But he would be at her breakfast. Jordan rose and brushed off his dusty hands, then threw the invitation atop his desk. "Someone I met tonight is planning to attend." He had Ian to thank for that piece of information. "I suspect she'll not be as glad to see me as Lady Astramont, however." Until he discovered the truth about this Emily/Lady Emma woman, he would dog her steps, unsettling her at every opportunity.

He studied the invitation, then groaned. "Two P.M.? Whoever heard of serving breakfast at that ridiculous hour?"

"If I may interject, my lord, that isn't unusual for these breakfast affairs."

"I'm sure you're right. But I can accomplish mounds of work by the time these women begin breakfast. Very well. Two P.M. it is. Send a message over in the morning."

Now that the matter was settled, he leaned against the desk and surveyed his servant. Hargraves's duties extended far beyond those of the average butler. It was Hargraves who'd kept an eye on Jordan's stepsister when she'd still lived here, and Hargraves who'd found someone to protect her on her disastrous trip to New South Wales. The man also had a knack for using the servants' gossip network to find out information useful to Jordan at Parliament and elsewhere.

"Hargraves, do you ever speak with any of Lord Nesfield's servants?"

"No, my lord; that lot keeps pretty much to themselves. But that's not to say I couldn't. I believe their coachman is courting the parlormaid at Langley House, and she's the sister of our own Mary's husband."

Jordan squelched a smile. "I see. And does all of that mean you could get an introduction to the Nesfield coachman if needed?"

"I believe so. Yes."

"Good. I want you to find something out for me."

"Certainly, milord. If the coachman will not tell me what you need to know, I'll find another avenue."

That was what Jordan liked about his stalwart butler—the man was determined and devious. His small frame and servile manner took everyone off their guard, and his surprising ability to drink anyone under the table had resulted in more than one valuable piece of information for Jordan. Even better, he never asked questions of his employer. He took his orders, then set out to do the job with a thorough attention to detail. The man should have been a Bow Street Runner.

But Hargraves was better than any Bow Street Runner, because his best quality was discretion. In this instance, discretion was something Jordan valued highly.

"Here's the situation, Hargraves." He crossed his arms over his chest. "There's this young woman . . ."

Chapter 7

⁓⁓◗◗⁓⁓

*We are truly indefatigable in providing for
the needs of the body, but we starve the soul.*

Ellen Wood, English playwright,
writer, journalist, *About Ourselves*

Ophelia settled her ample body on the settee
across from Randolph's chair, then slipped
her aching foot out of her slipper and propped it
on a horsehair footstool. She was certainly paying
for so many hours on her feet last night. And now
her brother was on the rampage. It was too much
to be borne.

"Well?" Randolph groused. "Where is the
blasted chit?"

"She'll be down shortly, I'm sure." Ophelia
yawned. "You must give the girl time to sleep, or
she won't suit your purpose."

"As if she suits my purpose *now*. I still have not
heard what happened at the ball. Is that why you
sent her right up to bed last night, even though I
told her to report to me at once? Were you protecting her because you knew she had not discovered anything?"

"I sent her up to bed because she was dead on
her feet."

"After one trifling ball that ended barely after midnight?"

"No. After dancing lessons and a full day of shopping for accessories and *then* a ball during which she danced every dance."

"At my expense, too."

She rolled her eyes and leaned forward to rub her foot. "If you didn't want to do this right, you should've told me. I would've dressed her in sackcloth and ashes and stuck her in a corner at every event."

Randolph's sole response was to scowl. He never had appreciated her particular sense of humor. "Well, the girl had best have something to tell me when she comes down. I shall not keep up this entertainment for her if she cannot produce anything."

"Entertainment?" Ophelia's short bark of laughter sounded loud in the early-morning quiet of the town house. "She seems to consider it torture." When Randolph looked at her with narrowed eyes, she added very deliberately, "I can't imagine why, though. If she didn't want to come, all she had to do was say so. Am I right?"

He jerked his gaze from hers, his mouth puckering sourly.

Time for a more direct approach. "Randolph, what did you tell Emily to make her agree to your plan? Clearly, she finds this scheme distasteful. You should have seen her after the ball last night. She was skittish as a mouse in a cat's paw."

"Did she behave like that at the ball, too? That is not what we agreed upon, you know. I wanted her to—"

"Randolph! Silence your wagging tongue for a moment, will you?" He glowered at her, but thankfully kept quiet. "You needn't worry about Emily.

During the ball, she was as bold and impudent as you could wish. She had every man in the place eating out of her pretty hand and thinking her the most 'original' creature alive."

"Then why was she skittish?"

"Because she obviously found the experience taxing and intimidating."

Ophelia was certain that Emily's encounter with Blackmore had been partly responsible for the girl's somber mood on the way home, though Randolph needn't know that just yet. She'd prodded Emily to reveal what had happened between her and that rapscallion, but the girl had evaded her questions.

There was something going on there; Ophelia would stake her life on it. And that was trouble indeed. From what she'd heard, Blackmore would chew up a little thing like Emily and spit her out. Ophelia didn't wish to see that, for she was growing very fond of the child.

"As for my original question," she continued, refusing to let Randolph draw her away from her immediate concern, "why is she willing to help Sophie at the expense of her own integrity? What hold do you have over poor Emily?"

"Hold?!!" He puffed himself up like an adder. "Hold, indeed. Her father owes his livelihood to me. That is all the hold I have over her." Casting her a sidelong glance, he added, "Besides, I am sure you have already asked the girl that very question, since you like to stick your nose where it does not belong. What does *she* say?"

His question told her at once that he was hiding something. "She won't tell me anything, as I'm sure you know. Thanks to you, she doesn't trust either of us."

Looking relieved, he stood and limped over to

the fireplace. "Nonsense. She knows her duty, that's all."

Ophelia sighed. She ought to press the matter further. But she'd learned long ago that if she forced Randolph into a corner, he would risk the bite of the deadliest snake before he'd tell her anything. And Randolph already had quite enough venom coursing through his veins.

But she could work on the girl. Emily didn't like lying, that much was clear. If only Ophelia could gain her trust. . . .

As if conjured up by the thought, Emily herself entered, already dressed for the breakfast at Lady Astramont's. With approval, Ophelia noted the girl's choice of the rose corded cambric. Emily had a natural sense of style that made everything so much easier.

With a quick glance at Randolph, who was staring into the fire with his back to the door, Emily crossed to Ophelia and handed her a cheesecloth bag.

"This is for your foot," she said in a low voice. "Mix these herbs with hot water. They make an excellent soak for sore feet."

Ophelia took the bag with a smile. "Thank you, my dear. It's very kind of you to make it up for me."

Randolph whirled around. "What? What are you two about?"

Quickly Ophelia hid the cheesecloth bag in her skirts. For some reason Randolph didn't approve of Emily's ministrations, although anyone could see the girl had a talent for physic. "She's saying good morning, you fool. What do you think?"

"It's about time you showed up," he growled at Emily. "Kept me waiting all night, you did. Sit down. I want a full account of the ball."

Emily settled carefully on the edge of a wing-backed chair to keep from mussing her gown. "How much has Lady Dundee told you?"

"Nothing at all, blast her. Who danced with you? Did anyone ask for Sophie?"

"Let me see. I danced with Mr. Pollock, Lord St. Clair, Lord Wilkins, Lord Radcliffe, Lord Blakely, and Mr. Wallace."

How odd that she didn't mention Blackmore, Ophelia thought. Hadn't she danced with the earl, too? Ophelia wasn't entirely certain.

"All of them expressed their condolences for Sophie's illness," Emily went on, "but only Lord St. Clair and Mr. Pollock seemed overly interested. Both of them asked repeatedly when Sophie would be attending social events again. And as you know, Lord St. Clair called on her yesterday."

"Yes, I know about that. And I do find it curious. St. Clair is something of a mystery. I heard he was estranged from his father for some secret reason that no one will discuss. He left England for several years, and no one knows why. He only returned last year. But I've heard the most dreadful stories of what he did while he was on the continent . . ."

And of course, Ophelia thought, Randolph believed every word. His own son had run off to the continent, so he was suspicious of any other young man who'd done the same.

Randolph began to pace, stabbing his cane into the Aubusson carpet every few steps. "Anyway, he and I had a bit of a talk once, and I told him that rumor had it he was not fit to marry any young woman. I let him know that I would not countenance any union between him and my daughter. You know what the impudent scoundrel had the audacity to say? That Sophie was the only person whose opinion he cared about." He snorted. "As if a girl of that age knows what she wants. A pretty lad—that is all a girl of eighteen looks for."

"That's not true," Emily retorted. "I think your daughter has more sense than to choose a man simply because he has nice features."

Ophelia wasn't so sure herself, but said nothing on that score. She didn't know her niece that well. "We set a trap for St. Clair," Ophelia told Randolph. "We told him we'd be at the breakfast and that Sophie would be here alone. If he comes here—"

"If he comes here," Randolph put in, "I shall be on the lookout. We will see how he acts and if he goes snooping about the house without permission. That would certainly tell us he was the one."

"Do try to control yourself," Ophelia cautioned. "We mustn't scare away the prey or show our hand prematurely. If word of what happened to Sophie leaks out because you approach some man too soon, it'll ruin her chances in the future. St. Clair may behave quite innocently, in which case you mustn't approach him."

"I think I can be trusted to show caution." Randolph halted his pacing, then peered through his lorgnette at Emily. "What about Pollock?"

"I'm not sure. He seemed only moderately interested."

"Pollock has a fortune, but is merely a mister," Randolph said. "He knows I would never accept the suit of any man with rank less than a viscount. Sophie deserves the best."

Sophie deserved to be paddled soundly for putting them to all this trouble, Ophelia thought. Yet sometimes she almost sympathized with the girl. Having Randolph for a father couldn't have been easy.

"What if one of these men really cared for her?"

Emily ventured. "What if Sophie were in love with one of them—"

"In love? Trust me, Miss Fairchild, love makes no difference. It soon vanishes, and then, if you have chosen the wrong partner, you find yourself unhappily yoked with someone who causes you only shame."

Heavens, Ophelia realized, Randolph was alluding to his own disastrous marriage! Apparently fancying himself in love, he'd married a girl much beneath him who'd turned out to be a vulgar and outspoken little twit prone to embarrassing him with great frequency. She'd given him a son who'd been a constant disappointment. But she'd had the decency, in Randolph's words, to die giving birth to Sophie, thus sparing Randolph a lifetime of mortification.

Unfortunately, with no one else around to garner Randolph's attention once his heir ran off, Sophie had become the center of his domain, the only one he could control. It was killing him to have her out from under his thumb, which was why he was going to all this trouble.

"In any case," Randolph blustered on, "what Sophie wants is immaterial. I know what is best for the girl. Neither Pollock nor St. Clair is acceptable. We must focus our attention on those two, since both are likely candidates. But was there no one else? No one who paid particular attention to you even if he said nothing of Sophie?"

When Emily colored, Ophelia waited for her to mention Blackmore. But the girl only murmured, "No one," as she cast Ophelia a pleading look.

Ophelia debated keeping the girl's secret. But that was pointless. Randolph would find out one way or the other about Blackmore's interest in her, and there would be hell to pay if they had kept it from him. Besides, Ophelia wanted to see how Emily would react to mention of the rapscallion.

"What about the Earl of Blackmore?" she said, acting as if she misunderstood Emily's look. "He spoke to you at length before we left."

As the color crept across Emily's face until even her ears were red, Randolph pivoted to face the young woman.

"Blackmore?" Randolph punctuated the word with a loud rap of his cane. "That scoundrel approached you? How could you forget to mention him after what happened at the Drydens' ball?"

Very interesting, Ophelia thought. "What happened at the Drydens' ball, Randolph? Do tell."

"The blackguard danced with my Sophie, that's what. Him with his reputation, presuming to touch a pure girl like Sophie! It was an outrage, and I told him so when I wrested her away from him!"

Ophelia could easily imagine the awful scene her brother had made.

"Lord Blackmore spoke to me only briefly last night," Emily protested. "And he didn't even mention Sophie."

"He wouldn't," Randolph growled. "That one is a fox, too clever by half. But he is a more likely candidate than the other two, I promise you."

"Don't be absurd, Randolph. Why would Blackmore try to elope with Sophie?" Blackmore most certainly had his eye on a particular young woman, but Ophelia would wager a king's ransom it wasn't her insipid niece. "The man's no fortune hunter. Besides, he can have any heiress he wants merely by crooking his finger, so he needn't endure your wrath for Sophie."

Randolph leaned forward on his cane, his eyes lit with malevolence. "I'm not saying he had any intention of marrying her, mind you. His sort delights in debauching women as an amusement."

"Oh, really, Randolph—" Ophelia began.

"You think I exaggerate. But he and I *are* enemies, and I humiliated him in front of all those people at the Drydens' ball. He might have decided to humiliate me by ruining my daughter. It is exactly the sort of thing a scoundrel like him would do."

Ophelia tried to imagine Blackmore being humiliated by her brother's making an ass of himself at a ball. More likely, Blackmore had laughed his head off. "You really are insane, you know. If Blackmore had carried Sophie off, then refused to marry her, he would have blackened his name in good society for the rest of his life. No one would countenance such behavior. He's never done anything of that sort, and I see no reason for him to begin it now."

Randolph grew sullen at her appeal to logic. Ophelia marveled at his amazing irrationality regarding Sophie. Any fool knew Blackmore wouldn't stoop to such petty vengeance.

Emily listened to the discussion with growing trepidation. She'd never considered Jordan a candidate for Sophie's lover, but certain niggling memories now assailed her. His kisses when they were out in the carriage. His behavior toward Lady Emma in the garden. He claimed not to care for young innocents, but there were essentially three to whom he'd made advances, if she considered both her personas and Sophie.

And yet . . . those had all been instances of impulse, and in the case of Lady Emma, most assuredly provoked. Would he truly set out to defame a young woman? He hadn't seemed the least concerned about Lord Nesfield's behavior toward him at the Drydens' ball.

She couldn't believe he would ruin Sophie for

such poor reasons. Still, he might have tried to elope with her. After Lord Nesfield had shown his disapproval, Jordan might have thought elopement the only way to ensure his success with Sophie.

Even Jordan's treatment of her last night could be interpreted that way. He'd been suspicious of her—perhaps because he feared a trap. Otherwise, why would he be so determined to unmask her? Why care if she was an impostor? And he *had* attended a marriage mart, which was certainly out of character. Had he been looking for Sophie?

Then again, he'd always protested violently that he didn't want a wife. And why had he kissed Emily and Lady Emma with such passion if he loved Sophie? The very thought of him caring for Sophie made jealousy explode in her brain. No, she wouldn't believe it. He wouldn't make advances to her if he wanted Sophie.

Unless his advances were an attempt to trick her into telling him what was going on! She scowled and rubbed her temples. Trying to guess Jordan's motives was giving her the most awful headache.

Suddenly, she realized both Lady Dundee and Lord Nesfield were staring at her.

"Do you feel all right?" Lady Dundee asked.

Sophie dropped her hands from her temples and pasted a smile on her face. "Yes, of course. I'm tired, that's all."

"You listen to me, young woman, and you listen well," Lord Nesfield growled. "Blackmore is as much a suspect as the others. Keep your eye on him, you hear me? And tell me everything he does, every word he speaks to you. You can begin by telling me what he said last night."

Her headache immediately worsened. Now she had to invent more stories—she certainly couldn't tell him the truth.

When this was over, she would never get herself into such a fix again. It would be truth and honesty from then on out. Lying was much too taxing.

Lady Astramont proved to be a little humming-bird of a woman, giddy and silly and prone to exaggeration. As soon as her butler ushered Emily and Lady Dundee into her wide marble foyer, she fluttered toward them, all smiles.

"I'm so glad you could come, Ophelia!" The woman had a trilling voice to match her hummingbird figure. "How many years has it been? Fifteen? Twenty? I swear, you don't look a day over twenty-five! That Scottish air must be good for the skin."

"It's not the air, Hortense, but good Scottish food that keeps me young." Lady Dundee tapped her plump cheek. "It fills out all the wrinkles."

Looking flustered by Lady Dundee's forthright allusion to her amplitude, Lady Astramont quickly turned to Emily. "And this must be your daughter. My, my, she is a pretty one. She takes after you, doesn't she?"

"Oh, yes." Lady Dundee's eyes sparkled with mischief. "She's a veritable copy of her mother."

"I can see that," Lady Astramont said earnestly.

Emily had to stifle her laughter as Lady Astramont led them through the foyer toward the parlor. Emily did her best not to stare, but it was hard to ignore the ostentation of Lady Astramont's house. Lady Dundee had said that Lady Astramont had more money than sense, and that was certainly evident in the vulgar display of wealth that surrounded her. Gilt vases, marble statues everywhere, lavish curtains of gold silk . . . it was bright enough to blind a person.

And all Emily could think was how much food for the poor such wealth could buy.

"Everyone's in the garden," Lady Astramont explained as they crossed the parlor to a set of French doors of cut crystal. "The weather was so nice, we set up the tables out there. But you won't believe the excitement. It's all anyone can talk about."

"What's that?" Lady Dundee asked.

Lady Astramont stopped, peeking over her shoulder before she lowered her voice to an annoying twitter. "You'll never guess who accepted my invitation." She paused for effect. "Lord Blackmore. The great earl himself. At *my* breakfast! Oh, I shall never have to worry about acceptances again after this. He rarely attends anything, and then only the most fashionable affairs."

Emily's blood thundered in her ears. Jordan. Coming here. Dear heavens, she wasn't ready for this. It was all she could do to keep her eyes focused straight ahead when she felt Lady Dundee's questioning gaze on her. Jordan had said they weren't finished. Obviously, he'd meant it.

"It's the most exciting thing to happen in years!" Lady Astramont blathered on. "And you, my dear friend, here to see it! Isn't it wonderful?"

"Yes, wonderful," the countess said dryly. "Is Blackmore already here?"

"Oh, dear me, no. That would be too much to ask. I'm sure he'll arrive late, which is his prerogative, of course. He is Blackmore, after all. But he sent his acceptance this very morning, so I believe he truly intends on coming."

As it happened, it was another hour before the earl made his appearance. Though Emily tried not to notice when he arrived, it was impossible to ignore. His entrance into the garden with Lady Astramont on his arm was like a stone thrown into a lake, producing ever-widening ripples of gossip and speculation.

Apparently, no one had believed Lady Astramont's assertions that the earl was planning to attend a breakfast that only those of little consequence attended. They'd assumed Lady Astramont was lying in a futile effort to enhance her social standing.

Now that he was here, everyone had to offer a whispered opinion to their neighbors on why he'd condescended to attend. And since nearly everyone had heard about his dancing with Lady Emma at the ball, most of the speculation focused on her.

Oh, why couldn't they all hush? She'd never imagined that such a lot of gossips and frivolous rumormongers ruled London society. Clearly, nobody had enough to do. For goodness sake, how could they move about a city like London every day and not notice all that needed to be changed and all the people who needed help? If they'd only channel their energies into something useful instead of repeating mindless tales, the world would be vastly improved.

Lady Astramont's chirping voice carried across the lawn. "Lord Blackmore, I hope you find everything to your satisfaction. Do try the roast duck. It's your favorite, is it not? And there's an apple tart and . . ."

As she babbled on inanely, Emily cast a quick glance at Jordan. Although he had a faintly pained look on his face, like that of a man wearing shoes that pinched, he responded to the woman's gushes with a charming smile and some murmured words about how glad he was to attend.

It took Emily by surprise. After the way everybody had spoken of him—as if he were the Deity Himself—she'd half expected him to be cold and barely civil to their fawning hostess. Although she didn't like Lady Astramont any more than he probably did, she felt kindly enough toward the woman not to wish her to be treated condescendingly in her own home. It warmed her that he felt the same.

Still, Emily could hardly blame him when he extricated himself from Lady Astramont's clinging arm as soon as possible. He spared Emily a long glance that told her exactly why he'd come, then took his time making the rounds of the other guests, like a tiger toying with his prey.

He waited until Lady Astramont carried off Lady Dundee, the second most important guest at the breakfast, for a tour of her house. Then he sauntered toward where Emily sat on a garden chair beneath an oak.

Thankfully, she wasn't alone. Mr. Pollock, who'd apparently also decided to attend at the last minute, had been at her side throughout the breakfast. Until then, his plaintive complaints about the bright sun and "ghastly" poached salmon had begun to wear on her. Mr. Pollock had the tendency to act as if their acquaintance was more intimate than she recognized. Still, she was grateful to have him nearby now that Jordan was here.

Pollock scowled as Jordan reached them. "Afternoon, Blackmore."

"Good afternoon, Pollock. Lady Emma."

She nodded coolly. "Where's your friend Lord St. Clair?" Was he even now falling into their trap?

"Ian doesn't attend many social occasions."

"Can't say I blame him for missing this one," Pollock retorted. "I'm surprised to see *you* here, Blackmore. It's not like you to socialize with Lady Astramont."

"Nor you. But I dare say you're here for the same reason I am." Jordan's gaze drifted to Emily. "I came to see Lady Astramont's garden, of course. I've been told it contains some truly *original* flowers."

When hot color flooded her cheeks, Pollock positively glowered at Jordan. "Yes, I forgot—you like trampling flowers underfoot, don't you?"

"Not at all. The perfect flower needs the perfect setting, however, and I'm here to ensure that it gets one."

"Oh? What do you consider the perfect setting?" Pollock said sourly. "In your buttonhole?"

"No. In the country." He cast Emily a lazy smile. "That's where flowers belong, don't you think?"

Emily met his gaze, every nerve ending screaming with the urge to tell him to go away and leave her alone. In the country, indeed. How could any man look so . . . so handsome and be such a beast? She'd never seen him in anything but evening dress, and his casual attire today only enhanced his attractions by making him look accessible, even to a rector's daughter like her.

And younger, too. He leaned against the oak's trunk like a youthful swain in a pastoral poem, the afternoon sun glinting off his auburn hair and setting it ablaze. His expression was anything but pastoral, however. It taunted her, challenged her to engage in his battle of words.

He thought he was so clever. *Say what you think*, Lady Dundee had advised. That would be perfectly easy with Jordan. "I'm not sure I understand your trite metaphor of the flower correctly, Lord Blackmore. Do you mean I should return to Scotland?"

"Not at all. I don't think Scotland would suit you. The English countryside seems more appropriate for a girl with your . . . attributes."

Pollock glanced from her to Jordan in bewilderment. "Are you insulting the lady, Blackmore? Because if you are—"

"Insulting her? Of course not. I'm paying her a compliment. Scotland is too barren and cold for a woman as lovely as she. Our English countryside is much warmer and better suited for such beauty."

"Not all of Scotland is barren and cold," she retorted, determined not to let him have the last word. "Parts of it are quite lush and green."

"All I've seen is Edinburgh and the land surrounding it," he responded, "but it wasn't to my taste. I prefer our simple English meadows. They're not quite so . . . wild and unpredictable."

She flushed at his reference to her behavior last night. He was still convinced that she was an impostor, and now he was bent on exposing her publicly. Heaven help her.

"Haven't been to Scotland myself," Pollock interjected, determined to jump into the conversation. He cast Emily an oddly possessive glance. "What's it like?"

"Yes," Jordan said coolly, "do tell us what it's like, Lady Emma."

Emily went blank . . . until she caught sight of Lady Dundee, looking out one of the upstairs windows. Bits and pieces of what the countess had told her floated into her mind, spoken in the woman's homesick tones. Lady Dundee had made her see Dundee Castle and its lands with perfect clarity. After all, what was a place but what one saw in it?

She gazed up at Jordan, but in her mind, she looked into Lady Dundee's face, heard her wistful voice. "Scotland as a whole? I can't begin to describe it all. But Dundee Castle in Campbell Glen, where we live, stands at the top of a grassy hill with slopes as soft as silk that careen down toward a perfect, clear lake."

"The Scottish call them 'lochs,'" Jordan said dryly.

"Yes, of course. I didn't think you'd know that, being English." She went on. "Beyond the loch is a craggy mountain where we played as children. The wind and rain have carved the rocks into fantastical shapes, so that it looks like gargoyles watching over us when we swim."

"Swim?" Pollock said. "Isn't the water too cold for swimming?"

"Most of the year, yes." She stared off in the distance, lost in the tales the countess had spun for her. "But in the middle of summer, it's warm enough. Even Mama swims then. And when the sun sets behind the hill, reaching out its fingers of gold and crimson as if to clutch the earth close a bit longer, there's no place lovelier."

"It sounds beautiful," a female voice said. "Like something out of a dream."

Only then did Emily realize she'd drawn the rapt attention of several of the ladies.

Jordan rolled his eyes. "Yes, like something out of a dream. Or a fairy tale."

Mindful of her audience, she said, "The Scottish who live around Campbell Glen do claim that fairies live in the forests beyond Dundee Castle." She lowered her voice to a whisper. "If you venture into the woods at night, you can see them, like a thousand fireflies, swirling in circles with their tiny, gossamer wings."

When Jordan snorted, the women glared at him, then moved their chairs closer to her. "Do tell us more. You've *seen* the fairies?"

"No, I'm afraid not." The general sigh of disappointment led her to add, "But I've seen traces of them, of course. Circles in the grass on the hill-side."

"How lovely," a young woman gushed. "I've always thought Scotland the most romantic place."

"Which only demonstrates that you've been reading too many far-fetched tales by that idiot Walter Scott," Jordan said.

"Have you no romantic feeling in you?" the woman retorted. "Can't you see how such poetry and stories enrich the soul?"

"Yes," Emily said mischievously, "have you no romantic feeling in you, Lord Blackmore?"

"Blackmore doesn't have feelings at all, much less romantic ones." Pollock lounged back in his flimsy wooden chair. "He doesn't even believe in love. Just last night, he told me love was a fickle emotion for fools to indulge in. Ladies, you see before you a man incapable of romantic feeling."

Emily's gaze shot to Jordan.

"Pollock has caught me out, I'm afraid." Jordan's voice was as chilly and black as a coal cellar in winter. "I don't waste time on poetry and 'romantic feeling' and such nonsense. As for love, it's a luxury I can't afford. I'm much too busy to waste time on spurious emotions."

"Then your life must be dreary indeed," Emily said sincerely. "Life is worth nothing without such luxuries. I pity anyone who has no time for them."

His eyes narrowed to slits, yet she didn't regret her words. Someone should have said them to him long ago. He shouldn't go through life believing himself above the very human emotions of his fellow men and women. No wonder he had a reputation for coldness, for being completely controlled.

Every eye was on the two of them now, but Emily ignored their audience, assailed by a profound curiosity to know what had shaped him into this ice figure. It must have been something very tragic. Or perhaps he was just the rare creature born without the urge to love. If so, she pitied him even more.

When the silence stretched out and became awkward, Pollock suddenly said, "Lady Emma, would you take a turn with me about the garden? I don't believe you've seen Lady Astramont's roses yet."

Dragging her gaze from Jordan, she cast Pollock a smile. "I certainly haven't. I'd be pleased indeed if you would show them to me."

Pollock offered his arm and she clasped it eagerly, glad to escape Jordan's dark looks and bitter opinions. But as they walked away, Jordan called out, "Lady Emma?"

She halted and turned her head to look at him. "Yes?"

"After you're done with Pollock, I want a word with you."

He said it as if there was no question of her agreeing. Everyone's eyes were on her, and they clearly expected the same. After all, he was quite an eligible catch. If he wanted a word with her, she was expected to drop all other amusements to indulge him.

But she knew what he wanted to discuss. He wanted to trick her into revealing the truth, especially now that she'd roused his fury by criticizing him. She daren't allow that.

"I'm afraid that will be impossible, Lord Blackmore. I promised Mama that we could leave as soon as she finished seeing Lady Astramont's house, and she must be nearly done. I'm sure she'll meet up with us while we are in the gardens."

An angry flush darkened his handsome face. Being refused anything by a woman was clearly as unfamiliar to him as taking tea on the moon. Well, too bad. As long as he couldn't be certain she was Emily Fairchild, he wouldn't dare to expose her.

"Another time perhaps," he clipped out.

"Yes, another time." Feeling more sure of herself, she walked off with Pollock.

Another time, indeed. If she had her way, it would come when pigs flew and fish took ferries, and not a minute sooner.

Chapter 8

*Whom do we dub as Gentleman? The
Knave, the fool, the brute—
If they but own full tithe of gold, and
Wear a courtly suit.*

Eliza Cook, English poet,
"Nature's Gentleman"

Minutes later, Jordan stormed out of Lady
Astramont's after taking quick leave of his
hostess. How dare Lady Emma rebuff him before
a crowd of people!

He leapt into his carriage and ordered Watkins
to drive to his club, her words still burning his ears.
Then your life must be dreary indeed. The little chit
had actually pitied him! Him! The Earl of Blackmore! A man who'd accomplished more in his lifetime than a dozen noblemen!

Just because he didn't wander the streets in a
perpetual state of infatuation like that fool Pollock
didn't mean his life was hollow and meaningless.
No, indeed. He was respected, envied even, by all
who knew him.

Perhaps he did go to bed alone most nights. And
there was the occasional time—more often, now
that his stepsister had moved out—when his house

felt like a pharaoh's rich and cavernous tomb.
Sometimes life worked out that way. Chasing after
love's dubious promises only brought disappointment, as he'd learned very young. If one allowed
oneself to crave affection and happiness and to
hope for more than simple contentment, one suffered pain. It was a fact of life.

Yet her voice still troubled his thoughts. *Life is
worth nothing without such luxuries.*

As if a woman her age knew anything about life!
He snorted as he gazed out the window at the
dingy dusk laying a gray, unforgiving cast over
every muddy walkway, especially in this part of
London. An aging strawberry seller trudged si-
lently homeward, tugging a cart of half-sold berries
with bare, chapped hands. Farther along, a whore
stood under the oil lamp seeking companions before the sun had even hidden its face.

Though he'd been raised with wealth and privilege, he'd seen a great many such sights, especially
once his reformer stepmother had married his father. Indeed, sometimes he felt guilty that he'd escaped such penury. Anyone who did escape it
should feel fortunate enough, without asking for
more.

Yes, love was a luxury, more so than Emily . . .
Lady Emma . . . *whoever* she was . . . could ever
know. Until Nesfield and Lady Dundee had
dressed her up and set her on display, she'd never
even left the country. What did she know of love's
fickle nature, the way some people held out a
promise of it, then snatched it away?

He curled his fingers into fists. She was a babe
in the woods with her teasing and flirting and lofty
statements about life. She thought that because she
wore satin gowns and spoke eloquently, because
her companions lapped up her every fanciful word,

she could say what she pleased and act irresponsibly.

Well, she was wrong. Such behavior would bring her a great deal of attention in the worst quarters. If she weren't careful, men would treat her as some fast-and-loose sort, and she'd be in deep trouble.

If she were Lady Emma, she would find herself compromised by some fortune hunter. And if she were Emily in masquerade? He scowled. Nesfield wouldn't help her one whit if she got herself into trouble. Jordan couldn't fathom what Nesfield was about—or Lady Dundee, for that matter, who'd seemed to be an intelligent woman—but it was obvious the man hadn't created this masquerade to help Emily. Nesfield would merely take what he wanted from her, and leave her with nothing. So whatever she planned to achieve was doomed to failure, no matter what she thought.

Ah, they'd reached Brook's at last. He left the carriage and hurried inside. Brook's was the favorite gentlemen's club of many Whig members of Parliament and almost as old as its predominantly Tory counterpart, White's, across the street. Its sedate atmosphere and stodgy décor generally soothed his temper immediately.

Not today, however. He didn't understand it. Here, among his sensible peers, he ought to be able to relax. There were none of Astramont's silly tittering females around, with their talk of fairies and romantic feeling.

But there was also no Lady Emma. She was back at Lady Astramont's, with Pollock. Pollock was the one brushing against her, smelling her lavender scent, listening to her melodic voice. Deuce take the man! And deuce take her, too. How dare she choose Pollock? Of course she'd done it to evade Jordan's interrogations. It had to be. Still, whether she were Lady Emma or Emily, no one else had the right to her but him, and he'd make Pollock understand that the next time he saw the devil.

The servant took his greatcoat, informing him in respectful tones that Lord St. Clair awaited him in the Subscription Room. He muttered a curse. He'd forgotten all about his appointment with Ian.

When he entered the Subscription Room it took a few moments to find the viscount through the haze of tobacco smoke, but at last he spotted him in a corner. Ian lounged in a chair beneath a sconce, with a pipe in one hand and his pocket watch in the other. He glanced up and saw Jordan, then tapped the face of his watch as Jordan approached.

Jordan settled into the armchair opposite him and grumbled, "I'm here, Ian. You can put away the watch and the incredulous look."

With a grin, Ian snapped the watch cover crisply shut, then restored it to his waistcoat. "That's twice now, Jordan. Since you're never late, I can only assume this is the early onset of senility. If you're not careful, you'll soon be doddering about with unlaced boots and talking to yourself."

"Very amusing, I'm sure. Last night was Pollock's fault. Tonight, I simply forgot. It happens, you know, even to me. I've a great deal on my mind these days."

"Lady Emma perhaps?" When Jordan scowled at him, he added, "You said you were planning to attend Lady Astramont's breakfast, but I really didn't think you would. You find her as annoying as the rest of us."

Jordan took a cheroot from the gold case sitting on the table between them with its array of the *Times* and other papers. He lit it, then drew the soothing smoke into his lungs. "Yes, but Emily

Fairchild was there. And I told you, I'll do what I must to prove she's an impostor."

Drawing deep on his pipe, Ian shrugged. "Why not just write to Miss Fairchild's father and ask where she's staying in London? If he gives you Nesfield's town-house address, then you know Lady Emma and Miss Fairchild are one and the same."

"I already thought of that, but I doubt it would do any good. Her father would have to be part of the scheme, or else why would he have let her come? Besides, the minute a letter arrives from me, questions will be raised about how Emily knows the Earl of Blackmore. You know how those country towns are: nothing but gossip."

"Why is that a problem?"

"Because I was almost caught having a tête-à-tête with her in a carriage a couple of months ago."

"You in a carriage with a complete innocent?" Ian tapped his pipe on the arm of his chair. "You really are entering senility. How the bloody hell did *that* happen?"

A business acquaintance approached from behind Ian, looking as if he might speak to them, but Jordan's patented scowl made the man redirect his steps in a hurry. Then Jordan told Ian what had happened that night, leaving out the kisses, of course. "So you see, it wasn't either of our faults, and we got out of it fairly well. But a letter from me would make people wonder about the night we were thought to be together. And if by some chance I'm wrong about Emily—"

"Ah, so you admit you could be wrong. You saw her by moonlight, for God's sake."

"I know." Jordan puffed hard on the cheroot. And Lady Emma had described Castle Dundee in such loving detail. Yet there was something about her . . . "I don't think I am. But I can't take any chances. If Lady Emma isn't Miss Fairchild, I wouldn't want to ruin the latter woman's reputation. The Miss Fairchild I met didn't deserve to be gossiped about."

"There may be another, perfectly logical reason for Lady Emma's resemblance to your friend Miss Fairchild."

"Oh?"

"Lady Dundee is originally from the same area, is she not?"

"Yes. The Nesfield seat is in Derbyshire. I imagine the countess spent her childhood there before she married."

"Then she and the Fairchilds may be distant relations. Plenty of second sons go into the clergy. Perhaps Mr. Fairchild is Nesfield's cousin or something. That may even be why he was given the living."

Jordan drummed his fingers on the carved oak arm of the chair. He hadn't considered that. An uneasy knot formed in his belly. What if all this time he'd been tormenting the woman for no good reason? Though both women shared similar features and spoke their minds, Lady Emma did differ markedly from Emily. Her coy flirtations bore no resemblance to Emily's moralizing. And the way she kissed . . .

Good God. He could be completely wrong. And that changed everything.

"If you want to know for certain," Ian continued, "why not go to Derbyshire?"

"I fear that wouldn't be any less discreet. But I could send Hargraves, if he can't find anything out from Nesfield's servants."

A dark look passed over Ian's face. "I don't

know how much luck you'll have there, even with Hargraves tackling the task."

"Why not?"

"While you were at the breakfast, I went to Nesfield's town house, hoping to speak to Lady Sophie. But the servants very politely rebuffed me, saying she was too sick for visitors. Don't you find it odd that she should be ill so long?"

Jordan blew out a puff of smoke. "Not necessarily. If ever a young woman was prone to illness, it's Lady Sophie."

"True, but I think it's her bloody father's fault. I suspect that if she escaped his iron thumb, she'd be fine. Unfortunately, I have to go through Nesfield to get to her."

Jordan cast his friend a covert glance. This new preoccupation of Ian's with marrying was beginning to disturb him. "I'm sure she'll be well in a few days, and you'll find a way around her father's objections."

"I'm counting on Lady Emma to aid me with that."

"Lady Emma?"

"If I can speak to her alone. But for that I need your help."

Jordan regarded his friend thoughtfully. "I'll be glad to help. As long as you help me speak to her alone as well."

Ian scowled. "See here, if you're planning to browbeat the girl—"

"I won't browbeat her. I merely want to ask her some questions."

"I can well imagine," Ian said with a snort.

"I won't do it any other way."

With a sigh, Ian set his pipe aside. "You're really interested in her, aren't you?"

Lady Emma/Emily consumed his thoughts, be-

deviled his sleep, and made him behave like a slob-
bering dog in a butcher shop. No woman had ever
blown him off the carefully plotted course of his
life before.

Jordan glanced away. "I'm interested in deter-
mining the truth, that's all."

"I take it your sally into the dark caves of Astramont proved pointless?"

"You could say that."

"You couldn't draw near your prey? Or when
you did, she proved too wily for you?" The mocking way he said "wily" made Jordan bristle.

"The girl evaded my questions, if that's what
you mean," Jordan snapped. "If you're dying to
know everything that happened, ask Pollock. He
was there, too."

"Pollock witnessed this great contretemps? This
grows more interesting by the minute. Perhaps I'll
have Pollock help me with Lady Emma instead."

Jordan spoke without thinking. "If you do, I
swear I'll hang that preening popinjay with one of
his own ridiculous cravats!"

Ian broke into a grin. "By God, you're jealous!"

"Jealous! Of that dandy? Don't be absurd!"

But when Ian's grin widened, Jordan busied himself with stubbing out his cheroot and hunting in
the case for another. He wasn't jealous. It merely
disturbed him to think of an exquisite creature like
Lady Emma with an idiot like Pollock. Unfortunately, thanks to his own fit of temper, she was
probably strolling through the extensive Astramont
gardens with Pollock at this very moment.

What if she truly were some laird's daughter
looking for a husband? Could she possibly think
Pollock would suit her, a man whose idea of entertainment was to drive about town in his phaeton
showing off his newest gaudy waistcoat?

And what if Pollock got her alone? What if the fop were treated to the same kind of kiss she'd given Jordan the other night?

A red haze filled his vision. To think of her standing under a cherry tree in Pollock's arms, teasing the man to kiss her, to caress her, to—

Devil take it, he should never have left her with that fool! Pollock could be quite smooth-tongued when he wanted to impress a woman, and judging from the leers the bastard had cast her at Lady Astramont's, Lady Emma was exactly the sort of woman Pollock would want to impress.

Well, if she took up with Pollock, she'd regret it. Jordan snatched up his second cheroot and lit it with a snarl. He would show her how vain and pompous Pollock was.

Never mind that until two days ago, Jordan had considered Pollock a casual friend. Now Pollock was the enemy. Anyone who stood between him and Lady Emma—Emily—was the enemy.

Even Ian. "Well?" Jordan glanced at his friend. "What's your plan? Am I in?"

"You're in. I can't miss the chance to watch you make a fool of yourself over a woman." Before Jordan could retort, he continued, "Here's what I thought we'd do . . ."

This was Emily's second walk with Mr. Pollock through the gardens. During the first, he'd questioned her about her love of Scotland. She hadn't been able to turn the conversation to Lady Sophie before Lady Dundee had joined them.

Though Emily had wanted to leave, this was the perfect time to question Mr. Pollock, especially with Jordan gone. Somehow she'd conveyed to Lady Dundee her desire to stay, but it had taken more contrivance to gain this second walk with Mr. Pollock.

At last they were alone. Everyone else had retreated into the house since the afternoon light had waned, so the gardens felt more intimate and exotic. The gazebo added to the effect, with its nymphs for columns and its ornate roof. As they approached it, the only sounds were those of their boots crunching the gravel walkway and a nightingale trilling a twilight song.

"You certainly put Blackmore in his place this afternoon," Mr. Pollock murmured confidentially. "I wager he won't bother you again."

She wished that were the case, but suspected that Mr. Pollock's remark merely revealed his hopes. Lord St. Clair was right: the young man did seem to resent Jordan. She couldn't imagine why, unless it was because Jordan had the title and status Mr. Pollock was unlikely to obtain.

But then, Mr. Pollock possessed things Jordan did not. Like a heart that *wasn't* made of granite.

"I wasn't trying to put him in his place," she said truthfully. "I was trying to make him stop mocking everything."

"You'll never succeed at that, I fear." They had reached the gazebo now. Mr. Pollock took out his handkerchief and dusted off one of the marble benches for her. "But let's not talk about Blackmore, shall we? I wish to talk about you."

"Me?" Warily, she took the seat he offered. "What is there to say about me?" She'd rather talk about Sophie.

The dying sun caught his thoughtful expression. "I could spout the usual platitudes—your hair is like spun gold and your lips like rubies—but I fear a woman of your sophistication is so used to hearing them you'd find them tedious."

A woman of her sophistication, indeed. If only he knew the truth. "Tedious, no. Ridiculous, yes. I am no more than an ordinary woman with perfectly ordinary hair and lips, I'm sure." She toyed nervously with the fan attached to her wrist, wondering how to turn the conversation elsewhere. Then inspiration struck. "My looks don't compare to my cousin's. That creamy complexion and jet hair. Don't you think she's stunning?"

"Lady Sophie can't hold a candle to you." To her surprise, he sat down and seized her fidgety hands in his well-manicured ones. "Just as the moon fades to nothing when the sun rises, so does her beauty compare to yours."

Dear heavens, she'd never had a man speak poetically to her—but she didn't imagine it boded well for keeping their acquaintance casual. She tried to extricate her hands, but he only clasped them tighter. "Mr. Pollock, really, you must release me!"

"Not until I say what's in my heart." The dusk light muted his features, but didn't hide the glitter in his pale blue eyes. "I think you might have some small feeling toward me, or you wouldn't have rebuffed Blackmore on my account. And your contriving to come out here with me alone confirms it."

Goodness gracious, she'd given him the wrong idea entirely. "Mr. Pollock—"

"Don't speak yet. Let me first tell you how I feel. Doubtless you have many suitors; I only ask that you count me among them and give me the same chance to further our acquaintance that you give the others."

This was disastrous. "I don't understand. I thought you were enamored of my cousin." She tugged her hands free, then slid away from him. "I never dreamed you might think of me in that way. You hardly know me."

He slid closer on the bench. "I know you well enough after today. I scarcely knew your cousin any better when I courted her. But you came along and put an end to any thought of that when I realized that the least of your family's jewels had been displayed first. The best was kept for last— you, a diamond of the first water."

Flowers, heavenly bodies, and now jewels. Did he ever speak in plain English? Obviously, his feelings for Sophie had been inconsequential if he could dismiss them so easily. She couldn't let him go on like this, no matter what Lord Nesfield expected. "Please say no more. You and I could never . . . that is, it wouldn't be possible for—"

"I know what you're going to say," he interrupted.

It's a good thing, she thought, *since I haven't the foggiest idea.*

"I know your father might disapprove of your being courted by a man without a title. But you Scottish aren't so fastidious about such things as we English. Surely, if you explained that I'm well able to provide for you, such a thing wouldn't matter."

Eagerly she seized on his reason. "You're wrong. It matters very much, not only to my father, but to Mama. She's determined to have me marry well. When it comes to such things, she's very English." When he looked crestfallen, her tender heart was pricked. "Of course, you know that *I* don't care about titles and such. You're a very nice man, and I'm sure you'll make a fine husband for someone. But I couldn't flout my parents' wishes by allowing you to court me. I'm sure you understand."

Her attempt to soften the blow of rejection only

further encouraged him. His face lit up, and he seized her about the waist, tugging her next to him on the bench. Her fan dropped from her fingers to dangle from her wrist.

"I don't care how your parents feel," he whispered, now close enough that the cloying scent of his toilet water filled her nostrils. "If that's all that concerns you, you needn't worry. Parental permission isn't *always* required for marriage, you know." He raised one eyebrow suggestively. "As you must realize, in some parts of the country men and women can marry as they choose."

His words gave her pause. Some parts of the country? As she must realize? He meant Gretna Green in Scotland, didn't he?

Had he said these same words to Sophie? "Mr. Pollock, you're being premature. You can't be implying that . . . that we should elope."

"Not unless we have to, but I wouldn't let a paltry thing like parental permission stand in the way of our mutual affection."

Did he mean it? Was Mr. Pollock so eager for a wife that he would resort to such persuasions to acquire one?

She forced a light tone into her voice. "Really, you must be joking. Is this how you always court a lady, by suggesting she throw aside her family and run away to some uncertain future?"

"If you're questioning my sincerity, madam, I assure you I'm perfectly serious. I'll do what I must to have you. I give you fair warning."

A chill shot through her as his seemingly frail arm became a restrictive band about her waist. She dared not linger here any longer. "You mustn't speak to me of such things." She tried to escape his embrace, but he only clutched her tighter. Alarm swelled in her chest. "Truly, sir, I could never ignore my parents' wishes, and certainly I could never elope. You must approach my parents in the proper way."

His other arm snaked about her waist to strengthen his hold. He might be a dandy, but his arms were surprisingly strong. "You've already said they would never allow a courtship between us, so that leaves us only one choice. Besides, I know you aren't always so careful of the proprieties." Anger stiffened his putty features. "I followed you and Lord Blackmore when you entered the gardens at Merrington's. I saw how you kissed him."

The fine hairs rose on the back of her neck. He'd seen them? Goodness gracious. She needn't tax her imagination to realize what he thought of her.

Every cautionary tale she'd ever heard leapt into her mind—of men carrying young women off against their wills, of men so desperate to marry that they would do anything to obtain the woman of their choice. Frantically, she scanned the garden beyond the gazebo, but no one was in sight. Her plan wasn't going well at all.

"That wasn't what you think—" she began.

"Oh, I don't hold your behavior against you. Blackmore can be very persuasive. The fact that you eventually rebuffed him last night and then again today emboldened me to speak for myself. Clearly, you understand that he's too cold for a woman of your passion and depth of feeling." He splayed his fingers over the small of her back. "But you and I are two of a kind, as you must realize. I can satisfy your needs as much or more than Blackmore."

He reached up and clasped her chin, then forced her head up so he could kiss her. Wet, hot lips smacked against her mouth. It was like being slapped with a boiled eel. Utterly disgusted, she pressed against his chest, but he wouldn't let go. She tried wrenching her mouth away, but like a leech he clamped himself to her and seemed intent on taking even more liberties. His thick tongue groped at the seam of her lips, and his perfumed breath nearly gagged her.

Sheer panic set in when he tried to drag the edge of her bodice down, pinching her breast in the process. She shoved against his shoulders, and when that didn't work, she jabbed him in the thigh with her closed fan. He dropped back from her, a curse tumbling from his lips.

She leapt to her feet, fumbling to straighten her dislodged clothing. "How dare you, Mr. Pollock! I have *not* given you permission to touch me in this familiar manner!" She sounded more like the prudish Emily Fairchild than the bold Lady Emma, but she didn't care. She wouldn't let the fool debauch her right here in the garden!

A peevish expression crossed his face as he rubbed his sore thigh. "You gave Blackmore permission. I saw the way you let him caress you. What kind of teasing wench are you?"

"I didn't give Blackmore permission to take liberties, I assure you!"

"It didn't look that way to me." His voice was decidedly nasty. He rose from the bench. "You were arching your back and purring like a cat in heat. And I'll have you doing the same for me, I swear, before this evening is out!"

When he stepped toward her, she pointed her fan dagger-fashion at his crotch. She didn't know much about the male anatomy, but she did know one thing: men were very careful of their groins. She'd seen boys in the village crumple to the ground in agony when attacked there. Her fan's spokes narrowed to points at the end, and closed, it looked positively lethal.

"If you come any nearer, I'll skewer you. Do you hear me?"

His gaze dropped in alarm, and she saw him hesitate as he assessed the danger to his privates. "You wouldn't—"

"She would," came a feminine voice from very near. As both Emily and Mr. Pollock jerked their heads in its direction, Lady Dundee stepped into the clearing surrounding the gazebo. Her expression was grim indeed. "My daughter has the blood of the Scots flowing through her veins, you fool. She won't hesitate to carve you into bits."

Relief flooded Emily, but Mr. Pollock went white and backed away from her as if she were a garden snake he'd suddenly discovered to be a viper. "Lady Dundee. This is not what it seems. I . . . I—"

"I know precisely what it is." Lady Dundee stalked up to the gazebo. "And you may be sure that I won't allow it to happen again."

His expression turned sullen. "Then you'd best keep a tight leash on the minx. I'm not the only man she's been meeting in private places."

Emily stifled a groan. Dear heavens, if he told Lady Dundee about Jordan . . .

The countess cast him such a frosty look that his sneer instantly vanished. "Mr. Pollock, I understand that you move in more exalted circles than you perhaps deserve."

He tugged nervously on his billowing cravat.

"Therefore," she continued in clipped tones, "if I ever hear that you repeated such lies to anyone . . . indeed, if I ever hear that you've spoken of my daughter in anything but the loftiest terms, even to the kitchen maid in the lowliest household of the most remote section of England, I'll make sure you become persona non grata in decent society. Unlike my daughter, *I* am equipped with something more than a fan. And I'll take great pleasure in using my position and contacts to eviscerate you. Understood?"

As Mr. Pollock lost all color in his cheeks, the countess faced Emily, her voice only a trifle less icy. "Come, Emma, we must go. We mustn't be late for the Winstead ball."

"Yes, Mama," she said quickly, nearly vaulting off the steps of the gazebo.

Lady Dundee's hand on her arm was like a vice as she half steered, half dragged Emily through the garden. Emily didn't blame her for her anger. The woman must think awful things of her, especially after Mr. Pollock's snide remark.

"Lady Dundee," she finally brought herself to say, "I am so sorry—"

The woman stopped just short of the entrance into the house and fixed her with an incredulous look. "Sorry? Whatever for? That incorrigible, half-witted . . ."

Words seemed to fail her as she stared back in the direction of the gazebo where Pollock sat with his head in his hands. She lowered her voice. "I blame myself, not *you*, for heaven's sake. I knew what you were trying to do when you arranged to walk with him, but I should never have allowed it. You're just a child. You have no idea how beastly some men can be. But I'm old enough to know better. I allowed Randolph to send a lamb to the slaughter, and for that I should be soundly beaten."

"You mustn't blame yourself! I'm *not* a child! I knew the dangers when I came out here. I simply misjudged Mr. Pollock's character. I'll be more careful next time."

"There won't be a next time." The older woman set her broad shoulders with determination. "I'm ending this masquerade. It was an idiotic idea from the beginning, but I allowed it because you seemed willing. No more, however. I won't stand by and watch while a hapless innocent is sacrificed for my foolish niece."

"But you *can't* stop it now!" Emily knew Lord Nesfield too well. He'd make good on his threats!

"I most certainly can. I'll tell Randolph tonight that he must finish it on his own. He has three likely suspects. Let *him* discover which is the culprit."

"No, I won't let you!" When the countess looked at her askance, she stammered, "I-I mean, I made a promise to your brother, and I shall keep it."

Lady Dundee scowled at her. "Nonsense. Forget your misguided sense of loyalty. I'm sure your father studied hard to warrant the living he receives from Randolph. You owe my brother nothing."

Lying was hard enough for Emily. Lying to Lady Dundee was like lying to her father, a distinctly unpleasant experience. Yet she must. "It's not loyalty to Lord Nesfield, but loyalty to Sophie."

"Poppycock! When you first heard our plan, you refused to participate. You were perfectly willing to let Sophie marry any fool she wanted. You only agreed to it after Randolph spoke to you. What did he say? You can tell me, you know. I can help you."

No one could help her. If she told Lady Dundee, Lord Nesfield would hand her over to the authorities with lies about Mama's death that she couldn't refute. It was as simple as that. "There's nothing to tell."

"Yes, there is. Tell me, my dear. It's all right." Lady Dundee's tone was that of a woman used to being obeyed. It reminded Emily of Jordan's attempts to get the truth out of her. Curse all these charming lords and ladies with their commanding voices!

Well, she'd fight the countess as she'd fought Jordan. "You promised me I could have an entertaining time in London and wear expensive gowns and dance till dawn every night. Shall you renege on your promises?"

Lady Dundee's eyes fairly snapped. "You can play that role with others, Emily, but don't play it with me. Remember, I know you're not some frivolous laird's daughter whose only aim in life is entertainment."

"The frivolous laird's daughter is part of me. Isn't that what you said?"

The countess apparently disliked having her words thrown back at her. "Emily—"

"If you tell Lord Nesfield that I mustn't do this, and I tell him I choose to do it anyway, what do you think will happen?"

Lady Dundee crossed her arms over her ample chest. "You can't continue the masquerade without me, so don't even think it. How would it look if Lady Emma's mother abandoned her daughter in the midst of her coming out?"

"How would it look indeed? Lady Emma's mother would either have to invent a story to explain, or else tell everyone the truth and ruin the reputations of herself, her brother, and perhaps even her real daughters." Emily swallowed hard. "Not to mention the reputation of Emily Fairchild."

For a long moment, the countess glared at her. Then a grudging smile touched her lips. "For a girl sired by a rector, you have an unlimited supply of impudence."

"I didn't start this, my lady. You and your

brother did. But I *will* finish it, with or without you."

"You leave me little choice, do you?"

Emily nearly collapsed with relief. "Truly, you needn't worry about me. I can handle myself. Besides, Mr. Pollock was the only one to take liberties. Every other man has been a perfect gentleman in my presence."

"Even Blackmore?"

The woman's perception was uncanny. Emily hesitated only a fraction of a second before lying. "Yes, even the earl."

Now would come the questions about what Mr. Pollock had meant with his accusations. What could she say? How could she explain?

But apparently, Lady Dundee was as reluctant to probe that sore spot as she. "Very well. We shall go on as before." When Emily started to thank her, she added, "Though I shall be a better chaperone from now on. I don't want another occurrence like this."

"Nor do I," Emily said sincerely. Not even Lord Nesfield could expect that of her.

Chapter 9

*Our opposers usually miscall our quickness of
thought, fancy and flash, and christen their own
heaviness by the specious names of judgement and
solidity . . .*

Mary Astell,
An Essay in Defence of the Female Sex

The language of the note Emily received the
day after Lady Astramont's breakfast was
formal. The meaning behind it was not.

For the fourth time since it had arrived yesterday
morning, Emily scanned the words scribbled on the
back of Lord St. Clair's card, trying to read between
the lines.

Dear Lady Emma,

*I would be honored if you would accompany me
to the British Museum tomorrow. Lord Elgin's
marbles are on exhibit, and I believe you would
enjoy seeing them. I could call for you at eleven
a.m. if you decide to join me.*

*Your friend,
Ian, the Viscount St. Clair*

She'd sent her acceptance at once, of course. She wasn't about to pass up this opportunity. Still, the invitation intrigued her, coming from a man who proclaimed to be more interested in her cousin than in her. Tucking the card in her reticule, she walked over to where Lady Dundee stood in the foyer, choosing a cloak from among several that Carter, the butler, held up before her.

"Perhaps Lord St. Clair just intends this to be a friendly outing," Emily said.

Lady Dundee raised her eyebrows. "Yes, and perhaps goblins truly do exist. St. Clair intends something more than a friendly outing, I assure you."

"He certainly does." Lord Nesfield had been watching them from his seat by the foyer table, his lorgnette bobbing back and forth as they talked. Now he scowled through it at Carter. "Lady Dundee can handle that herself. I will call you if we need you."

They kept their silence while Carter walked away. The servants didn't know about Emily's masquerade, because neither the countess nor the marquess trusted them with the knowledge. Having never met Lady Dundee or her children, the servants had accepted Emily as the countess's daughter without question.

Lady Dundee had even concocted a story to allow Emily to receive letters from her father without arousing suspicion. She'd told them that Emily, an expected guest, was traveling extensively before coming to London, and that they were holding her mail for her. That had allowed Emily to answer her father's letters without alerting him to what was going on. All the subterfuge, however, made it difficult to talk when the servants were around.

As soon as Carter was out of sight, Lord Nesfield

said, "The other night when St. Clair was here he questioned the servants about Sophie most thoroughly. I nearly revealed myself, I was so sure he was our man." He sighed. "But then he left without so much as trying to bribe them to let him see her. I swear, I wish I knew what that scoundrel was about."

"We'll find out today," Lady Dundee said.

"I do not see how," he grumbled. "With you hovering about, he is not likely to say anything to Miss Fairchild. Let the chit go alone with him. She will find out more that way."

"Randolph, I'm ashamed of you!" Lady Dundee picked up a snowy lace pelisse and handed it to Emily. "You would never send your own daughter on an outing unchaperoned. Have you no notions of decency?"

He scowled. "As if anything about this outing is decent. He is taking her to see the marbles, for God's sake. Matters have come to quite a pass when a young man thinks that showing a young lady scandalous Greek art is the proper way to court her. I do not see what one more indiscretion will hurt."

"That's because you have peculiar notions about propriety." The countess snorted. "Letting a young woman see great works of art is scandalous; letting her risk her virtue is not."

"If you really want a chaperone, why not send Hannah?" Hannah was the lady's maid they'd hired for Emily. "She is a timid sort. She will not prevent him from speaking to Miss Fairchild in private."

"That's precisely what I'm afraid of," Lady Dundee muttered under her breath as she chose a parasol for herself.

"What? What's that?" the marquess asked, peering through his lorgnette.

"Nothing, dear." Lady Dundee winked at Emily. "Randolph, you mustn't fret. We'll gain Emily a few minutes alone with the man. It'll suffice, I'm sure. With any luck, we can eliminate St. Clair as a suspect and focus on Mr. Pollock. After Lady Astramont's breakfast, Emily and I both believe Pollock to be quite capable of running off with Sophie. He does stand to gain the most by marrying her."

"Do not forget Blackmore," Lord Nesfield put in. "He is a suspect as well."

Lady Dundee paused in her search through the parasols. "At first I thought that was a silly idea; now I'm not so sure. He *has* been hovering about Emily a great deal. I suppose we should consider him a possibility." She glanced at Emily. "Did he say anything to you at Lady Astramont's breakfast, my dear? Ask you about Sophie?"

"We had no chance to be alone, I'm afraid," she said truthfully, praying that Lady Dundee hadn't heard about her public refusal to walk with him. She'd considered telling Lady Dundee about Jordan's suspicions, but now feared it would only prompt Lady Dundee to end the masquerade and spark Lord Nesfield's anger. No, she would have to weather this alone.

Lady Dundee chose a parasol. "A pity you couldn't speak to him. Oh, well, there will be other chances."

That's what Emily was afraid of. Even this outing worried her. After all, Lord St. Clair and Jordan were friends. Lord St. Clair might have invited her only so he could question her on Jordan's behalf.

But what if Jordan were the very one they sought? Despite Lord Nesfield's silly theory, she hadn't dismissed the possibility that Jordan might have cared for Sophie, and the only way to determine that was to speak to him alone.

At the sound of horses clopping along the pebbled drive outside, then halting, Lady Dundee pushed Emily toward the parlor. "Quick, my dear, go in there. It won't look good to have you standing about waiting for St. Clair. Randolph, you must disappear. You don't want to scare the man off, do you? Oh, where has my reticule gotten to? I swear, sometimes I think these bits of cloth are sewn small purposely to thwart me! Carter, come here!"

As Lord Nesfield limped off down the hall, Emily wandered into the parlor. She wished she'd thought to make a fortifying tincture for herself. She needed one today.

Lady Dundee hurried into the parlor, and shortly afterward they both heard the opening of the entrance door and a murmur of male voices in the hall. Then Carter entered and announced Lord St. Clair.

As soon as the viscount came in, he cast Emily a warm smile. He really was a charming man most of the time, even if he occasionally disquieted her. With his black hair and blacker eyes, he reminded her of a panther she'd seen in a book, all sleek and quiet and deadly.

Today, however, he was quite friendly. The requisite greetings were made, the polite bows and curtsies. Lord St. Clair didn't even seem to flinch when Lady Dundee announced her intention to join them on the outing.

"So I have not one, but two lovely ladies to squire about. A fine day it will be indeed." He rubbed his hands together. "Well, are you ready to see the marbles?"

At their murmurs of assent, he offered them his arms and accompanied them to the front door. As they began to descend the stairs, Emily glanced down and spotted Jordan, standing beside the carriage—*his* carriage.

She halted abruptly. Wearing a chocolate-brown frock coat and form-fitting tan trousers, he looked casual, confident, and handsome as always. His eyes were on her, full of smug challenge. As her heart began to beat a wild and foolish tattoo, she dug her fingers into Lord St. Clair's arm.

"I hope you don't mind that I invited Lord Blackmore to join us," Lord St. Clair said smoothly. "My carriage is much too small to accommodate three people comfortably, and Lord Blackmore gallantly offered his in exchange for the privilege of going along."

Stop staring at him like a ninny, Emily chastised herself. *That's what he wants—to unnerve you.*

She didn't realize she still hesitated on the steps until Lord St. Clair said in a concerned tone, "Lady Emma, are you all right?"

Fighting to regain her composure, she forced a smile to her face. "Yes, of course. I . . . I just have a bit of a headache, that's all, and coming out into the sun aggravated it."

"If you have a headache, I'm sure St. Clair can postpone," Lady Dundee put in.

"Indeed I can," Lord St. Clair added, though he sounded disappointed. "Do you need to sit down?"

She wanted so badly to say yes, to flee into the house and claim that her headache would prevent her from going. But if she ran from him like a coward, Jordan would be even more convinced of her identity than before.

His mocking smile decided her. "No, I'm fine. It's not that bad. I wouldn't miss this outing for the world."

As they reached the bottom of the steps, Lord St. Clair turned to hand Lady Dundee into the carriage, then followed her in, leaving Emily with Jordan. Their contact as he handed her in was brief, so brief no one would have remarked upon it, but Emily felt it clear to her toes. His fingers, supple but strong as they curled around her gloved hand . . . his thighs brushing her skirts . . . his other hand resting in the small of her back, warm and hard and shamefully familiar.

At least she didn't have to sit beside him. Lord St. Clair had properly taken the seat facing backwards, leaving her to sit next to Lady Dundee.

Having Jordan facing her, however, proved no better. His carriage was roomy, to be sure, but not roomy enough to keep his booted feet from meeting her slippered ones. As the carriage set off, he stretched one leg out next to the door. Then Emily felt his calf brush against hers, the movement blocked from Lady Dundee's view by her skirts.

She sucked in a breath as her gaze shot to him. Had he done it purposely?

His gaze met hers, knowing and sinful. Oh, yes, he'd done it purposely. When he smiled, letting his gaze trail meaningfully over her attire, she went all liquid inside.

It didn't matter that she was wearing a perfectly respectable walking gown, with a pelisse layered over it and thick stockings beneath. It didn't matter that gloves covered her hands, and a bonnet nearly all of her hair, leaving the oval of her face as the only bare skin showing.

She might as well have been naked. She felt his gaze over every inch of her skin beneath her clothes . . . like a forbidden caress. Then he stroked her leg with his foot, slowly, deliberately, making her blood pour hot through her veins, a fiery liquor warming every extremity.

She inched her leg away as unobtrusively as possible. The wretch merely inched his over in the same direction, and this time he laid it against hers with abject insolence. She couldn't move any farther away without the others noticing. Curse him!

She tried to ignore the limb pressed so intimately against hers, tried to tell herself that it meant nothing because he was wearing Hessians and she was wearing stockings.

But when he rubbed his calf against hers in another long, sensuous stroke, her breath stopped in her throat. All her attention was focused on that terrible, delightful contact between them. He stroked again and again, his leg making love to hers with an easy, subtle motion.

The carriage was suddenly far too small. When his next caress sparked a deep, sinful urge in her most private areas, she shuddered involuntarily.

"Are you cold, Lady Emma?" Jordan asked in a mocking tone.

She cast him a pleading look, but he smiled and very deliberately ran the toe of his boot halfway up her calf, eliciting another shudder.

He grinned. "Would you like a blanket? I'm sure I have one somewhere."

"I'm . . . I'm fine, Lord Blackmore," she managed to stammer. "I'm quite comfortable, thank you."

Lord St. Clair shot her a searching glance, and when Jordan traced the curve of her ankle with the toe of his boot, he scowled, making her wonder if he'd seen it.

"Let's tell them about the marbles, shall we, Jordan?" the viscount suddenly remarked in a hard voice.

Jordan smiled at her, oblivious to his friend's disapproval. "Certainly. You tell them."

Lord St. Clair hesitated. Then with a calculating glance at Jordan, he said, "The marbles are beautiful, priceless sculptures from the Parthenon. Lord Elgin brought them back to England during his tenure as ambassador to Greece, and sold them to the British Museum two years ago. Now they're on display."

"Brought them back?" Jordan scowled, and his leg went still against hers. "He stole them, you mean, just as surely as if he'd crept into someone's house at night and palmed their silver."

This was obviously a subject that Jordan and his friend had discussed before.

Lord St. Clair glanced down at her skirts, then went on, a mischievous smile on his face. "But Jordan, Elgin had permission from the Ottoman government to take them."

Jordan snorted and straightened in his seat, thankfully moving him out of range of her leg. "You might as well say he had Napoléon's permission. The Ottomans invaded Greece as surely as Napoléon invaded Italy. They have no right to give the Parthenon away. The Greeks are the ones Elgin should have asked. But he didn't, and from what I've heard, they were none too happy about it."

Now that Jordan had stopped tormenting her, the conversation was beginning to interest Emily. "I don't understand. He just took these sculptures from the Parthenon and carted them back here?"

"That's exactly what he did." Jordan's eyes burned with a sudden zeal. "Thanks to Elgin, half of the Parthenon has been sent piecemeal to England. It defaced the building abominably."

"But Jordan," Lord St. Clair said, "the building

had already been defaced by the Turks and God knows who else. The Greeks weren't taking care of it. And if it hadn't been for Elgin, the French might have taken those sculptures."

"At least the French wouldn't have let them sit in a dank storage shed for six years deteriorating while Elgin tried to persuade the British Museum to buy them. Do you think that did the marbles any good? My contact at the museum—a man charged with cleaning them—said they were terribly damaged by sitting in the damp London air all that time. What right had Elgin to destroy a historical monument of enormous importance for his own personal gain?"

"But how could anyone allow him to do such a thing?" Emily asked as the enormity of it hit her.

Jordan let out a sound of disgust. "How indeed? Our countrymen didn't so much as censure the devil."

"That's not true," Lord St. Clair said dryly. "You've publicly censured him enough to make up for the rest of us. I'm surprised you even agreed to come along to see them."

"I'm on the museum's board of directors. I like to keep an eye on how the marbles are treated." For a moment, his mouth was taut, his expression angry. Then he looked at Emily, and his anger seemed to fade. "Besides, I couldn't resist the chance to accompany two such lovely ladies."

When he punctuated his comment by stretching out his leg again and laying it against hers, Emily glared at him, then ground the heel of her slipper into the top of his boot—a totally pointless endeavor. His only response was to hook his boot behind her calf and caress her halfway to the knee.

Curse him!

Lady Dundee said, "Well, I, for one, am quite

eager to see the sculptures, no matter how they got here. We seldom have the opportunity for such enrichment in Scotland, do we, dear?"

That gave Emily an idea. "Oh, don't say that, Mama. You will only confirm Lord Blackmore's poor opinion of our country." She smirked at Jordan.

"Poor opinion?" the countess asked, eyes narrowing.

Emily eagerly enumerated all his insults to Scotland from the breakfast party, forcing Jordan to explain his words to Lady Dundee. Let him fend off the countess for a while—the scoundrel deserved it.

As Jordan frowned, she and Lord St. Clair exchanged congratulatory looks. By the time they'd reached the British Museum, Lady Dundee had been waxing poetic over Scotland's glories for several minutes, and Jordan was scowling as thunderously as the god of war himself. It was all Emily could do not to laugh.

Her glow of triumph continued when Lord St. Clair made sure he handed both women down from the carriage. Even better, Lord St. Clair took her arm, leaving Jordan with Lady Dundee. Emily wanted to kiss the man. Obviously, he had been completely aware of how Jordan had been annoying her.

But she was surprised a few minutes later when Jordan suddenly expressed a desire to show Lady Dundee a painting in a separate room, and Lord St. Clair said that he and Lady Emma would stay behind to finish viewing the works in the room they were in.

She hadn't expected this, though it was certainly convenient. Not only was she rid of Jordan for a while, she was also able to speak to Lord St. Clair in private.

With a quick glance to make sure their companions had gone, Lord St. Clair led her into one of the rooms that contained the Parthenon Marbles Exhibit. Emily caught her breath when she saw the first one—a horse's head so intricately carved that each hair on its mane bristled and the jaw muscles flexed.

How exquisite! It was almost worth Jordan's misbehavior to see this.

From there, they circled the room to admire first the headless sculpture of two women whose draped gowns left nothing to the imagination, and then the caryatid, a full sculpture of a woman that had served as a column in the Parthenon.

That's when Lord St. Clair finally spoke. "She looks a bit like Sophie."

"Yes, she does, doesn't she? It's the eyes. They're so innocent."

He touched the marble briefly, then dropped his hand. "How is she?"

"She's doing better. You needn't worry about her."

"She's been ill for weeks. When I visit, she doesn't even send down any messages." His brow was furrowed. "Did she know you were to be with me today?"

"Yes, of course."

"And she gave you no message for me, no word of anything."

Emily debated making something up. But the greater the supposed silence on Sophie's part, the more anxious he would become and thus the more likely to confess something. "No." She couldn't resist adding, "But she was sleeping when I left."

He raked his fingers through his hair in distraction. "When I visited yesterday—while you and Lady Dundee were out—the servants wouldn't even let me see her. What kind of illness could be so awful that visitors aren't allowed?"

His obviously genuine concern was touching. What if he *had* been the one? And what if he truly were in love with Sophie? Would it be so terrible to let them be together? Lord St. Clair didn't seem a bad sort, no matter what Lord Nesfield thought.

"It's not the nature of her illness that keeps visitors from her, but simple female vanity, I assure you," Emily lied. "What young woman wishes her friends to see her when she looks pale and sickly and cannot dress in her best gowns?"

His mouth tightened into a thin line. "That doesn't sound like Lady Sophie. She never struck me as vain. Indeed, I've never met a more straightforward, simple girl. That's why I chose to offer her my attentions."

Chose to offer her my attentions? That was more the language of a man picking out a prize cow than the language of love. Perhaps she'd been too hasty in her assessment of Lord St. Clair's feelings.

"Besides," he went on, "I don't trust the lady's father. I think he might keep her closeted away from visitors to prevent her from making an unwise match."

Emily's heart pounded. His words were too near the truth to be accidental. What should she tell him? How could she get him to say more? She must be certain of him before Lord Nesfield could risk accusing him.

She tried a more direct approach. "Are you saying that matters had progressed so far between you and my cousin that her father would *need* to use such tactics?"

He clenched his jaw, his eyes still fixed on the

statue. Goodness gracious, how could she tell anything when she couldn't see his eyes? She held her breath, waiting for his answer.

Suddenly, he sighed wearily. "I don't know what I'm saying. The last time I saw her, she and I came very near to discussing marriage. Then her father interrupted the discussion, and I haven't seen her since. I don't know what to make of it."

Dear heavens, he *had* to be the one! Relief coursed through her. She would no longer need to fear exposure; she could put an end to the dreadful lies.

But maybe she was being too hasty. She needed more evidence.

"Have you approached Uncle Randolph with an offer?"

"I don't wish to do so until I'm sure of her feelings. This silence from her makes me wonder if I was wrong about the way she felt. If she hasn't even told *you*, her own cousin, about me—"

"Oh, but she has!" He mustn't become too discouraged or she'd never find out for certain if he was the one. "We talked about you at length after my first ball."

"What did she say?"

"Um . . . well, I can't tell you that." Thinking fast, she shot him a coy smile. "Sophie would never forgive me if I told all her secrets."

His gaze swung to her, and in the depths of his black eyes, she saw suspicion. "Are you playing games with me, Lady Emma?"

A shiver passed over her. This was the side of him she'd suspected lay dormant. The dangerous side. "Not at all. But if you're not even willing to approach my uncle with an offer, I don't see why I should tell you everything about my cousin. It wouldn't be fair, especially when he doesn't approve of you."

He stared at her as if debating something. "I have a confession to make." When he paused, she held her breath. "You see—"

"So *there* you are," boomed a loud, feminine voice as Lady Dundee swept into the room, followed closely by Jordan. "We thought we had lost you."

Emily cast the countess a withering glance. She'd been so close, curse it all! He'd been on the verge of telling her about the elopement—she was sure of it! And now, thanks to Lady Dundee's overprotective instincts, Emily would have to try again. It was enough to make her cry, for goodness sakes!

Lady Dundee seemed oblivious to Emily's distress, or to Lord St. Clair's, for that matter. She strode up to them, waving her arm as if to indicate the entire building. "It's all so fabulous, don't you think? I'm quite pleased you invited us, St. Clair." She flashed a smile at Emily. "Isn't it lovely, my dear?"

"Yes, Mama, it is."

Lady Dundee sighed. "But all this walking has tired me enormously."

"Perhaps you should rest a moment before we go on," Lord St. Clair said quickly, once more his amiable, courteous self. He offered the countess his arm. "I believe there are benches in the next room."

Hooking her hand in his bent elbow, Lady Dundee paused to look around, then made a face. "Good Lord, I must have left my shawl in one of those other rooms. I have no idea where. Would you mind looking for it, Emma?"

"Not at all, Mama."

"And take Lord Blackmore with you. He knows his way around here."

With a smug smile, Jordan offered her his arm. Emily couldn't even protest, not when her "mama" had sanctioned the encounter. Lady Dundee was certainly in great form today, managing to allow not one, but two private meetings so that Emily could do her work.

Oh, if only Lady Dundee knew what she'd done.

With a sense of impending doom, Emily allowed Jordan to lead her into the other room. What was she to do now? How was she to fool him?

As soon as the others were out of sight, she tried to take her hand from his arm, but he wouldn't let her, clamping his other hand over it forcefully. "I do believe I'm growing fond of your mother," he bent to whisper in her ear. "Clearly, she knows what's best for you. Or should I say, she knows *who's* best for you?"

Curse the wretch! Tossing her head back, she fixed him with a cool smile. "Don't flatter yourself, Lord Blackmore. Mama might have set her sights on you, but I have not."

"Haven't you? You didn't have to come on this outing. I almost thought you weren't going to— that nonsense with the headache and all."

"Oh, it wasn't nonsense, I assure you," she said sweetly. "The sight of you always gives me a head-ache."

As they passed quickly through the room, Emily looked for the shawl. He clearly did not.

"We both know why I give you headaches," he murmured.

"Because you're a nuisance and an arrogant, in-sufferable bore?"

He laughed at the outrageous lie, then stroked her hand, beginning with the edge of her short glove before trailing his fingers down to the tips in a caress that made her catch her breath. "I give you headaches for the same reason I made you shiver in the carriage earlier." He paused. "Because it makes you *remember*."

"Remember what?" She jerked her hand from his arm as she faced him. "The way you pawed me at the ball two nights ago?"

Their gazes met, and he held the look, his eyes darkening. "No. Not then."

Curse him for all his suspicions and hidden meanings! She should never have allowed this! Whirling away, she stalked off toward the entrance to another of the rooms. "I shan't stand here and listen to your nonsense. *I'm* going to look for Mama's shawl!"

He caught her arm, then steered her in another direction, that infernal smile on his face again. "Then you're headed the wrong way. Lady Dundee and I didn't go in that room. Try this one over here."

The doorway he steered her toward was smaller than the others, and the door to it was closed. Perhaps if she hadn't been so furious, she would have noticed the guard and the fact that he bowed deferentially to Jordan. She might even have paused to wonder why he had to unlock the door as they approached.

But as soon as she stepped inside the cavernous room and the door was shut behind them, she knew she'd made an enormous error. There was no one else inside.

They were completely alone.

Chapter 10

Who would not rather trust and be deceived?

Eliza Cook, English poet, "Love On"

Excellent, Jordan thought as the door clicked shut. As usual, his plan had worked perfectly. Thanks to Lady Dundee and her inexplicable help, it had worked more than perfectly, saving him the trouble of using an elaborate story to get Emily in here. She'd followed him without a protest.

Her acquiescence wouldn't last, however. Already, she'd whirled toward the door. When she heard the guard lock it, her lovely eyes went big as saucers, and she rounded on him in a fury. "What do you think you're doing! Are you insane? Tell him to unlock the door! Tell him at once!"

"Calm down. It's not what you think. This room isn't open to the regular museum visitors, so the door must remain locked as long as we're in here. He'll open it when we're ready to leave. All we have to do is knock on it."

"I'm ready to leave now!"

She darted for the door, but he caught her before she reached it. "You can't go before you see this."

He gestured behind her, and with a scowl, she pivoted in that direction.

Then she froze, her mouth dropping open. "Goodness gracious." Awe filled her face as she fixed her wide eyes on the great stone sitting atop the scarred wooden worktable before her and propped against the wall. "Why, it's . . . it's—"

"A centaur," he finished for her. "It's carved in what is called a metope."

She stepped forward, and he let her go, watching as she approached the sculpture. The single panel of marble was about four feet by four feet. Its left half was covered with a dusty length of muslin, but the headless centaur on the right half was carved in such high relief that he appeared to be attempting his escape from the marble.

"It was taken from the Parthenon's south side," he said softly. "Incredible, isn't it? I thought you would like it."

"Oh, I do! It's the best I've seen so far."

Her obvious delight made him smile. Although this had merely been a ruse to lower her defenses against him, he was pleased that she appreciated the artistry that had so captivated him the first time he'd seen this piece.

"It's from a depiction of a battle between the centaurs and the Lapith men," he said.

"May I touch it?"

"Of course."

She stretched her hand out over the table to press it against the centaur's marble flanks. "So real. You can see the ribs beneath the skin, as if he were an actual creature."

"Yes, the craftsmanship on this piece is very fine." He went to stand beside her. "That's why I wanted you to see it."

While she examined the metope, he drank in the

sight of her. Talk about fine craftsmanship—she was about as fine a piece of work as a man could want. Her skin rivaled the marble for smooth creaminess, and the curves apparent beneath her gown made his mouth water and his fingers itch to touch her.

Why did women always dress in those gauzy, thin materials that made one think of delicate fruit pastries with light, feathery crusts? Didn't they know how it made a man want to tear the damned layers away to taste the silky, hot center?

And all that lace, like powdery sugar. There was white lace everywhere . . . dripping from the ends of her sleeves and on the scarf that draped her bodice. For God's sake, her entire pelisse was made of the stuff. And yards of it covered the bonnet that he detested because it hid her luscious hair.

She glanced up at him, her expression still full of wonder. "Why is it locked away? It should be on display with the others."

It took him a second to remember what she was talking about. "The metope? They're cleaning it. After years in Elgin's back garden, it was filthy. I imagine it'll be some weeks before it's put on display."

"So why are we allowed to see it?"

"As I said before, I'm on the board of directors."

"Oh, of course. That's why the guard knew you." A pleased smile touched her lips. "I can't thank you enough for using your influence to let me have a look at such a piece of work." She stroked the sculpture again with a gentle touch, and he felt a jolt of lust so intense he nearly groaned aloud. He wanted those fingers to touch *him*, to caress *him*. He wanted it as badly as he'd ever wanted anything.

"Here," he said softly, taking her hand. Slowly,

he unbuttoned her glove and drew it off to expose her slender fingers. "You can feel it better this way." He pressed her hand against the marble, fervently wishing he were pressing it against something now equally as hard.

She stilled as he molded her hand to the marble. For him, the sculpture had ceased to exist. He was aware only of the delicacy of her bones, the shape of her fingers beneath his, the way her breath had quickened.

They stood there a moment, linked together, each so aware of the other that the silence in the room was deafening.

Then she slid her hand back, forcing him to drop his. She kept her gaze fixed on the sculpture as she murmured, "It's a crime to think of this lying in the dirt. It's so beautiful."

He gazed down at her upturned cheeks and wistful smile, both as fragile and smooth as the marbles themselves. "Yes, beautiful," he choked out, fighting back the urge to seize her and kiss her senseless.

God, how he wanted her. But he mustn't scare her off before he could attend to his first priority. He cleared his throat. "Would you like to see the rest of it—the part under the cleaning cloth?"

Her eyes lit up. "Oh, certainly. I . . . I mean, if it's allowed."

The eager anticipation in her face sparked a brief moment of guilt. He was planning to play a very dirty trick on her. Still, he wanted to know the truth, didn't he?

Ignoring his conscience, he yanked off the swath of muslin and fixed his gaze on her face. He didn't have to look at the sculpture to know what she was seeing. He'd purposely chosen this metope because of the veiled figure.

Under the cover was a headless sculpture of a Lapith man. He was apparently grasping the centaur by the mane, possibly preparing to cut off the head that nature had already worn away from the stone. The man's body was brilliantly carved to show each muscle and rib, and draped over his arm was a splendid cloak, with every ripple and fold lovingly depicted.

Except for the cloak, however, the figure was naked from head to foot.

There was no way on earth she could ignore *that*. And if, as he thought, she was Emily Fairchild, her reaction would have to be dramatic.

Dramatic indeed. Her mouth dropped open and her eyes widened. She blushed from the roots of her hair to the edge of her bodice, filling him with a quick burst of satisfaction. She was Emily—she had to be.

After a moment of stunned silence, she said in a hushed whisper, "My word, he's magnificent."

Magnificent? He nearly choked. "You're not shocked?"

She shrugged. "Why should I be? I'm from Scotland, where the men wear nothing under their kilts."

Amazement followed upon amazement. How could Emily be spouting off about kilts with such nonchalance?

When she peered closer at the carving, he actually found himself jealous. "This half of the carving seems even more to your liking than the other."

"Of course. The man is quite well rendered."

Well-rendered? Did she mean well-hung? "So his nakedness doesn't bother you," he said inanely, unable to leave that subject.

"Certainly not. The human body is nothing to be

ashamed of. The Greeks knew that, even if we aren't so wise."

She couldn't be so calm about this. It was unthinkable! Then his eyes narrowed when he saw her rest her hand on the table as if to support herself. Ha—she was merely pretending not to be shocked. That was it. He'd try his other trick on her. "What you're saying is, 'Naked I came from my mother's womb, and naked I shall return there.' And that makes it all right." He held his breath, waiting for her to respond to the bit of scripture.

"I suppose. What poet are you quoting? This Lord Byron everyone seems so interested in?"

Byron! She thought it was Byron? Emily Fairchild would have been familiar with such a well-known biblical passage—even if he'd had to spend hours looking for it in the Bible he never touched. But Lady Emma . . .

Her gaze traveled casually up the sculpture to fix directly on the man's flaccid member, and he choked back a groan. His own member supplied the arousal the stone figure's lacked.

Deuce take her! He could believe her lack of shock had been a pretense, and he might even believe she didn't know the scripture he'd quoted—but there was no way Emily Fairchild would peruse a man's privates with such curiosity.

Ian must be right. The girl was precisely who she claimed to be: Lady Emma. She was probably a distant relation of the rector's daughter, nothing more.

He didn't know whether to be disappointed or ecstatic. If she weren't Emily, then he'd been right about the rector's daughter and her purity. The young woman hadn't been deceiving him; she was probably still tucked up in her rectory reading Bible verses. And Emily was the woman he wanted.

Or was she? He watched as Lady Emma stepped back from the sculpture to take a better look at the overall effect, and a surge of lust hit him as strongly as before. Good God, he was still attracted to the chit! Why was that, if she wasn't his Emily?

Because she was exquisite, with a mind like a man's and a body decidedly female. The women he met in society paled next to her. She inflamed his senses and tempted his wicked loins. And she was accessible. He needn't be careful of her the way he'd been careful of Emily. Lady Emma was no innocent.

She sighed, a darling utterance that sent hot urges careening through his unruly body. "I suppose we'd best return to Mama before she sends the museum guard after us." When she pivoted toward the door, he caught her arm to halt her.

"Don't go yet, Emma," he said softly.

"I mustn't let Mama worry about me—"

"You weren't so concerned about your mother at Merrington's ball. As I recall, her wishes didn't affect you one way or the other."

Her gaze swung to his, full of fear and something else. Panic. What had happened to the flirtatious wanton?

As if she'd read his thoughts, she flashed him a sudden coy smile. "If Mama charges in here with half the museum guards in tow, you won't be happy, I assure you."

"I won't be happy if you leave without giving me a kiss." He tugged her toward him, his heart thudding erratically. "Just one. I went to a great deal of trouble to have the chance for it. Surely you won't disappoint me by turning missish all of a sudden."

He clasped her chin lightly, then rubbed his thumb over her moist lower lip, feeling her suck in an urgent breath. She wanted him, too. She pretended otherwise, but she wanted him. The desire was like a primeval force between them, going out from him and reflected back by her.

"You don't play fair," she whispered, her eyes wide and needy.

"I never have." Then he brought his mouth down to meet hers.

She tried to break the kiss at once, but he clasped her head in his hands, dislodging her bonnet and sending it tumbling to the floor. Then he held her still to explore her lips. They were warm . . . pliant . . . luscious, like marzipan hot from the oven. And not nearly enough to satisfy his sudden, unbearable sweet tooth.

He pressed his tongue against her tender, adorable mouth, feeling triumphant when she opened it and moaned. Driving his tongue deeply into the velvet warmth, he reveled in the way she accepted him.

But it still wasn't enough. After days of burning and aching for her, he wanted more, needed more. Dropping his hands to her waist, he clutched her close, melding her body to his from chest to thigh as his hands roamed freely over her ribs and waist and hips.

He kissed her long and hard, with all the hunger of a man who'd never been so reckless. She didn't fit his usual pattern. She was a marriageable girl, but not an innocent. And she wasn't Emily.

Still, he kissed her. And when her slender arms crept about his waist, he groaned, then backed her toward the table a few paces away. He didn't stop to think, didn't break the kiss. He merely set her on the table and fit himself between the thighs that parted naturally under her loose skirts.

Something otherworldly had seized him, shattering all thoughts of propriety or sense. He had to touch her all over, feast on her, stroke the legs and arms and breasts that had driven him mad.

She tore her lips from his, shock written in her face. "Wh-What are you doing?"

"Playing with fire," he muttered, then seized her mouth again.

Fire, Emily thought as Jordan swept his large, knowing hands along her sides to her waist, then down her thighs. Yes, fire ... heaps and heaps of coals bursting into flame. That's what it felt like all over ... in her breasts ... in her belly ... in the secret place between her legs. His mouth and hands sowed sparks all over her body, and like a fool, she gave herself up for kindling.

Surrendering to the urge to touch him in return, she threaded her fingers through the auburn hair that looked like dark flames in the midday sunlight streaming through the windows. His thick hair was soft and yielding, so different from the hard, firm hands taking liberties with her body.

God help me, she thought as he slid one of those hands beneath her skirt and glided knowing fingers up the length of her stocking to her garter, stoking more fires as he went. She should never have let him kiss her. She should never have used her saucy persona to fool him when he'd tried his blatant attempts to unmask her.

It had worked; he'd called her Emma, not Emily.

But now she was reaping the results of her foolish game. Lady Emma was wild and unruly. Lady Emma craved a man's touch, a man's kiss. The wicked Lady Emma had taken her over.

And with a seducer's unerring instincts, he knew it. There was none of the reticence he'd shown to Emily Fairchild that night in the carriage; he was transgressing every boundary. One of his hands now caressed her thigh sensuously; his other rested on her waist.

Not for long, however. Drawing back, he lifted his hand to seize the lace scarf loosely knotted over her bodice. "Let's get rid of this useless bit of fluff," he muttered as he deftly unknotted it and tossed it aside to bare the tops of her breasts.

Her breath caught in her throat. His hot gaze was fixed on the swells pushed up by her short corset until they nearly spilled out of her gown. She ought to cover herself, but her hands inexplicably stayed tangled in his hair. Starting in the hollow at the base of her throat, he dragged his index finger slowly down between her breasts.

"Don't . . . you shouldn't . . . be so wicked, Jordan."

"Wicked?" he rasped. "I've not been nearly wicked enough with you." Hooking his finger beneath her bodice and chemise, he tugged the muslin down on one side. Her breast sprang free as if eager to flaunt itself for him.

Shocked at her own acquiescence, she dropped her hand to her bodice, but he caught it, imprisoning her fingers while his other hand reached for her exposed breast. His eyes met hers in a look as potent as opium and just as mesmerizing. Wordlessly, he ran his thumb over the nipple, which puckered into a tight little knot beneath his deft touch.

"Goodness . . . gracious," she gasped when he stroked and teased it again. Curse the seductive wretch. It felt so . . . so thrilling!

She couldn't bear looking at him, at the triumph in his face. But as her eyes drifted shut, she didn't stop him from touching her either. The urge to experience his caresses overwhelmed her modesty as the exquisite sensations turned her knees to putty and her resolve into air.

When he took her mouth again in a searing, sensuous kiss, she rose to it, welcomed it, slid into it as if into a waking dream. She was as boneless as a sleeping cat, except that she wasn't asleep. She was awake, and so very alive, more alive than she'd ever been in her life.

Somewhere in the swirl of wild, ungoverned excitement, she realized that his hands launched twin assaults—one freeing her other breast while his other hand inched above her garter to stroke the soft, inner skin of her upper thigh. At the intimate caress, she abandoned all pretense that she might resist. The reckless Lady Emma had completely possessed her, filling her with a fierce urge to feel his hands on her.

How could she have spent so many years in complete ignorance of what a man could do... could tempt a woman to do? She craved every glide of his fingers across her sensitized nipples, every wispy caress, every sweet, tormenting motion.

His parted lips left hers to trail openmouthed kisses over her cheeks, her closed eyelids, her temples. She couldn't think or move or do anything but be. Her world had shrunk to this alluring exchange of intimacies. The scent of marble dust and the rough wooden table beneath her curling fingers were her only links to the physical world beyond him.

Then his mouth followed a path down the slope of one breast, and before she knew it, he was devouring it as he rolled the nipple of the other between his thumb and finger.

Goodness gracious! How wanton, how sinful!

How delightful. A moan escaped her lips as she

arched back, letting him suck her breast so hard she nearly shot up off the table from the sheer pleasure of it.

"Jordan," she whispered as she raised her hands to grip his shoulders. "My God . . . Jordan . . . this is . . . this is . . . so . . . so . . ."

"Scandalous?" he murmured against her breast.

"Heavenly!"

He drew back from her with a grin. "That's what I adore about you," he said as he took his hands off her long enough to remove his coat and toss it on the table, then unbutton his waistcoat. "You aren't ashamed of a little honest pleasure."

Somewhere in the depths of her fevered brain she registered that he shouldn't be removing his coat. But then he caught her hands and placed them inside his waistcoat to rest against his ribs, and the urge to explore his body the way he was exploring hers became almost painful. Shamelessly wishing he would also remove his linen shirt, she felt along his sides with curious fingers, molding the muscles as she went. They were as firm as the sculpted ones of the naked figure behind her, hard and lean and very male.

When her hands reached his waist, he groaned, then unbuttoned the top two buttons of his trousers. Grabbing her gloveless hand, he slid it inside. "Touch me," he whispered, his gaze hot on her as she resisted feebly. "Touch me as you touched him."

"H-Him?"

"The statue." His voice was hoarse with need as he pushed her hand down to where something long and hard strained against his stockingette drawers. "The centaur."

"I didn't . . . touch him like this."

"You might as well have," he choked out. "You

made me jealous of the damned statue, for God's sake."

His admission thrilled her. It was surely wrong to put her hand on his groin and certainly beneath his trousers, but she wanted to touch him very badly. Besides, looking at that statue had roused her curiosity. Timidly, she curled her fingers around him as he bade.

The hard thing leapt to life in her hands, and she let go with a gasp.

"No, don't," he groaned, then pushed her hand back to cup him. Her mouth went dry as his hand urged hers to stroke him. "God, yes, like that. Don't stop."

He thrust against her hand a couple of times, his eyes closed, his expression one of sheer need.

But when she tightened her grip on him out of curiosity to see the effect, his eyes shot open and he jerked her hand out of his trousers with a curse. "That's too good. No more. I can't take any more."

His wanton gaze locked with hers as he reached for the hem of her skirt and drew it up so high it bared her legs nearly above the knees. "Your turn," he whispered with a teasing smile that froze her breath in her throat.

What did he mean?

He showed her. Smoothing his hands up her thighs, he caressed her lightly above her garters. Then she felt his fingers open the slit in her drawers. She tried to clamp her legs together, but his body between them prevented that. "Jordan, I don't know if you—"

The first caress made her jerk. The second made her sigh. By the third, she was aching for more, her hips writhing on the table in her attempt to get closer to his teasing fingers. "Dear heavens, Jordan . . . *Jordan* . . ."

"Yes, Emma?" He stroked her again, and she gasped. "Do you like that? Have I pleased you?"

"Goodness gracious—"

Whatever else she might have said was lost in the needy kiss he gave her. He fondled her devilishly, driving her to madness. She no longer cared what happened to her. She was in the arms of the man she'd dreamed feverishly about for weeks, and he was showing her what passion was all about. Everything else paled by comparison.

Her hands gripped his shoulders, flexing and unflexing as he made her twitch and wiggle. When he slid his finger inside her, she was beyond being shocked. This was what she'd been waiting for, what she wanted. It was delicious. She liked it—she loved it!

"God, how I've wanted to do this from the first moment I saw you," he rasped out. "I've wanted to touch you, to have you in my arms like this, to be inside you, my sweet, adorable darling."

The endearment sent a thrill coursing through her.

"I've thought of nothing but you since we kissed," he said fervently, his finger driving deep inside her.

Somehow she'd grown damp inside, making it easier for him to stroke her. "And they say you have no romantic feeling," she whispered as she clutched at his shoulders. "How wrong they are!"

He delved inside the slick passage between her legs with a particularly insolent caress. "This isn't romantic feeling, my dear. This is desire, pure and simple. I've never lacked for that. Not for you."

It took a few seconds for his words to drift through the haze of seduction, but when they did, she froze and drew back to look at him. "Wh-what did you say?"

He nuzzled her ear, his finger still thrusting inside her. "I said I've always wanted you. Surely you knew that."

His words were like a cold bucket of water dumped on her head. All her rampant urges and shameful impulses died at once.

The . . . the lecherous wretch! She'd thought he wanted her, but he'd just wanted *this*! Oh, mercy, she was going to be sick. She'd been such a fool!

Frantically, she grabbed at his arms, trying to get his hands off of her.

"What the devil are you doing?!" he cried when she dragged his hands from beneath her skirts. The incredulous look on his face was exactly what she deserved for being so stupid.

"Get away from me!" she cried desperately. "I don't want your hands on me!"

"Damn it, Emma," he growled as he reached for her. "What nonsense is this?"

"It's not nonsense!" She batted his hands away, then shoved free of him and leapt off the table, hurrying to the opposite end of the room. She turned her back to him. "I won't . . . I *can't* do this shameful thing! It's wrong!"

As tears of mortification and anger welled in her eyes, she fumbled with her clothing, trying to straighten it, trying not to think of the things she'd let him do. And all because she'd been foolish enough to think he actually cared for her! She would have fully given herself to him if she'd thought he was in love with her.

But no, not Jordan. Not him, with his hard heart. It had been lust and nothing more. For goodness sake, it hadn't even been for *her*, but for Lady Emma! And only because he thought the woman from Scotland was as experienced as those . . .

those fancy women he spent all his time with. The bastard!

"Emma, there's no shame in making love," he bit out as he came up behind her.

He laid his hands on her shoulders, but she shrugged them off. "No shame for you," she whispered. "But no matter what you think of me, I do have a reputation to uphold. And if I throw my virtue away—"

"Throw your virtue away," he said sarcastically. "It's a little late for that, isn't it?"

Horror gripped her as she swung around to face him. "You don't mean that what we just did . . . that I . . ." She knew something of how a woman lost her virginity, but not in great detail. He'd put his fingers inside her. Was that the same as . . . did that mean he . . . "Did you take my . . . my virginity?" she asked, appalled by the possibility.

"What the devil! Don't you know?"

"Of course I don't know!" she cried in sheer frustration. "I've never been with a man like . . . like that! How would I know?"

His jaw went taut, and he looked decidedly ill. "I thought . . . from the way you acted in the garden, the way you kissed me . . . hell, from the way you acted just now, the things you allowed me to do, I thought—"

"I did those because I believed you cared about me!" she burst out, then instantly regretted the confession. "I was curious, and you were so . . . so—"

"Persuasive." His voice was now under his wretched control. "Yes, I have a talent for persuasion. And I wanted you, Emma. I still want you. But that's all there is to it. If you think that this little encounter shall result in marriage—"

"Oh, for goodness sake," she snapped, remembering their first time in the carriage. "I've never seen a man so convinced that women are trying to trap him into marriage!" Rage made her reckless. "*I'm* not the one who dragged you in here! *I'm* not the one who wanted 'one kiss'! In case you hadn't noticed, I've had my share of suitors since I came to London. I don't need to trick some hapless man into marriage, Jordan!"

For a moment, he looked stunned. Then his eyes narrowed, and his tone grew icy. "You've said that before, Emily."

She started to retort, then froze. She *had* used those exact words—the first time they'd met, in the carriage. And he'd just called her Emily, not Emma.

Her heart sank. Dear heavens, he knew. He knew because he'd made her so angry she'd forgotten her role. A thousand curses upon him! She couldn't even take it back or invent some explanation for her words. Playing a role was beyond her at the moment, when her emotions were raw and he was standing there, his hands clenched in fury.

Panic-stricken, she darted toward the door.

"Emily, no!" he growled as he lunged toward her.

But he was too late to prevent her. Praying that the guard was still there, she pounded furiously on the door and shouted, "We're ready to leave! You can let us out now!"

"Yes, milady," a muffled voice answered.

Relief coursed through her at the welcome sound of a key being inserted in a lock. Then Jordan pinned her against the door so hard she could feel his arousal against her backside. "Devil take you, Emily, we have to talk," he hissed under his breath.

She shook her head violently. "Let go of me! I don't want to talk to you anymore." The door shuddered beneath her fingers. "Release me or I swear I'll scream."

He hesitated, his breath hot and hard against her cheek. She felt the guard trying to open the door, but Jordan still had her braced against it.

"Milady, is there something blocking the door?" the guard called out through the door. "I can't seem to move it."

She twisted her head to glare at Jordan, daring him to attempt keeping her in there. For a long moment, he glared back, and she feared he might actually do it.

Then with a curse he stepped away, allowing her to step away from the door, too.

It swung open at once. The guard looked suspiciously from Jordan to her. "Is everything all right, milady?"

She forced her voice to be calm. "Everything's fine, thank you." She walked out, grateful that there was no one else in this part of the museum at the moment.

"Wait!" Jordan said behind her.

She paused, all too aware of the guard's gaze on her. "Yes?"

"You've left your bonnet and glove behind, Miss Fairchild," Jordan said acidly.

She faced him slowly, hardly able to meet his implacable gaze. He held the items out, and she took them, not even bothering to correct him. It was silly to go on pretending with him. He knew who she was now.

The enormity of that fact suddenly struck her. She couldn't just walk away, not without making some attempt to salvage the situation. She cast the guard a pointed look. "Excuse me, sir, would you give us another moment alone?"

The guard scowled at Jordan, whose missing coat and waistcoat surely demonstrated that something had been going on in the room besides simple admiration of the arts. But if he noticed, he didn't say anything. With a curt nod in her direction, he turned away. "All right. But I'll be over here, miss, if you need me."

As he moved off a few paces, she forced herself to meet Jordan's livid gaze. "I have a favor to ask of you. I have no right to it, I know, but I'm asking you . . ." She swallowed, staring down at her hands. "I'm entreating you not to tell anyone your . . . suspicions about me."

"They're not suspicions anymore, Emily."

"I realize that. But only you know the truth, and I—"

"The truth?" Stepping toward her, he lowered his voice to a hiss. "I don't know the goddamned truth. All I know is you're masquerading as Lady Dundee's daughter. I don't know why or how or—"

"And I can't tell you."

He glowered at her. "Why the devil not?"

She drew on her glove, then forced herself to meet his gaze. "It's . . . complicated. But please believe me, I have good reason for this pretense. If you reveal the truth to anyone—your friends, your servants, anyone at all—it could ruin not only my life, but the lives of several other people." She swallowed her pride. "I'm begging you. If you care even a little for me, you'll keep silent."

A muscle worked in his jaw. "You want me to keep silent, but you'll give me no answers. Why are you doing this? Why be guided by Nesfield and his sister? What purpose does it serve? If you'd just tell me, I'd keep your secret!"

Yes, of course he would—except for where it concerned his good friend, Lord St. Clair. She and Lady Dundee were so close to finding out who Sophie's lover was, that Emily couldn't risk frightening off their most likely suspect now. Or suffering Lord Nesfield's wrath. "I'm sorry, Jordan, I can't tell you. It's not my secret alone."

"And if I refuse to keep quiet unless you tell me everything?"

Tears welled in her eyes, but she fought them back furiously. She would not let him see her cry. She wouldn't! "Then the first person you'll destroy is me. Isn't it enough that you've taken my . . . virginity? Must you take everything else?"

Remorse filled his features, and his voice gentled. "I didn't take your virginity. Your virtue is intact."

"Well, at least there's that," she said in a whisper. "But it doesn't change anything. I still can't tell you."

"Devil take it, Emily! Tell me, damn you!"

She cast him a pleading glance. "Why do you care so much about this? It has nothing to do with you." He'd given her no indication that he'd ever been interested in Sophie, so there was no point in continuing to suspect him, no matter what Lord Nesfield thought. "Keeping my secret won't hurt you. Do you despise me so much for trying to fool you that you won't rest until you destroy me?"

His expression was stark, drawn. "I don't despise you, for God's sake. I could never despise you, and I certainly don't wish to destroy you."

"Then keep my secret."

"Why can't you trust me with the truth? Haven't I proved I care about you?"

He could say that now? After what had just happened? "Oh, yes, I heard how much you cared! 'This isn't romantic feeling, my dear,' " she quoted bitterly. " 'It's desire, pure and simple.' You desire me, that's all." She hugged herself, feeling the hurt slice through her again. "No, you don't even desire me! You desire that wanton Lady Emma! Yet you

want me to trust you with my entire future! How
dare you?'' Tears began to stream down her face,
and she wiped them away furiously. ''You have no
right to ask that of me, you . . . you bastard!''

He groaned, his expression shifting from anger
to guilt as he stepped forward, reaching for her.

Quickly, she backed away, stammering, ''I . . . I
have to go now. I d-dare not stay here any longer.''
Turning on her heels, she hurried off.

''Please, Emily,'' he bit out behind her. ''Can't we
talk about this?''

She didn't answer but kept on going, a fervent
prayer tumbling from her lips as she hurried
through the rooms. *Dear God, don't let him tell. If
you'll keep him from exposing me, I'll never do anything
like this again, I swear.*

She only hoped God heeded the prayers of wan-
tons.

Chapter 11

Sabrina Jeffries

To act the part of a true friend requires more conscientious feeling than to fill with credit and complacency any other station or capacity in social life.

Sarah Ellis, English missionary and writer,
Pictures of Private Life

Ophelia looked askance at St. Clair as she rose from the bench. "What do you mean, you can't find them? They must be here somewhere."

He seemed to share her concern. "I've searched every room, but they're nowhere to be found." He handed her a scrap of woven silk. "I did find your shawl, however. It was only a couple of rooms away."

Of course it was. She'd purposely left it close by. So where on earth were they? A pox on Blackmore, that rascal. She should've known this would happen, especially after yesterday. And now it would be on her head, as well it should be. She was the one who'd let the girl in for this trouble.

"When I get my hands on that scoundrel . . ." she muttered as she hurried across the room.

St. Clair marched grimly beside her. "You can have him after I'm through. I swear, I had no idea

189

he'd try something like this. Jordan isn't generally irresponsible. Some might even say he's too responsible sometimes. But he has this fool notion about your daughter that—"

When St. Clair broke off, she stopped and grabbed his arm. "What fool notion?"

He raked his hand through his hair. "Nothing. It's nothing."

"Tell me what Blackmore is up to with my daughter!"

"It's ridiculous. It's just that—"

"Hello, Mama," came a cheery voice from behind her. "I'm afraid we didn't find your shawl. We've been looking everywhere."

Ophelia turned to find Emily and Lord Blackmore approaching, a few paces apart. Though the girl was smiling, the smile was patently false. Her bonnet was on crooked and her face was flushed. And Blackmore was looking as fierce as those carvings of the soldiers she'd just seen.

Something had happened, something monumental. Tension emanated from them, as taut as a wellstrung bow.

"Where in God's name have you two been?" Ophelia asked, her angry gaze fixing on Blackmore.

Blackmore met it with unrepentant insolence. She found it a tad unnerving.

It was Emily who answered, the words coming out in a rush. "I'm so sorry if we worried you, Mama. When we couldn't find your shawl, we spoke to the guards, but they hadn't seen it, so we went out to the carriage and looked there. Didn't we, Lord Blackmore?"

He hesitated a moment, his scowl deepening, if that were possible. "Yes," he finally clipped out. "Of course. We went out to the carriage."

A blatant lie if she'd ever heard one. But if they

hadn't gone out to the carriage, where had they disappeared to?

Ophelia held up her shawl. "St. Clair found it for me. How odd that you missed it. It was only a couple of rooms away."

Emily wouldn't meet her gaze. "Yes, how odd." She looked as if she were thinking, then added, "Oh, I know. That must have been the room we skipped because Lord Blackmore said you hadn't gone in it." She cast him a wan smile. "I *told* you we should check all the rooms, you silly man. But you were so insistent—"

He met her gaze, the muscles flexing in his jaw. "Yes, I'm nothing if not insistent. I eventually always get my way, you know."

A fresh blush stained the girl's cheeks as she returned her attention to St. Clair. "Well, in any case, I'm . . . I'm afraid I'll have to cut our outing short, Lord St. Clair. That headache of mine—"

"Of course. I should have insisted that we change it to another day the moment you said something." St. Clair shot Blackmore a stern glance. "I can be insistent myself, can't I, Jordan?"

The two men stood glaring at each other until Ophelia cleared her throat. Since no one was going to tell the truth, and since they were all obviously ready to throttle each other for things they wouldn't discuss aloud, they might as well go home. "Well, then, I suppose one of you gentlemen should call for the carriage."

"I will," Blackmore growled, then stalked off toward the entrance like some prowling beast.

As soon as he was gone, Emily visibly relaxed. St. Clair took her arm and led her in the same direction Blackmore had gone, with Lady Dundee following behind.

He gazed down at Emily with concern. "Are you all right? You look a little peaked."

The smile she flashed him was brittle and far too bright. "I'll be fine as soon as I can lie down in a quiet room with a cold cloth on my head. You mustn't worry."

"With your cousin sick, I can't help but worry," he answered smoothly. "You might be suffering from the same ailment."

Yes, indeed, Ophelia thought, an ailment called *men*. They were a plague upon women everywhere. Except for her dear Edward, of course.

She missed Edward. She'd known he wouldn't approve, so she hadn't told him of this farce. Still, she wished he'd come to London. This was becoming more complicated with each passing day, and she could use his advice. He was an excellent judge of character—he'd know what to make of St. Clair and Blackmore.

The ride back to Randolph's town house was so quiet, she could practically hear each hoofbeat of the horses. But the silence failed to dispel the air of suppressed anger between Blackmore and Emily that vibrated like two tines of a tuning fork.

Somehow she would find out what had happened during their absence. Emily would not put her off this time.

When Blackmore's carriage clattered up in front of the town house, St. Clair practically bounded out, as if in a hurry to escape the tension. Blackmore, however, didn't move. "I'll wait here for you," he told St. Clair, as the viscount helped first Emily, then herself from the carriage.

Good riddance, Ophelia thought as they left Blackmore behind. She was more than ready to escape both thorny men. As soon as they entered the house, she began assuring St. Clair that he needn't give any more thought to them and could leave at once. Though he hinted broadly at his wish to see Sophie, she ignored him and watched with profound relief as he left, looking tense, discouraged, and more than a little angry.

Although she wanted to talk to Emily before Randolph could corner the girl, Carter approached her before she could even usher the girl into the parlor.

"There's a Mr. Lawrence Phelps waiting to see you, milady. I thought I would wait until his lordship left to mention it. 'Tis very strange. The young man claims to be Miss Emily Fairchild's cousin. Of course, I told him that Miss Fairchild will be coming soon to stay with Lady Sophie, but the young man insists that Miss Fairchild is here now and demands to see her. I put him in the parlor."

"Thank you, Carter," Ophelia said, dismissing him with a look. As soon as he left, she turned to Emily. "Is this Mr. Phelps truly your cousin?"

"Oh, yes." Emily sighed. "He's a barrister here. Papa must have written to tell him I was in town. What should I do? If I talk to him, the servants will wonder. Nor can I tell him what I'm doing. He's very moral and might tell Papa."

"Were you unable to elicit the truth from St. Clair or Blackmore? Must we go on with the masquerade?" Ophelia cast a quick glance at the closed door of the parlor.

"You interrupted just as Lord St. Clair was about to confess something important." Emily whispered. "I'm nearly certain he's the one. But not certain enough. I need more time."

Ophelia thought a moment. "All right. I'll handle your cousin."

"What will you tell him?"

"You'll see." She nodded toward the door that

led to the dining room, which adjoined the parlor. "You can listen from in there if you want. Now go on with you. We don't want the lad to grow impatient and come out where he can see you."

Emily nodded quickly, then hurried off into the dining room.

Ophelia waited until Emily disappeared, then entered the parlor, only to catch the young man in question sifting through the letters that sat on a salver on the tea table. He whirled around, knocking the letter opener to the floor.

"Good morning, Mr. Phelps. I'm Lady Dundee. I trust you found our mail in order?"

Chagrin clouded his face. He bent to pick up the letter opener, but when he straightened, all hint of embarrassment was gone. "Good morning, my lady. I merely wondered if my cousin was receiving her letters."

Secretly admiring his insolence, she swept to her favorite chair, then sat down, indicating that he do the same. "We're keeping your cousin's letters for when she arrives. I promise she'll receive them all then."

He took the chair she indicated. "I don't understand. My uncle's letter stated quite clearly that Emily was in town and staying at Lord Nesfield's town house with Lady Sophie. I thought to pay her a visit, and instead was fed some Banbury tale about her being en route."

Impudent puppy. She examined the young man more closely. He was handsome, lacking the sober, pinched look of some barristers, and brazenly returned her gaze. He had the appearance of a man used to rummaging through myriad facts to find the truth. An intelligent fellow, no doubt. This would be tricky.

But Ophelia hadn't reached her pinnacle of success in polite society for nothing. Spinning tall tales was her special gift. "Miss Fairchild *was* here. But she and Sophie left two days ago to visit a country estate. They won't be back for some time."

"My uncle didn't mention anything like that."

She leaned forward conspiratorially. "May I be frank, Mr. Phelps?"

"Yes, of course."

"We didn't tell him. Miss Fairchild feared that her father might not allow her to go, since the woman hosting the visit is . . . shall we say, more acceptable in my circle than among people of your father's strict moral code." When Mr. Phelps drew himself up in righteous indignation, she added hastily, "The woman is perfectly respectable these days, mind you. But before she married her husband, the earl, she was—" She lowered her voice to a whisper. "An actress. And I know how clergymen feel about such things."

The young man's eyes narrowed. "You packed your niece and my cousin off to the country estate of some unsavory woman without asking my uncle's permission? Who is their chaperone? Why aren't you with them?"

"I'll be going there in a few days, but my brother is with them. They're perfectly safe." Pray heaven Randolph didn't return from White's before Mr. Phelps left.

The barrister settled back in his seat and eyed her with suspicion. "How odd that Lady Sophie should leave town in the midst of her coming out."

"It's not often done, I'll admit, but in this case, it's perfectly warranted." She thought quickly. "You see, Sophie no longer has to make the rounds. She's accepted an offer of marriage." Thankfully, he wasn't apt to move in any circles where he could learn she was lying.

He looked momentarily stunned. Then his pale blue eyes glittered beneath the dark, scowling brows. "Really? So soon after her arrival in London?"

Ophelia shrugged. "That's to be expected for a girl with her attractions. In fact, her fiancé is one of the guests at our friend's estate."

He glanced away, staring off into the fire a moment as if considering her words. "I see." Then his gaze swung back to her as he rose. "Thank you for clarifying matters, Lady Dundee."

Ophelia rose as well. "You're welcome. Be sure to visit when Miss Fairchild returns."

"I certainly will." He headed for the door with her a few paces behind, then stopped short. "Why don't you give me the address of that estate where Emily is staying? Then I can write my cousin and ask her to pay me a visit upon her return."

Really, this young man was growing troublesome. Did he have some other, deeper interest in Emily? Cousins sometimes did marry, after all.

How excessively inconvenient his interference would be now, when they were close to discovering the truth. Ophelia mustered all the frosty dignity she could manage. "I'm sure your cousin will have little time for letters in the country, nor would I wish to trouble her host with taking mail for her. That's why we're holding her mail here." She stepped toward the door, and opened it for him. "I'll tell her of your interest when I get there. I'm certain she'll write you as soon as she has the chance."

He glanced from her to the open door, looking as if he might say something else. Then he gave a sketchy bow. "Very well, Lady Dundee. Sorry to trouble you. I'll await my cousin's letter with eager anticipation."

"You do that. Good day, Mr. Phelps."

She watched as Carter showed him out, then sank onto the settee, her heart pounding in her chest. Pray heaven that was the last she saw of the impertinent creature. She was getting too old for these games.

Emily burst into the room. "Thank goodness he's gone! You did that very well. I don't think he suspected anything, do you?"

Privately Ophelia thought he suspected a good deal. But she couldn't tell the poor girl that, not when Emily had so many other things on her mind. "I think we're rid of him for the moment."

"Yes." The young woman forced a bright smile. "Well then, I suppose I'll go rest for a while. My headache, you know."

She had already turned toward the door when Ophelia said, "Wait one moment, my dear. Before you run off to hide, I wish to discuss what happened at the museum."

The girl's back went rigid as a poker. "Nothing happened. I told you, Lord St. Clair—"

"You know quite well that's not what I'm referring to."

Emily's heart sank as she faced the countess. She'd hoped to avoid this, prayed that Lady Dundee wouldn't question her too closely. She should have known better.

The countess patted the seat next to her on the settee. "Come here and tell me what happened with Blackmore."

Emily nearly rebelled. Hadn't she been through enough today? Merely thinking of her encounter with Jordan made her want to cry. The hungry glide of his hands over her body . . . the shocking things she'd let him do! Every moment had been the sweetest torture. And to know that it had meant absolutely *nothing* to him ... She could never reveal that shame to Lady Dundee.

On the other hand, she needed advice. What if Jordan did tell everyone? What was she to do? The only person who could help her with this was the countess. Heaven knows telling Lord Nesfield would be a disaster.

"Well?" Lady Dundee said, jolting Emily from her reverie.

Wearily, she took the seat next to the countess. Perhaps it was time she explained Jordan's interest in her. She could tell the truth without revealing all of what happened this afternoon. "Lord Blackmore and I visited a 'private' part of the museum."

"I knew it! All that nonsense about the carriage ... Did he try to make advances? I swear, I'll strangle the scoundrel if—"

"It wasn't about that." She paused, swallowing hard. "You see, he knows who I really am."

The countess gaped at her. "What? But how?"

Unable to look at Lady Dundee, she explained. How she'd met Jordan. What had happened. How he'd recognized her later, then spent his time trying to prove who she was. Without revealing what else they'd done, she told Lady Dundee that he'd finally trapped her into revealing her identity in the museum.

"So you see," she finished, her gaze dropping to her hands, "his interest in me is motivated only by a desire to unmask me. And today, thanks to my blundering, he succeeded."

She waited in utter fear for the countess's reaction. Would Lady Dundee lecture her for not revealing this before? Or, God forbid, would she head straight to Lord Nesfield with the news?

When the countess said nothing, Emily couldn't bear it any longer. She glanced up, fully expecting the woman to be wearing a look of censure. But the countess was smiling. Smiling, for goodness sake!

"This is interesting indeed. So he's known your true identity all along? And he hasn't said anything to anyone? How very strange."

"Not 'known.' Suspected. I don't think he would have said anything without being sure."

"Hmmm. But today he learned he was right. You say you asked him not to tell anyone?"

"Yes. I don't know if he will."

"He kept quiet this afternoon, didn't he?"

"That's true." Emily considered that, then shook her head. "On the other hand, he's not the kind to make public pronouncements. If he tells Lord St. Clair, he'll do it in private. We must watch the viscount carefully; his behavior will indicate if he knows."

Lady Dundee straightened. "While you and Blackmore were gone in the museum, St. Clair invited us to join him at the opera this evening. He's taken a box. I thought it might be a good idea, so I accepted. What do you think? Are you up for it?"

"Yes, of course. Then we can determine what Jordan—I-I mean, Lord Blackmore—has told Lord St. Clair. I'd rather go and learn where we stand."

"What if Blackmore is there?"

Emily lifted her chin. "It doesn't matter. I'm not afraid of him, you know."

But she *was* afraid of him. She was afraid of the sinful urges he roused in her, afraid that she was slipping into an infatuation that would wreck her life. And terrified that he would reveal her secret. He'd said he cared, but what did that mean? He'd made it quite clear he wasn't the sort of man influenced by something so silly as pity.

"You're in love with him, aren't you?" Lady Dundee said softly.

Emily's eyes widened. "In love? Certainly not! How could I be in love with a man so far above me? He would never marry me. For goodness sake, even when he thought I was Lady Emma, he wasn't interested in me beyond—" She stopped short, reddening.

"Beyond the physical attraction, you mean?" Lady Dundee settled her feet on the footstool. "You think not? Trust me, a man of his sort doesn't follow a woman about town simply because he's randy. He can go other places to fill those needs."

"He followed me about town because he wanted to expose me," she said bitterly.

"Did he? Seems like an awful lot of trouble merely to prove that some nobody is an impostor. What would he gain by it?"

"I don't know. I've been asking myself why he's so persistent. I can only assume it offends his moral sensibilities to have me impose on his friends with this masquerade."

"Moral sensibilities? Blackmore? From what I hear, he reserves his moral sensibilities for his reform efforts in Parliament. In private, he seems no more nor less moral than his peers. No, he's interested in you—I'd stake my honor on it."

"Then your honor would be ruined," Emily bit out.

"We'll see. Tonight. And remember, if he *has* told his friend, it's not your fault."

"I only wish your brother felt the same." A sudden terror struck her heart. "You won't tell Lord Nesfield all this, will you?"

"Of course not. Randolph will overreact, as he always does. And you mustn't worry about it anymore, do you hear?" Lady Dundee regarded her intently for a moment. "Now run along, dear, and get some rest. You'll need it for tonight. You and I will see this through, never you mind."

A sudden surge of gratitude made Emily grab the countess's plump hand and kiss it. "Thank you, Lady Dundee, for not revealing my secret to your brother. And for not insisting that I stop the masquerade."

Amusement lit the countess's eyes. "Stop the masquerade? Now that it's become interesting? Certainly not." Emily rose to walk off, and Lady Dundee added, "Oh, and dear? Wear the red velvet tonight."

Emily blushed. She'd sworn never to wear that particular gown. "But it's so . . . so revealing. Don't you think it's much too low in the front for a girl at her coming out?"

"Pish-posh. This is the opera. Everyone dresses that way. Go on now, be a good girl. Everything will be fine. You'll see."

With his hands shoved in the pockets of his greatcoat, Jordan walked briskly along the Strand. After watching Ian disappear inside the Nesfield town house, Jordan had abandoned the carriage to his friend.

Ian would think he was avoiding the inevitable discussion about "Lady Emma." It was true, but it wasn't his main reason for setting off on foot. Walking helped him cope with frustration and anger, and right now, the knot of both was wound so tight and large in his gut that it would take a great deal of walking to unwind it.

What to do about Emily? He couldn't expose her, not after the way she'd begged him. Good God, she'd looked so desperate, so terrified. He'd bet a fortune she'd been trapped into this masquerade against her will.

And for what? What could Nesfield and Lady

Dundee possibly gain by it? How had they even convinced her to cooperate? The Emily Fairchild he'd met in Derbyshire had been honest to a fault. She'd been the most open, artless . . . genuine woman he'd ever met. This masquerade wasn't in her character. Her reason for doing it must be compelling—she wouldn't relinquish her will easily.

Except when it came to lovemaking. Good God. Guilt lashed at him, making him feel like the lowest cur. The look on her face when he'd made that comment about her virtue . . . it had driven a knife in his gut. She'd been so deuced innocent that she hadn't even known whether she'd lost her virginity!

In that respect, he'd been a blind idiot about her. Any fool could have seen that Lady Emma's flirtations were desperate attempts to hide her identity. The truth of who she was had been obvious—her looks, her evasion of him from the beginning. She'd even called him Jordan in that damned room at the museum. He'd never given Lady Emma leave to call him by his Christian name, but he'd urged Emily to do so. Yet even though her use of it had registered somewhere in the back of his mind, he'd ignored it.

Why? Because he'd wanted to believe she was Lady Emma. Emily Fairchild was inaccessible, but Lady Emma was fair game. He'd desired Emily so badly that he'd been willing to believe she was somebody else so he could have her.

And he'd almost taken her virginity! He'd almost ruined her, because he hadn't wanted to acknowledge the truth.

A carriage rumbled up beside him, but he ignored it until it halted, and a voice said, "I thought I might find you on the street. Get in, Jordan."

He glanced over to see Ian holding the door

open. "Go away. I'm not in the mood for lectures right now."

When he walked off, Ian stepped out of the carriage and caught him by the arm. "I don't care what you're in the mood for. Get in the carriage, or I'll throw you in."

"How dare you!" Jordan whirled on him, his hands clenching into fists. He was spoiling for a fight, and at the moment didn't much care whom he fought.

Ian's determined expression altered at the sight of Jordan's fighting stance. "Don't be a fool. This should be settled in private, not in a public brawl."

The itch to hit something, anything, seized Jordan with almost overwhelming power. But Ian was right. A public brawl would make the papers and provoke unwanted speculation about why they were fighting so soon after being seen with Emily and Lady Dundee. He dared not draw undue attention to Emily.

Without a word, he lowered his fists, then climbed into the carriage, throwing himself into the seat.

Ian got in and told Watkins to drive to his town house, then turned to Jordan. "What happened between you and Lady Emma?"

"It's none of your concern," Jordan ground out.

"I'm the one who invited her. I'm responsible if something happened—"

"Nothing happened."

"Are you saying she dislodged her bonnet and got marble dust on the back of her skirts purely by accident?" When Jordan's gaze shot to his, he added, "Oh, yes, I noticed. That and other things. Like her missing scarf. It's a wonder Lady Dundee didn't notice it herself. I swear, if you compromised that young woman—"

"I didn't compromise her!" But he nearly had. And he'd wanted to. Jordan's gut twisted into an even tighter knot. Had it been so obvious as all that? "Why are you so concerned about the good Lady Emma anyway?" he retorted. "I thought it was Lady Sophie you wanted."

"It is. But I like Lady Emma, and don't want to see her harmed."

"Neither do I, believe me."

Ian rubbed his chin thoughtfully. "I see. Do you still think she's a rector's daughter masquerading as a lady?"

The impulse to tell his friend the truth was almost more than he could bear. But Emily had begged him not to, tears filling her eyes. Good God, he couldn't make her cry again. "No, of course not. It was a stupid notion, nothing more."

"So that means you're no longer interested in her."

"I didn't say that," he retorted.

Of course he was still interested in her. He wouldn't expose her, but nothing prevented him from trying to find out what hold Nesfield had over her. He'd be discreet and careful, but he *would* learn the truth. Someone must rescue her from this madness, for God's sake, before she was found out. Obviously her father wasn't trying to do so.

"Let me see if I have this right," Ian said dryly. "You're interested in a woman of marriageable age and station."

The word "marriageable" caught his attention. He scowled at Ian. "It's not what you're thinking. I enjoy her company. She's an intriguing acquaintance, that's all."

"Liar. Thanks to this mere acquaintance, you've—" Lifting his hand, he ticked them off one by one. "Arrived late for an appointment. Attended the breakfast of a woman you despise. Tried to seduce said acquaintance in the midst of a crowded museum where being caught would mean public censure for you and humiliation for her. Threatened to trounce your closest friend." He paused. "Am I missing anything?"

"My fist in your jaw," Jordan ground out.

"Make that 'twice threatened to trounce your closest friend.' Do tell me what you've done with the real Earl of Blackmore."

"Very amusing. As for trying to seduce her, any man with eyes would attempt it."

"*I* haven't." Ian leaned forward. "Are you in love with her?"

"Good God, what a question." He forced a cynical smile to his lips. "You can ask that of me? The man with the granite heart, as Pollock calls me?"

"Pollock is a mercenary masquerading as a romantic. You, however, are a romantic masquerading as a mercenary. Unless I miss my guess, you're particularly vulnerable to Lady Emma."

"Horrible thought. No, you're wrong. This is lust, nothing more. It'll pass."

A voice played suddenly in his head. *You desire me, that's all . . . Yet you want me to trust you with my entire future! How dare you? You have no right to ask that of me, you . . . you bastard!*

Devil take her! One thing had nothing to do with the other! He was an honorable man; he would help her if she'd only tell him the truth. He could be trusted. After their night in the carriage, she should know that.

Yes, of course—after you practically seduced her in the museum without stopping to think what it would do to her. And her so innocent that she didn't even know she was still a virgin when you were done mauling her, for God's sake! I'm about as trustworthy as a snake.

All the same, he must help her. She was unhappy with this situation—any fool could see that. Somehow he must help her out of it.

"Merely lust, is it?" Ian said, breaking into his thoughts. "Then it must be difficult for you to be around this 'acquaintance,' since you're too honorable to seduce an innocent without marrying her, and you have no interest in marriage."

"You have no idea," he muttered under his breath. That was precisely why he should keep his distance from her. Yet that was impossible under the circumstances.

He glanced out the window, relieved to see Ian's town house up ahead. "Looks like we're here, old friend. Will you be making the rounds of the balls tonight?"

Ian thankfully didn't comment on Jordan's abrupt change of subject. "I don't know. What about you?"

"Perhaps." If he asked Ian if he knew where Emily would be, the man would torment him mercilessly. "I haven't made any plans."

The carriage halted. "One word of advice. If you're truly only interested in Lady Emma for her physical attractions, you should probably stay away from her."

"Advice? That sounds more like a command to me."

Ian climbed out and slammed the door. "Take it however you want, my friend."

"I will." Jordan pounded on the ceiling. "Home, Watkins!"

Stay away from her? The devil he would. As Watkins drove off, Jordan scowled blackly. Ian had always been gallant toward women, but this time he was treading dangerous ground. Emily was *not* Ian's concern. She was his, and his alone. And he would find out what the woman was up to if it killed him.

After several minutes of contemplation, Jordan concocted a plan. As soon as he arrived home, he strode inside, bellowing for Hargraves.

The butler appeared in a flash, running after him as Jordan hurried up two flights of stairs and into his study. "Yes, milord? What do you need?"

"Pack your bags, man. You're taking a trip." Jordan opened his safe and removed a fistful of pound notes.

Hargraves blinked a couple of times. "Now?"

"As soon as you can be ready."

"Where am I going?"

"To Willow Crossing."

The butler coughed discreetly as Jordan counted out the notes. "Er . . . isn't that where Miss Fairchild is from? The woman you think is masquerading as Lady Emma?"

"Not think. Know. She told me the truth herself today."

"You don't say!"

"Yes. Unfortunately, she wouldn't tell me why." He stopped counting. "You haven't discovered anything more, have you? Other than what you told me this morning about when Lady Dundee and her daughter arrived in London?"

"Actually, I have. It's not much, but perhaps you'll know what to make of it. It seems Lady Sophie is not in residence. She hasn't been for some weeks. They say she's ill and had to go home, but they're not supposed to tell people where she is."

"That's curious." Did Emily's masquerade have to do with Sophie and her illness? But how?

"Something else, milord. When I asked about Miss Emily Fairchild, they said she's coming for a visit soon. They've been told that she's traveling and can't receive mail, which is why they're holding her mail for her, but they all think it a mite odd that her father would write her so many letters when she can't yet answer."

"That *is* helpful, Hargraves. I'll wager that her father doesn't know about this masquerade. I can use that." He didn't want to threaten to tell Emily's father yet—she'd never forgive him. But he would if he must. Somebody had to look out for her.

"Nesfield has a hold over her," he mused aloud. "I don't know what it is, but I want you to find out. That's why I'm sending you to Willow Crossing. You haven't found anything here, so you might as well see what you can find there. You don't mind a trip to the country, do you?"

"Indeed not. I've been itching to escape the city, milord."

"Good. I want you to leave today. Spend a few days there, ask questions. But be discreet. Don't tell anyone you're looking for me, all right? Just find out what you can about the Fairchilds and Nesfield. It shouldn't take long in a small town like that."

"I'll take care of it, milord. You can count on me."

"I always do."

And while Hargraves was in Willow Crossing, Jordan would find some way to discover the truth here. No matter how much she protested, he wouldn't let Emily go on like this alone. Not any longer.

Chapter 12

Going to the opera, like getting drunk, is a sin that carries its own punishment with it.

Hannah More, English writer,
reformer, philanthropist, Letter, 1775,
to her sister, *The Letters of Hannah More*

Emily had never attended an opera. Willow Crossing had an ancient orchestra that played at assemblies, and a traveling troupe of actors that sometimes presented Shakespeare. But no operas, to be sure.

The Marriage of Figaro, by Mozart, was entirely beyond her ken. Thankfully, although it was an Italian opera, this production was in English. Not only could she understand the story, but she was enjoying it beyond anything, drooling over the music like the country fool she truly was. The voices rang so clear, so perfect! The orchestra actually knew all their notes, even the high ones!

Her enjoyment was enhanced by the fact that Lord St. Clair had shown no signs of having learned any dark secrets about her that afternoon. When he'd come in behaving like his usual self, she'd relaxed, especially since he'd come without Jordan. Perhaps everything would be fine after all.

209

Perhaps Jordan would be satisfied with proving to himself that he'd been right about her identity. For the first time since the Merrington's ball, she felt free to enjoy herself.

The character named Cherubino, a woman playing the part of an adolescent boy, launched into an aria, and Emily strained forward. How could such lush sounds emerge from such a tiny woman? Emily's musical abilities were tolerable at best, but she did love to listen. By the end of the second act, she'd smiled so much her face hurt.

The chandelier with its hundreds of candles was lowered for the interlude, and Lady Dundee rose from her seat. "I see that Lady Merrington is here tonight. I believe I'll go speak to her."

"I'll join you," Lord St. Clair said as he also rose. "These chairs aren't made for men with long legs." He held out his arm to Emily. "Are you coming, Lady Emma?"

The soft, elegant strains of a violin wafted up to their box, and she sighed with pleasure. "Would you mind very much if I stayed here and listened to the music?"

Lord St. Clair chuckled. "It's just the interlude."

"Yes, but it's beautiful, don't you think?"

Lady Dundee cast her an indulgent smile. "Indeed it is, my dear. Come along, St. Clair. Let her have her fun."

Emily smiled gratefully, then returned her attention once more to the stage, where the musicians were playing a duet for violin and harp. She so loved the harp. The schoolteacher in Willow Crossing owned a harp, but it wasn't as pure or sweet as this one. There were advantages to living in the city. She would miss this.

Faintly, she heard the door open behind her and assumed that Lady Dundee had come back for something she'd left behind. Then a husky male voice said, "Good evening, Emily."

She froze. Jordan. He was here.

Her pulse raced and her heart fluttered. Oh, foolish, foolish heart—to be enamored of such a man.

She heard rather than saw him advance to the front of the box. Flipping up his tails, he took the chair next to her. She sat rigidly, not daring to look at him after the intimacies they'd shared that afternoon. She wiped her clammy hands on her skirts and wished fervently that he hadn't come.

But when he said nothing, she couldn't resist a glance at him. As usual, his cutaway was impeccable, his cravat immaculate. Why couldn't he wear ill-fitting coats or have warty hands or something else to dislike? No, he had to be perfect in every way. The perfect, beautiful, forbidden earl who kissed like the devil and held her fate in his hands.

He met her gaze, and she dropped hers at once, mortified to be caught staring.

Then he cleared his throat. "You're looking lovely this evening. Though I must say that your gown is a little . . . snug, don't you think?"

He sounded as if he'd been gargling nails. And what did he mean? That she was too plump for the gown?

She glared at him. "Lady Dundee said it would be acceptable for the opera."

His gaze flickered briefly to where the gown pushed her breasts up scandalously high, much like all the other women's gowns she'd seen this evening. He swallowed, then jerked his gaze back to her face. "For some other woman perhaps. On you, it's deadly."

For goodness sake, what did he mean? Now that he was certain she was a rector's daughter, did he think she had no right to wear such beautiful clothes? The arrogant wretch. "If you're going to insult me, you might as well leave!"

"Insult you? I wasn't insulting you. At least, I don't think I was." He sighed. "Don't throw me out yet, not after I went to so much trouble to find out where you were."

"What trouble? I'm sure your friend told you we were attending the opera."

"My 'friend,'" he said with a hint of sarcasm, "didn't tell me a thing. I've been to two dances, a party, and an early ball looking for you. I finally had to go to Ian's house and badger his servants to find out where he—and therefore, you—might be."

Her foolish heart fluttered again. "You went all those places in search of me?"

"I had to talk to you. We left things unsettled this afternoon."

She squelched her disappointment. Of course that was why. God forbid he should wish to see her for some other reason.

Well, she needed to talk to him, too. But how to broach the subject? "You've missed half the opera."

"No, I haven't; I've been in my own box. I keep one year-round, mainly for my sister when she's in town." He gestured to a box across the theater, where the curtains were half-drawn. His tone hardened. "I've been in there watching all the men gawk at you."

Was that jealousy she heard? She sighed. Of course not. Jordan would never be jealous of her, or of any woman for that matter. "Why didn't you join us?"

"I didn't know if your 'mother' would allow it after what happened this afternoon. I suppose she's ready to skin me alive."

Should she tell him that Lady Dundee knew

about their previous association? No, she'd best not. Then he might feel free to badger the countess about what was going on. "She . . . didn't suspect anything," she lied.

He glanced off across the theater, drumming his fingers on his knee. He seemed agitated. "That's a shock. Ian suspected everything. He spent half the afternoon lecturing me about toying with innocent young women."

She froze. "And did you tell him why . . . I mean . . . what we spoke about and—"

"No." His gaze shot to her, deeply serious. "I didn't tell him anything. That's why I'm here. To assure you that I'll keep your secret."

Relief swamped her, so intense she nearly reeled with it. "Oh, thank heavens! I was so worried!"

He scowled. "You didn't really think I'd be so callous as to expose you without knowing what was going on, did you?"

"I didn't know what to think. Until now, you've been so . . . so insistent about finding me out, it seemed logical that you would want to let everyone know—"

"Good God, you don't think much of me, do you?" He jumped to his feet and began to pace the small area at the front of the box. "Well, my dear, you should have trusted to your feminine tactics. Your tears and your begging were very effective, I assure you. I'm not made of stone."

"They weren't tactics!" Wounded by his cold words, she struck back. "Besides, Mr. Pollock says you boast of your granite heart, so I guess you *are* made of stone, aren't you?"

He whirled on her, eyes narrowing. "Pollock? Is he still sniffing around after you? He only told you that because he resents me, you know."

"Oh? So you never boasted of it to him?"

With a muttered oath, he glanced away from her. "All right, so I might have said . . . something like that. But I'm not as bad as he makes me sound. Just because I don't crumble in the face of a woman's tears doesn't mean they don't affect me. I'm not the unfeeling wretch you take me for."

He seemed so insulted she took pity on him. "Apparently not," she said, softening her tone. "At least you're going to keep my secret."

"Yes. But I still want to know why you feel compelled to masquerade like this. You can trust me. I swear it. Just because I tried to seduce you this afternoon—"

"I don't want to talk about this afternoon!" Dear heavens, she couldn't bear it if he talked about *that*. Setting her reticule on the seat beside her, she rose and hurried to the back of the box near the door. "Perhaps you should go now."

He followed her. "Emily, I was merely trying to assure you that it won't happen again."

"I realize that. Now that you know who I am, you're not likely to touch me, are you? It was Lady Emma you wanted, not me."

"What the devil are you talking about?"

Dear heavens, she'd said far too much. "Nothing. It's nothing."

He grabbed her arm. "Obviously it isn't 'nothing' or you wouldn't have said it. Surely you don't think I kissed you this afternoon only because I thought you were Lady Emma."

"It doesn't matter." She fought to keep her tone even, unruffled, though inside she was aching. "I . . . I understand. Truly, I do. You're used to more sophisticated women. You thought I was a wanton, so you tried to seduce me. But now that my lack of experience is . . . painfully apparent, I needn't worry about that, need I?"

"Good God, if only that were true." He raked his fingers through his hair. "There's only one problem with your theory, Emily. I knew who you were this afternoon, and I still wanted you."

She shook her head. "You thought I was Lady Emma, that . . . that wild girl from Scotland."

"I told myself you were Lady Emma, because then I could allow myself what I really wanted—to make love to you. I have no desire to take any woman's virginity, and I thought that Lady Emma wasn't a virgin, so it would be all right."

When she flinched, he drew her behind the velvet curtain that shielded the unused seats in the back of the box and now hid them. Then he lowered his voice. "But it was Emily Fairchild I really wanted, I promise you. It's Emily Fairchild I *still* want. I've watched the men ogle you all night, wanting to challenge each one to a duel just for looking at you in that excuse for a gown."

"Stop it! Stop saying these things just to make me feel better!" She turned her face away, tears welling in her eyes. "I hate it when you pity me!"

"Pity you?" He forced her against the wall, then lifted her chin to make her look at him. "Pity you, for God's sake! Have you no idea what you do to me? If this weren't a public place, we wouldn't be having this discussion. I would already have rid you of this deuced piece of seduction you're wearing. I'd be feasting my eyes on every inch of your beautiful body. We'd be on the floor, and I'd be kissing you in every place you can imagine and some you can't. You wouldn't leave here a virgin, I swear."

She couldn't doubt his words now. They were echoed in his hungry look, his husky voice, his quickening breath. His body felt hot against hers compared to the cool wall against her bare back.

Lush harp notes trickled into her consciousness, tripping almost as quickly as her pulse. But not quite.

Then his hand slid down her neck in a lingering caress that branded her skin with his need, and her pulse went mad. He dragged one large finger slowly down her throat and chest until it rested between her breasts, which rose and fell in her vain attempt to breath normally.

He hooked his finger behind the edge of her bodice. "Good God, if we were anywhere else but here . . . if we were really alone . . ."

He didn't have to say any more. If they were alone, he'd be tugging her bodice down and sucking her breasts, fondling them as he had this afternoon. Shameful woman that she was, she wanted him to. Oh, how badly she wanted him to.

He dropped his hand to grab hers and flatten it against the thickness in his breeches. "Do you feel that?" he growled. "That's how much I desire you. I can't even see you without feeling *that*. It doesn't matter if you pretend to be Emma or the damned Queen of England. You're still Emily, the woman I lust after so much that I don't get any sleep. I've lusted after you ever since the night we were alone in the carriage—"

Now he was telling falsehoods. She jerked her hand away. "That night in the carriage, you pushed me away—you didn't want anything to do with me."

He leaned forward until his mouth was at her ear. "Then why did I kiss you?" He pressed a kiss to the shell of her ear, then the lobe, then the sensitive patch of skin beneath it. He smelled of soap and tobacco. And desire. Most assuredly desire. Tiny shivers of anticipation danced along her spine.

He continued in a hard voice. "Trust me, I do not kiss women I don't desire. And I knew that I shouldn't, *couldn't* desire you."

"Because I'm a rector's daughter and too far beneath you."

"No," he said firmly. "Because you're sweet and innocent and a virgin."

She turned her head toward him. Their mouths were inches apart, so close she could practically taste his wine-scented breath. "What's wrong with wanting a virgin?" She couldn't keep the hurt out of her voice. "Most men prize virginity."

"Virgins are dangerous creatures. They believe in love and 'romantic feeling' and all the nonsense I gave up on long ago. A virgin expects a man to sell her his soul, and I can't do that. It's not in my nature."

There was nothing like hearing the truth to ruin a good seduction. She dug her fingernails into her palms to keep from crying. "Oh, yes, I forgot. You're the man with the granite heart, aren't you? You only feel . . . desire."

His gaze locked with hers, and for the first time, she thought he looked uncertain. Then his face cleared. "Exactly. I see you finally understand me."

Shoving him away, she moved back into the muted candlelight, hugging herself tightly. "I will *never* understand you. How can a man live without love, without the softer emotions? How can you even bear to get out of bed in the morning?"

"I have no trouble getting out of bed, I assure you. I don't need 'love' to get through the day. That's something I found out quite young."

"What do you mean?"

His expression turned as smooth and hard as glass. "I didn't come here to discuss the state of my heart. It has nothing to do with whether you can trust me. I may not be a sentimental fool, but I'm a decent, honorable man who hates watching you engage in a masquerade I know you detest. I want to help you, Emily. You can trust me with your secrets. I'll do what I can to protect you from Nesfield and Lady Dundee."

Alarm surged through her. "N-Nesfield?"

"It's obvious they have some sort of hold over you. You wouldn't agree to this insanity otherwise. And I can help you with them. I know I can."

Panic filled her. If he started to question Lord Nesfield—"No one can help me, but especially not you. Please, Jordan, just leave it be!"

"I can't."

"Why not?" She wrung her hands as she approached him. "It doesn't concern you. It'll all be over soon. Then I'll return to Willow Crossing and disappear from your life, and you won't be bothered by me anymore."

"Deuce take it, Emily, I'm not bothered by you! I want to help!"

"I don't want your help! Can't you get that through your thick head? The only way you can help is by staying out of it!"

"You won't tell me what's going on?"

"No!" She lowered her voice. "Please promise me you won't interfere. You mustn't interfere!"

"I won't interfere. But I won't stay out of it either."

"A curse upon you, Jordan! Why are you so intent on ruining my life?"

"I'm not ruining your life. I'm trying to keep *you* from ruining it." He gestured to her gown. "This . . . this role of yours seems to involve your enticing men and gadding about scantily clad. That's more dangerous than you realize, especially if you flirt with them as nonchalantly as you flirted with me!"

She wanted to take hope from the jealous edge in his voice, but she knew better. "The only man dangerous to me is you!"

"Really? And Pollock? He hasn't touched you? He hasn't made advances?"

The question so took her by surprise that she blushed before she could stop it.

"I thought so," he growled. "Devil take the bastard—"

"It was nothing I couldn't handle," she broke in. "I'm not as stupid and naive as you think. I know how to deal with men like him!"

He laughed harshly. "Yes, I could tell that this afternoon."

Her blush deepened. How dared he remind her of how wantonly she'd behaved!

The interlude music had ended, and she could hear people milling back into the opera house. Soon Lady Dundee would return with Ian. She couldn't deal with Jordan and them, too. Besides, she was tired of his insinuations.

Briskly she walked to the door and held it open. "Get out! Get out and stay away from me!"

He glanced at the filling theater, then stalked toward her. Halting at the doorway, he fixed her with a piercing look. "I'll leave—for now. But depend on it, I'm not staying away from you. Not until I get to the bottom of this."

And with that, he stormed from the box.

Ophelia decided that St. Clair knew nothing of Emily's identity. She'd given the man plenty of opportunities to discuss it, and he hadn't said a thing. So Blackmore had apparently kept Emily's secret. Wasn't that interesting?

They were returning to the box when she spotted Blackmore himself emerging from it. She stopped short and grabbed the viscount's arm. "Would you look at that?"

As St. Clair followed the direction of her gaze, he went rigid. "Bloody hell. I'm sorry, Lady Dundee. I'll go after him, and tell him he's not welcome—"

"Don't you dare!"

He gaped at her. "What do you mean? After this morning, I thought—"

"Well, you thought wrong. I like Blackmore. I think he's interested in my daughter."

"You could call it that," St. Clair muttered.

"I distinctly detect sarcasm in your voice. Are you saying I'm wrong?"

"Not in the least. God knows I've never seen a man more interested in a woman. But . . . well . . ."

"His interest is merely physical. Is that what you're trying to say?"

He looked taken aback by her candor. "I'm not sure. It's what he claims."

"Pish-posh. Men always claim they're only interested in the physical. It keeps their pride intact. They don't want anybody thinking they might be enamored of a mere woman. Blackmore is a very proud man, after all."

St. Clair smiled. "Yes. And 'enamored' is a good word for what Jordan seems to feel for Lady Emma. But being enamored of a woman and doing something about it—something honorable, that is— are two different things."

"Are you saying he would debauch my daughter, then walk away?" She held her breath. If so, this couldn't go any further. Emily wasn't prepared to fend off the full seductive power of a man like Blackmore, and Ophelia didn't intend to send the girl home ruined.

"I don't think so. He's always steered clear of innocents."

"Well, he's not steering clear of her, is he?"

St. Clair looked thoughtful. "No, he's not." He cocked his head to stare at her. "Lady Dundee, are you trying to catch Jordan for your daughter?"

"Of course! Emma is in love with him. And if my daughter wants a man, I'll do what I can to get him." It was the least she could do for Emily after involving her in Sophie's mess.

"In love with him? She told you that?"

"No. She denied it violently. The girl doesn't know her own mind. But I know young women, and I'd wager my husband's fortune that she loves the scoundrel."

St. Clair rubbed his chin. "I must trust your maternal instincts on that one. And it's conceivable he's in love with her as well."

Ophelia's eyes lit up. "Do you think so?"

"He denies it, too. But I've never seen him act this way around a woman. He can't let her out of his sight or stop talking about her."

"Aha! Well then, we must do something about this."

"What do you have in mind?"

She paused to look St. Clair over. Even in the poorly lit hallway, he was arresting, if a little rakish. He was tall—Ophelia had a partiality for tall men—and he had quite good bone structure. What was more important, he had all the qualities of a fine gentleman—courtesy, tact, a sense of humor. True, sometimes he was a trifle somber, as if the weight of the world lay on his shoulders. But she suspected St. Clair would make a good husband for any woman, even a silly girl like Sophie.

As for Randolph's fears about his character ... Well, she couldn't believe them. Yes, there were times when St. Clair seemed a bit . . . well . . . dangerous, but so had her Edward, and he'd turned out fine.

Nonetheless, before she took the monumental step of telling him where Sophie was, she wanted to be more sure of her decision. And there was a way to do that while at the same time giving Blackmore the chance to court Emily properly.

With a glance at the crowd around them, she pulled St. Clair into a nearby empty box. "Do you like entertaining, Lord St. Clair?"

"What kind of entertaining?"

"Dinner parties. Picnics. Diversions. You do have a house in town, don't you? It would be no trouble at all for you to entertain. I'd do it myself, but it might look suspicious. And if two people who might not otherwise take the initiative to meet should happen to be invited, no one could blame you, could they?"

"Yes, but—"

"I should very much like to see your house, you know. If you're as serious about Sophie as you seem, I think it only fair that I assess your potential."

His eyes narrowed. "Fair indeed. Would your niece be equally interested in seeing my house?"

"I'm sure she would—if she were in London. But my brother has sent her off somewhere to keep her safe from certain unsuitable men."

The expression on his face was priceless. "Like me, you mean. Damn it, I knew there was something suspicious about her illness!"

"Yes, well, Randolph overreacts sometimes." She cast him a sly glance. "But if I determine that a man is *not* unsuitable after all, I might just be in a position to influence my brother. Or otherwise ensure that a wedding takes place, if you know what I mean."

He gave her a long, assessing look. "Lady Dundee, are you blackmailing me into having dinner parties at my house?"

"Not at all. I'm merely pointing out the great advantages that you, your friend, and my daughter could derive from such parties." When he seemed to mull that over, she added, "And that would allow me to assess Blackmore's potential for my daughter as well, wouldn't it?"

A reluctant smile creased his lips. "You are a sly, manipulative woman."

"Thank you. I try very hard to arrange the lives of my family so as to ensure the most happiness for them and the least inconvenience for me."

He chuckled. "Very well. I won't stand in the way of your machinations. I need an ally, and Jordan clearly needs a wife, even if he won't admit it. Since this is your idea, do you have any proposals about whom I should invite? Aside from you, Lady Emma, and Jordan, of course."

"Mr. Pollock, for one."

"Pollock? Why?"

"Blackmore seems jealous of his interest in my daughter, don't you think?" That was just a guess, of course. Her real reason for including the odious man in their party was to determine once and for all if Pollock might be the one after Sophie. She prayed he wasn't. She couldn't stomach having that man in the family.

"I wouldn't trust Pollock around Lady Emma if I were you," St. Clair said with a grim look on his face.

"I don't. But Blackmore will make sure the man treats her with respect, don't you think?"

"I suppose." His scowl faded. "Well, then, anything else?"

"Oh, I have a million suggestions. But come, we must return to the box before Emma wonders what has become of us. You and I will take care of the details later."

It was high time to end this foolishness. And before it was all over, she planned to make sure that Emily got something of worth out of it.

Chapter 13

One must choose in life between boredom and torment.

Madame de Staël,
Letter to Claude Rochet, 1800

A dinner party, of all things. Jordan still couldn't believe it. He climbed out of his coach at Ian's town house, shaking his head at his friend's odd behavior. Before his absence from England, Ian had kept to himself at his country estate. Jordan certainly never remembered his giving a dinner party. This sudden burst of conviviality was very uncharacteristic.

But then, so was the man's search for a wife. Jordan had never thought to see the day when Ian would be dancing attendance on the simpering girls at marriage marts. Soon Ian would be married, and there would be no more lazy afternoons fishing at Jordan's estate or hours spent debating politics in the Subscription Room at Brook's. Ian would be done with all that. He'd have little need for his friends, because he'd have a wife to keep him company, to share his thoughts and life.

To keep the loneliness at bay.

The thought shook Jordan. That was one thing

to be said for marriage: it meant the end of loneliness.

Or did it? His mother had been lonely, painfully so. And his father, too. Marriage didn't always end loneliness. Sometimes, it brought about a much worse loneliness, the kind that came from living side by side with a stranger.

He sighed. Pray God Ian chose his wife carefully and found someone who wouldn't ignore him. Jordan wouldn't wish his parents' sort of marriage on anyone.

The door opened as he reached the top of the marble stairs, and a footman took his greatcoat and top hat. A familiar female laugh drifted down to him from the drawing room upstairs, sparking a sudden anticipation in his belly. Was *she* here? Two days had passed since he'd spoken to her, though he'd seen her at several social functions. But if she were here . . .

How could she be? Surely Ian, with all his protective instincts, wouldn't have invited her. Still, his palms grew clammy as the servant led him upstairs. And when he entered the drawing room to find a knot of men gathered around Emily, drinking wine and relating stories that she laughed at with feminine delight, his throat went raw.

She was here, all right, and making the men lust after her as usual. For God's sake, why didn't Lady Dundee do something instead of sitting there and watching Emily with fond indulgence? Did the deuced countess *want* Emily to be hounded by a lot of lecherous fools?

At least Emily's gown was demure tonight, unlike that piece of scarlet seduction she'd worn to the opera. Rich folds of pale rose satin swathed her form, making her lips and cheeks look petal pink and soft. Sprigs of white orange blossoms encircled her golden hair like a fallen halo, and a strand of equally white pearls nestled between her breasts with a contented glow, drawing his envy. To rest between those soft mounds of flesh would bring contentment indeed.

"Well, if it isn't the good earl himself," said a cold voice. Jordan tore his gaze from the delectable image to find Pollock standing by the window, a wineglass of delicate crystal cupped in one equally delicate hand. "Welcome, Blackmore. You're missing a fine burgundy." Pollock held up the glass, then shifted his gaze to Emily. "And even finer company."

Pollock? Here? Had Ian gone mad? Didn't he realize Pollock had his eye on Emily? Oh, how he'd like to smash that dandy's face for even daring to look at her!

By some miracle, he made himself sound nonchalant. "Good evening, Pollock. If I'd known you were here, I would've hurried. I wouldn't want to miss your latest riveting account of your trip to your tailor."

At his sarcasm, the ladies tittered, the gentlemen smirked, and Lady Dundee cast him a calculating smile. Only Emily ignored him, turning her back deliberately to him.

Pollock gestured dismissively with one manicured hand. "At least I know what the ladies want to hear. You'd bore them with stories about your precious reforms."

"Ah, yes. God forbid we should discuss anything important, like how to feed the poor and provide the workingman with a decent wage. We're much better off focusing on the cut of your fancy coats."

"Why, you—" Pollock broke off as the glass he was holding shattered in his fist. "Damn you, Blackmore! Look what you've made me do!"

A pall fell on the room, the other guests staring in horror, uncertain what to do, where to look. This sort of thing just wasn't done.

Pollock grabbed at his hand, now studded with glass shards. "It's bleeding, for God's sake!" It was indeed, dripping down over Pollock's other hand and onto Ian's Moroccan carpet, the blood and burgundy mingling into a vermillion stream. "Somebody do something! Get a doctor!"

Whirling around, Emily hurried to Pollock's side. "Let me see that."

When he resisted at first, she caught his wrist and took out her handkerchief. "Stop it! You've cut an artery! Do you want to bleed to death?"

He went limp, his face turning ashen as she dragged up his lace-edged sleeve, then wound the handkerchief tightly around his forearm in a tourniquet.

Her commonsense reaction and lack of aversion to blood took Jordan by surprise, until he remembered the night he'd first met her, when she'd given Sophie some elixir and the two women had discussed her penchant for doctoring.

"Come over here," she commanded, leading Pollock to the settee. "We must pick the glass out of it. I'm afraid you've got quite a nasty gash. I may have to sew it up." She scanned the room, her eyes fixing on Ian, who was calming his guests. "Lord St. Clair, I'll need some towels and clean rags, a bowl of hot water, a needle, and some clean thread. Ask your cook for garlic, rosemary, or mint. And bring some brandy. Mr. Pollock will need it."

Ian called for a servant and passed on Emily's instructions, then returned his attention to his hapless guests, who were now milling around the chair where Emily sat.

"Rosemary and garlic?" Pollock snapped, as she

bent her head over his hand. "Sounds like you're making a soup."

"Both are good for treating wounds. I'd prefer eucalyptus," Emily muttered, "but I doubt Lord St. Clair keeps that on hand."

"What does a mere girl know about doctoring anyway? It's not exactly the pastime for an earl's daughter."

Jordan's blood chilled in his veins. There was a vague suspicion in Pollock's tone. The man couldn't possibly know anything. Still . . .

"Surely you've heard of the Scottish penchant for physic," Jordan said. "I believe it's common for even their women to learn such things. Isn't that true, Lady Dundee?"

The countess raised one eyebrow. "Oh, certainly. My Emma has learned from the best doctors. You're in safe hands with a Scot, Mr. Pollock."

"I never heard any such thing about the Scottish," Pollock grumbled. Emily dug out a piece of glass, and he jerked his hand. "Ouch! Are you trying to murder me?"

"I will if you don't sit still! Would you rather we send for a doctor? Then you can bleed to death while you wait for him to arrive."

Pollock lapsed into a resentful silence. The servant entered, bearing the items Emily had requested, and Ian tactfully offered to take the ladies on a tour of the house so they wouldn't have to watch. The other men left with them, as did Lady Dundee. Only Jordan remained. He wasn't about to leave Emily alone with Pollock for one minute.

"Staying to gloat over my pain?" Pollock snapped at Jordan.

"Not at all. But Lady Emma might need something else."

"Yes, make yourself useful." Emily's calm, clear

gaze met his for the first time all evening. She handed him a rag. "Tear that into strips, will you?"

"Don't give that to him," Pollock muttered peevishly. "He might put poison on it."

Jordan bit the ragged edge with his teeth, then tore a strip loose. "I *ought* to poison you. The world would be better off without men foolish enough to cut themselves on wineglasses."

"Why, you arrogant ass!" Pollock said, half-rising in his seat.

"That's enough, both of you!" Emily jerked Pollock back down. "You're not helping matters, Mr. Pollock." She glared at Jordan. "Nor are you. This is all your fault, you know. If you hadn't provoked him—"

"How was I to know he couldn't take a joke?" Jordan said unrepentantly as he handed her the strips of rags.

She took them with a scowl. Crushing rosemary and garlic together between her fingers, she pressed the pulpy mass against the wound, then wrapped the bandage around it. "It wasn't a joke. It was just another case of your showing contempt for anybody who doesn't meet your high and noble standards."

The words of rebuke brought him up short. Was that what she thought of him?

Pollock watched them both, a slow smile curling his lips. "Exactly, Lady Emma. You know the man well. He looks down on us mere mortals. And he certainly doesn't understand men with sensitive tastes like me." He covered her hand as she bound his wound, and his gaze drifted down to ogle her breasts. "Or women of kindness like you."

Jealous fires seared Jordan. And when she went still, blushing to the roots of her hair, the fires flamed even higher.

Quickly, she finished binding the wound, then mumbled, "The servant forgot the brandy, and I know you must be in pain. I'll fetch it."

As soon as she had gone, Pollock leaned back and cast him a taunting glance. "I was wrong, after all. She's very good at doctoring, isn't she? She has a soft touch."

Jordan could hardly see for the anger clouding his vision. "You stay away from her, Pollock, do you hear me? She's not your sort."

Pollock smiled, examining his bandaged hand with fastidious interest. "I suppose you think she's *your* sort."

"Stay away from her. That's all."

"I will if she will. But as you can see, the woman can't keep her hands off me."

"Don't be absurd." He added snidely, "She amuses herself by helping idiots."

Pollock's gaze shot to him, resentful, devious. "Really? Is that what she was doing that night she and I were together in Lady Astramont's garden?"

The blood drained from Jordan's face. He told himself that Pollock was lying to pay him back for making a fool of him in front of Ian's guests. But there'd been that blush of Emily's every time Pollock was mentioned, and what she'd told him last night about Pollock's advances . . .

"You know, Emma kisses like an angel," Pollock remarked. "And those breasts, so ripe to the touch—"

"You bastard!" Jordan reached Pollock in two strides and jerked him out of the chair. "You keep your filthy hands off her!"

Pollock smirked at him. "Don't tell me you've taken a fancy to her. She's more my sort than yours, you know. At least *I'd* marry her."

The words were a shock of cold water in his face.

At least I'd marry her. Would Pollock marry her? Even if he knew who she really was?

More importantly, would she marry Pollock? Why else would she have let the man touch her, if not to gain a rich husband?

No, he couldn't believe that of her! He couldn't!

He thrust Pollock away with an oath. "Get away from me, before I shove all your lies down your dirty throat!"

"Lies, eh?" Pollock said smugly as he dusted off his frock coat. "Perhaps you should ask Lady Emma what we were doing in Lady Astramont's garden the night of the breakfast." He shrugged. "Or perhaps you'd better not. You might not like the answer."

With thunder in his brow, Jordan advanced on Pollock.

The scoundrel stood his ground, a cruel laugh escaping his lips. "So the man who can't feel has finally met his match, has he? Good. I hope she breaks your frigging heart." Then Pollock turned on his heel and walked out.

Jordan stood there, Pollock's nasty words careening through in his brain. They were lies, nothing but lies! She wouldn't have let Pollock put his hands on her. She wouldn't have!

The source of his torment made the grand mistake of entering just then, bearing a bottle of brandy in her lily-white hands. She looked startled to see him alone. "Where's Mr. Pollock? He may want this brandy for the pain."

"Such elaborate concern for a reprobate," he snapped. "I wonder why Mr. Pollock's pain should disturb you so much."

"I don't like to see *anyone* hurt. At home, I always patched people up. It's my specialty."

"And is letting them make free with your body your specialty, too?"

She stiffened. "If you're talking about what happened between you and me in the museum—"

"I'm talking about what happened between you and Pollock at Lady Astramont's, deuce take it!"

The blood drained from her face. "He . . . he told you about that?"

No denials. No protests. Just guilt. He felt as if his guts were being wrenched out with a pitchfork. "Oh, yes, he was quite happy to boast of how he kissed and fondled you!"

"He didn't!" She paused, confusion in her face. "I . . . I mean . . . well . . . it wasn't like that—"

"So he told the truth." The words tasted like ashes in his mouth. "And how many other men have put their hands on you?"

Her confusion faded, replaced by fury. "How dare you! It's acceptable for *you* to put your hands all over me, even though you freely admit you never intend to marry. But no one else must touch me, is that it? Only you can 'make free with my body'?"

"If you're nurturing some foolish notion that Pollock will marry you, you'd best forget it. Once you tell him who you really are, he won't come near you. You can lay money on that!"

"Thank you for reminding me yet again of my inferior class," she said bitterly. "I'm good enough for you to maul, but not good enough for either of you to marry, is that it? Don't worry, Jordan. I've no intention of forgetting my place—with you *or* with Mr. Pollock."

It dawned on him how his words must have sounded just as she whirled on her heel and opened the door. "Now, Emily, I didn't mean—"

But she was already walking out the door, her

head held so high it was a miracle it didn't fall off her elegant little neck. Cursing himself for being so blunt, he started after her, then spotted Ian and the others coming down the stairs from the second floor. Quickly, he ducked back into the drawing room. The last thing he wanted was to make polite conversation when jealousy raged through him like a wild bull.

He heard a servant in the hall announce that dinner was served. Then Ian said, "Why don't all of you go down to dinner? I'll just fetch the others."

Jordan glanced about the room, looking for an escape. But there was none. Next thing he knew, Ian was sauntering into the room.

The viscount looked around, bewildered. "Where's Pollock? And Lady Emma?"

"Who knows?" He couldn't prevent the acid edge to his voice. "She's probably off 'comforting' him the way only a woman can. You might try one of the bedrooms."

Ian arched one eyebrow. "Your jealousy is showing, Jordan. You know quite well Lady Emma would never go off into a bedroom with Pollock."

"Wouldn't she?" He stared unseeing into the fireplace, feeling a sudden childish urge to kick at the embers. "Pollock seems to think otherwise. He implied he'd come close to having her."

"Pollock will say whatever he can to provoke you. You know that. It's just lies."

"Then why didn't she deny it?"

"You actually repeated Pollock's words to her?"

At Ian's incredulous tone, Jordan faced his friend. "Yes. Why not?"

"Bloody hell, have you no sense at all when it comes to respectable women?"

"No," he growled. "If you'll recall, I don't usually deal with them."

"Well, you don't accuse a well-bred woman of being free with her affections, unless you deliberately want to insult her. And you especially don't tell her you heard it from some idiot, then actually believed it."

Jordan strained to remember the entirety of their conversation. "She admitted she'd been alone with him."

"And she admitted that he'd touched her?"

"Not exactly. But she blushes every time his name is mentioned."

"I see. And this is your evidence. I wish you could hear yourself. If any other man had told you such a tale, you would have laughed him out of countenance." He shook his head. "Why do you care anyway? If you've no interest in marrying the girl, what does it matter if Pollock courts her?"

Jordan shoved his hands in his pockets. Emily had said much the same thing. "He's no good for her. You know that. He'll take advantage of her, then refuse to marry her." *When he finds out who she really is.* "Why did you invite the bastard anyway?"

Ian hesitated before answering. "Actually, inviting Pollock was Lady Dundee's idea. I wouldn't have, but she insisted upon it."

Good God. What if Lady Dundee and Lord Nesfield had some strange idea of marrying Emily off to Pollock? "What does Lady Dundee have to do with this?"

"The dinner party was her idea. She promised to press my courtship of Sophie with Nesfield. But first she wanted some idea of my potential as a husband."

Ian's words caught Jordan by surprise. "What do you mean? Have things advanced so far with Lady Sophie? Why, you haven't even seen the girl in weeks!"

"That doesn't change anything. I still have very serious intentions toward her."

Jordan remembered what his butler had told him that morning. "I think there's something you should be aware of, my friend. When Hargraves was asking Nesfield's servants about Lady Emma, he discovered that Lady Sophie isn't in town. She hasn't been for some time. I'm not even sure she's ill."

"Yes, I know."

"You know?"

"Lady Dundee told me. Apparently Nesfield whisked his daughter away to the country to protect her from 'scoundrels' like me." He smiled. "But the countess has decided that her brother is a fool. She says that if I prove acceptable, she'll find a way to get around Nesfield's objections."

"Ah." That made perfect sense. It was just like Nesfield to do something so dramatic, and just like Lady Dundee to do as she pleased. So Sophie's absence apparently had nothing to do with Emily's masquerade. Or else the countess and the marquess hadn't wanted Sophie around mucking up things while they finished their plot.

But what *was* their plot?

Inviting Pollock was Lady Dundee's idea. Devil take it, this had something to do with Pollock. Otherwise, why would Emily ever have gone near the man? And now that he thought about it, she'd spent a great deal of time with Pollock at that first ball as well.

The thought of Pollock and Emily together made his skin crawl.

"Are you all right?" Ian asked. "You're looking pale."

"I'm fine. Just a little hungry."

"Then I guess we'd best go down to dinner."

Jordan followed Ian out of the room. He was hungry, all right. Hungry to know what was going on.

At least now he had a way to make Emily tell him the truth. Oh, yes, he had a little surprise to spring on Emily once he could get her alone. And no amount of tears and begging would put him off this time.

Emily glanced across the dining-room table to where Jordan sat beside an attractive and decidedly well-endowed young widow. Thank heaven his attention was drawn to his companion. Perhaps the wretched woman would even convince him to leave the party early. Emily would be quite happy if she did. Truly.

"You want to scratch her eyes out, don't you?" Mr. Pollock whispered in her ear.

A curse on Lord St. Clair for seating her next to Mr. Pollock. The daughter of an earl was *not* supposed to be taken in to dinner by a mere mister. Perhaps Lord St. Clair, being a bachelor, didn't know such things. He *had* said this was his first time to give a dinner party. Still, Lady Dundee should have set him straight in the drawing room.

Of course, the viscount hadn't erred in the least with the rest of the seating. Oh, no. That's why Jordan was seated between Lady Dundee and the beautiful countess. The countess whose eyes Emily indeed wanted to scratch out, although she'd never admit it to anyone.

"I have no idea what you're talking about," she blithely lied to Mr. Pollock as she concentrated on slicing a piece of roast beef.

"The merry widow sitting with Blackmore. She's just his sort, you know."

Emily's hand on the knife shook. She knew only

too well. The woman was perfect for him: sensuous and lush and obviously available, if one was to judge from the way she kept thrusting her ample breasts up in his face and leaning on his arm. Well, let the widow have him. Since the man only seemed to want tarts, he deserved her.

"I know we got off to a bad start," Pollock whispered again, "but we could put all that behind us. I promise I'd do better by you than Blackmore." He laid his bandaged hand on her thigh. "Any man who prefers common crockery to fine china is a fool."

The scoundrel never gave up, did he? Laying her knife carefully down, she slipped her hand under the table to grab his wounded one and squeezed it just until she heard him curse under his breath. "Mr. Pollock, if you touch me again, I will smash a piece of fine china on your head. Do we understand one another?"

Lifting his hand, she dropped it in his lap, then returned to cutting her meat.

"You're saving yourself for *him*, I suppose," Pollock said in a nasty voice as he nursed his hand. "Well, he won't marry you."

"The last thing in the world I want is to marry Lord Blackmore."

What a blatant lie. For days now she'd pretended to herself that she didn't care what he thought or did, that his lack of interest in her as a prospective wife didn't matter. And all the time, she knew she cared far too much. She wanted to ravage the face of the woman across from her, the one with the good fortune to be an attractive widow. She wanted to rail at Jordan for his coldness and his absolute control over his emotions. She wanted to hate him for believing all the nasty things Pollock had probably said about her.

But she couldn't hate him. If this had been any other place and time, if she and he had been of equal standing and wealth, she would have risked anything to have him.

Curse him for that!

As if he'd heard her thoughts, he glanced her way, his gaze flicking first to Mr. Pollock, then to her. His jaw tightened. Then he turned his head abruptly and leaned to whisper something in the widow's ear that made her laugh.

Emily colored, wondering what he was saying and, worse yet, doing. Was he touching the widow beneath the table as Pollock had tried to do to her? Or making an assignation to meet the woman later? Her heart constricted painfully at the thought.

It seemed an eternity before the meal was over and another eternity before she and the other women could retire to the drawing room and escape the men. How wonderful to be away from them all! If this interminable masquerade were ever over, she would never speak to one of their gender again! They were more trouble than they were worth!

Unfortunately, she had scarcely settled into a comfortable chair when yet another male appeared at her side. Everyone looked up as the footman handed her a folded handkerchief and said, "You forgot this in the dining room, madam."

"But it's not mine—" she began as she took it from him. Then she saw the Blackmore monogram and felt the stiff crackle of paper inside the cloth. "Oh, I'm sorry. Yes, it is mine. Thank you."

She waited until everyone's attention turned elsewhere, then carefully opened the note in her lap.

Make some excuse to leave, it said. *I'll meet you in the hall. I have something to discuss with you.*

Cursing inwardly, she balled the paper up into a tiny knot. She could just imagine what he wanted to discuss. No doubt he wished to make more filthy insinuations about her and Mr. Pollock. The wretch! Did he think she was at his beck and call?

Yes, he did. And with good reason. He held the knowledge of her real identity in his hand. He could make her dance to his tune whenever he wanted, and he knew it.

She waited until Lady Dundee's attention was diverted, then murmured to the woman nearest her that she was going to use the necessary. Thankfully, no one paid her much mind when she slipped out the door.

There he was, in the hall as he'd promised, leaning against the wall with his hands shoved deep in his coat pockets. Pushing away from the wall, he caught her with a look designed to strip away her defenses.

She wrapped her lace shawl protectively about her body. "What do you want?"

Gripping her arm, he led her down the hall a short distance. "We must talk. But not now. Tomorrow morning I shall come to take you riding, and you will go with me, do you understand? Find some way to leave your maid and Lady Dundee at home. You and I shall have a very long, very private chat, and you will tell me the truth at last."

"Will I indeed? Why do you think I'll be more likely to do that now than I was before?"

A smug smile touched his lips. "Because now I know more about what you're up to. This has something to do with Pollock, doesn't it? If you don't tell me the truth, I'll tell Pollock everything I know." His smile faded abruptly. "That ought to put an end to whatever your scheme is."

So he'd figured that much out, had he? Or was

he just guessing? She crossed her arms over her chest, trying to hide her trembling. "Tell him what you wish," she bluffed. "It doesn't matter. I shan't go riding with you tomorrow, and I certainly shan't tell you anything."

His mouth thinned into a grim line. "Very well. I'll speak with Pollock in the morning. But first I shall confront Nesfield. I know that he's behind this. Perhaps he won't share your nonchalance when I tell him I'm planning to reveal your identity to Pollock."

Horror swept through her. Lord Nesfield! If he told Lord Nesfield—

"You can't! You mustn't!" she protested, dropping all pretense of unconcern. "Please, Jordan, don't do this!"

"Why? Just tell me that, and you have my silence."

She was tempted, oh so tempted to tell him everything. But that was impossible. Once she told him that this concerned Sophie, he would realize that it concerned Ian as well. He'd never stand for having his friend's chances for happiness destroyed. He'd go to Lord Nesfield anyway, and then Nesfield would make good on his threats.

The thought made her shudder. "I-I can't."

"Then tomorrow I'll pay Nesfield a visit."

"But you promised me you'd keep silent! What kind of honorable man reneges on his promises?"

He scowled. "The kind who sees the sort of danger you're getting yourself into. The kind who wants to protect you from the likes of Pollock and Nesfield."

"Pollock? That's what this is about, isn't it? You're jealous of Pollock and the other men around me, so you—"

"I'm not jealous!" he bit out. But his rigid stance

and angry expression belied his words. "My reasons don't matter. Either you tell me everything, or I go to Nesfield. It's as simple as that." When she stared at him, frantically wondering how to change his mind, he added, "You have tonight to make your decision. But in the morning—"

"In the morning, you will ruin my life!"

His jaw tightened. "Don't be so melodramatic. Any connection between you and Pollock would be far more ruinous to you than my mild interference."

Mild interference? Oh, if only he knew. "It's not . . . this awful thing you're imagining, I assure you. You know I could never engage in something truly distasteful."

"Do I? What do I really know about you? You're adept at masquerades, and you can quote scripture when it suits you." His gaze flickered over her body. "And you have a talent for making men want you. That's all I know. You've toyed with Pollock, and God knows you've toyed with me. And for what? Tell me that."

"You . . . you make it sound so . . . sordid."

"From where I'm standing, it certainly looks that way."

Curse him! He had a right to be suspicious, but what more could she tell him? How was she to escape this thorny mess?

Suddenly a voice called to them down the hall. "Blackmore, is that you?"

It was Lord St. Clair. She cast Jordan a pleading look.

"Don't worry, I won't say a word to Ian. But tomorrow, I will reveal your identity to whomever I wish." He strolled past her toward his friend, as casually as if he'd been carrying on the most insipid conversation with her. "I was just coming to see you, Ian. Sorry, but I have to leave."

"So early? Don't you wish to stay for the dancing?"

"You're having dancing? Good God, that isn't like you."

The viscount shrugged. "Perhaps I've been too long away from society."

Jordan looked grim. "Or perhaps you're letting certain people influence you." When Lord St. Clair scowled at him, he added, "In any case, I can't stay. Business and all that. You understand."

Lord St. Clair's gaze shot past Jordan to her. "Not really. But you'll do exactly as you please as usual."

Jordan glanced back at her, a taunting smile on his lips. "Good night, Lady Emma. I'll be at your town house at ten tomorrow. Don't forget."

She glared at him. Forget! He knew quite well she wouldn't forget! She would never forgive him for this—never!

Lord St. Clair showed his friend out, then came back to where she was still standing, her hands working her shawl into knots.

"Lady Emma, are you all right?" Gently, he took the corner of her shawl from her clenched fingers. "My friend seems to have distressed you."

"Your friend *always* distresses me! At the moment, I'd like to see his head on a platter!"

He laughed. "A bloodthirsty sentiment for a lady."

But I'm not a lady, she thought sourly. *That's the trouble.*

Too bad she couldn't tell him that. Donning her best Lady Emma persona, she cast him a haughty look. "We Scots are a bloodthirsty lot. And we don't take kindly to arrogant English lords who meddle in other people's affairs."

"I hope he wasn't discussing Pollock with you again."

Her eyes widened. "Jordan told you about that? Never mind about his head on a platter! It belongs on a spike!"

"Calm down, Lady Emma. I came upon him when he was angry, and he spoke out of turn. But I defended your honor to him, I assure you, and reminded him of what an idiot Pollock is. Jordan would normally ignore the man's lies, but he's prone to jealousy where you're concerned. You should be flattered: no other woman has ever succeeded in making him jealous."

"Yes, I'm quite flattered," she said with heavy sarcasm. "What woman wouldn't want the attentions of a man who has no desire to marry, yet has the audacity to be jealous of every man who smiles at her?" Tears welled in her eyes, and she cursed them, turning away from Lord St. Clair to hide her face. She shouldn't have said so much. He would guess the true nature of her feelings.

"What do you mean—'has no desire to marry'?"

She blotted her eyes with the end of her shawl. "You know what I mean. Everyone knows about Jor—About Lord Blackmore. How he only consorts with 'experienced' women like that . . . that widowed countess, how he has a heart of stone." Her voice sounded overwrought, yet she couldn't calm herself. "He's proud of his immunity to normal human emotions, for goodness sake! He boasts of it!"

Lord St. Clair was quiet a long moment. Then he laid his hand on her arm. "That's true. But I think he boasts of it precisely because he fears those emotions. He's not as impervious as you think."

"Yes, he is," she whispered, remembering his cold refusal to consider her pleas.

"Lady Emma, shall I tell you a bit about my

friend? It might help you to understand his strange behavior."

"Nothing could make me understand him!"

"All the same, come with me to my study. I think you'll want to hear this."

She nodded, allowing him to lead her down the hall. She might as well hear him out, though he could say nothing to change her mind. Jordan was just one of those men who were empty inside. The sooner she accepted that, the better.

Chapter 14

The best way to get the better of temptation is just to yield to it.

Clementina Stirling Graham,
Scottish writer, *Mystifications*

Hours later, Emily stared out the window of the carriage, thinking of what Lord St. Clair had told her about Jordan. So much heartache, so much pain for a child. It was no wonder he prevented himself from feeling. In his place, she might have done the same.

"You're very quiet this evening, my dear," said Lady Dundee. "Didn't you think the dinner went well?"

"I suppose." A thought suddenly occurred to her. "Were you able to learn anything from Lord St. Clair? I'm eager to end my masquerade." If Lady Dundee had discovered anything conclusive, then they could tell Lord Nesfield. Lord Nesfield would take action, and then it would be too late for Jordan to interfere.

Yes, Lord Nesfield would take action: to ruin Lord St. Clair. She bit her lip. Then Jordan would truly hate her, wouldn't he? She was helping Lord Nesfield destroy his friend's hopes.

"I'm afraid I didn't learn much," Lady Dundee said, her eyes sparkling with an irritating merriment. "We shall just have to go on a bit longer."

Emily wanted to scream. "But we can't! Lord Blackmore has figured out that this concerns Mr. Pollock, and now he's threatened to tell Mr. Pollock everything!"

The woman looked maddeningly nonchalant about the entire matter. "Really? Blackmore said that?"

"Yes. He said he'd give me tonight to make up my mind. In the morning he's calling for me, and if I still won't tell him the truth, he'll reveal my identity to Mr. Pollock. The wretch! You know Mr. Pollock will delight in tearing us all down publicly. What's more, it will put Lord St. Clair on his guard and effectively end our chances to find out if he's the one."

Lady Dundee waved her hand dismissively. "Oh, Blackmore won't do such a thing, depend upon it. He'll threaten, but he won't act. Not as long as *you* are involved."

"I fear you're wrong. Especially after what I learned tonight." She turned in her seat to face Lady Dundee. "Tell me something. You must be about the same age that Jordan's mother would have been if she'd lived. Did you know her? What was she like?"

"Lavinia? She was a flirt, that's what. She enjoyed men and balls and never paid any attention to what her parents said. But then, I was a bit like that myself."

"And Jordan's father?"

"Oh, he was nothing like her at all. That was certainly a mismatch. He was the sober sort. Unlike his son, he didn't spend his time with . . . ladies of the evening. In other respects, however, they're

very much alike. He was earnestly devoted to reform and rarely attended social functions. Everyone was quite surprised when Lavinia, of all
people, captivated him so much that he married
her."

Emily hesitated a moment, wondering if she
should reveal what Lord St. Clair had told her. But
she so badly needed advice, and she knew she
could trust Lady Dundee to keep quiet. Besides,
she needed to impress upon the countess the gravity of the situation. "Actually, Jordan's father *had*
to marry Jordan's mother. One day when they happened to be alone, the earl became overcome by his
desire for her and they . . . well . . . you know. Then
she found herself *enceinte*, so she was forced to
marry the earl."

"Poppycock."

"It's true! Lord St. Clair says so! Jordan told him
about it when they were boys. According to Lord
St. Clair, Lady Blackmore hated her forced marriage so much that she drank a great deal and
made Jordan's life a misery."

"Oh, I don't deny that Blackmore's father probably impregnated Lavinia. She was a pretty girl
and very fast. Nor do I doubt she was the kind of
mother you describe. Married to a man who preferred to spend his evenings discussing Horace's
poetry and who probably wouldn't humor her
whims, Lavinia *was* the sort to turn to drink. The
poor girl had few resources within herself to create
her own entertainment."

Her voice grew grim. "But I'd wager a fortune
she was the one to seduce the earl, and not the other
way around. Lavinia's father was a mere baronet
and had little money besides. The earl would have
been quite a catch for her. I imagine she thought it

would be grand fun to be married to an earl ... until she actually was."

Emily considered that a moment, the creaking of the springs the only sound in the carriage. Then she sighed. "If that's true, it only makes it more awful. Lord St. Clair says she always blamed her unhappy life on Jordan and his untimely conception. She used to tell him that he'd ruined her life, that she was in hell because of him."

Lady Dundee pursed her lips. "What a dreadful thing to say to an innocent child. Lavinia never could take responsibility for her own actions."

"That's why he won't trust his heart to anyone. In his experience, opening your heart to someone is dangerous, if not disastrous." He must find her masquerade very suspicious. It probably looked like the sort of scheming his mother had engaged in. In a way, it was. "So he won't hesitate to make good on his threats. I know he won't."

"But he's already opened his heart to you a little, hasn't he? He has yet to reveal your secret. And I don't think he will." She cast Emily that mysterious smile again. "Even if he does, it won't be so bad. It might hasten matters."

"You don't understand! I tried to tell him I didn't care if he told Mr. Pollock, but he said he'd also try to get the truth from your brother! He's very persistent!"

"Then let him speak to Randolph. What does it matter? It might even be a good thing: Randolph might be forced to end this foolishness. Then I can convince him to accept St. Clair as Sophie's suitor."

The countess's vaguely smug voice struck fear in Emily's heart. "Oh, don't even think that! You know your brother won't accept the viscount! And he'd blame *me* for destroying all his plans! He'd never forgive me!"

"Pish-posh, what if he doesn't?" When she saw Emily's agitation, she added, "If it's your father's living you're worried about, there's no problem. I suppose Randolph has threatened to cut your father off. That's why you've been so worried, isn't it?"

Emily just stared at her, her fingers curling into the satin upholstery in frustration.

"Well, you needn't concern yourself about that. Even if Randolph did as he threatened, which I can't imagine he would, I'd make sure that your father found another equally attractive living." She smiled and patted Emily's hand. "So you see, there's nothing for you to worry about. You must leave it all to me."

Nothing for her to worry about! Lord Nesfield was willing to see her hanged, and she had nothing to worry about? How she wished she could explain that to the countess! But Lord Nesfield had promised to keep silent only if she did, too. She was wretchedly trapped between Lady Dundee's meddling and Jordan's obsession.

"So don't you worry about Lord Blackmore, my dear," Lady Dundee went on, apparently thinking she'd solved all of Emily's problems. "We will weather the storm if he speaks to Pollock or Randolph."

It was all Emily could do to paste a false smile on her face and give the countess a nod. She'd find no help here. She'd have to discover a way out of this mess on her own.

But how?

The coach slowed almost to a stop, and the sounds of horses and loud voices assailed their ears. Lady Dundee peered out the window. "Oh, dear, the ball at Mrs. Crampton's must be quite lively. There are carriages and hackney coaches everywhere blocking the road. We'll have to walk the last little bit, I'm afraid."

They were nearly in sight of the house, so walking wasn't too awful, especially with the footmen to aid them in the more crowded spots. Indeed, Emily was glad to get out into the night air. She only wished it was the bracing, clean air of Willow Crossing, not London's smoke-choked ether. She badly needed to clear her mind, to figure out some plan.

Gingerly, they picked their way among the horses and coaches, trying not to soil their gowns. "It appears we're in for a long night," Lady Dundee complained as a coachman shouted to one of his friends. "We won't get any sleep with all this racket. A pity. You'll need all your wits about you for meeting Lord Blackmore in the morning." She cast Emily a sidelong glance. "You know he only torments you because he cares for you."

"Cares for me?" she said in a burst of anger. "And all this time I'd thought you a wise woman. Obviously, I mistook madness for wisdom."

"Sometimes they're the same. Madness can be a symptom of wisdom. Those who know the truth aren't always happy to hear it, you know." She smiled and lowered her voice so the footman at her side couldn't hear her. "But in this case, I'm neither mad nor wise. I'm merely stating what any woman my age knows. Men are peculiar creatures very different from us, my dear. When they want something badly, they don't like to admit it. No man wants to need a woman for anything. But since they *do* need us, and for more than merely our presence in their beds, their only recourse is to hound us while stoutly proclaiming they only want their desires fulfilled."

"Lord Blackmore does only want his desires fulfilled," Emily whispered. "Sometimes it's as if he's angry at me because he desires me and can't have me."

"I'm sure that's part of it. Though I suspect that even if you were to leap into his bed and give him exactly what he wanted, he would still be unfulfilled."

Emily blushed at the countess's frankness. Lady Dundee was wrong. Jordan wanted only one thing from Emily. If she were to give it to him, he'd go away at once and leave her alone.

She straightened. That's exactly what he'd do! Leave her alone!

He professed to be concerned for her, but she knew he only wanted to find out the truth because he was jealous. And his jealousy came from a lack of having his desires satisfied. He wanted her in his bed, but he wouldn't take her if it meant having to marry her.

So what if she offered him what he wanted, making it clear she didn't expect anything in return? Perhaps after his appetites were appeased, he'd give up this foolish obsession with knowing everything. Then his interest in her would wane, and with it, his interest in her masquerade.

"Emily, have you heard a word I said?" Lady Dundee remarked.

In sudden fear that the countess might guess the direction of her thoughts, she lowered her gaze to the paved street, pretending to watch her step in the darkness. "Yes."

"I said even if you gave him what he wanted, he would still be unfulfilled."

"I know what you said." She just didn't believe it. For too many years, Jordan had hardened himself against feeling anything but lust. After a lifetime of merely satisfying his carnal appetites, he wasn't likely to change now. No, if she gave him what he wanted, she would be free of him.

But at what a cost!

As they reached the house, she entered behind Lady Dundee, her thoughts in a turmoil. If she offered him her body in exchange for his silence, she would save Papa. And ruin her future. She might even find herself with child, like Jordan's mother.

Well, she could only pray that wouldn't happen. And if it did, it was a small price to pay to keep from going to the gallows. Compared to Lord Nesfield's plans for her, one night with Jordan would be no risk at all. And it must be tonight, before Jordan could make good on his threats.

A sudden dreadful thought popped into her mind. What if he refused to accept her bargain?

Carter helped her remove her pelisse, and she glanced down despairingly at her satin gown with its modest cut and girlish color that made her look like the virginal rector's daughter she truly was. Jordan would never agree to this. He'd restrained himself from touching or kissing her at the opera, even when he'd wanted to, and all because of his aversion to innocent young women and the complications they could bring to his life.

She stiffened. All right then, it wouldn't be the pure Emily Fairchild who went to him: it would be Lady Emma. His words this evening proved that he already doubted her character; she'd use that to her advantage. Tonight she would strike a bargain with him, even if she had to seduce him, and yes, lie to him about her virginity.

Or was she considering this only because she desired him? Because she wished to experience lovemaking with the only man she'd ever truly wanted?

Surely she couldn't be that wicked. No, this was

her best course of action. Her only course of action.

Carter shot the lock to in the massive oak doors behind them, and the sound reverberated through her brain. How could she sneak out of this fortress and find her way to Jordan's town house? Dear heavens, she didn't even know where he lived!

The slurred voices of drunken hackney coachmen drifted inside from the street.

Hackney coachmen, Emily thought with a smile. *Perfect.*

"You go on to bed now, my dear," said Lady Dundee. "Try to get some rest."

Emily's smile faded. That was one thing she was unlikely to get this evening. Rest—of any kind.

Jordan lay comfortably stretched out on the chaise longue in his study. He was in his shirt-sleeves with his boots off and a brandy snifter cradled in one hand as he tried to read through a proposal for workhouse reform. He couldn't concentrate, however. He finally laid the proposal down and stared off into space.

Tomorrow he would know everything. She would tell him for certain. The fear in her face had made that clear. He didn't like frightening her, especially when he had no intention of making good on his threats. He wished he could get the truth from her some other way, but he couldn't. And he must put an end to the men preying on her. Even if Pollock had been lying or had only kissed her once, the bastard would take more if he had the chance—and he might *get* that chance if Emily continued to associate with him. No, this couldn't go on. Jordan would force her to end it before disaster struck.

A knock came at the closed door, startling him. "Go away! I told you I wasn't to be disturbed!"

"But there's a female here to see you," the servant replied.

A female. He laid his snifter aside with a groan. That was how his servants referred to his soiled doves, but surely no tart would dare to come here without a summons. He hadn't even brought so much as a randy widow home with him in months. Not since he'd met Emily.

Emily. As if any other woman could capture his attention now.

"Give her some money and send her away," he ordered.

"I tried that, milord. She won't take it. I told her you didn't want to be disturbed, but she insists. Says her name is Emily, and you'd want to see her."

He sat up straight. Emily? Here? Was the woman insane?

In an instant, he was at the door and flinging it open. "Why didn't you say so, for God's sake? Show her up here at once!"

The servant nodded and hurried off, wearing a look of complete bewilderment. Jordan glanced down at his stocking feet, then over to where he'd tossed his cravat, cutaway, and waistcoat across a chair. Should he put them back on? Should he at least pretend this wasn't the most improper situation she'd ever put him in?

What was the point? If she were fool enough to come here alone and risk her reputation just to beg him to relent, then she deserved to be shocked.

"Miss Emily," announced the servant.

Jordan turned to the door as the servant ushered her into the room, and his jaw dropped. She wasn't likely to be shocked by *his* attire, for God's sake. Look at what *she* was wearing.

The scarlet gown from the opera, the one he'd

wanted to tear off her. Only this time it was worse, for he'd swear she wore nothing under it—no petticoats, no corset, perhaps even no chemise. As she entered the room, the shimmering velvet clung to her legs and her delicious curves like gilt wrapping paper encasing every man's dream of a birthday gift.

Except that he couldn't open it, wasn't allowed to open it, damn it. He sucked in air, futilely trying to catch his breath as she approached. Her lavender scent surrounded him like a cloud of temptation, yet all he could do was gape at her.

"Milord?" said the servant. "Will that be all?"

"Yes," he said in a strangled voice. "And this time I truly do *not* wish to be disturbed."

Emily colored but said nothing as the servant left, closing the door behind him.

"What the devil are you doing here?" he exploded. "How did you get here?"

She swallowed. "I climbed out a window and took a hackney coach. I found one who knew where you lived."

"You took a hackney? In *that*? It's a wonder you weren't mauled!"

"I wore a cloak until I got here, but your footman insisted upon taking it from me."

"I'll kill him tomorrow," he muttered. No one should ever be allowed to see her like this. No one but him.

Sternly, he reminded himself of why she had probably come. Crossing to the chaise longue, he picked up his brandy snifter and took a great gulp of the fiery liquor. If only it could smother the greater fire in his loins. But that wasn't likely. Only one thing would smother that fire, and although she stood before him wearing the most enticing of gowns, she wasn't available.

He refused to look at her. If he did, he couldn't be responsible for his actions. "I suppose you've come here dressed like that because you think it'll distract me from my purpose."

"No."

The softly spoken answer took him by surprise. He whirled to stare at her. "You're not hoping to make me give up my plans?"

"Actually, I've come to . . . offer you a bargain." Her chin was trembling and her hands, too, but she held herself as proudly straight as if she were dressed in a Quaker's prudish woolen dress. "You said at the opera that you want me. Well—" She hesitated a moment, as if gathering her courage. Then she swept her hands downward to indicate her body. "You can have me."

For the first time in his life, he found himself utterly speechless. Surely she didn't mean what he thought she meant. Not his virginal rector's daughter.

At his silence, she went on more nervously. "I'll give you my body freely for one night. In exchange, you must promise not to speak to Lord Nesfield or Mr. Pollock." She took a deep breath, then went on in a rush. "I won't expect anything of you other than that. I don't want you to marry me. I merely want you to keep quiet."

And for that, she would do this? For a moment, he actually considered the offer and all it would mean. He could strip off her gown and caress each golden curve. He could fondle those sweet breasts, part those slender legs, and bury himself deep inside her with impunity. He could find release. Finally.

After all, he'd never really intended to go to Nesfield. It had all been a bluff.

But if he gave in, accepted her offer, he'd lose his

only method of convincing her to tell him the truth—he couldn't give that up. She offered him this because she was desperate, not because she wished to share his bed. She was as skittish as a filly at her first mating. She couldn't seem to stop fiddling with the deuced gown, and her eyes swept his study as if searching for the monsters sure to be lurking behind his bookshelves.

Devil take her for this. "Your scheme means so much to you that you'd prostitute yourself to save it?"

She flinched at the word "prostitute," but it didn't seem to halt her in her purpose. "Yes. The purpose of my masquerade is more noble than you think, and if you end it before—" Anger flashed in her eyes, then was gone. "You must believe me. Many people will be ruined if you speak to Lord Nesfield. And yes, I'll do anything to keep that from happening." Reaching up, she removed the pins from her hair, sending the rope of golden silk cascading down about her shoulders. "Anything you want."

A jolt of desire turned his knees to rubber. The scent of lavender teased him, and when she shook out her long hair, he thought he'd gone to a rake's heaven.

Or a rake's hell. "What kind of man do you think I am?" he choked out, as much to convince himself as her. "Do you really think I'd take your innocence for any reason?"

"You needn't . . . worry about that." She tilted her chin up. "It's not a concern."

His blood ran cold. He couldn't have heard her right. "What do you mean?"

She drew a shaky breath. "There's no 'innocence' for you to take. I'm not as pure as you think."

"I don't believe you."

"Why not? How do you think I could play Lady Emma so convincingly? Even *you* weren't sure who I was. Do you know any virgins who behave as I did?" She thrust out her chest, taunting him to look at the breasts that fairly burst to be free of the velvet. "Would they wear a gown like this to an unmarried man's home?"

She was playing Lady Emma now, wasn't she? The experienced Lady Emma. The tempting Lady Emma. It was all a role. Wasn't it?

Sidling up to him, she removed the brandy snifter from his numb fingers and set it down on the nearby desk. Then she laid her perfect little hand on his chest and began to unbutton his shirt. "Come now, Jordan, surely you've wondered if I might be . . . less than pure. If you hadn't, you wouldn't have believed Mr. Pollock's tales."

"I didn't . . . believe them," he murmured, though his throat had suddenly shrunk to a tiny passageway that barely allowed air in or out of his body. If she didn't step away from him soon . . .

Another button. Another. "Yes, you did. And with good reason."

Jealousy exploded behind his eyes. "So you did let him kiss you?"

She wouldn't look at him. "He kissed me, yes. And . . . and touched me."

"Is he the one who—"

"No, of course not." Her hand went still on his shirt front. "It happened before I came to London. You don't know the man."

That roused his suspicions, though she didn't seem to notice. Oh, no, she merely went on unbuttoning his shirt, edging so close that he could only watch in utter fascination as her breasts lifted and fell more quickly with each breath.

At least *she* could breathe. He'd given up on it altogether.

"Who was he then?" he rasped. She was lying. She had to be. When she shrugged, he goaded her. "Your cousin perhaps. The one with you at the Drydens' ball."

"Certainly not!"

Her outrage confirmed his suspicions. *She's only acting a role*, he told himself. He'd rather believe that than believe he'd misjudged her character.

Glancing up, she caught the suspicion in his gaze, then added stubbornly, "Lawrence is a prude. He would never touch me." With a half smile, she slid her hand inside his shirt to caress his chest. The feel of her fingers on his bare skin was incredible, like being stroked by an angel. "It doesn't matter who it was. I don't care about him. I want *you*. I've always wanted only you."

She bent her head to press a kiss to his chest, and he jerked beneath her touch. If she was acting, it was certainly a convincing performance. "It can't be true. I know you are—"

"Innocent? Do you? As you said before, what do you really know about me?"

Devil take her, she was muddling his brain. Her hand swept lightly over his ribs, and he sucked in a breath. If she were what she claimed, then he could have her. Here. Tonight. For her willingness to share his bed, he would give her whatever she wanted.

But she *wasn't* willing. She was only pretending to be willing, the way she had at the museum. And doing a damned good job of it, too. Her fingers were skimming down his waist now, light, sensuous. He wanted them lower, much lower.

She cast him a seductive smile. "Let's enjoy each other as you always wanted. Then you can give up this nonsense about going to Lord Nesfield and causing trouble."

That reminded him of why she really was here. He caught her hand, squeezing it hard. "I won't agree to your bargain. I don't believe you're not an innocent. I won't believe it."

For a moment, he thought he saw worry flicker in her face. But it was gone so fast, he wasn't sure. In its place was a look of frightening determination . . . the look of a woman bent on seduction.

"Then I shall have to convince you." Taking him by surprise, she laid her hand on the bulge in his trousers. The traitorous thing leapt at her touch. He groaned as a purely feminine look of satisfaction covered her face. This role of hers was becoming far too real.

Her fingers explored him through his trousers, caressing and intimate, stroking him with a surety that gave him pause even as he went hard as iron. Cursing under his breath, he caught her hand and shoved it away. Deuce take the teasing wench! How could she know just how to tempt a man?

Grabbing her by the shoulders, he looked for some sign of uncertainty in her eyes, but there was none. A slow smile touched her lips as she curved her hands around his waist and then had the audacity to slide both hands down to cup his buttocks. She squeezed, and he nearly erupted right there.

"Well? Shall we go on?" she asked in the silken tones of a lover.

His body declared mutiny. It was needy and hungry and ready to take her on the floor. She was offering herself, and God help him, he would accept her offer. Now.

He caught her in his arms, kissing her with all the desire that had built in him since the day he

first saw her. Her soft response, the way her body
melted and her mouth opened beneath his, filled
him with such possessive, damnable gladness that
it frightened him. Good God, the taste of her . . .
the scent of her, luscious and beguiling . . . it would
make any man forget himself. Wildly he stabbed
his tongue inside her warm mouth, now almost
mad to join himself with her.

Her body undulated against his as fluidly as a
cat's. He could almost imagine her purring as she
twined her arms about his neck, threading her fingers through his hair to clutch him close.

Then the clock struck midnight, startling them
both.

Tearing his mouth from hers, he glanced at the
clock, then around the room at his somber study.
He didn't know if he could wait another second to
have her, but she deserved better than this.

"Come on," he said as he dragged her toward
the door.

"Where are we going?"

"To my bedchamber. I won't take you here on
the floor like some savage."

She halted short of the door. "Does this mean
you agree to my bargain? You'll keep silent?"

Her words reminded him uncomfortably of why
she was doing this. He glanced at her, wishing he
had the will to refuse her and knowing he didn't.
One look at her tumbled hair, reddened lips, and
eyes glazed with need was enough to make him
abandon any scruples. "Keep silent? I'd bind my
tongue forever just to have you in my bed tonight."

Triumph briefly glinted in her eyes. Then she
touched her finger to his mouth, tracing the outline
of his lips with a sensual gesture that made lust
rage through his body. "I can think of other, better
uses for your tongue."

He caught her finger in his teeth, sucking on it until a sigh escaped her lips. When he released it, he was harder than before, if that were possible. "So can I. Come with me, and I'll demonstrate just how many."

Chapter 15

Vice is detestable; I banish all its appearances from my coteries; and I would banish its reality, too, were I sure I should then have any thing but empty chairs in my drawing room.

Fanny Burney, English novelist
and diarist, *Camilla*

Jordan's bedchamber wasn't what Emily had expected. To be sure, it had a massive canopied bed perfect for seduction, with lush damask hangings of midnight blue dripping down from an ornate mahogany cornice.

But where were the lewd paintings, the erotic sculptures meant to excite one's lust? For a man who spent his nights in the arms of tarts and merry widows, his bedchamber was oddly sober and sparsely furnished, with only a neat dressing table and writing desk to accompany the bed.

"Here we are." He shot the bolt, and the sound echoed loudly in her ears.

"Yes." Dear heavens, she really was here. In his bedchamber. Alone with him.

"Let's get rid of this, shall we?" He approached her from behind and pushed her hair aside so he could unbutton her gown. She felt the cloth parting, exposing her back a little at a time to the chilly air. She shivered, partly from the cold, partly from apprehension. When he was kissing her senseless, she forgot the enormity of what she was about to do. But having him undress her—that was a reality she could hardly ignore. After this was all over, she would be thoroughly and truly ruined.

By a man who would rather eat nails than marry.

Not that she could imagine being married to him anyway. One thing this visit had accomplished was to remind her of the vast difference in their stations. This room alone was twice the size of all the bedchambers at the rectory put together, and this was only his town house. He probably had more than one estate. His wife would have to be a consummate hostess, a woman with skills Emily had never dreamed of.

A woman like Emily could only be suitable as a mistress. Yet she would fail at even that. The very way he unlaced and unbuttoned and untied the many fastenings of her gown showed that he had experience she lacked. He'd obviously done this many times before.

She hadn't even done it once. If she made it through this without his guessing the full extent of her inexperience, it would be a miracle.

Of course, once he took her he would discover the truth. She'd been told that losing one's virginity involved blood and some pain—she could hardly disguise *that*. But by then, it wouldn't matter. His only reason for not wanting a virgin was his dislike of inexperienced women . . . and his fear of being forced into marriage. The latter she would reassure him wasn't a concern.

But the former—

She must have stiffened or made some unconscious movement that revealed her fears, for he paused as he finished unhooking her gown. "What's wrong?"

"What do you mean? N-nothing is wrong."

He turned her around, his gaze searching her face. "One would think to look at you that you'd never been undressed by a man before."

She swallowed. "Don't be silly," she said with a brittle laugh. "How could I have experienced the delights of love without being undressed? I'm just . . . concerned that I might not please you. After all, you've known a great many women, or so they say."

Like a fiery torch, his gaze drifted down over her loosened gown. "None like you. Trust me, Emily, it would be impossible for you not to please me tonight."

Then she was in his arms and his mouth was on hers, making her forget everything but him. He tasted so good, the brandied heat of his lips driving out the chill of her fears. He shoved her gown off her shoulders, and it whispered to the floor, leaving her in only her knee-length chemise.

"Mine," he whispered in a guttural tone, like a starving man marking his possession of the single loaf of bread fallen from the baker's wagon. "All mine." And his dark, probing kiss was a blatant repetition of the word.

His. She wanted to be his, if only for tonight. From the moment he'd first stepped into that carriage with her, he'd roused a strange restlessness in her that had lain dormant until then. His first kiss had cut her free of a lifetime's moorings, setting her adrift in a wildly unfamiliar sea of unfathomed temptations. Now she never wanted to go back. This might be all she'd have of him, but it would be enough. One delightful night to cherish in her heart and last forever.

As his mouth mated with hers, she burrowed her hands inside his shirt to mold the warm skin. It was so different from hers, so rough with hair, the muscles beneath it taut and firm. They bunched into fine ropes beneath her touch.

He groaned, tearing his lips away. His fingers tangled in the straps of her chemise, drawing it down until it pooled in the center of her scarlet gown like a camellia surrounded by roses. She was completely naked.

Unable to mask her shyness, she reached for him, but he swept her hands aside. "I want to look at you. Let me look at you."

Color crept over her skin from her face down. No one, not even a maidservant, had ever seen her like this. She'd been taught it was wrong to bare one's body except for the length of time it took to bathe or dress. Her parents had often recited the passage in the Bible where Noah placed a curse on his youngest son for having seen his nakedness.

Yet as Jordan continued to stare at her with unabashed admiration, all those strictures, all her shame at violating them, slipped away.

"You're exquisite," he said in a voice hoarse with need. "If you only knew how many times I've imagined you like this. And how far short my imagination fell of the reality."

It was Lady Emma who answered, for surely Emily couldn't have been so bold. "Shall we see if *my* imagination falls short of the reality?" she teased, stretching out her hands to strip the shirt from his shoulders.

She marveled at her own audacity. Amazing how a man's admiring gaze could free a woman to be so terribly naughty. But he didn't seem to mind. He obligingly yanked off his trousers, then his stockings and drawers, leaving him as naked as she.

Naked. And completely unashamed. She sucked in a startled breath, and he grinned.

"Well? Do I meet with your approval?"

What was there to disapprove? He had a broad chest with hair that held just enough red tint to make his body appear gilded in antique bronze. His waist showed no signs of thickening, and between his lean thighs . . .

She jerked her gaze back to his face, somehow managing to hide her alarm. "You'll do, I suppose."

Do? she thought. He would split her in two with that . . . that male appendage of his! Obviously she'd misunderstood this matter of mating entirely. Surely women weren't built to accommodate such a thing. Surely God had made an error when creating Jordan's private parts.

Never mind about ruining her—Jordan would kill her!

But it was too late to escape, too late to protest her lack of experience. Already, he'd caught her in his embrace and was backing her toward the bed with clear intent, his member jutting against her thighs. "You 'suppose' I'll 'do'? We'll see about that, my darling Emily. When I'm through with you—"

I'll be dead for sure, she thought in a panic just before he tumbled her back on the bed, parting her legs so he could kneel between them.

His gaze was hot on hers as he caught her hands, pinning them on either side of her head. It left her open and exposed in a way she'd never felt before, and her panic increased when he lowered his head to her breasts. The instinct to fight him surged up in her . . . until his mouth closed over her nipple and his tongue swept it in a caress as thrilling as it was gentle.

She went limp beneath him. Oh, dear heaven. When he did that, she almost believed he *wouldn't* kill her. At least not with pain.

No, pleasure was his weapon, one he used most cleverly. Everywhere his mouth touched there was heat, excitement, secret enjoyment. And his mouth was everywhere . . . sucking each breast until she arched beneath him, then trailing down to taste her navel. His evening's growth of whiskers rasped against her skin, but that, too, was a seduction, reminding her that he was a man and she was very, very much a woman.

Their fingers were entwined now as he marked a path of kisses along her lower belly with skilled lips and tongue. He made her acutely aware of her body, treating each hollow and slope and indentation to lavish caresses that made her squirm and sigh. She'd never guessed that a man's mouth could provide such wanton luxuries.

And such torture. He made her want things she couldn't put a name to, made her ache in places she'd never ached before. He seemed to be aching, too, because more than once he groaned and the muscles of his face were tight with restraint.

What he was restraining himself from doing, she wasn't sure. But if this was only the beginning of his seduction, she would never make it to the end.

Then he took her by surprise, pressing a kiss into the thatch of hair between her legs. She nearly shot up off the bed. While she watched in shocked fascination, he released her hands so he could part her curls and bare the soft folds of her flesh for a second, more intimate kiss.

Something curled up tight inside her, something urgent and most assuredly wicked. "Wh-What are you doing?" she whispered before she could stop herself.

He cast her a secret smile. "Has no man ever done that to you?"

What should she answer? Did every man behave so outrageously in bed? Her mother's terse description of lovemaking had made no reference to such wild acts.

Thankfully, he supplied the answer himself. "Apparently not." He caressed her with his mouth again, this time lingering over her until it felt as if a spring were twisting inside her, tighter and tighter with every touch of his tongue to her too sensitive skin. She grabbed fistfuls of damask coverlet to keep from clasping him to her and showing him just how wicked she was.

But she couldn't keep the small cries of pleasure from escaping her lips. "Yes . . . oh, goodness gracious . . . Jordan . . . *Jordan* . . ."

"Do you like that? Does it please you, my darling Emily? Or shall I stop?"

"No!" Shame swept her at this evidence of her wantonness, but her hips moved toward his mouth of their own accord. "I mean . . . I don't know . . . please, Jordan . . . please. . . ."

He didn't stop. His tongue was inside her, stroking her . . . tightening the spring until she could almost not bear it anymore. So much tension . . . it was too much . . . she would never endure it . . .

Then suddenly it snapped, spinning outward to shoot pleasure through every limb and vein and muscle. It tore an animal cry from her as her body arched up off the bed, then collapsed in a great shudder of release.

When she could think again, she found him watching her with a grin of pure male satisfaction. She was smiling, too, and couldn't seem to stop.

Every part of her body felt soft and languid and delicious.

"I will 'do,' will I?" he growled as he moved back up over her, planting his hands on either side of her shoulders. Sweat plastered tendrils of auburn hair to his forehead, and his face wore a look of raw desire. "Now we shall see if *you* will do, my darling."

Her pleasurable languor vanished as she felt his member probing between her legs until it found the entrance and inched inside.

Oh, dear, what was she supposed to do now? She had no idea! What did he expect of her?

"Good God, you're so tight . . ." he murmured as he slid deeper, his eyes closing in obvious satisfaction.

Tight wasn't the word for it. He filled her so utterly she couldn't think of anything else. Surprisingly, her body seemed to stretch to accommodate him. Still, there was pressure . . . a great deal of it. It widened her most uncomfortably.

Surely this was as much of him as she could hold. Surely he couldn't move inside her any more. Yet he did, sliding farther and farther until she thought he might cleave her in two. She shifted beneath him, trying to make him seem not quite so . . . so . . . intrusive.

Suddenly, he gave a forward thrust that seemed to tear something inside her, wringing a cry from her lips. He froze and his eyes flew open to fix her with a look of shock. "Good God! Damn it, Emily, what—"

He broke off as she gazed up at him guiltily.

Every muscle in his body went taut. "You lied to me. Devil take it, you lied!"

She nodded, feeling more than a little relief that

she needn't pretend anymore. "I'm sorry," she whispered.

"I think the damage . . . is done. But I can stop—"

"Don't!" If he stopped, he might not see a reason to keep his end of the bargain. Desperately, she clutched at his hips, anchoring him to her. "Finish it, please. You promised!"

His eyes glittered bleakly. "But I've hurt you. I should have taken more care."

"It always hurts the first time."

"So they say," he bit out.

She wriggled her hips a little, surprised that some of the pressure had eased. "Truly, it's not so bad."

He clamped his eyes as if in pain. "If you keep that up, I swear I *will* finish it."

"Good." When his eyes shot open, tormented and still angry, she undulated against him again and whispered, "I want you, Jordan. Virgin or no, I want you . . . so badly . . . please . . ."

The anger seemed to drain from him. "Then hold on, my darling. I'll try not to hurt you any more."

Her only answer was to lean up and kiss him squarely on the lips. With a groan, he kissed her back, driving his tongue deep into her mouth as he began moving inside her again.

This time there was no pain, and the uncomfortable tightness seemed to ease even more. A sweet tension swelled inside her loins, like the one she'd felt when his mouth had caressed her. As it grew, a restless need to swivel her hips against him overcame her.

When she did, he tore his lips from hers with a gasp. "Good God, Emily . . . such an innocent . . . and such a wanton. You are . . . amazing . . ."

"So are you."

Amazing and wonderful. The feel of him inside her, driving into her, possessing her, was so incredible that she was glad, *glad*, she'd given herself to him.

His gaze burned into her, possessive, fierce. "Now you truly are mine," he rasped. "Mine. All mine."

"Yes." She would always be his, no matter what happened after this night. She could never be anyone else's.

She clasped him to her, trying to memorize the feel of his slick skin, the faint, musky scent that clung to him, the unbelievable pleasure of his body fused to hers. *My love*, she thought, realizing with some sadness that it was true. She loved him. She'd always loved him. And after tomorrow, when it was all over, she would still love him.

But she couldn't tell him. He didn't want love or "any of that nonsense." So instead she showed him, giving up her body to his hot thrusts, reveling in the way they sent her reeling into a mindless dream.

"My darling," he whispered as he drove into her with an almost frantic pace. "Yes . . . yes, Emily . . ."

Then he plunged into her so deeply, she thought he'd reached the very center of her soul. And at that moment, the tension broke inside her with a burst of light and unbearable release. She was still arched against him, her fingers digging into his back, when he cried out her name and spilled himself inside her.

For a moment, the world ceased to exist. There were only the two of them joined together, suspended in sweet intimacy.

Then he collapsed on top of her. And as she floated slowly back to consciousness, sated and rapt and near to swooning with pleasure, it dawned on her that it was over. Now. Forever. She would never have him again.

That's when she turned her face aside and wept.

At first Jordan was conscious only of the most marvelous sense of fulfillment he'd ever experienced in his life. Emily was completely his. Despite his fears for her, she had entered into their lovemaking with an enthusiasm that was endearing. He felt sure he'd pleased her. God knows she'd pleased him.

He buried his face in her slender neck, marveling once more at the softness and delicate fineness of her skin. Then he heard the sobs.

She was crying! He pushed himself off her in alarm. Good God, he'd hurt her more than he realized!

Stretching out next to her, he cupped her cheek in one shaky hand. "I tried not to hurt you, darling. I'm sorry, so sorry."

She shook her head wildly, struggling to regain her breath between hiccuping sobs. "You didn't . . . hurt me."

The tension in his chest eased a little. "Then why are you crying?"

Scrubbing tears away with her hand, she gazed at him with reddened eyes. "Because it was so . . . wonderful. And I'll never get to do it again."

A laugh escaped his lips before he could stop it. "Even I can't do anything about that. I'm afraid a woman can only be deflowered once in her life."

The words sobered him: only once. He'd done the unthinkable—he'd taken a woman's innocence. He waited for the anger to come, the sense of betrayal that she'd managed to accomplish with trickery what no other woman had. Yet all he felt was happiness that it had been him and no one else.

"I . . . I don't mean the deflowering," she stammered. Color suffused her face as she glanced away. "I mean, you and I shall never make love again."

"I don't see why not." He stroked her golden hair, a strange peace settling over him as he made the only possible decision he could. He'd always known what would be expected of him if he ever made love to a woman like Emily. But he hadn't thought he'd be so pleased about it. "Certainly we must be discreet until we marry, but after that—"

"Marry!" She sat up, crossing her arms over her breasts in a vain attempt at modesty. "You aren't going to marry me, Jordan! You can't!"

Her reaction surprised him. "Of course I can. And I will, now that I've taken your virginity. I'm not such a cad as to debauch a woman, then send her home without so much as a fare-thee-well."

"Then give me a fare-thee-well. But you needn't marry me—I told you that from the beginning. This was a bargain, that's all. It was the only way I could think of to keep you silent."

Slipping from the bed, she hurried to where her chemise lay and pulled it on. He stared down at the red stain she'd left behind. *A bargain, that's all.* The horrible words pounded into his brain. Did she truly see it that way?

Well, it didn't matter how she saw it, he thought wearily. It didn't change anything. He sat up, wishing she hadn't left the bed so quickly. "Emily, be practical. We must marry. It's the only thing that will save your reputation."

"No one knows of this. It needn't affect either of our lives."

"Too late for that." He climbed from the bed and approached her. He gathered her in his arms, and though she stood stiffly, she let him hold her. "I could never let you walk away now. What if you find yourself with child?" Tipping her chin up, he stared into her anxious face. "Would you deprive the child of his father?"

"No, but . . . it's not likely, is it? We only . . . I mean, it was just once—"

"Believe me," he said bitterly, thinking of his parents, "just once is all it takes."

Her face turned ashen. "I'll deal with that problem if it happens. But I shan't let you marry me. I know you must think that I planned it all along, but truly, I didn't come here expecting you to marry me!"

"I *know* that."

"I-I thought you would be delighted to have me without any obligation. I didn't expect anything else. Truly, I didn't! I would never force you into marriage!"

He didn't know whether to be pleased or insulted by her frantic eagerness to convince him. "I believe you, darling." He cradled her close. "I'm offering marriage because I choose it. I *want* to marry you."

"No, you don't. You've said a thousand times you have no use for virgins."

"I know what I said. If matters had been different, I wouldn't have sought one out. But I've already had the virgin, so honor dictates I must marry her."

She twisted away from him, her face filling with hurt. "Honor? That's why you wish to marry me? To preserve your honor?"

"Now, Emily—" he began in a soothing voice as he reached for her.

Swatting his hands away, she caught up her

gown and pressed it to her chest like a shield. "I don't want your honor!"

With a scowl, he found his drawers and drew them on. This was turning into a lengthy discussion, the last thing he wanted right now. What he wanted was to take her back to bed and make love to her again.

But it appeared she would have none of that. Obviously, she wanted him to make some foolish vow of love. Well, she was *not* getting that from him. Bad enough he was so obsessed with her that even the thought of marrying her made his blood race and his hands itch to hold her again. That was all the power over him he wished to give her.

"We are going to be married, Emily," he said evenly as he advanced on her. "That's the only way to fix this situation."

"There is nothing to fix!"

"Isn't there? Come now, Emily, you were so desperate for my silence that you ruined your entire future to obtain it. I'd say there's a great deal that needs fixing, and marrying me will certainly do it! Nesfield won't be able to touch you then."

Frantically, she scrambled into her gown. "You don't understand! I have to continue my masquerade, and you mustn't stop me! I won't let you stop me!"

"Why?" He grabbed her by the shoulders as she tried to pull up her gown. "What is so important about this masquerade that you'd go to such lengths to protect it?"

For a moment, he thought she might actually tell him. She looked as if she wanted to tell him. Then her face stiffened, and she shifted her gaze to the door behind his back. "Let me go, Jordan. Unless you intend to keep me a prisoner here, I'm leaving. Now."

He dug his fingers into her shoulders, fighting the urge to shake her senseless. "What do I have to do to prove I have only your welfare at heart? You said once that you couldn't trust me because I felt only lust for you. But I've offered you marriage. If that doesn't prove you can trust me with the truth, what will?"

She slumped in his arms. "It's not a matter of trusting you. If I . . . tell you, then I risk a more certain ruin than anything so paltry as the loss of my virginity. More than that I cannot say."

"Nesfield, devil take him. I won't let him hurt you, do you hear?"

"You can't stop him."

He thrust her away and strode to where his clothes lay on the floor. "We'll just see about that," he snapped as he dressed.

"No!" She jerked up her gown, then ran to him and grabbed his arm. "No, Jordan, you *must* leave him alone!"

"He's taking advantage of an innocent young woman. I will *not* leave him alone!"

"You promised!" she cried as she clung to his arm. "You said if I came to your bed, you would keep silent!"

He froze, looking down at her pale face and the panic in her eyes. Her unfastened gown—that damned scarlet gown—hung so low he could see the lacy edge of her chemise, and beneath it, the creamy swell of one breast.

"I did my part," she said in an aching voice. "Won't you do yours?"

Deuce take her. He couldn't refuse when he knew how much she'd relinquished for his silence.

And yet . . . She'd asked him not to say anything to Pollock or Nesfield. He could only assume that she would also consider his speaking to Lady Dundee a violation of their agreement.

But there was one person whom he *could* speak to, someone who could make her recognize the wisdom of marrying him.

"All right." When she stared at him warily, he straightened her gown on her shoulders so that it hid her most obvious temptations. "I won't say anything to Nesfield or Pollock, if that's what you wish."

"That's what I wish."

"As for marrying you—"

She touched a finger to his lips. "No more about that. I don't expect you to sacrifice yourself for propriety's sake."

"It wouldn't be a sacrifice," he whispered, and meant it.

"All the same, you needn't marry me." When he went rigid, she added, "Please, let's not discuss it anymore. I only want to go, before they discover I'm missing. The hackney coach is waiting outside—"

"I'm not letting you ride about town in a hackney at this hour," he said firmly. "I'll take you home in my coach."

"What if someone sees us together and guesses—"

"At three A.M.? No one will see us. And if it makes you feel better, I'll stop a short distance from Nesfield's."

She looked relieved. "Thank you. To be truthful, I didn't fancy the long ride back with that . . . that awful man in the hackney coach. I think he was a little drunk."

"No doubt. Now, why don't you get out of that gown and wash up over there." He gestured toward the basin of water on his dressing table. "I'm sure I can find one of my sister's gowns for you to wear home that's not so . . . provocative."

At her blush, he nearly smiled. Somehow even in her "fallen" state, she managed to be as pure as ever.

"While you're dressing," he added, "I'll rouse the coachman."

And tell him to prepare for a trip—a long trip. Because no matter what she thought, this night was not over yet.

Chapter 16

If all the good people were clever,
And all clever people were good,
The world would be nicer than ever
We thought that it possibly could.

Elizabeth Wordsworth,
British educator,
"The Clever and the Good"

Emily climbed into the Blackmore carriage and sat on the far end of the seat facing forward. Her gown was a little snug and too long—Jordan's stepsister must be tall and slender. But at least it didn't show as much of her as the other one had.

When Jordan entered a few moments later, he sat next to her. After ordering Watkins to drive on, he took her hand in his. "You look tired. It's been a long night for you, hasn't it?"

"Yes." In truth she was utterly exhausted. Seduction had its pleasures, but it was certainly draining.

He closed the curtain, casting them into nearly complete darkness. Then shifting so that he sat with his back braced against the side of the coach, he drew her onto his lap and cradled her head against his chest. "Here, why don't you rest a bit? I'll wake you when we arrive."

As he wrapped his arms around her, she relaxed against him. She *was* tired. If she could only close her eyes for a moment . . . "I'm not hurting you?"

"Not at all. Besides, it might be the last time I can hold you like this."

Sudden tears filled her eyes, and she was thankful he couldn't see them in the darkness. Yes, the last time. Although lying in his embrace was an indulgence she could ill afford, she couldn't bear to throw the moment away.

But she doubted she'd be able to sleep. So much had happened, so much she wanted to think about. . . .

It seemed like only seconds later that she was startled awake by a rumbling noise. A somber gray light filtered into the carriage from behind the curtains, dulling the brilliant gold of the brocade cushions.

Still, there was enough light that she could see everything in the carriage clearly, where before it had been pitch-black. They must be nearing her street, which was well lit by oil lamps.

Another low rumble sounded from behind her, and she shifted to look up at Jordan. He was snoring, of all things. That was what had awakened her. She smiled. It was an endearingly normal activity, one she wouldn't have connected with the Earl of Blackmore. Earls weren't supposed to snore. Or sneeze or eat or do any of those human things the rest of the population engaged in. They were supposed to have servants to do those things for them, she thought wryly.

Who would ever have thought that she'd grow so familiar with an earl that she'd be listening to him snore?

She touched his cheek, rough with its evening growth of beard, and gazed fondly at the features relaxed in sleep. A bittersweet pang made her jerk her hand away. It was too tempting to look at him like this, to think that she could see this sight every morning if she were only willing to sacrifice her self-respect.

She couldn't believe he'd offered to marry her. She'd expected him to be delighted not to have to wed her after bedding her. Obviously, she'd misjudged his character entirely. If she'd guessed he would feel that way, would she have been so ready to offer herself to him?

Glancing up at his slightly curving mouth, she sighed. Yes. She was such a weakling. She didn't regret a single moment of their night together. It was no wonder young women fell so easily under the spells of wicked men. If other men were half as adept at seduction as Jordan . . .

For a moment, she imagined what being his wife might be like. They could make love whenever they wanted. During the winter they would cuddle under the blankets, kissing and touching and doing all those scandalous things he'd done to her tonight. During the summer, they could make love in the garden—

She blushed. The very idea! To make love outside where anybody might see them . . . What a wanton thought! It proved how far she'd fallen.

Yet nothing had changed from before. He was as forbidden to her as ever. Perhaps she might ignore the difference in their stations, the fact that he'd spent his entire life avoiding marriage, and even the fact that he didn't love her—but there was still one glaring reason she couldn't marry him.

Her masquerade. Once he found out why she'd been pretending to be Lady Emma, once he discovered that Nesfield wanted to ruin his closest friend's plans for happiness, he would recoil from her in disgust. How could he forgive her for deceiving his friend and thus deceiving him?

With a sigh, she gingerly disentangled herself from Jordan's limp arms, then slid off his lap and took a seat opposite him. She drew the curtain aside, fully expecting to see the lambent glow of oil lamps on wet streets.

But there were no cobbled streets, no houses looming dark in the still night like hulking beasts awaiting the dawn. Dawn was already here—overcast and gloomy, but still dawn. And all she could see through the drifts of dust raised by the coach's wheels were miles and miles of green fields crisscrossed by hedges.

She jerked the curtains open, her heart skipping a beat. For goodness sake, they were not in London—they were in the country!

"Wake up, Jordan!" she cried, leaning forward to jerk his arm. "Your mad coachman has taken us into the country!"

Jordan's snoring halted abruptly, and he opened his bleary eyes to stare at her. "What the devil—"

"We're not in London! I don't know how far outside the city we are, but it's morning, so we must have gone quite far! You must make your coachman turn back! If I don't get into the house before someone discovers I'm gone . . ." Despair overcame her.

Jordan sat up, then groaned. "Deuce take it, my leg's gone to sleep." He rubbed it with both hands.

"All of you went to sleep, curse you!" She grabbed one of his arms. "Stop that! There's no time to waste! Make him halt and turn back!"

"Who?"

If she'd had a reticule, she would have hit him over the head with it. "Watkins, of course! Your fool coachman has taken us into the country!"

As if finally comprehending what she'd been trying to tell him for the last few minutes, he glanced out the window. "I think you're right."

Exasperation made her voice strident. "Then stop him, for goodness sake! Make him turn back!"

"I can't."

"What do you mean, you can't? Of course you can!"

"When Watkins gets it in his head to go off for a drive in the country, there's no stopping him. We'll just have to settle back and enjoy the ride."

"Don't be ridiculous! You don't have to—" She broke off, eyes narrowing. He looked entirely too nonchalant. Obviously, the wretch had planned this. "Where are we going, Jordan?"

"I have no idea."

"Curse you, this is no joking matter! Answer me! Where are we going?"

His eyes met hers, steady and clear. "You're right, of course. This is not a joking matter."

"*Where are we going?*"

"North."

That stymied her. "North?"

"As I said earlier, we *are* going to be married."

It took a moment for his meaning to sink in. But when it did, she stiffened in outrage. "You're taking me to Gretna Green? Against my will? You . . . you wretch! You despicable, deceitful—"

"Watch it, my dear, you're talking to your future husband," he said with a smirk.

She pounded on the ceiling with her fist. "Stop the coach, Watkins!" she shouted. "Stop it now!"

The coach rumbled on.

"He won't stop unless I command it," Jordan said. "Besides, what good would it do if he set you down here in the middle of the road? Will you walk back to London?"

"If I have to!"

"You might as well stop fighting it. You know marrying me is the only solution."

"You can't *force* me to say the vows. You'll have to drag me kicking and screaming into the church!"

Her vehemence seemed to startle him. Then his eyes narrowed. "If I have to," he echoed her earlier words.

A howl of rage tore from her as she looked for something, anything to throw at him. His hat sailed across the carriage and then his leather gloves. He dodged them both, alarm crowding his features.

She'd just lifted one of the cushions when he grabbed her hands. "Pax, Emily! Good God, you'd think I was taking you to your execution!"

The fight drained out of her all of a sudden, and she slumped against the seat with a groan. What would Lord Nesfield say when he found out she was gone? How long would it be before he assumed she had simply run off? Then how long before he took it upon himself to act?

"You don't know what you've done," she whispered mournfully.

He squeezed her hands. "Then tell me, darling. I promise, I'll do whatever it takes to free you from Nesfield's control."

She lifted her gaze to his, torn unbearably between the urge to unburden herself and the sure knowledge that she couldn't. If she told him about Lord Nesfield's threats, he'd no doubt race back to London in a rage and threaten the marquess with bodily harm. A lot of good *that* would accomplish. Lord Nesfield had an ironclad case against her, and no blustering or threats on Jordan's part could change that. Indeed, Jordan's interference would prompt the marquess to act on his threats. And there was nothing Jordan could do to stop it.

No matter how much influence Jordan had, he couldn't undo the events leading to her mother's death. Or to the strange quirk of fate that had given Lord Nesfield power over her.

Much as she longed to tell him, she couldn't. She mustn't.

Her only recourse was either to convince him to turn back . . . or find some way to escape him between here and Gretna Green. The journey was long, after all, and they'd have to stop periodically. That's when she would make her escape. And if she did it soon, she might even reach London before too much damage had been done.

She glanced at his expectant face. In the meantime, she had to put him off.

"Emily?" he prodded. "Why don't you tell me all of it?"

"It doesn't matter anymore."

He grimaced, apparently sensing how close she'd come to revealing the truth. "It matters to me."

"I'll tell you. But not now."

"When?"

What could she say that would pacify him until she could make her escape? It came to her in a flash of brilliance. "I'll tell you after we're married."

Suspicion darkened his eyes. "So you've changed your mind? You're saying you'll marry me?"

She hated lying to him, especially about this, but what choice did she have? "Yes."

"Why?"

She threw her hands up in a helpless gesture. "Because you're giving me no choice, you ninny. I'm practical enough to realize I can't fight you. So I'll marry you." When he still looked skeptical, she added bitingly, "Though you can't expect me to like it."

His lips tightened into a grim line. "You needn't make it sound like a death sentence."

"I'm sorry. It's just that . . . this will alter my life dramatically."

"For the better, I hope." Releasing her hands, he leaned back against the cushioned seat. "There's no reason to wait until we're married to tell me the truth, you know."

"Once we're married, I'll be sure I can trust you. Then I won't be afraid to reveal everything."

His eyes glittered darkly. "Devil take it, you know you can trust me now."

It tore at her to see the hurt in his face, especially now, when he looked so unlike an earl, all rumpled from sleep with his hair tousled. But she had no choice. "Please, Jordan," she said softly, "you've already won. What does it matter if you wait a week or two to hear my sad tale?"

A strange light flickered in his eyes. "A week or two? No, I don't suppose it does matter."

She relaxed against the seat. Now she must figure out how to escape him. First, she had to stop the coach. Then she had to distract him long enough to escape. Hardest of all, she had to procure transportation to London. How in the world could she manage that?

Suddenly her stomach growled, providing her with a flash of inspiration. "Are you planning to starve me until we reach Gretna Green?"

"I wasn't planning to starve either of us," he said tersely. "I thought we'd eat breakfast in Bedford. I'm known at the White Cloak Inn. They'll take good care of us."

She didn't want to be taken good care of, and

she certainly didn't want an inn where he was known. "How much farther?"

He knocked on the ceiling and repeated her question to Watkins. The answer made him frown. "I'm afraid it'll be another couple of hours or so. You woke up sooner than I expected."

"So," she clipped out, "you *do* intend to starve me. What a wonderful way to begin a marriage."

He sighed. "All right then. We'll stop at the next inn we come to. Will that be to your satisfaction, milady?"

"Perfectly."

"You'd best eat hearty," he grumbled. "I'd like to reach Leicester by this evening."

Not if she could help it. Though she would dearly love to wait until tonight to escape, she didn't dare let that much time elapse.

The first inn that came into sight was a wretched affair indeed, aptly titled The Warthog. A ramshackle, timber-framed house with a weathered sign, it nonetheless had a bustling inn yard filled with carts and mail coaches and the occasional gig. It obviously catered to travelers of a poorer class, who could only afford the few pence it took to purchase sausages and oat bread for their breakfast.

Even her pinchpenny father would never have stopped at a place like this. But it suited her needs perfectly, for its customers were the sort of people more likely to help her than those of a richer and more wary class.

"Here," she announced. "Let's stop here."

Jordan cast a contemptuous look over the inn yard. "Well, my dear, you're nothing if not brave. Aside from the unwashed customers with whom you'll be rubbing elbows, you're likely to find a rat or two at your table."

"I don't care. I'm hungry." She tossed him a

taunting glance. "Besides, you're an earl. Can't you make sure we have a private dining room?" That would make everything so much easier.

"Trust me, I intend nothing else." A calculating look passed over his face. "I'm never averse to privacy. *If* the innkeeper can produce such a thing."

As it happened, the innkeeper, whose bristly chin and warty nose seemed appropriate in light of the inn's name, was happy to oblige, especially when Jordan laid an impressive number of sovereigns in his hand. The man was already staring at Jordan with undisguised awe, but at the sight of the gold, he looked positively radiant.

"My wife and I want a private room, the best you have," Jordan stated. "I want a substantial breakfast brought up as soon as possible. And make sure my coachman is fed as well." He added another sovereign, then with a glance at Emily, murmured something else in the man's ear.

The innkeeper's head bobbed so furiously, Emily thought it would surely fly off at any moment. "I have the perfect room for you, milord! I've no doubt your lordship will be pleased. This way. Watch your step. There's a loose board here . . ."

She took Jordan's arm when he offered it, trying not to dwell on the pleasure it had given her to hear him refer to her as his wife. She could not, must not let that temptation sway her. Marriage to a man unable to love would be disaster, even if there weren't all those other considerations.

As they followed the babbling innkeeper up rickety stairs to the second floor, she cast a quick glance around her. She'd be leaving in a hurry, and it wouldn't do to get lost on the way out.

The innkeeper ushered them into a room with cheery curtains and surprisingly clean floors, though the place smelled of coal and fish, and the simple furnishings were worn. "I'll have breakfast brought to you presently, milord."

It was only after the innkeeper left that she noticed the bed. She was still gaping at it when she heard Jordan lock the door. Whirling toward the sound, she fixed him with an accusing gaze. "This isn't a dining room! It has a bed in it!"

His knowing smile curled her toes. "So it does. I thought we might . . . satisfy our appetites in more than one respect."

She blushed. Dear heavens, he wanted to bed her again. The very thought of it made her hot and weak. And why not let him? After all, she'd be leaving him before the day was out. Then there'd be no more chances for lovemaking.

Could it hurt to have one more hour in his arms?

She shook herself. Of course it could! If she let him make love to her again, she would never be able to leave him. Besides, the more often they made love, the more likely that she'd find herself with child afterward.

He took a step toward her, and she backed away. "Now, Jordan, this isn't the time for this. You said you wanted to make Leicester today."

He stalked her, a grin spreading over his handsome features. "We'll make Leicester, don't you worry. Come now, it'll be a while before they bring us breakfast. There's plenty of time to indulge ourselves."

When he approached too near, she darted away, putting the bed between them as she fumbled for some reason to put him off. "Do you really wish to have the innkeeper burst in upon us in the midst of . . . of . . . well, you know?"

As he edged around the bed, he laughed. "Lovemaking, darling. It's called lovemaking. And the door's locked, remember?"

She backed up, only to run squarely into the coarse wooden dressing table. Glancing back, she spotted the earthen water pitcher that stood beside the washbasin atop the table. An idea took shape in her mind.

Shifting so that her body blocked his view of her hands, she groped behind her for the pitcher. "I intend to eat as soon as the food arrives. We're not married yet, you know. If you wish to exercise your husbandly rights before the wedding, you must at least feed me first."

He lunged for her, catching her in his arms just as her fingertips touched the pitcher's handle. "All right then. How about a little taste before the main meal?" He planted a light kiss on the end of her nose. "Something to get me through breakfast."

Then his lips were on hers, coaxing and tender and oh, so tempting. For a moment she let herself enjoy the kiss, let him open her mouth with his tongue to plunge inside, hinting at what he wanted to do to her, what other parts of her body he wanted to possess. His hands swept up her ribs until the thumbs rested beneath her breasts.

But when he covered the soft flesh with expert fingers, she tore her lips away from him. What was she doing? Shifting a little in his arms, she grasped the pitcher's handle, praying he wouldn't notice.

He didn't. His eyes glittered with unquenched desire, and his breath came in jerky gasps as he bent his head toward her mouth again.

"I'm sorry, Jordan," she whispered just before he could kiss her.

Then she conked him on the head with the pitcher.

Chapter 17

I hate the noise and hurry inseparable from great Estates and Titles, and look upon both as blessings that ought only to be given to fools, for 'tis only to them that they are blessings.

Lady Mary Wortley Montagu, Letter, March 28, 1710, to her husband

When Jordan came to, he was lying in a puddle of water on the rough wooden floor. Staring up at the stained ceiling, he tried to figure out why he was wet and his head hurt like the dickens. He sat up with a groan and rubbed the knot on his head. How did he come to be lying in such a shabby room?

Then he saw the cracked pitcher a few feet from him, and everything came back to him.

"Devil take her!" he growled as he lurched to his feet. Standing up made the throbbing in his head worse, but rage spurred him on.

The chit had actually run off! And after he'd begun to believe she'd resigned herself to their marriage! That's what he got for underestimating Emily Fairchild.

Stumbling toward the door, he tried to open it,

but it was locked. Damn it! She'd locked him in.
He pounded on the door, roaring at the top of his
lungs for the innkeeper. He heard a flurry of voices
in the hall, a woman's and then a man's raised in
debate.

"She said he kidnapped her," the woman's voice
muttered.

The second voice was almost assuredly the innkeeper's. "Yes, but my dove, he's an earl! We cannot keep an earl prisoner!"

"Open this door!" Jordan thundered, their discussion only enraging him further. "Open it or I
swear I'll have every magistrate in the county
down on your head!"

There was a pause, but it was thankfully short.
Then he heard the key turn in the lock, and the
door swung open to reveal the innkeeper wringing
his hands, accompanied by his scowling wife.

Ignoring them both, he hurried down the creaking stairs as quickly as his aching head would allow. He didn't know how long he'd been out, but
it didn't matter. He would find her. And when he
did . . .

He burst into the dining room, but a cursory survey revealed she wasn't there. He whirled upon the
innkeeper, who'd followed him down the stairs
babbling apologies.

"Where is she?" Jordan growled, taking a step
toward the innkeeper.

"She . . . she . . . said that you kidnapped her
against her will. She . . . she—"

"Where is my *wife*!" Jordan thundered.

The innkeeper gestured toward the door with
one shaky finger.

Jordan hurried out into the inn yard, more in
control of his faculties now. Thankfully, she hadn't
hit him hard enough to do any permanent damage.

At the other end of the crowded yard, he saw Watkins remonstrating with a burly man who was handing Emily into the driver's seat of a small gig.

"Unhand my wife!" Jordan roared as he shoved his way through the throng.

Emily's eyes widened at the sight of him. "Hurry up!" she urged her would-be rescuer. "Get in!"

When the man hesitated, his startled gaze fixed on the sight of a lord of the realm hurtling across the inn yard toward him, she took up the reins, but Watkins stepped forward, grabbing them away from her before she could do anything.

Glaring first at Watkins, then at Jordan, she stood up in the gig. "I'm going back to London, and there's nothing you can do to stop me!"

"Don't count on that," Jordan bit out as he stalked up to the gig.

The burly man stepped in his path. "The lady don't want to go with you, guv'nor. And she paid me well to carry her back to the city."

"Paid you—" He fumbled in his coat pocket for his purse, but it was gone. She'd not only hit him over the head with a pitcher and locked him in, she'd actually had the audacity to steal his money! "I assure you, your gallantry is misplaced. Whatever fool tale she might have told you, this woman *is* my wife, as my coachman can attest."

Watkins nodded vigorously, more than ready to lie for his employer, but Jordan's challenger would have none of it. "She said you'd say that. She said you been lying to people to keep her from escapin'. Well, I ain't gonna let no bleedin' swell with debauchery in his mind hurt no proper young lady."

Jordan glared up at his challenger. Deuce take her, she'd chosen her protector well. The hulking brute outweighed him by five stone and was taller by a couple of inches, even though Jordan wasn't a small man himself. The man smelled of sweat and field labor, and probably hefted boulders for a living.

Which only enraged Jordan further. "Step aside, or I will make you," he hissed in a low voice, conscious that half the inn now filled the yard behind him, watching the excitement unfold.

"Make me?" the man laughed. "Make me? Why, you impudent little—"

The man swung one of his beefy fists at Jordan's head, but Jordan ducked it, countering with a swift blow to the man's soft belly.

His challenger had just enough time to cast Jordan a look of complete bewilderment, as if shocked that an earl could pack a punch like that, before Jordan gave him a right uppercut to the chin.

The giant staggered back, but didn't fall. Then he took Jordan by surprise with a blow to the eye that sent Jordan reeling back. Dimly, Jordan heard Emily cry out, begging them to stop, but stopping was out of the question.

The man had tried to steal Emily. And nobody was going to steal Emily. Quickly, Jordan shot his left fist into the man's face, then put all his strength into smashing his right fist into the giant's stomach, the man's weakest area. That did the trick. Emily's hapless Galahad crumpled to the ground, clutching his belly.

Not for nothing had Jordan spent time at the Lyceum studying pugilism for the past five years. One thing he'd learned—size didn't matter nearly so much as the placement of one's blows.

"Next time, don't come between a 'swell' and his wife," Jordan muttered as he stepped over the moaning form and headed to where Emily still stood in the gig, her mouth agape.

Before she could even protest, Jordan swung Emily down and into his arms. Ignoring her gasp, he carried her toward his coach.

"Put me down!" she cried, pounding on his chest. "Curse you, Jordan, I will not go with you!" When he merely threw her over his shoulder like a sack of wheat and nodded to Watkins to open the carriage door, she cried out, "Somebody stop him! Help me, please!"

Grimly, he tossed her into the coach, then faced the grumbling crowd. Thanks to Emily and his complete miscalculation of her determination not to marry him, he was now in a rather delicate situation. More than one face looked upon him with suspicion, and a knot of beefy laborers had tumbled out of a cart, armed with pitchforks and shovels.

Crossing his arms over his chest, he feigned a nonchalance he didn't feel. "Please forgive my wife for any trouble she's caused. She and I argued, and this is her way of punishing me."

"You . . . you liar!" she protested through the open door to the coach. "You scoundrel, you—"

He shut it in her face, then leaned against it, glad that his coach was sturdy enough to muffle her voice. "As you can see, she'll say anything to strike back at me."

"She says you kidnapped her," a belligerent voice called out from the crowd.

He snorted. "Come now, do you really think I need to kidnap a woman for companionship? Besides, I told the innkeeper she was my wife when we entered. She didn't protest it then, and she had every opportunity to do so. But she wasn't angry at me then." He cast them a rueful look. "Or at least not as angry as she is now."

His challenger stumbled to his feet, looking wary and stubborn all at the same time. "The lass said you wanted to take advantage of her. That's wot she tole *me*."

"I must plead guilty to that." He forced a smile to his face. "I quite often take advantage of my beautiful wife, but then, who wouldn't?"

To his relief, there were a few titters in the crowd.

"Unfortunately," he went on, "she detests leaving her fancy friends behind in London for a week at my estate, and she made her wishes quite plain a few moments ago." He gave an exaggerated sigh. "But alas, business calls, and I do so like having my wife with me in the country where I can ... take advantage of her."

He could sense their sudden indecision. Their strong belief in the immorality of noblemen was being challenged by their equally strong belief in the frivolous whims of noblewomen. And the latter, coupled with his ability to trounce a man nearly twice his size, seemed to be winning, though he didn't intend to stay here and find out for certain.

To further clinch the matter, he turned to his challenger. "You may keep the money my wife gave you. You deserve it."

He made sure his look amplified his words, reminding the hulking brute that an earl was no one to trifle with, especially one whose "wife" had stolen his purse. When the man blanched and mumbled, "You ought to keep a tight leash on that one, guv'nor," Jordan knew he'd won his point.

He turned to the innkeeper. "Thank you for your hospitality, but I'm afraid we must be on the road before my wife gets any other fool notions in her head."

"Yes, milord, I understand."

Jordan reached for the door handle, and the inn-keeper cried, "Wait!"

He froze, wondering if he were about to be stoned by a mob after all. Turning to the innkeeper, he fixed him with as haughty a gaze as he could manage.

"You and your wife will be needing your break-fast," the innkeeper stammered. He motioned to a servant girl who disappeared into the inn, then hurried back out with a gingham-covered basket. "I took the liberty of having this prepared."

"Thank you." At least one person knew on which side his bread was buttered. Jordan's smile was genuine this time. "Perhaps this will take the edge off my wife's anger long enough for me to take advantage of her."

Amid a more general laughter this time, he opened the coach door and climbed in.

Emily sat stonily on the seat, facing forward. Setting the basket on the other seat, he collapsed next to her and ordered Watkins to drive on.

As they rumbled out of the inn yard, he fought to compose himself. He wanted to throttle her and feared that if he looked at her, he might do so. But in his heart, he couldn't blame her. He *was* kidnap-ping her, after all, even if it were for her own good.

He blamed himself more than anything. He should have realized when she'd acted so skittish at the inn that she wasn't as resigned to the mar-riage as she'd pretended.

When he could trust himself to speak civilly, he said, "I hope you don't intend to repeat this farce at every inn where we stop."

"Would it do me any good?"

He glanced at her, but she was staring ahead as if in a trance. "I doubt it."

A slight tremor in her face belied the seeming

calm of her voice. He looked down to see that her hands were clenched into fists in her lap.

"I told the truth," she said bitterly, "but they believed you. All you had to do was speak a few glib tales, and they were quite eager to let me be carried off."

Her tone was so hurt he couldn't help but feel a twinge of guilt. It made him angry. "Did you really expect them to risk their livelihoods for you? Despite all those poets extolling the idea of the noble savage, the lower classes are no different than you and I. Survival is their first priority. Ideals like chivalry and generosity fall a far second."

"What a cynic you are."

She said it without rancor, as if merely making an observation, but it struck him to the heart. He wasn't a cynic, but a realist. A cynic took a dim view of everything, whereas a realist merely viewed the world in practical terms. Couldn't she see that?

No. Right now, she probably considered him second only to Satan Incarnate. And all because he was doing the right thing by her.

She ought to be grateful! This wasn't how a woman should react when a man proposed marriage after ruining her! Here he was, breaking all his rules for the first time in his life, and she didn't even appreciate it!

He'd never proposed marriage to anyone, and he'd certainly never expected to propose marriage to some wide-eyed innocent. Strange how natural it had felt to proclaim her his wife in that inn yard. The words should have tasted like ashes in his mouth. But during his confrontation with that laborer, he'd never thought of her in any other terms. As far as he was concerned, she was already his wife. They lacked only a piece of paper to sanctify it.

If he could get that far. "Tell me something, Emily," he said, unable to keep silent any longer. "Why are you so reluctant to marry me that you would proclaim me a kidnapper to escape it? Do you find the idea of marriage to me that repellent?"

He held his breath for her answer, marveling that it should mean so much to him. When she didn't answer at once, a hollow anxiety settled in the region of his heart that was more disquieting than her answer could possibly be. "Never mind," he said tightly. "It doesn't matter."

She glanced at him, then sighed. "Of course I don't find the idea of marriage to you repellent. Under other circumstances—"

"What other circumstances?"

Her gaze dropped to her hands. "The kind of circumstances most people marry under. You seem to forget I'm one of those foolish virgins you keep harping on." She paused, as if afraid to say more. "I . . . I want love, Jordan. I know you think it's silly, but it's what I want all the same."

It didn't surprise him to hear her say it, but he found himself incapable of giving her the response she wanted. The thought of saying he loved her terrified him. And it wasn't true. It couldn't be. Besides, she hadn't said a word about loving him.

The realization disturbed him more than he liked.

It was several moments before he could manage to speak at all. "And you don't care that not marrying me would mean your ruin?"

"Marrying only to save one's honor is ludicrous. You know too well that it leads to disaster. Your parents—"

"My parents? What do you know of my parents?"

She gave an uneasy shrug. "Lord St. Clair told me they were forced to marry. He said they were dreadfully unhappy together."

"Oh, he did, did he?" Devil take Ian. If Jordan had wanted her to know all that, then he deuced well would have told her himself.

"I don't want you thinking that I tried to trap you into marriage the way your mother did your father. I couldn't bear to be in a marriage where you blamed me for ruining your life."

"I don't blame any of this on you," he bit out.

Her gaze shot to him. "Yes, you do. You think all women are alike, that they're all like your mother—trying to trap you into doing something you don't want."

A surge of anger made him scowl. "Do you really think I'm so narrow-minded as to distrust an entire gender because of something one woman did?" When she merely stared at him, he ground out, "Except for that night in the carriage, when I made some admittedly unfounded accusations, have I ever implied that I thought you were trying to trap me into anything?"

A small frown creased her forehead. "Well, no, but—"

"For God's sake, Emily, I don't even blame my mother for what happened in my parents' marriage, so I certainly can't blame you for this."

"What do you mean? Of course you blame your mother! That's why you avoid young virgins!"

He shifted in his seat to face her. "I avoid young virgins because I don't want to make the same mistake my father made."

"Exactly. A woman tricked him into marriage, and you don't—"

"No. Being tricked into marriage was not his mistake. Being so deeply in love that he lost his sense of perspective was." He gazed steadily at her. "Every man with money and power knows that some women will do anything to obtain it, just as some men will do anything to obtain an heiress. We put ourselves on our guard, and we learn to spot the signs. I assure you, my father couldn't have reached the age of twenty-six unwed without developing such instincts."

When she looked at him uncomprehendingly, he sighed. "My mother did set a trap for my father, and yes, they were forced to marry. But she'd been taught by her parents that snagging a husband with a grand title and even grander fortune was the most noble achievement to which any young lady could aspire. She merely behaved as she'd been taught. I don't blame her for that."

He took Emily's hand in his. Gazing down at the strong, capable fingers and the skin that had probably never seen an exotic lotion, he thought how utterly different she was from his vain, grasping mother. "My father, too, had been taught. He knew to be wary of such attentions. But my mother was a beauty, and my father wasn't the most handsome or charismatic man. He was bookish and shy. So when a blazing beauty flirted with him, he forgot all his caution."

Jordan's voice tightened. "His lovesick mind mistook shallowness for naïveté, a frivolous nature for youthful enthusiasm. Whatever she lacked, he supplied in his mind, for the simple reason that he let a blind emotion—and a not-so-blind cock—guide him."

Instead of looking shocked at his deliberate crudity, Emily was watching him with complete absorption. With a scowl, he released her hand. He hadn't intended to reveal so much; it had just come out.

But if they were to marry, it was best she know why he didn't cater to such frivolities. "Eventually," he went on, "my father emerged from his fog to realize that she wasn't what he'd made her to be in his mind. But by then it was far too late. She was with child, and he had to do the honorable thing. He woke up to find himself an intelligent, quiet man saddled with a stupid, selfish wife who didn't share his deep feelings of love or his sensibilities."

He sucked in a harsh breath. It all came back to him so painfully—the constant fights, his father's refusal to indulge his mother's whims, her heavy drinking. And amidst it all, the knowledge that if it hadn't been for his untimely birth . . .

With an iron force of will, he shoved away the memories. "Marriage became a torment for him. He loved and was appalled by her at the same time, so he withdrew from the marriage to keep sane. And Mother, deprived of her fawning suitor, looked elsewhere for companionship. In a bottle." He went on in a bitter voice. "That's what your foolish 'love' did to two sadly mismatched people. In the end, Father's dalliance with Cupid led to disaster. Can you blame me for finding the emotion dangerous?"

"But Jordan, that's merely one instance. Your father married a second time, didn't he? Or wasn't he in love then?"

"Oh, he was in love, all right. Father never could learn his lesson."

"So she wasn't a good person either?" Emily whispered.

His expression softened as he thought of Maude.

"She was an angel." He cast Emily a half smile. "Sometimes you remind me of her."

She flushed, but didn't look away. "There, you see? Love doesn't always end in disaster."

"You don't understand. They had a few wonderful years together. Then she contracted a horrible illness, and Father fell apart. He put so much of himself into his love for her that losing her was more than he could bear." His voice grew somber. "At the end he was a ghost of a man, completely devoted to her, consumed by despair that nothing could be done to save her. He died shortly after she did, because he couldn't live without her. As far as I'm concerned, it was Cupid who shot the arrow that killed him, leaving his son and stepdaughter to grieve without either parent for comfort."

For a long moment, they were both locked in silence, the thudding of the hooves on the muddy road the only sound. Then she sighed. "I'm so sorry," she whispered. There was pity in her face, a pity that roused his anger.

"I'm not telling you this to sadden you or make you feel sorry for me. I merely think you should know the truth. Even if I wanted to love you, I couldn't. I taught myself to resist such unstable emotions long ago." When she blanched, he added, "But that doesn't mean we couldn't have a comfortable, contented marriage. Indeed, if it's not clouded by emotion, it will likely be better than most."

"You think so, do you?" She lifted her chin, her green eyes soft with regret and hurt ... and some other deep emotion. "And what if I'm in love with you?"

To his disgust, his first reaction to the simple

statement was sheer joy. Emily, *his* Emily, in love with him?

Then his practical side reasserted itself, and he forced himself to say, "You aren't. You're confusing desire with something else, which is understandable under the circumstances."

"Don't patronize me, Jordan," she snapped. "I may be naive and young and all those things you despise, but I'm not stupid. I know what I feel."

Uneasily, he realized he had no desire to argue with her on this particular point. How selfish could one man be, to be pleased that she loved him even though he didn't feel the same?

Yet he couldn't stop being pleased. He chose his words carefully. "If that's true, I see no reason it should hurt our marriage. As long as you understand that I don't . . . have the capacity to love."

"Did your father understand that your mother didn't 'have the capacity to love'?" she retorted. "Is that what made their marriage such a success?"

She couldn't have chosen a better weapon. He stiffened. "It's not the same. My parents weren't well suited. You and I are."

She laughed bitterly. "Oh, certainly. You're an earl; I'm a common rector's daughter. You take for granted your box at the opera; I count myself blessed to have attended once. You're on speaking terms with the Prince of Wales; I'd never even seen his portrait until my farce of a coming out. I wouldn't know the faintest idea how to seat people at a dinner party and—"

"None of that matters to me," he said fiercely.

"Not today, perhaps. But it will. One day you'll wake up and find yourself ashamed of me." She glanced out the window at the dark forest they were passing through now. "If you loved me, you might overlook my lack of sophistication and my ignorance of society, but as it is, those things can only be an embarrassment to you."

"You're forgetting your other admirable abilities—your gift for physic, your quick wit, your sweet nature . . ."

"What does an earl need with any of that? For physic, you have the best doctors money can buy. For wit, you have the greatest minds at your command. And I doubt that a sweet-natured woman is of any use to you at all."

She was wrong. Her sweet nature was the first thing that had attracted him. But she would never believe that, as self-effacing as she was.

There was one thing she would believe, however. "You're forgetting a certain, very significant ability." He caught her chin and tipped it up until she was gazing into his face, her eyes uncertain, almost wary. "The ability to please me in bed."

Her gaze didn't waver from his. "That's the easiest thing to purchase, as you should well know, having paid for your share of tarts and merry widows, my lord."

He frowned at her deliberate use of his title. "Not as easy as you think." He threaded his fingers through her hastily dressed hair and dislodged the few pins, letting her hair cascade around her shoulders like a golden robe. His voice grew husky as he caressed her flushed cheeks, the vibration of the carriage making his movements ragged. "I've never had a night as enjoyable as last night. For that alone, I'm willing to give you my name."

He brought his mouth to within inches of hers. If he couldn't convince her to marry him with words, then he would use any other means possible. But he *would* convince her. He might not be in love, but he'd decided that a wife could be a very handy thing. Especially when the wife was Emily.

Desire flared in her features, though she tried to hide it. "And what happens when you tire of bedding me?"

The very absurdity of the statement made him smile. "I shall never tire of that." And before she could summon up any other arguments, he covered her mouth with his.

Good God, she was soft, so soft. She had lips made for kissing, their delicate contours and natural color more tempting than the painted mouth of any whore. Deeply, repeatedly, he drove his tongue inside her mouth, mimicking what he really wanted to do to her. The scent of lavender crowded his senses, lending a sweetness to a kiss that was already more sweet than he could bear.

He had a rabid urge to touch her, all of her, to brand her as his. But he wanted to do it slowly, to make sure that he built her own need to feverish heights first. He stroked the smooth skin of her neck, then down the slope of her chest to where the lacy edge of her bodice ran high along the tops of two perfect swells of luscious, female flesh.

Though she allowed him to kiss her, he could feel the tension in her . . . the uncertainty. He would banish it thoroughly, he vowed. If it took him all day, he would make her want him as badly as he did her.

His hands slid deftly along the bodice to where a placket hid rows of hooks and eyes. Thankfully, her pelisse-robe opened in the front, so it was an easy matter to unfasten the hooks and bare her chemise.

She jerked back, her fingers flying to hold closed the half-opened bodice. "Jordan, you mustn't . . . you can't . . ."

"Why not?" He bent to slip his hands beneath her skirts, then skimmed them up her calves, his fingers gliding over the silken stockings until they reached her ribbon garters and tugged them loose with one quick motion.

She flattened her hands over her skirts. "We're not married yet!"

"That didn't bother you last night." He stripped one stocking off, then the other.

"Yes . . . but . . . but . . . here? Now? In broad daylight?"

"The broad daylight I can take care of." Without even looking, he yanked the curtain shut over the only exposed window. With the day already overcast, the carriage was lit with only the faintest gray light, enough to show her wary expression. "Come now, my darling. We nearly made love that first night we met in my carriage. This isn't so different from that, is it?"

She scooted back from him on the seat. "It's *very* different. You stopped it then. You didn't want me."

"I have always wanted you."

Though she dragged in a shaky breath, she shook her head. "Not me. My body. You want my body, but you don't want *me*, the innocent with foolish hopes of love."

"You forget you're not so innocent anymore," he rasped. He removed his coat, then his waistcoat. "And I do want you. All of you."

Edging closer, he reached for her bodice again. She caught his hand. "I don't think we should do this."

He gazed at her, at the parted lips and torn expression. "I see. You can seduce me when you want, but I'm not allowed to do the same. That hardly seems fair."

"It wasn't fair for you to kidnap me and force me to marry you."

"True. I didn't want to be seduced, and you didn't want to be kidnapped." He lowered his voice. "But both of us want this."

"I . . . I don't . . ." she said weakly when he slid his hand beneath her skirts again. "Please, Jordan, you shouldn't . . ."

"You say that only out of anger at me for thwarting your plans. But you don't mean it. What possible reason could you have for denying us both what we want? Especially when you know we're going to be married anyway."

"Because . . . because . . ." She faltered as he glided his hand up past her loose stockings to her upper thighs. He found the patch of hair and tangled his fingers in it, caressing her lightly, easily.

She sucked in a ragged breath. "Goodness gracious . . . oh, dear . . ."

He delved into her, his blood quickening to find her wet and warm and ready for him. Stroking her in time to the rocking of the carriage, he whispered, "Listen to your body. It never lies."

He found her little nub and rubbed it until her eyes slid shut and a flush of pleasure lit her face. "You are . . . a very wicked man," she choked out.

"Wicked is as wicked does." He caught her head in his free hand, holding it still as he lowered his mouth to hers. "And I am going to do so very many wicked things to you, my darling . . ."

She sighed, a small sigh of acquiescence, and he swallowed it with his kiss. He took great pains not to frighten her with the intensity of his need, but it was all he could do to keep the kiss tender when what he truly wanted was to ravish her like a marauding Viking.

At first she responded timidly, hesitantly. But as their tongues mated and twined, she arched toward him, grasping his waist to pull him closer.

Before he knew it, she was clutching handfuls of his shirt and tugging it loose from his trousers.

He unfastened the buttons of his trousers, then his drawers, eager to help her. Her hands slid down his sides and around to his back. But when she slipped them inside his loosened trousers to cup his buttocks, he nearly lost all control.

"Good God," he muttered as he tore his mouth from hers, "you never cease to amaze me."

Her eyes were glazed with desire, and a sultry smile touched her lips. "If you can do wicked things to me . . . then I can do wicked things to you—"

His kiss cut her off, and this time he couldn't contain his need. His tongue drove into her, possessing her mouth, while the fingers of one hand probed between her legs, seeking her slick inner core. She shifted to give him better access, but nearly fell off the seat and had to move back. Their positions made it awkward to touch her like this, especially with the carriage motion threatening to toss them onto the floor any minute.

With a growl, he removed his hand and sat back on the seat. Shoving his trousers and drawers down past his knees, he grabbed her around the waist and lifted her onto his lap. As her mouth went round in surprise, he maneuvered her until she was straddling his thighs, her skirts hitched up past her knees.

She planted her hands on his shoulders and gazed at him wide-eyed. "Wh-what are you doing?"

Reaching for her bodice, he unhooked her gown, peeling it away until she wore only her sheer chemise. "There's more than one way to make love, Emily. I took you like a rutting savage last night, so today you shall set the pace."

A blush stained her cheeks as she stared down at his rampant erection. "I . . . I don't understand."

He grinned. "Oh, I think you do." Clasping her waist, he drew her closer so that his member jutted up against her, the tip brushing the bunched-up chemise covering her belly. "Put your knees on the seat. Yes, like that. Now rise up on them and . . ."

That was all the direction she needed. Though her face was a brilliant shade of red, she nonetheless positioned him beneath her, then slid slowly down, encasing him in her sweet velvety warmth.

"Oh, God . . ." he groaned. "You feel so good . . . so damned good . . ." If he'd ever guessed she'd be this willing and adept a learner, he would have proposed marriage the first night he'd met her. Obviously, he needn't worry that she would want to make love with the candles snuffed and the curtains drawn.

Indeed, there was a light in her face now—excitement at her success, surprise, and certainly the hot flush of enjoyment. She wiggled experimentally on his lap, and he gasped.

Casting him a delighted smile, she did it again. It only served to torment him, since she didn't continue the motion. He writhed his hips beneath her, trying to get her to move the way he wanted, but she merely sat there.

"You have to move, darling," he ground out. "Up and down."

"I know how it's done, Jordan." A mischievous grin spread over her face. "I was there last night, too, remember? But you said it was my turn to set the pace, and that's what I'm doing. I think I'd rather sit here a moment and look at you."

First she stripped his shirt from him, then dragged the tips of her fingernails slowly down the front of his chest.

"Emily . . ." he growled.

"How about this?" With a smile, she slowly, maddeningly, rose up on her knees and came back down on him by tortuous degrees. His fingers dug into her sides as he gritted his teeth. She did it again, even slower this time, though she finished with a little shimmy of her hips that drove him absolutely insane.

"Has anyone ever told you you're a tease?"

"Me? I didn't start this, and you know it."

With an oath, he glared at her. "Move, damn you!"

"You mean, like this?" Her face was the very picture of innocence as she slid up the length of him, then back down by what seemed like quarter inches. "I am doing it right, aren't I?"

Sweat formed on his brow. She thought to torture him, did she? Well, two could play that game. He insinuated one finger in the place where they were so tightly joined and groped for her sweet, sensitive center. She gasped when he stroked the nub so lightly, it was almost not a caress.

Now she was the one to groan and undulate toward his hand.

"You like that, don't you?" He touched her again, briefly and certainly not enough to satisfy. "Is that how you want it?" He mimicked her earlier words. "I am doing it right, aren't I?"

"Please . . . Jordan . . ." She leaned into him, her fingers pinching his shoulders. Her breasts hovered inches from his mouth. Even when draped by her nearly transparent chemise, they were too tempting to ignore.

He sucked one through the muslin, then blew on the wet, gauzy material until she shuddered, her nipple a swollen nubbin beneath the cloth. "More?" he asked wickedly. He bestowed the same treatment on the other one, his tongue darting out to give the nipple a fleeting caress. "Or shall I stop?"

"Curse you for always having to win," she said even as she dragged off her chemise, then shoved her lovely bare breasts into his face. The motion shifted her on his lap, tightening her grip around his erection.

He groaned. "I think we should both win." He thrust his hips up beneath her, reminding her of what he wanted. "Move, Emily, move . . ."

And finally, she did.

It was exquisite. It was utter torture. She found the perfect rhythm, smooth and rapid and enticing. She even managed to blend the rocking of the carriage with her own rocking in a precise symphony of movement that wrung him like a hot hand.

Good God, having her make love to him was incredible. The scent of lavender spiked his senses, and her shimmies and innocent twists sent him reeling. He could hardly hold back his release to await hers. But hold back he did. After last night, he wanted her to know complete satisfaction.

So he focused all his efforts on laving her breasts with his tongue and stroking the hot silk of her between her legs.

"My goodness, Jordan . . ." she whispered when he tugged on her nipple with his teeth. "Do that again . . . yes . . . oh, yes . . ."

Her unvarnished enjoyment was a curse, for it made it nearly impossible for him to restrain himself. He had to close his eyes to keep from seeing the pleasure shining in her flushed features, the amazingly erotic image of her riding him. As an innocent, she was overpowering; as an experienced woman, she would be annihilating.

God preserve him until the annihilation.

Her rhythm increased, her body descending like a goddess's to torture him with pleasure. The rush to release became unstoppable, especially when she caught his mouth with hers and began to probe boldly inside with her tongue. He sucked on her tongue with almost frantic eagerness.

Suddenly she broke off the kiss, her body arching above him. "I love you, Jordan!" she cried as she undulated around him. "I love you ... I love you ..."

That was all it took. With a guttural cry, he spilled himself inside her and felt her shudder around him at the same time.

I love you, her words echoed in his head as he clasped her fiercely to him. *I love you.*

Chapter 18

And, after all, what is a lie? 'Tis but
The truth in masquerade.

Lord Byron, *Don Juan*, cto. 11, st. 37

Later, Emily sat in her chemise, drawing on her stockings. Jordan, dressed in only his drawers, leaned forward to rummage inside the amply filled basket from the inn. A surge of affection filled her when she noticed the freckles on his back, a dark smattering of them across his well-defined shoulders.

He was hers. For a brief time, only a few hours perhaps, he was hers.

Her mind clamored to be heard. *You shouldn't have told him you loved him. You shouldn't have let him make love to you. You should have stayed strong.*

She ignored all of it. Someone should have warned her that lovemaking had varied delights. Perhaps then his seduction wouldn't have taken her so by surprise. Perhaps she wouldn't have cried out so feverishly that she loved him or exposed herself so wantonly.

Oh, but the look on his face when she'd teased him at the beginning . . . She stifled a giggle. She

316

would have to do that again sometime, once they were married.

She sobered at once. What was she thinking? They were not going to marry. She *must* return to London, even if it meant attempting an escape everywhere they stopped. With each passing hour they moved farther north, and there was no telling what Lord Nesfield would do once he discovered her gone. Lady Dundee might hold him off for a while, perhaps even a day or two, but eventually when she didn't appear . . .

A hollow fear settled in her chest. When that happened, it would all be over anyway. So she must be strong. She must find a way to escape Jordan.

"The sausage is cold, I'm afraid," Jordan said as he drew out a greasy, paper-wrapped parcel. "But I think there's toast and jam. Oh, and here's a fruit tart. Do you want it?"

He held it up to her, his gaze meeting hers. "What's wrong? You look as if you'd seen a ghost."

A ghoul was a better term for the looming image of Lord Nesfield in her thoughts. She forced a smile. "I . . . I'm merely tired, that's all. And hungry."

He handed her the tart, then sat back and unwrapped the package of sausages. "There's plenty of food here. And you can have a nice long nap after you eat."

She munched on the tart, but it tasted like wood in her mouth. "Aren't we going to stop at all?"

He seemed suddenly very interested in the sausages. "Yes, of course. We'll stop for dinner."

"I assume we'll spend the night in Leicester."

This time his answer was longer in coming. "Probably."

Then he changed the subject. Feeling temporarily

reprieved—after all, she couldn't just leap from the carriage—Emily seized on the chance to find out more about him. They talked as new lovers do, each wanting to know the other's secrets. It didn't surprise her to hear that he'd been dreadfully lonely as a child, or that he missed his mother despite her callous treatment of him.

And his zeal in talking about reform made him seem less different from her than she'd thought. At least he made the attempt to understand the concerns of ordinary people. Many of his peers—like Lord Nesfield—had no use for such things.

What was painful to hear about was his close friendship to Ian. Clearly he'd do anything for the friend who'd helped him through the dark hours of his childhood. It saddened her to think how much he would hate her, truly hate her, once he learned the truth, once Lord St. Clair had been exposed and Lord Nesfield took action. If only . . .

No, she couldn't risk it. For Lord St. Clair, exposure would mean embarrassment and the end of his hopes for marriage to Sophie. For her, however, exposure could mean her life.

Jordan tried to turn the conversation to her parents, but she skirted that discussion with only a few terse words about her mother's death.

Later in the day, she learned what Jordan meant by "stopping for dinner." Although they halted twice in the morning so she could relieve herself by the side of the road, the first time they stopped for more than a few minutes, she wasn't allowed to leave the carriage. Apparently, Jordan was taking no more chances. He stayed inside with her while Watkins entered the inn and paid for their dinner, which he carried back to them.

That alarmed her, but she clung to the fact that they couldn't go on this way for the entire trip.

Scotland was a good two weeks' journey—Watkins had to sleep sometime.

For herself, she slept in the afternoon, lulled by the rocking of the coach. She woke up to Jordan's tender kisses, and they made love again, slowly, leisurely, as if they had all the time in the world.

Afterward, he fell asleep with his head propped against the side of the carriage. She watched him, thinking how perfectly adorable he looked asleep, with his hair so unruly and his usually hard features soft. He claimed to be incapable of love, but she no longer believed it. It would come harder, but that would make it all the more precious when it came.

If only she could stay with him to watch it happen . . . She sighed, a bitter disquiet spoiling her peace. Dear heavens, she must make sure they stopped soon. She couldn't bear this limbo much longer, this place where he was hers and not hers, too.

Shortly after sundown, she had her wish. They halted at an inn, and Jordan ordered another private dining room for them. To her dismay, however, there was no bed in this one, and Watkins joined them for the meal.

As they sat eating roast mutton and poached salmon in a room twice as spacious as the one at The Warthog and four times more luxurious, she glanced at the yawning coachman, then leaned toward Jordan. "Aren't we going to spend the night here?"

"We're not to Leicester yet," he said calmly.

"But your man looks exhausted."

"Yes, I know."

That was all he would say. But when they were on the road again, Watkins had an assistant, some man Jordan had hired at the inn. She thought it odd that Jordan would be so insistent on making it to Leicester that he would hire a man for only a few hours, but she supposed it was his prerogative. He could certainly afford it.

Once in the coach, she slept again, determined to be awake and alert once they stopped in Leicester. Thus she was shocked to discover when she opened her eyes again that the next day had already dawned.

She sat up and looked at Jordan, who was sitting across from her wide-awake, peeling an orange with his pen knife. "Why didn't we stop? Surely we've passed Leicester."

"Yes." He propped his feet up on the seat next to hers, crossing them at the ankles with utter nonchalance.

We must be well past it by now, she thought. *We must be almost to Willow Crossing.*

Alarm bells went off in her head. Willow Crossing lay off the main road to Scotland, yet as she glanced out the window, she thought she saw a familiar grove of trees. A sudden horrible fear made her legs grow weak.

"This isn't the road to Scotland," she stated.

"No." He concentrated on peeling the orange. "We're not going to Scotland."

"What do you mean, 'we're not going to Scotland'! You said—"

"I said we were going to be married. You asked where we were headed, and I said 'north.' And we're going north."

The truth hit her all at once. "You're taking me home."

He met her gaze. "Yes. I intend to do this right, and that means asking your father's permission for your hand."

Dear heaven, she could only imagine what Papa

would think when they arrived and Jordan announced that he wanted to marry her! How could she explain? Even if she could spin some tale about her sudden appearance with Jordan, she doubted Jordan would keep quiet about her masquerade. Oh, no—that was probably the very reason he'd brought her here.

And in the end she'd have to tell Papa that Mama killed herself. No. No!

"It won't work," she protested. "If you bring me to Papa's, I'll tell him that I won't marry you. Then you'll have to give up your plans."

"If you refuse to marry me, Emily, I'll tell him what you've been doing for the past month. I'm sure he'll find it very interesting."

"He knows already," she lied. "It won't accomplish anything."

"He doesn't know. My man learned that much from the servants at Lady Dundee's, who were speculating wildly about why Miss Fairchild's father kept sending letters to her there."

Her throat tightened, and she dropped all pretense of nonchalance. "Jordan, you promised—"

"I promised not to speak to Nesfield." His feet hit the floor as he leaned forward, fixing her with a dark gaze. "I didn't promise not to try to protect you some other way. You've been drawn in by a man who'll bring about your ruin if you continue to do his bidding. I won't stand by and watch it happen. And since you won't tell me why Nesfield is forcing you to masquerade and you won't let me speak to him, you give me no choice but to take you away from him, as far away and as permanently as I can manage. If that means speaking to your father—"

"You will kill Papa," she hissed. "You don't understand what you're doing."

"Then make me understand."

She stared at his implacable face, at the eyes that promised her no quarter. Glancing out the window, she was alarmed to see that they were now traveling down the main road that led through town. In five minutes or less, they would be at the rectory. She had to tell him something, anything that would make him stop!

Perhaps if she told him the reason for her masquerade . . . Yes, that might satisfy him. Perhaps if he knew the reason, he wouldn't press her on why she'd agreed to it. Of course, he would hate her for her part in putting an end to his friend's hopes, but she couldn't help that.

"All right," she whispered. "But stop the coach. Please."

His eyes narrowed, as if he were trying to discern whether she were in earnest.

"Stop the coach!"

He did as she asked, ordering Watkins to pull over to the side of the road.

She slumped against the seat with relief. Then, seeing his expectant look, she said wearily, "This has to do with Sophie."

"Sophie?" He looked astonished. Obviously, he hadn't considered that.

With halting words, she recounted how Sophie had tried to elope and how Lord Nesfield and Lady Dundee had asked her to act as a spy in an attempt to unmask Sophie's would-be husband. Emily glossed over her reasons for agreeing, focusing on her explanation of their plan.

She knew at once when he made the connection between her masquerade and Lord St. Clair.

Straightening in his seat, he uttered a foul oath. "Ian was one of your suspects, wasn't he? Not only Pollock, but Ian. That's why you've been so cozy with him. That's why the dinner parties and the outings to the museum and the dancing at the ball."

The chill in his voice made her wrap her arms tightly over her chest. "Yes. Lord Nesfield even suspected you, because you paid so much attention to me, but I told him that was ludicrous."

He drove his fist into the side of the coach. "I should have realized that all this concerned Ian. But I let my jealousy of Pollock blind me to the obvious." He glowered at her. "You've been spying on my closest friend, knowing that Nesfield will destroy him if he discovers Ian is the one."

"Destroy him? No! Lord Nesfield said he would offer the man, whoever it is, money or . . . or something that would make him agree to leave Sophie alone."

He looked at her in disgust. "Emily, you aren't stupid. Do you really think Nesfield will stop at offering money? What if this lover of Sophie's refuses Nesfield's money? Will Nesfield threaten to ruin him? Or will he arrange for the man to be . . . disposed of?"

Her eyes went wide. "Y-You mean, murdered?"

"Of course. I wouldn't put it past Nesfield. He won't propose a duel—he knows he wouldn't win. Instead he'll hire footpads to accost Ian in some dark byway—"

"He never said anything about murder! Surely he wouldn't—" She broke off in horror. A man who would threaten to send a young woman to the gallows if she didn't do his bidding would certainly not hesitate to have someone murdered.

She took a shaky breath. "In any case, I don't know who it is. It mightn't be Lord St. Clair at all."

"Or it might be. I don't think Ian would carry off an heiress, but who can know for certain?" He leaned forward, his face taut. "Even if it isn't Ian, you were helping that snake Nesfield see to some poor man's ruin. Why?"

"Sophie is my friend," she said stoutly, seizing on the explanation she'd given Lady Dundee. "I . . . I didn't want to see her married to some . . . some—"

"Fortune hunter? What rot! If your friend was in love with the lowliest shepherd, you would have gone to the ends of the earth to help them find happiness. I know you. You believe in such idiocy." His expression tightened. "What happened to your aversion for lying? Am I to believe you took on a masquerade you loathed, dressed in provocative gowns, and paraded yourself in front of every man in London merely to help your friend? I don't believe it!"

"I don't care what you believe!"

"You'd *better*. Because I'm returning to London as soon as I leave you at your father's. I *shall* get to the bottom of this, if I have to strangle Nesfield to do it!"

Panic descended on her. "You can't! Talk to Lord St. Clair if you must, and Pollock, too. Warn them to keep away. But please, don't go near Nesfield!"

He clasped her shoulders and shook her. "Why, damn it? What has he threatened to do to you?"

Tears coursed down her cheeks. "I . . . I can't . . . tell you! You can't do anything about it and if I tell you—"

"Is it your father's living? Is that it? He's threatened to take away your father's living? Damn it, Emily, I can give your father *ten* livings, wherever he likes!"

"It won't matter!" She stared distractedly about her. "Lord Nesfield knows things about me . . . he says he'll . . ." No, she couldn't tell him. He would rush back to Lord Nesfield for certain then, no matter how much she begged. Jordan was the sort to act, and he would never accept that he couldn't prevent the marquess from having her prosecuted. So he'd blunder in and threaten Lord Nesfield and accomplish nothing but her ruin. She could think of only one way to prevent that.

She clasped his coat. "I'll marry you, Jordan. I'll be your mistress . . . I'll do whatever you want! Just don't go to Nesfield! Take me back to London with you, and I'll . . . I'll talk to him myself!"

He was staring at her now as if she were some loathsome insect. Releasing her shoulders, he tore her clenched hands from his coat, then fell back in the seat. "'Things?' What kind of 'things' does Nesfield know about you that are so heinous you'd offer to be my mistress to keep from having them exposed?"

"It doesn't matter. We'll get married, and then perhaps he won't . . ." She trailed off. "What am I saying? He hates you. If we marry, he'll be even more likely to use what he knows against me." Jordan was looking at her with such wariness, her heart twisted in her chest. "Besides, you don't want a wife with dark secrets, do you? It's one thing to lower yourself to marry a mere rector's daughter, but God forbid you should marry a woman who keeps things from you, who might be a thief or a . . . a murderer."

"That's enough!"

"I'd ask you to trust me," she whispered. "But you won't do that, will you? Not the mighty Earl of Blackmore. No, you must know everything, have control over everything. You would never be so foolish as to trust somebody else."

"Damn you, Emily, shut up!" His eyes blazed like two torches in the blackest night. Then he rapped sharply on the ceiling. "Go on to the rectory, Watkins!"

The coach rocked, then rumbled forward. She stared at Jordan. "What are you going to do?"

He didn't answer. A disquieting stillness had come over him, tense and frightening.

"You're going to speak to him anyway. Even though I've asked you not to. Even though you promised not to if I gave myself to you."

That made him flinch. "I should never have made that promise. Nothing good has come of it."

"You're going to break it then."

"Don't you see? I have to. It's for your own good. Nothing you've said has changed my mind about this situation. I'm leaving you at your father's and returning to London." He glanced away. "But I'll be back. No matter what you think of me, Emily, I won't abandon you. I don't need the tie of some dubious emotion to do right by you. We'll be married, no matter what Nesfield says or does or—"

"If you speak to him on my behalf, there will be no marriage."

"What do you mean?"

She had meant that Lord Nesfield's attempts to destroy her and her family would put an end to any thoughts of marriage. But now something else occurred to her. He wanted everything his way. He made promises, but broke them if he deemed it necessary. All the control must be on his side, because if he gave it up to anyone, then he was revealing the chink in his armor. And she couldn't marry a man like that, no matter what happened.

"I mean, I won't marry you. I don't blame you for warning your friends—that's to be expected. But your only reason for going to Lord Nesfield is to 'help me,' or at least that's what you claim. What gives you the right to decide what's best for me when you don't know the entire story? You refuse to trust my judgment. You refuse to honor your promises. Well, if you can't do something as simple as that, then I don't see how we can marry!"

He gave a dismissive gesture. "Your father will make you marry me once he hears—"

"That you've taken my innocence? No, he won't. Not all men are like you, Jordan. Some of them actually care about what their women want or need or—"

"I care, devil take it! If I didn't care, I wouldn't have offered marriage!"

"Yes, but you don't care enough to honor my wishes or keep your promises. So I will not marry you!"

"You're making me choose? Between speaking to Nesfield and marrying you?"

She nodded.

His voice grew bitter. "I thought you said you loved me."

"I do. I love you enough to want us to have a real marriage, not one where you run everything and I merely play the adoring wife."

"So you love me only as long as I do what you wish!"

"No. I love you no matter what you do. But I can't marry you if you won't consider my wishes, too."

The carriage halted in front of the rectory, and she glanced out at it, thinking how strange it was to be home with everything still in such a turmoil. She thought of her parents' love, strands of caring woven into a magnificent cloth heavy enough to withstand any tempest.

"This is absurd," he was saying. "Our marriage has nothing to do with such matters. It's merely a practical way to deal with the fact that you've been compromised. Love has no place—"

"You know something, Jordan? You've spent your entire life avoiding love. You say it's because your father ruined his life by loving your mother when she wasn't worthy of it." She drew in a ragged breath. "But you've got it all wrong. Your parents' marriage wasn't a disaster because your father loved your mother too much. It was a disaster because your mother didn't love your father in return. It's not love that destroys. It's the lack of it."

He looked as if she'd slapped him. "You know nothing about it!"

"Oh, yes, I do. I can spot a man who's starved for love when I see one. But love requires trust and a willingness to give as much as one gets." She reached for the door handle. "What a pity those are beyond you."

Opening the door, she climbed from the carriage.

"Emily, wait—" he protested as he climbed out after her, but she turned around to block his path before he could take two steps up the walk.

"What do you plan to do? Go in and tell my father that you've compromised me, that I've engaged in all manner of wickedness? Then trot off to London and ruin my life while I endure his lectures? No. Leave me some dignity at least."

"Come now—"

"No. Go back to London. Talk to your friend. I wouldn't want to be the cause of any harm to him. Just remember that if you speak to Nesfield, that is the end of anything between you and me."

He glared at her, his face ashen, but she simply crossed her arms over her chest and continued to block his path.

"All right," he finally said coldly. "If that's the way you want it."

Turning on his heel, he climbed back into the carriage and ordered the driver to drive on.

She held her breath until the carriage was out of sight, wondering if Papa was watching out of the window even now. It didn't matter. She would have to tell him everything, no matter how much it hurt him. He was her only hope. If she impressed upon him the seriousness of the situation, he would surely help her return to London.

If she could reach London before Jordan, she might find a way to convince Lord Nesfield that this mess wasn't her doing. And she might actually beat Jordan there: Jordan and Watkins were exhausted, and they wouldn't share her sense of urgency.

Hurrying into the house, she fumbled about in her mind for how to tell Papa why she was here. But she stopped short at the sight of not only her father, but Lawrence sitting in the drawing room.

Surprise gave way to relief. "Thank God! Lawrence, you can take me back to London. How did you get here? On your horse? I can ride. If we hurry—"

"Slow down, child," her father interrupted. "What are you doing here? How did you come? Lawrence has been telling me the most astonishing story—"

"There's no time for that, Papa!" She turned to Lawrence. "We must leave for London at once!"

"What's wrong?" Her cousin's face grew drawn. "Is it Sophie? My God, what have they done to her? If that beast of a father has hurt her, I'll . . ."

He trailed off as he saw the confused expression on her face.

"Sophie?" she whispered. "You're concerned for Sophie?"

Color suffused his face, and that's when she knew. Dear heaven. "You. You're the one."

"The one?" Casting her father a helpless look, Lawrence mumbled, "I-I don't know what you're talking about."

"Oh, yes, you do, devil take you!"

"Emily!" her father said sternly. "How dare you use such language!"

She wanted to laugh. If only her father knew . . . All the things she'd done, the words she'd spoken, and for what? Because she hadn't seen what had been right under her nose all this time. Lawrence's dramatic response to Sophie . . . Sophie's dramatic response to him. She should have realized they were attracted to each other.

Granted, Lawrence had claimed to despise the "snobbish" Lady Sophie. Yet after the ball, he'd not been so vehement in his dislike. He'd even asked a casual question or two about Sophie and her family, but she'd assumed . . .

"How did you manage to court her when her father keeps her so secluded?" she asked, trying to make some sense of it. "I know he never allowed it."

"Court her?" her cousin said in feigned surprise.

"Curse you, Lawrence, stop this foolish pretense! I know you tried to elope with Sophie!"

It was her father's turn to be confused. "Lawrence tried to elope with Lady Sophie? But when? How?"

"In London a few weeks ago," Emily explained tersely. "Lord Nesfield caught her as she was leaving the house, and Lawrence was forced to flee."

All this time, and it had been Lawrence. She might as well put the noose around her neck herself. Her own cousin! Lord Nesfield would never believe she'd had no part in Lawrence's plans.

"Lawrence," her father demanded in his most ministerial voice. "Is this true?"

Lawrence looked from her to her father. Then he crumpled. "Yes."

"May God have mercy on us all," her father muttered. "Lord Nesfield will have my hide for this."

He'll have more than that, Emily thought morosely. "Oh, Lawrence, if you only knew what trouble you have caused—"

"I don't care," he said with all the selfishness of a man in love. "I love her. She loves me."

Emily gave a shaky, nearly hysterical laugh. "Young love. A pity Lord Nesfield doesn't understand the concept. He thinks a fortune hunter has put her under a spell."

"That bastard! I don't care about his money. He has the sweetest daughter in Christendom, and he doesn't even know it."

"That's the trouble—he does know it." Emily sank into a chair, more weary than she could express. Her masquerade, her foolish masquerade, had all been for nothing. The lies and the games and her shattering night with Jordan . . . all of it, pointless. She was completely ruined, her reputation in a shambles and her life soon to be at risk, and all because she'd been blind to her cousin's change in affections. And her friend's.

"When did this happen?" she whispered. "You seemed to dislike her so."

Lawrence began to pace the room, his hands clasped behind his back. "I thought she was beautiful, of course, from the first. Even then, I envied the man who would have her. But she seemed too haughty, too cold. Then at the ball, when you told me all those things about her shyness, I began to reconsider."

Another mad laugh escaped her lips. Wonderful. She could thank herself for that.

"Then I lost sight of you for a while. I thought we were going to leave the ball, but I couldn't find you."

Emily sat up in the chair, casting her father a nervous glance. That had been when she was with Jordan in his carriage.

"Since the last person you'd talked to was Sophie," Lawrence continued, "I went in search of her to ask where you were. I found her alone and very distraught." He stopped, anger marring his features. "Some fool had joked within her hearing about the scene on the dance floor with her father, and she was mortified, nearly in tears. I . . . I did the only thing I could think of to cheer her up. I asked her to dance."

Emily sighed. She could almost imagine it. Lawrence, struck by gallantry at the sight of Sophie's distress, and Sophie, grateful to him for his kindness in the wake of other people's cruelty.

Her cousin's face softened into the dreamy countenance of a lover. "We danced two dances. They were utter bliss."

Lawrence dancing twice? And calling it "utter bliss"? Her cousin truly had been shot by Cupid's arrow to bring about this transformation.

"And on the basis of two 'blissful' dances, you eloped?" she said in astonishment.

"No, of course not." Lawrence averted his gaze. "When I returned to London, I knew she was there for her coming out. So I . . . er . . . tracked her down."

"Tracked her down?" her father said, eyes narrowing.

"I hired a Bow Street Runner to find out where she was staying. Then one day when she went shopping with her maid, I followed her and—" He glanced guiltily at his uncle. "I pretended to . . . accidentally meet her on the street."

"You mean, you lied to her."

Lawrence squirmed under her father's accusing look, and it was all she could do not to cry. Lawrence's pretense paled compared to what she'd been doing for the past few weeks. When her father found out, it would probably send him to an early grave.

"It was a small lie, and the only one," Lawrence said defensively. "She wanted to see me as much as I wanted to see her, so after that, we met regularly."

"And when did you get it into your head to elope with a woman far above your station and out of the range of your purse, young man?" her father growled.

Lawrence straightened, towering over the older man. "I'll have you know that I make a very tidy living. And she doesn't care about all that anyway. She loves me. That's all that matters."

"You think so?" Papa shook his head. "We'll see if you're so certain when she's complaining about not having her own carriage and begging you to buy her some expensive bauble. Like is meant to stay with like, my son."

Truer words were never spoken, Emily thought bleakly.

"I don't care what you think, Uncle," Lawrence said haughtily. "I shall marry Sophie. When I find her, that is." He approached Emily, a determined expression on his face. "I've had the London house watched, and I've questioned the servants there and here, but I can discover nothing."

Kneeling before her, he startled her by grabbing her hands, his face the very picture of a tormented man. "Please tell me where she is, dear cousin! You're her closest friend—you *must* know! The servants said she was in the country, but she's not here. And I didn't for a minute believe that tale of Lady Dundee's about the house party you were both attending. What have they done with her? Is she truly engaged to be married as Lady Dundee claimed?"

Emily sighed. Curse the fool, he was so distraught, so deeply in love that it hurt to look at him. If only Jordan felt that for her ... No, it was just as well he didn't. By the time Lord Nesfield finished with her, there would be nothing left for him to love.

"Cousin?" he prodded.

"She's not engaged." She slumped against the chair. Now she had a choice—she could tell Lawrence where Sophie was ... or refuse to tell him and give him over to Lord Nesfield. But after what Jordan had told her, she was sure the marquess would destroy Lawrence. Sophie would be miserable, and Lawrence would most likely be ruined or dead, for he'd never take Lord Nesfield's money. Not her moral, rigid-minded cousin.

What's more, Lord Nesfield would probably still blame Emily for what had transpired, especially if Sophie persisted in her feelings for Lawrence. After all, Emily had introduced the two of them, and behind the marquess's back, besides. That would give him reason enough to act on his threats.

She sighed. She might as well be hung for a sheep as a lamb. "She's in Scotland. At Lady Dundee's estate."

Lawrence looked suspicious. "But Lady Dundee is in London for her daughter's coming out."

Her father interrupted. "Her daughter's coming out? Lady Dundee's eldest is scarcely fifteen. Or so the marquess told me a few months ago, when I inquired after his family. Surely that's too young."

"The servants told me," Lawrence replied with some irritation, "that Lady Dundee and Lady Emma, her daughter, were in residence."

Her father frowned. "Her name's not Emma, it's—"

He broke off at the same time Lawrence's gaze swung to her.

"It's a long story," she whispered. "I'll tell you all about it, Papa, after Lawrence leaves." She turned to her cousin and quickly told him everything Lady Dundee had said about where her estate was situated. "Now go on. Go fetch your Sophie, but be careful of Lord Dundee. I'm sure he'll be watching out for his niece."

"Thank you, cousin," he said, shocking her by seizing her about the waist and kissing her cheek. "I shall never forget this service."

Nor shall I, she thought bitterly.

Now came the distasteful task of explaining everything to her father. He was watching her expectantly, giving her no choice but to plunge right in. She began with Lord Nesfield and Lady Dundee's proposition, but got no further than that.

"You agreed to this?" he thundered. "You agreed to deceive hundreds of people?"

"Lord Nesfield left me no choice." She swallowed. "Papa, there's something you don't know about how Mama died."

When she finished telling him about the laudanum and finding her mother dead with Lord Nesfield as a witness, his face turned ghostly pale. He dropped into a chair, his eyes staring at nothing.

Then to her alarm, he began to laugh, bitterly, angrily.

"Papa!" she said, hastening to his side. "Papa, you must take hold of yourself! I know it sounds dreadful, but—"

"I'm sorry, Emily." His voice cracked with pain. "I'm merely angry at myself. I've kept myself aloof from you, and in the process allowed you to be left to that man's mercy, when all this time I had it in my power to prevent it."

"Whatever are you talking about?"

He cast her an anguished look, then took her hand in his. "My dear girl, we've been silent on this subject too long. It's time I told you what I know of your mother's death . . ."

Chapter 19

*We are wrong to fear superiority of mind and soul;
this superiority is very moral, for understanding
everything makes a person tolerant and the capacity to feel deeply inspires great goodness.*

Madame de Staël, *Corinne*

Jordan had to make a decision. After another two torturous days of travel, they were nearing London, and he still didn't know what to do.

It would have been so much easier if he'd been able to find Hargraves before he left Willow Crossing. The man might have told him something that explained Emily's desperation. But a cursory search of the inns had revealed that the only man who'd recently come from London had left at dawn.

Jordan had faintly hoped to meet up with his servant on the road, but that hadn't happened. Now he had to decide. Should he go to the Nesfield town house at once and confront the snake in his hole? Or should he wait until he heard what Hargraves had to say?

The carriage hit a rut, one of endless thousands plaguing it on the road home. He remembered the

road north as having been smooth, without a single
jolt to mar it. Amazing how lust could lend a rosy
hue to one's surroundings. Except for the incident
at the Warthog, their trip had been as pleasant as
a day's sail when the wind is exactly right and the
waves are playful.

He groaned. Good God, he was waxing poetic
again. That was what Emily's talk of love had done
to him. He felt it again, the heart-stopping blow to
his gut. Love. She loved him. But she wouldn't
marry him if he questioned Nesfield. After a day
and a half of listening to her theories about what
comprised a good marriage, he knew she meant it.

Deuce take her and her ultimatums! He could
either open the door of Nesfield's nasty closet to
see what secrets about Emily the bastard had
stored up. Or he could keep silent and let her deal
with Nesfield alone. For God's sake, she was no
match for the marquess. She had no power, no
wealth, no title . . . nothing with which to threaten
him! She ought to be grateful that Jordan was willing to step in on her behalf!

Yet she wasn't. In her twisted perspective, his
interference merely reflected a lack of caring.

The truth was, he cared far too much, so much
that the thought of Nesfield knowing dark things
about her chilled his blood. They couldn't be anything substantial. His darling Emily had never
done anything truly wicked. He couldn't believe it.

But she'd been willing to ruin herself and behave
in a way she abhorred merely to keep Nesfield silent. For God's sake, what could prompt such behavior but something awful? He had a right to
know what lay in her past. If he was going to give
her his name, he ought to know what he was getting himself into!

You refuse to trust my judgment, do you? he heard

her saying. *Well, if you can't do something as simple as that, then I don't see how we can marry!*

Devil take her! Devil take her bizarre logic and her pleas and her refusal to see that he had only her welfare at heart!

What gives you the right to decide what's best for me when you don't know the entire story?

He groaned. She wouldn't *tell* him the entire story! How could she expect him simply to stand by and watch Nesfield ruin her life?

Well, he would find out the truth from Nesfield *and* she would marry him, no matter what she thought. She'd never make good on that ultimatum. He was the Earl of Blackmore, for God's sake! Her father would be insane to let her refuse such an advantageous proposal!

But what if he did? What if the rector was as principled as his daughter claimed? What if he stood by her and refused to countenance Jordan's suit? Jordan snorted. Then let her be ruined. Let her live her life in shame. It wasn't his fault if she were such a fool. He'd done more than anyone could expect. He didn't need a wife. He hadn't wanted one, and he'd be better off without one.

He half believed that. For about a mile. Then he drove his fist into the cushioned seat with a curse. The truth was, he couldn't bear the thought of not marrying her, of never having her in his life again. It made him almost physically ill. Call it fate, but from the moment she'd stepped into the carriage in Derbyshire, she'd been linked to him forever. The thought that he might lose her over this ate at him like an ulcer.

Damn her! This was what happened when a man let frivolous emotions control his destiny instead of reason. She thought to wrap him about her finger by speaking a few words of affection to him. She thought to use the enticing appeal of love to make him want her so badly he would do anything for her. Father had made that mistake—

He sat up straight. That wasn't true. Father had never heard words of love from Mother. She'd treated her husband with nothing but contempt. She'd ignored the incredibly valuable gift he was offering, taking it for granted and never offering it herself.

It's not love that destroys, Emily had said. *It's the lack of it.*

A sudden chilling realization gripped him. All this time he'd considered himself a wiser version of his father, a man who'd learned from his father's example that emotions were dangerous. But it wasn't Father he resembled. It was Mother.

No matter what he'd told himself, he'd been as starved for love as Emily had claimed. He'd reveled in her admissions that she loved him. He'd soaked up the affection like a greedy sponge. Like his mother, he'd wanted it all, without giving it back. All the fun, and none of the responsibility.

Yes, he'd offered Emily marriage, but that was a trifling thing. The way he'd envisioned it, she would give him her body and her heart and yes, her love, and he would give her ... what? His name? Money? She didn't want either one. Children? He didn't even know if she liked children. His companionship? A woman like her would never lack for companionship.

What she wanted, amazing as it seemed, was a real marriage. To him. But giving her that was a great deal harder than giving her his name or his companionship. He knew what a real marriage was like—his father and stepmother had shared one. Real marriage was difficult. It meant an exchange, an equal union. It meant sometimes compromising one's wishes for the other person.

It meant letting a person know you so intimately that he—or she—could destroy you if she chose. Trust. It meant trust.

If you can't do something as simple as that . . .

"Milord?" came Watkins's voice wafting down from the perch. "You said you'd tell me where to go once we reached the city."

Jordan hesitated only a moment. Then he took the first leap of faith he'd ever taken in his life. "Home, Watkins," he called out. "Take me home."

Clutching Blackmore's note in her hand, Ophelia called for her carriage, then paced impatiently while it was fetched. The summons to Blackmore Hall didn't surprise her in the least. She'd guessed almost from the beginning that Emily was with him. Of course, she'd told Randolph that the girl had taken off for home and would return in a few days. It was the only thing she could think of to prevent him from taking drastic action. She'd even prayed it wasn't a bald-faced lie. But in her heart, she'd known that the girl had gone to Blackmore. And he, damn his hide, had kept her.

Where, she didn't know. She'd been to Blackmore's house countless times in the past three days. His servants had protested that he'd left the city, and they had not said where he'd gone. But wherever he was, Blackmore had Emily. Of that, Ophelia was certain.

Now the blackguard had returned, destroying Ophelia's faint hope that he'd taken Emily to Gretna Green. She should have known better. Why marry the girl when he thought he could have her without benefit of clergy? After all, since he knew her true identity, he held all the cards. He knew only too well that neither Ophelia nor Randolph was in any position to protest his actions publicly.

That didn't mean, however, that Ophelia intended to let him get away with it. Oh, no. She'd make him marry the girl if she had to hold a pistol on him to do it.

The carriage arrived, and she climbed in, her voice shrill with impatience as she gave the order to drive on. As it clattered off, she opened the card with its terse message and read it again. The only thing she didn't understand was Blackmore's insistence that she come alone and not tell Randolph where she was going. That was curious. And for heaven's sakes, where had Blackmore been for the past three days?

By the time her carriage reached Blackmore Hall, Ophelia was in high dudgeon. She ignored the footman who handed her out of the carriage and brushed right past the servant who held the massive oak door open for her. "Where is the scoundrel?" she demanded, as the man took her cloak.

He quaked beneath the look she gave him, but he didn't need to direct her, for she heard voices coming through an open door upstairs. Recognizing one of them as Blackmore's, she hurried up the stairs toward them.

Just as she reached the door, she heard him say, "Where the devil is Hargraves? He should have been here before me. I fully expected him to be waiting here—"

When she burst through the entranceway, effectively cutting him off, she was startled by the sight that greeted her. Blackmore was there, pacing before the fireplace in what appeared to be his study. He looked most unkempt and certainly weary.

But St. Clair was present as well, and Emily was nowhere in sight.

Ignoring St. Clair's frigid gaze, she fixed all her attention on Blackmore. "Where is she? What have you done with her?"

The man seemed to have a maddening calm. With a quick glance in his friend's direction, he circled behind his massive desk, no doubt intending to intimidate her. "Good afternoon, Lady Dundee," Blackmore said coolly as he took his seat. "Thank you so much for coming."

"A pox on you, young man! Where is Emily?"

" 'Emily'? You're giving up the pretense so easily?" There was real surprise in his voice.

What had he thought? That she'd hem and haw in front of St. Clair when Emily's welfare was at stake? The blackguard!

"I don't care about all that! I want to know what you've done with the poor girl!"

His eyes narrowed. "The 'poor girl' is in Willow Crossing with her father, where she belongs. I took her there."

She gaped at him. Emily was at home? With her father?

Then the last part of his sentence registered. "Do you mean to tell me that you traveled with Emily for two days unchaperoned? You awful man! You know better! When I get through with you—"

"With *me*?" he thundered. Rising abruptly from his seat, he leaned forward and planted his fists in the center of his neat desk. "I took her there after she came to me alone at night. That 'poor girl' offered me certain liberties in exchange for my silence about her scheme! Yes, I took her home! What else was I supposed to do? Leave her to be further corrupted by you and Nesfield? At least with her father, she'll be safe!"

Ophelia felt the color rise in her face for the first time since her schoolgirl days. Emily had . . . had offered herself to Blackmore? For his silence? Good Lord in heaven!

She collapsed into the nearest chair, hardly able to comprehend it. The night Emily had spoken so earnestly to her, she'd never dreamed how desperate the girl really was.

"So don't speak to me about chaperones," he went on in a low, threatening voice. "For all I know, you or your pandering brother sent her to me in the first place."

Her head shot up. "Why, you impudent dog! I had no idea she would attempt something so desperate!"

"Didn't you?"

"No, indeed!" She turned her gaze to Lord St. Clair. "Tell him! You know I would never—"

"Frankly, I don't know what you might do, Lady Dundee. You told me you wanted her to marry Jordan. Perhaps you thought sending her to him might do it."

It was Blackmore's turn to look surprised. He faced his friend. "Lady Dundee said that to you?"

"Yes," Ophelia answered quickly. "But I wouldn't have tried to bring it about in such a shameless manner. And Emily knew nothing of my plans for her. Indeed, she was convinced you would never marry anyone."

A troubled look passed over Blackmore's face. "Yes, I know."

Ophelia rose from the chair and hurried to the desk. "No matter what I've said or done, you mustn't blame it on her. Yes, she participated in a masquerade at my request. I assume that you know why?" When Blackmore nodded, she went on. "But her intention was always to find the man who tried to elope with Sophie, nothing more."

"It wasn't me," St. Clair put in. "Let's be straight on that point."

She gave him a dismissive glance. "Whatever you say. It hardly matters now. I'd already decided you were perfect for Sophie. If Blackmore hadn't frightened Emily into taking desperate measures, I would have handed Sophie to you myself."

St. Clair looked startled. "Truthfully?"

"Enough of that, both of you," Blackmore interjected. "I don't care about Sophie and her troubles. I care only about Emily. You make it sound as if she participated in this masquerade merely because you asked it of her. But there's more to it than that. The night she came to me, she was frantic with fear. I want to know why."

Ophelia sighed. "If I knew, I'd tell you. She insisted all along that she was merely concerned for Sophie, but I knew there was something more. When we first asked her to do it, she refused. Then my brother spoke with her privately, and she changed her mind."

"And you didn't question that? You thrust a country innocent into London society, into the company of unscrupulous men like Pollock, without a moment's concern?"

"Now see here, Blackmore, I did my best to protect her. The night Pollock assaulted her in Lady Astramont's garden—"

"Assaulted her! I'll string him up by his ballocks!"

Oh, heavens. She'd made the mistake of assuming that Emily had told him about that little incident. "Don't worry, he didn't get beyond one kiss. When I came upon them, she was holding him off with the pointed edge of her fan and threatening to dismember him. Emily can take care of herself, whatever you may think. And when she couldn't, I tried to watch out for her."

"Did you really? Then how did I get her alone for so long at the museum? Tell me that!"

She fixed him with her haughtiest glance. "I made the mistake of assuming I was with gentlemen that day. How foolish of me."

A muffled snort from Lord St. Clair drew her attention. For some reason, the wretch seemed to find this all very entertaining.

Blackmore didn't share his amusement, however. "She shouldn't have been thrown into the situation at all—"

"I agree. Unfortunately, though I suggested ending the masquerade more than once, she refused. She was adamant about it. And since I had no idea why she wanted to continue, I had no choice but to go on."

That seemed to bring Blackmore up short. He raked his fingers through his hair distractedly. "Your brother has something on her—"

"I know. He won't say what, and neither will she. I even offered to give her father a living if she wanted to end the masquerade, but she refused my help."

"Mine, too," Blackmore bit out. "Damn! I'd hoped you might give me some answers. All you're giving me is more questions."

"I'm afraid the only one who knows the truth besides Emily is Randolph. And I doubt he'd speak to you."

"In any case, I can't talk to him," Blackmore surprised her by saying.

"Whyever not?"

His handsome features clouded over. Pacing to the fireplace, he stood staring into it a moment as if contemplating something. Then he said in a low voice, "She told me she wouldn't marry me if I questioned your brother."

"What?" both she and St. Clair exclaimed at once.

"You? Marry?" St. Clair added, his eyes alight with mischief.

Jordan shot them both a resentful glance. "A man has to marry sometime, doesn't he? And unless some new bill passed in Parliament while I was gone, an earl may still marry whomever he wishes."

Only with difficulty did Lady Dundee stifle the gleeful laugh threatening to erupt from her throat. Blackmore planned to marry Emily! Good Lord, the girl had pulled off the match of the decade, possibly the century! It was what she'd hoped for, but she hadn't dreamed it would come to pass.

She was careful to answer him diplomatically. "Of course you may marry." She paused. "I take it you've proposed. But has she accepted?"

Obviously this was a touchy subject. Lifting the brass poker, he stabbed it into the fire until sparks threatened to ignite all his furniture. "Not exactly. It depends on what I do about Nesfield."

"That's so strange," Ophelia mused aloud. "What could Randolph possibly know about her that would make her refuse to marry a man she loves?"

His startled gaze flew to her. "She told you she loved me?"

"Not in words. But whenever you walk in the room, it's as noticeable in her reaction to you as the scent of lavender in her hair."

That seemed to please him. Just as she was about to ask if he shared Emily's feelings, however, a new voice came from the doorway.

"Good day, milord. I understand you've been watching for me."

As all eyes turned to the ginger-haired man in the doorway, Blackmore exclaimed, "Hargraves! You're here! What took you so long? They told me in Willow Crossing that you left two days ago!"

"In Willow Crossing? You were there, milord?"

"Yes, I left the same day you did," Blackmore explained impatiently. "I'd hoped to catch up with you on my way back."

"My horse lost a shoe, and I had to stop in Bedford for a new one. You must have passed me on the road while I was at the blacksmith's there. I'm sorry, milord. I got here fast as I could."

Ophelia eyed the wiry figure with some suspicion. "Blackmore, who is this fellow?"

"My servant. At my request, he went to Willow Crossing to find out whatever he could about Emily."

Blackmore had been spying on the girl? He truly was enamored of her, wasn't he?

"Well? What have you learned?" Blackmore asked Hargraves in clipped tones.

Hargraves appeared a bit uncomfortable about speaking before so many people. "I asked people about any connection between Lord Nesfield and Miss Fairchild, and most said there was none. But the apothecary told me an interesting tale. Seems the girl's mother died more than a year ago. She'd had a wasting disease something like your stepmother's. She suffered pain a great deal, and Miss Fairchild was the one that made up her medicines, primarily laudanum for the pain. The day she died, she was found by her daughter." He paused for effect. "And Lord Nesfield."

Jordan stared at his servant, not sure what to think. No, he knew what to think. Emily would never willingly watch any creature suffer, especially her mother. Could she have given her mother more laudanum than she should have? And then Nesfield happened along?

Her voice trickled into his consciousness. *Lord Nesfield knows things about me . . . God forbid you should marry a woman who keeps things from you, who might be a thief or a . . . a murderer.*

Good God, that made perfect sense. It explained why she'd absolutely refused to tell anyone the truth. She'd committed a crime. Nesfield could have her hanged for it, and she knew it.

He ought to be appalled. They were talking about matricide, after all. But he remembered too well the horrible pain Maude had suffered at the end. He would eagerly have given her extra laudanum if he could have.

No wonder Emily had been almost frantic. No wonder she'd begged him to trust her! She'd thought, and probably rightly, that Jordan could do nothing if she were accused of murder. She might even have feared that he would despise her once he learned the truth.

Well, it wasn't her he despised. "Devil take him!" Jordan glowered at Lady Dundee. "Your brother Randolph is lower than the lowest snake!"

Apparently, she'd made a similar deduction concerning Emily and her mother, for she said, "Yes, he is."

A sick wave of fear gripped Jordan. Good God, if he'd gone to Nesfield first . . . no wonder she'd told Jordan to trust her. He might have risked her very life. Of course, if she'd confided all this to him in the first place . . .

But she hadn't trusted him enough for that, not knowing how he would react. Could he blame her? It was her life at stake, after all. Still, he fervently wished she could have trusted him with her life.

"What do we do now?" Lady Dundee said. "If Randolph has made the kind of threats I suppose, they aren't idle threats."

"No, they wouldn't be." Jordan thought a moment. A sudden idea struck him, so simple that he wondered he hadn't thought of it before. "Wait! I have the perfect solution to this." In a few words, he described his plan.

Lady Dundee regarded him with obvious admiration. "I believe that *would* work!"

A mere boy of a footman suddenly burst into the room, followed by one of Jordan's servants who was remonstrating with him.

The footman spotted Lady Dundee and hurried to her side. "Milady, you must return to the town house at once! Lady Emma has come back! She's brought an old man with her, and there's all sorts of strange doings and . . ." Suddenly conscious of four pairs of eyes on him, he trailed off. "A-Anyway, Mr. Carter thought you and Lord Nesfield should be sent for."

"I'll come at once," she told the footman, then pivoted to face Jordan. "What do you make of this?"

He shook his head. "I suppose Emily impressed upon her father the gravity of the situation, and he's come to lend a hand. Though I don't know what either of them can do. Our plan seems the best solution."

She started toward the door, then paused. "You're coming, aren't you, Blackmore?"

"Of course. I'll be there shortly."

When Lady Dundee was gone, Jordan leaned on the desk for support, suddenly weak in the knees.

"Are you all right?" Ian asked.

Jordan shook his head vigorously. "What if I

burst in there, and she takes that to mean I've gone against her wishes? Or God forbid, what if I make matters worse?"

"You're abiding by the spirit of her wishes, if not the letter. You promised her not to question Nesfield about her masquerade, and you're holding to that. And I don't see how you could make it any worse than it already is."

"Yes, but she might not see it that way, and if she doesn't—" He broke off, the very thought evoking an unfamiliar tightness in his chest. "I could lose her."

Ian looked bemused and pitying, all at the same time. "So the Earl of Blackmore is finally in love," he said softly.

Jordan started to utter his usual denial, then realized he couldn't. He literally could not speak the words. "Love? Is that what they call this detestable physical state? The cold sweats, the pounding heart, the absolutely choking fear that I might have to live without her?"

"So I've been told."

He stared at his friend, then groaned. "Then it's a damned nuisance, and I was right to be against it all this time. Good God, I don't think I could go through this more than once in a lifetime."

Ian smiled. "With any luck, you won't have to."

Chapter 20

Be plain in dress, and sober in your diet,
In short, my deary, kiss me, and be quiet.

Lady Mary Wortley Montagu,
A Summary of Lord Lyttelton's Advice

Emily sat down near the fireplace in the Nesfield drawing room, then jumped up again and paced in front of it, twisting her shawl into a labyrinthine knot.

"Emily, dear, calm down," her father said. "It'll all be over soon."

"I know." And then what? Marriage to Jordan? When he didn't love her? She didn't even know how he'd react to the news about her mother's death. He might not even want to associate with her family after this.

Where was he anyway? Had she and Papa actually reached London before him? She could hardly believe that. Her curiosity grew overwhelming. "Papa, I'm going to speak to Carter."

"The butler? Why?"

"It's nothing. I . . . I merely want to determine how long Lord Nesfield will be."

The truth was, she thought as she hurried from the room, she had to know if Nesfield was with

352

Jordan. Or if Jordan had come earlier and Nesfield had gone to begin the process of having her arrested. But she could hardly tell Papa that. He didn't even know about Jordan. She'd told him that a friend had brought her to Willow Crossing. It was true, of course, though Jordan was much more than a friend. But she hadn't dared mention her possible future with Jordan when she was still so unsure of her own feelings and so much was unsettled.

It no longer ought to matter if Jordan had spoken to Nesfield. Even if Nesfield tried to make good on his threats, Papa had the means to prevent him.

Still, it mattered to her. If Jordan couldn't trust her, what kind of marriage could they have? She could live without his love, perhaps. But without his trust? His consideration for her wishes? That would be the worst sort of alliance.

On the other hand, what she'd asked of him was almost too much for any man to do. Without knowing any of the circumstances, she was asking him not to interfere. Any man would find that difficult, but one like Jordan would find it next to impossible.

Worse yet, he might not even have reached London yet, and then she would never know for sure.

She found Carter in the dining room, overseeing preparations for the next meal as if things like this happened every day. "May I have a word with you?" she asked in a low voice, glancing at the other servants. "Alone?"

"Certainly, mil—Miss Fairchild."

The moment she and her father had arrived, he had insisted upon setting the servants straight about her identity. She would've preferred that he not, since it complicated everything and since Lady Dundee might have wished it done a different way.

But Papa was too much a man of God to compound a lie.

She took Carter aside. "You said Lord Nesfield had gone to his club. Was he . . . was he alone? Or did he receive some sort of summons to go there?"

Carter looked nonplused. "Summons? The only person receiving a 'summons' this morning was Lady Dundee. Lord Blackmore requested her presence at his town house. That's where she is now."

She stared at him with wide eyes. "Are you sure the request was meant only for her? It did not include Lord Nesfield?"

"I'm absolutely certain. Indeed, she told me not to tell her brother where she'd gone. She said that Lord Blackmore had requested that."

The full ramifications hit her with astonishing force. He'd done as she'd asked! She couldn't blame him for talking to Lady Dundee—that hadn't been part of the agreement, and he would have wanted to gather as much information as possible. But he hadn't gone to Nesfield. That certainly said something for the extent of his feelings for her, didn't it?

Despite reminding herself that it wasn't all over yet, she couldn't prevent the surge of delirious happiness that lightened her heart. Hastening back into the drawing room, she sat down beside her father with a secret smile. Jordan had done as she'd asked. Her Jordan. Yes, *her* Jordan. She could think that now. *If* he still wanted her after this was all over.

She and her father heard the carriage thundering up the street at the same time. He took her hand and squeezed it as the carriage halted outside. Then they heard voices in the foyer, but when someone finally entered the room, it wasn't Nesfield. It was Jordan.

She gazed at him in astonishment as he strode toward her, with Lady Dundee and Lord St. Clair following close behind. He didn't even give her time to introduce her father.

"Emily, Nesfield's carriage is right behind ours. We have only a moment. Listen, I know everything—about your mother and the laudanum and about Nesfield's blackmailing you." When she scowled, he added, "And I didn't get it from Nesfield either, if that's what you're thinking. I haven't spoken to him. I swear it."

"Then who could have told you?"

"There's no time for explanations." Bending on one knee, he took her hand and kissed it. "Now it's your turn to trust me. I have a solution that'll keep you safe without hurting anyone, but you must let me speak to Nesfield first."

"Emily, who *is* this chap?" her father put in, his eyes fixing on their linked hands.

"He's . . . a friend," she said lamely. "Papa, meet the Earl of Blackmore. Lord Blackmore, this is my father, Edmund Fairchild."

"I'm very pleased to meet you, sir," Jordan said quickly. "We have much to discuss. But later, I'm afraid." Ignoring the way her father gaped at him in ill-disguised awe, he returned his attention to Emily. "I won't speak to Nesfield without your permission. Will you let me do this for you? I know what I'm doing, I promise."

"He does know what he's doing," Lady Dundee interjected in a whisper, then glanced over her shoulder as she heard Carter speaking to her brother in the hall. "Let him speak first."

"Now see here," her father broke in. "We've got our own solution—"

"It's all right, Papa." Jordan had asked her permission? Mr. I-Must-Always-Be-in-Control Jordan?

A smile lit her face. "I want to see what Lord Blackmore has come up with. It can't hurt, can it?" She cast her father a meaningful glance. "Please? Do this for me?"

Her father barely had time to give his reluctant agreement before Lord Nesfield stormed into the room.

"All right, where is the damned chit?" he thundered, then drew up short when he saw his sister, his rector, the Earl of Blackmore, and the Viscount St. Clair all gathered about Emily like a phalanx of soldiers protecting their queen.

He recovered quickly, however. "Out, all of you! Except my niece. I wish to speak to her alone."

Emily laughed aloud. He was still trying to maintain the masquerade? Now? Even with Papa here?

"Do not laugh at me, young lady," Nesfield interjected. "You know what I will do to you."

Her father stiffened and started to rise, but Emily caught his arm to stay him.

Jordan stepped forward. "Oh? What will you do to her?"

A pity that Nesfield wasn't as familiar with Jordan's moods as she was, or he would've realized he was treading on dangerous ground.

"This is not your affair, Blackmore. Go away."

"I can't. I've come to speak to you about your 'niece.' I wish to marry her."

Emily scowled. If that was Jordan's idea of a solution, it wasn't going to work. Her father was beginning to look apoplectic, but she tightened her grip on his arm, urging him to silence.

"Marry her?" Nesfield sputtered. "I will not allow it. Now leave. And take your friend with you."

"Surely you'd prefer that I marry your niece rather than your daughter."

That flat statement got everybody's attention. Nesfield's gaze grew positively furious. "What do you mean?"

"I mean, *I'm* the one who tried to elope with your daughter Sophie. I know you've been searching for me. I've heard about the men you hired. Despite that, I had planned to try again, of course." He shifted his gaze to Emily. "But then I met your lovely niece, and I lost all interest in your daughter at once."

Emily stared at him, astounded and thrilled and delighted. He *had* come up with the perfect solution! First, claim to be the blackguard who Nesfield wanted to destroy, then eliminate Nesfield's reason for doing so by offering to relinquish his interest in Sophie. It was brilliant and perfect, and if they'd been alone, she would have kissed him for it.

"Lady Emma has completely stolen my heart," he went on in a tone that actually sounded sincere. There was certainly no denying the heat in the glance he gave her. "So you see, you must consent to the marriage, since I know you have no desire to see me wed your daughter."

Her father jumped up from his seat, unable to contain himself any longer. "Do not listen to this man, Lord Nesfield. He is *not* the one who ran off with your daughter, and I can prove it."

Jordan whirled around, his face mottled with anger to have his plan so quickly scuttled. "Mr. Fairchild, you don't understand the gravity of this situation!"

Emily decided she'd best step in. "It's all right, Jordan." She rose from her seat. "He *does* understand. Let him speak."

Jordan stared at her for a moment, then nodded tersely. But for the first time ever, she saw fear in his face. Fear for her. It warmed her to the very center of her heart.

"What do you know of all this, Fairchild?" Nesfield demanded.

"You may remember my nephew, Lawrence Phelps?" When Nesfield merely glowered at him, Papa went on. "*He's* the one who ran off with Sophie. And I say 'ran off' because he's probably in Scotland with her by now. I regret to tell you this, my lord, but I'm sure they'll be married before you can reach them."

This new development stunned everyone. Nesfield was thunderous, Lord St. Clair looked perplexed, since he'd obviously never heard of her cousin, and Jordan was scowling.

Only Lady Dundee seemed calm as she turned to Emily. "Mr. Phelps? That barrister who came to the town house, supposedly looking for you?" When Emily nodded, she burst into laughter. "Now that's a match made in heaven. He was all sobriety and protective concern, exactly what Sophie has grown used to from her father."

Emily hadn't thought of it that way before, but now that she did, she had to laugh as well. Of course, right now anything would make her laugh.

Unfortunately, her laughter only served to infuriate Lord Nesfield. "My Sophie shall *not* marry a barrister! I will obtain an annulment! I will kill him! I will—"

"You'll do nothing of the sort," Lady Dundee retorted. "And until you can behave civilly, I'll be happy to have my niece and her new husband stay with us in Scotland."

Deprived of one source of satisfaction, Lord Nesfield rounded on Emily, his expression livid. "This is all *your* doing, you bitch! I shall see you hang for this!"

Emily recoiled from the malevolence in his voice, but Jordan thrust himself between her and Nesfield. "Stay away from her, or I'll kill you, I swear it! And if you ever speak to her like that again—"

"Do what you wish, Blackmore, but you cannot prevent me from ruining her and her father." Lord Nesfield's voice grew nasty. "And I do not think you shall want to prevent me when you hear the truth about the little chit. You see, she killed her mother."

"I did *not*!" Emily cried at the same time that Jordan shouted, "I don't care!"

Then they both stared at each other.

"You didn't?" he said.

She gaped at him. "You actually thought I did?"

"Well, I...I...my servant went to Willow Crossing and he found out...that is, I deduced..." Seeing that he was sinking deeper with every word, he added fiercely, "It wouldn't matter, you know. She was in pain, and you have a tender heart. I understand that. I—"

"It's all right," she said as laughter bubbled up from her throat. She ought to be furious that he'd thought her capable of murder, but he obviously knew the circumstances. And any anger she might have felt was overshadowed by the realization that he'd been willing to make great sacrifices for her, even while thinking that she'd taken her mother's life. A giddy delight filled her. "It's all right, Jordan," she repeated soothingly. "But I didn't kill her."

Her father frowned at her improper amusement, then scowled at Nesfield. "No, she didn't. My wife killed herself."

The words stunned everyone but Emily into silence, more because of who was saying them than what he was saying. Now sure that he had everyone's attention, her father added, "What's more important, I can prove it." Reaching into his pocket, he whisked out a folded sheet of paper. "You see, my wife left a suicide note."

Once again, Emily felt an overwhelming sense of relief. She still felt guilty that it had been her laudanum which had killed Mama. But it made a difference to know that Mama hadn't simply succumbed to a sudden burst of pain and taken too much of a medicine Emily had carelessly left nearby. The note's thorough explanation of her mother's reasons for killing herself proved that she had planned her death—planned it and executed it. And Emily couldn't blame her—or herself—for that.

"What do you mean?" Nesfield said suspiciously. "You never said anything about a note."

Her father colored. "I know. That proved not only sinful, but a terrible mistake as well." He hesitated a moment, as if unwilling to reveal so much of his actions in front of strangers. Then he sighed, apparently realizing he had no choice. "The day of her death, when I came home to find you and Emily with my poor Phoebe, I was distraught, to say the least. I fled into my own bedroom—Phoebe and I had been sleeping apart because she rested easier that way—and that's when I found the note, on the dresser. Phoebe had left her sickbed long enough to stumble to the dresser."

Emily hurried to her father's side, feeling again all his anguish. He leaned on her for support. "My first reaction was horror. Phoebe had committed the ultimate sin. She was damned forever." He halted a moment, overcome by emotion. "And even worse was the knowledge that her pain had been so great she'd been driven to an unthinkable act."

He stared down into his daughter's face. "Then I began to think of other things, selfish things. If Phoebe's suicide were made known, I'd lose my living, I'd be disgraced. And what would become of my daughter? It would make it nearly impossible for her to marry or have any kind of a life—" He broke off, then lifted his head with a stubborn expression. "I'm not proud of it, but I don't think I was wrong to consider such things. In any case, that's when I decided to keep it secret, even from Emily. I thought she didn't know about the suicide. And to be honest, neither of us was willing to talk about Phoebe's death."

His hand gripped her arm fiercely. "But that was wrong. I see it now. At the very least, I should have told my sweet girl what went on."

"I should have told you the truth, too, Papa," she interrupted, unwilling to let him take all the blame. "But I wanted to protect you."

"And I you." He gave a bitter laugh. "So we both were punished for our silence. I deserved my punishment." His voice broke. "But my dear girl did not. If I'd ever dreamed, if I'd ever thought that she and Lord Nesfield knew or that he would use it against her—"

"You couldn't have known," she reassured him, tears streaming down her cheeks. It still amazed her that he'd held such darkness in him all that time. It was no wonder he'd been unable to forget his grief. And for her! He'd done it for her!

"Oh, Papa, I love you," she whispered.

"I love you, too, my sweet girl."

"A touching scene," Nesfield said in a hard voice. He stabbed his cane into the carpet. "But that note is no proof at all. How do I know you did not write it up yourself at your daughter's request?"

Her father glared at Lord Nesfield. "You may

have power and riches, my lord, but even you cannot dismiss a note written in the hand of a dead woman. Anyone who compares it to her other writing will see it was written by her. And since it's marked with the date of her death and states quite baldly that she plans to take her own life, that's all the proof we need."

Nesfield might be a blackguard, but he was no fool. He shook a little as he stared through his lorgnette at all the witnesses to this exchange. "You think you have won, the lot of you. Very well, perhaps I cannot prove murder. But that shall not stop me from ruining you, Fairchild. The world shall hear that your wife killed herself, and you will not be able to find a living anywhere—"

"I doubt that," Jordan interrupted. "Here stand three people more than eager to give the man a living." He came up to Nesfield, lowering his voice threateningly. "As for scandal, I'm sure the world would love to hear how the Marquess of Nesfield's daughter ran off with a barrister."

Nesfield paled.

"Or perhaps," Jordan went on more viciously, "I should tell the world how you used the suicide of your own rector's wife to force his daughter into masquerading against her will. That should make for very entertaining dinner conversation."

"You would not spread such a tale! It would shame Miss Fairchild, too!"

"Perhaps at first. But what does it matter once she's my wife?" When Lord Nesfield paled, he added, "Yes, I intend to marry her, now more than ever. And no one will dare say anything against her around me. It might even be seen as a grand melodrama, complete with villain. Lady Dundee can provide her side of the tale, and Ian can impress his friends by claiming to have seen through the masquerade all along. And your name will be vilified every time it's repeated."

"Enough!" Nesfield swayed where he stood, his face contorted in horror.

Emily had never seen him look so old. Or so helpless. Deprived of his daughter and of any possibility of revenging himself against the man who'd taken her, he looked shriveled and pathetic. If it hadn't been for everything he'd put her through, she could almost feel sorry for him.

Almost.

"All right," he muttered, gripping his cane in a shaky grasp. "None of what was said today shall leave this room."

"Not good enough," Jordan growled. "I don't want my wife forced into continuing a lie." He cast her a quick smile, which she answered with all the love in her heart. "Emily abhors lying, and I don't wish to upset her. But you've widely proclaimed her to be Lady Dundee's daughter."

He crossed his arms over his chest. "So this is what we shall do. We'll circulate an amended story of this travesty. Emily, concerned for her friend Sophie, agreed willingly to masquerade in order to find the blackguard who'd tried to elope with your daughter. It was a noble endeavor, but doomed to failure because I knew who Emily really was from the first."

When Nesfield looked startled, a wicked smile touched Jordan's lips. "You didn't know that, did you? In any case, our tale will say that I decided to help her and so did Ian. In the process, she and I fell in love. But when she discovered that it was her own cousin, a man of some means, who'd run off with Sophie, she threw herself on your mercy, and you, being the generous and fatherly man that you are, decided to accept her cousin as Sophie's husband, and to add two hundred pounds to Mr. Fairchild's annual stipend."

"You can't expect me—" Nesfield began.

"Never mind that," Emily's father broke in. "I don't want to have dealings with this wretch ever again."

Jordan shrugged. "Very well. That's easily fixed. Mr. Fairchild left your parish because of a more than generous offer from his new son-in-law."

"No one will believe any of this . . . this fairy tale," Nesfield croaked feebly.

"You're right," Jordan retorted. "But it doesn't matter. They'll speculate about the real story, and it'll be the topic of conversation for weeks to come, but with so many lofty personages involved, they can hardly find fault with any one person for participating in the masquerade. Besides, it was for a good cause and ended happily, with two sets of lovers united."

His tone grew heavily sarcastic. "And since everyone behaved well, a few minor deceits can be overlooked. My wife and Lady Dundee will be seen as noble defenders of young lovers, and your daughter will be lauded for her dedication to love. We shall neglect to mention, of course, that her new husband is a barrister. I only regret that *you* will come off looking like a saint."

Nesfield summoned up a bit of his old fire. "If you think I shall support this tale of yours merely so Miss Fairchild can keep her reputation intact—"

"Be careful, Randolph," Lady Dundee warned. "If your name is dragged through the mud, then mine will be as well, and I refuse to be a joke at dinner parties."

Jordan raised one eyebrow. "Well, Nesfield? Shall we all walk away from this relatively unscathed, with only an amusing tale to note its passing? That's better than you deserve. But since anything else will result in harm to Emily—and I will *not* have her harmed any further by you—it seems the only choice."

Nesfield visibly recoiled from the threat in Jordan's words. He glanced around at the people arrayed against him, two of them with respectable titles and fortunes and one of them his own sister. It suddenly seemed to dawn on him that bucking such a conglomeration would lead to disaster only for him.

"All right," he growled. "But the five of you can continue the farce without me. *I* am going to Scotland. There is still some chance I can stop my daughter from ruining her life." With that, the marquess stamped out of the room, calling for his carriage.

"Enjoy your trip," Jordan said in a menacing undertone.

Emily shivered. She had the distinct impression that Jordan would find some way to make Nesfield pay for what he'd done. She wouldn't want to be in the marquess's shoes just now.

Jordan surprised her by then turning to her father. "Can you support my tale, Mr. Fairchild? I know how much you disapprove of lying."

"I fully intend to tell the truth," her father answered. When Jordan looked alarmed, he added, "But that's easily enough done. I know nothing of all this but a lot of hearsay. Who am I to say what did or didn't happen while my daughter was in London?"

Her father cast Jordan a speculative glance. "First, however, I'd like to hear more about it from you and my daughter. You have now mentioned marriage to her several times, yet until a few minutes ago, I didn't even know you knew her."

At Jordan's frown, her father said quickly, "Don't misunderstand me. I'm most grateful for your interference today. I couldn't have handled Lord Nesfield nearly so well alone." He clasped Emily close. "Nonetheless, I find myself bewildered—and a bit disturbed—by your interest in my daughter."

"It's not such a strange thing," Jordan stated. "I first met her at the Drydens' ball in Derbyshire. Then, while she was here in London, we were much thrown into each other's company." His voice softened. "And I fell in love with her."

There was that word again. Love. It was one thing to pretend in front of Nesfield, but he didn't have to keep it up with Papa. "Jordan, there's no need to—"

He cut her off before she could say "lie." "The only trouble is, I've proposed to her, and she hasn't yet accepted me."

She couldn't believe it. The Earl of Blackmore was standing there, looking as awkward and uncertain as any man who'd come to propose marriage a second time and wasn't quite sure of his reception.

He glanced at Lady Dundee and Lord St. Clair, who were both beaming their encouragement. Then he looked nervously at her father. "I know this is asking a great deal, sir, but do you think you might give your daughter and me a few minutes alone? Afterward, I will be much better able to answer your questions."

When her father hesitated, she squeezed his waist. "Please, Papa?"

"As you wish," he grumbled, "but only a very few minutes." He released her and started to walk off, then paused to fix Jordan with a concerned look. "I think you should know, however, that while my daughter was packing to come here yesterday, a neighbor in Willow Crossing came to tell me of seeing a very important-looking carriage drive away from my house. Emily told me that a friend had brought her home, but now I wonder—"

"As I said," Jordan remarked with a touch of his old arrogance, "I will be happy to answer all your questions later."

Her father nodded, clearly reminded of the vast difference in their stations. Jordan might be a young man desirous of his daughter's hand in marriage, but he was also the famous Earl of Blackmore, and years of ingrained behavior would make it difficult to alter her father's awareness of that.

Lady Dundee and Lord St. Clair thankfully took her father's exit as their cue to withdraw as well. When she and Jordan were completely alone, he approached her with uncertain steps.

"Emily, I meant every word I said to your father. I've been in a state of absolute terror the past two days, thinking you might not marry me. The thought of losing you makes my stomach churn and my blood falter. I love you. There, I've said it. Now please, put me out of my misery and agree to marry me."

Her first impulse was absolute joy. He loved her! Jordan loved her! He'd actually spoken the words!

Then a second awful and mischievous impulse possessed her. After all his stout claims that he was impervious to love and after all the terrible pain he'd put her through, she couldn't resist tormenting him, if only a little. "Are you sure it's love, Jordan? What you're describing sounds more like an ague." She laid the back of her hand against his forehead. "Perhaps you're ill. After all, the Earl of Blackmore falling in love—"

"Enough, you teasing wench," he said in a warning tone, then caught her hand. "All right then. You want me to behave like a sentimental idiot, do you?" His voice actually shook when he continued. "I need you to make me whole, Emily Fairchild. I want you. And yes, I love you. I will always love you."

He pressed her hand against his heart. "The first time you quoted scripture at me, you chipped away a piece of my granite heart, and you kept chipping away until nothing was left but dust. Thanks to you, there's a real heart in its place. And it will always belong to you." He kissed her hand, then flashed her a wry smile. "Now then, my darling, is that enough emotional excess for you? Will you please agree to marry me?"

She kissed him then, a big, joyful kiss as full of love as she could manage.

When she drew back, he looked dazed. "I hope that's a 'yes.'"

She smiled broadly, her heart so full she thought it might burst. At last her forbidden lord was no longer forbidden. "It is indeed, my love. A very emotional and very sentimental 'yes.'"

Epilogue

My soul is an enchanted boat,
Which, like a sleeping swan, doth float
Upon the silver waves of thy sweet singing.

Percy Bysshe Shelley, *Prometheus Unbound*

The Christmas ball at his stepsister's estate was more crowded than Jordan would have liked, given Emily's still-delicate condition. She shouldn't be exposed to so much chaos when she was recovering from having their son a month ago, but she'd insisted that they accept the invitation, since the Worthing estate was close to Jordan's own. What could he do but indulge his wife, since indulging her few requests was his greatest enjoyment?

He was returning to her with a glass of punch when he noticed her in deep conversation with his stepsister. As he neared them, he heard his name spoken. A mischievous impulse made him duck behind the pillar next to them and strain to overhear their words.

"He's not the same person since he met you," Sara was saying. "Jordan used to hate parties of any kind, and I've certainly never heard him quote poetry as he did at dinner. He seems so relaxed

369

and happy. What kind of potion are you feeding my brother, Emily? You must give me some of it.''

"Surely you don't need any such thing for *your* husband.''

"No. To be truthful, there are certain situations in which I would prefer that Gideon *not* be relaxed, if you know what I mean.''

"I do indeed. And in similar situations, you can be sure that Jordan isn't the least relaxed himself.''

The two women laughed themselves silly over that one, and Jordan decided he might as well interrupt. "My ears are burning, ladies," he said archly as he rounded the pillar and handed the punch to his wife.

That sent them into another peal of laughter. Though he raised an eyebrow, he was secretly pleased his wife took such delight in the pleasures of the bedchamber. Too bad they couldn't indulge themselves for another week, or so the doctor had said.

It might as well be a year. He cast his wife a long, lascivious glance, fervently wishing she hadn't chosen her scarlet velvet gown for this occasion. True, it was appropriate for Christmas, and though he still thought it scandalous, he had to admit his sister's gown wasn't any more modest.

Yet every time he saw Emily in that gown, her translucent skin glowing like delicate china and her breasts pushed up high, fuller now that she was nursing their son, he went hard as a rock. That gown always reminded him of their first time, the way she'd offered herself to him with such ill-concealed innocence.

He took a large swallow of punch. Good God, if he made it through the next seven days without ravishing her, it would be a miracle. He could kill her for wearing that gown tonight. No, what he wanted to do to her was much more pleasurable.

"Jordan, are you all right?" Emily asked, her pale brow creased in concern.

"I'm fine." *Merely randy as hell, darling.* Trying to take his mind off his urge to rip her gown in half and feast on those lush breasts and sweet curves, he scanned the room. "I see that Sophie and Lawrence are here."

Across the room, Lawrence whispered something in his wife's ear, and her eyes lit up. Their faces were aglow, proving that everyone had been wrong to try to prevent their marriage. Jordan added, "I'm glad a few members of London society have accepted them."

"Mostly the ones who want to irritate Lord Nesfield," Sara responded. She shot Jordan a curious glance. "Not that it would take much to irritate him these days. I understand he's had a series of personal and financial setbacks. His club refused to honor his membership anymore, he's lost thousands of pounds in a shipping venture, and there's some sort of legal battle concerning a substantial piece of his property. What a terrible lot of bad luck he's had this year."

"Yes, very bad luck," Jordan repeated dryly, exchanging a glance with his wife. The man would have a great deal more bad luck before Jordan was through with him. Noting the speculation in his sister's eyes, Jordan changed the subject. "I wonder how Ian is adjusting to the marriage between Lawrence and Sophie."

"I suspect he was never in love with her," Emily said. "He hasn't seemed too disappointed."

In love, Jordan thought. Amazing how differently the words affected him now than a year ago. But then, he hadn't known he would find the perfect wife—a woman whose interests in reform meshed with his own, whose frankness always entertained him, and whose body . . . Good God, why couldn't he keep his mind off that subject?

"Ian didn't even flinch when he saw Lawrence and Sophie enter," Sara remarked, forcibly bringing Jordan back to the conversation. "And I saw him on the balcony not five minutes ago, kissing Felicity."

"Did you now?" Emily said smugly. "That doesn't surprise me a bit. I knew something was going on there."

"Nonsense," Jordan said with a snort. "Ignore my foolish sister, Emily. If Ian *was* kissing the girl, it was only a momentary flirtation, I assure you."

Sara wore a calculating expression. "I don't know if that's all it is, Jordan. You should have seen the way he was watching her earlier. He couldn't take his eyes off her. And he *is* looking for a wife, isn't he?"

"Sara," Jordan said condescendingly, "if you think Ian will consider marrying an opinionated bluestocking, you don't know him very well."

His wife and his stepsister exchanged knowing glances.

"You ought to trust your sister on this," Emily said, a slow smile touching her lips. "She has wonderful instincts. Sara, do tell him what you told me right before our wedding."

"Tell me what?"

Sara grinned, her eyes suddenly alight with mischief. "You remember the night of the Drydens' ball? When the two of you met? Gideon and I realized what was going on between you two before you even climbed into that carriage."

"What do you mean?" Jordan asked.

"You said you were taking a widow home, but Gideon had met both Emily and Lawrence, and

knew she was a rector's daughter and Lawrence
was her cousin. He told me he thought you'd made
a mistake."

"For God's sake, why didn't you say something?
I can see how that deuced pirate husband of yours
would think it was all a good joke, but surely you
knew better. You might have saved Emily consid-
erable embarrassment."

"Yes, but then she wouldn't have met you,
would she? Besides, I decided that a rector's
daughter might be exactly the thing for my
brother." She laughed. "You see? I *do* know a good
couple when I see one."

"That was sheer luck," he grumbled, unaccount-
ably irritated. It had always pleased him to think
that a whim of Fate had brought him and Emily
together, and he didn't like knowing that his sister
had been involved, even if it were only in the most
limited capacity.

"Would you rather we hadn't met?" his wife
asked quietly, misinterpreting his scowl.

Angry at his sister for bringing the entire thing
up, he cast her a pointed glance. She mumbled
something about having to find her husband and
hurried off, leaving them alone in their corner of
the room beside the balcony doors.

"You know the answer to that," he said softly.
He took his wife's hand and kissed it. "And if you
aren't sure, come outside, and I'll . . . remind you
of how I feel on the subject."

She glanced shyly away, though she let him lead
her onto the balcony. "Really, Jordan, in the middle
of a ball?"

In some ways, she was still the sweet innocent
he'd fallen in love with. Indeed, it was her peculiar
mixture of innocence and worldly instinct that al-

ways delighted him. "Yes." He drew her into his arms and kissed her hair.

She gazed up at him with a smile. "It's cold out here, you silly man."

"Exactly what I need. It'll keep me from ravishing you the way I've wanted to for the past two months."

"Ah, but you don't have to keep from ravishing me anymore. The doctor told me today that I can resume all 'marital activities.' Why do you think I wore this gown tonight?"

He caught his breath, his body giving an instant response. "What the devil are we doing here then? We're going home. Now!"

She laughed delightedly as he pulled her back into the room and headed toward their hostess. "Oh, good," he heard her whisper beside him. "I do so like doing it in the carriage."

Author's Note

The discussion about whether the Elgin marbles belong in England continues until this day. The Greek government has been fighting to have them returned, but the British Museum believes they should remain in England. To read more about this fascinating dispute, visit the Parthenon Marbles web site at *http://www.rethymno.forthnet.gr/marbles/index.html*.

Dear Reader,

If you're looking to put more romance in your life, then don't miss next month's romantic selections from Avon Books, starting with the return of those irresistible Cynster men in Stephanie Laurens' *Scandal's Bride*. Richard Cynster, known to his family as Scandal, has decided he'll avoid the fate of most Cynster men—he'll never marry. But then he meets beautiful Catriona Hennessy. Will Scandal soon be headed to the altar?

Next, it's the moment many of you have been waiting for—the next contemporary romance from Susan Andersen, *Be My Baby*. I know that Susan's *Baby, I'm Yours* is a favorite of her many, many readers, and if you haven't yet experienced the pure pleasure of reading one of Susan's fast-paced, sexy contemporary love stories...well, now is the time to start! It's contemporary romance at its finest.

Eve Byron has charmed countless readers with her delightful heroines and strong heroes, and in *My Lord Stranger* she gives both. It's a Regency-set love story you're not likely to forget.

Margaret Moore is a new author to Avon Romance, and *A Scoundrel's Kiss* is sure to please anyone who loves a rakish hero tamed by the love of a woman. Here, our hero makes a bet with his friends that he can seduce any woman in England...even the prim-and-proper heroine.

Enjoy!

Lucia Macro
Lucia Macro
Senior Editor

AEL 0299

Avon Romances—
the best in exceptional authors and unforgettable novels!